A Talent for Trouble

MATTESON WYNN

© 2020 Matteson Wynn

Cover art and design by Michael Tangent.

All rights reserved. This is a work of fiction. Names, characters, places, and incidents are used fictitiously. Any resemblance to actual events, or persons, living or dead, is coincidental. No portion of this book may be reproduced, or transmitted in any form or by any means, electronic or otherwise, without written permission from the author.

For Alesha

Chapter One

Someone needs to tell magic it can't have caffeine after noon. Maybe then it'll stop waking me up in the middle of the night.

Unfortunately, I was having no such luck on this particular night because a magical warning bell clanged in my head, jerking me out of a sound sleep.

"Okay Bayley," I said. "I'm up. You can turn the alarm off."

Mercifully, the bonging in my head stopped, and the lights gradually came on, giving my eyes a chance to adjust. Living in a magical house has its advantages.

Fuzzy woke up too. He leapt from the bed to the windowsill, fur raised, a low growl vibrating from him as he went into full guard-cat mode.

"That can't be good," I mumbled, rubbing the sleep from my eyes.

I sat up and tried to figure out what had happened this time. Concentrating on Bayley and the property, I scanned for signs of danger. A few realizations hit me at once.

The only people inside Bayley right then were me and Fuzzy.

There were no intruders on the property.

And it was raining.

"Oh no."

My stomach sank as my suspicion became a reality. Bayley showed me an image of Gram Murphy stepping out of the rain and onto the lawn in front of the house. He had his arms wrapped around a woman I didn't recognize, and she was resting her head on his shoulder. They stood there, just for a moment, hugging on my lawn in the rain. He leaned down to whisper something in her ear. Then I saw him look around, zero in on the light shining around the side of the house from my window, and head around the corner.

What the hell?

Well, at least I'd had a chance to wake up a little before I had to deal with whatever this was. I sent a silent prayer of thanks to my friend and lawyer, Nor, for making Gram sign a contract that forced him to send Bayley a magical warning anytime he was going to step through a rainstorm and onto the property.

I dropped my Bayley-vision, jumped out of bed, and joined Fuzzy at the window just as Gram and his girlfriend stepped into the square of light my bedside lamp was beaming outside.

"Finn," he hollered toward me.

As I reached for it, Bayley slid the window up for me. I gave the frame a little pat of thanks.

Then I leaned out and yelled back, "Are you kidding me, Gram? It's the middle of the night. When you got permission to visit, we didn't mean you could show up at three a.m."

My breath formed little clouds as I spoke, and I yanked my head back before I got drenched. It was almost cold enough for the rain to turn to snow, and the frosty, damp air bit the sleepiness right off me.

I expected Gram to snark at me. Instead he said, "Please Finn. May we come in?"

He was so humble and polite that my alarm level shot up three notches. Gram was never nice to me. That's when I noticed how badly the woman was swaying. She seemed to be struggling to stand up, despite leaning on Gram. He wasn't hugging her so much as supporting her.

Are they drunk? I wondered.

Stifling a groan, I said, "I'll be right down," and slammed the window shut.

I got dressed quickly, all the while trying to guess what Gram was doing here, and why he'd brought a date. It wasn't like we were friends. I wasn't even sure we were frenemies. Sure, he'd saved my bacon a month ago, but mostly because he'd been forced into it by my neighbor Zo. And I had a sneaking suspicion he'd agree to help because he knew he was so far on my bad side that it was his only hope of earning some brownie points.

Relieved as I'd been for the help, I'd been sure it'd come back to bite me in the ass. I just hadn't expected it to be at three in the morning.

Once I was dressed, Fuzzy took off for the front door, and I hurried after him down the front staircase.

The more I thought about it, it didn't seem like Gram's style to get wasted and then try to impress his date by showing off Bayley to her. Which could only mean that something was really wrong.

I yanked open the front door. Gram had come around the side of the house to stand in front of the porch. He'd made the rain stop, so when Bayley turned on the porch lights for me, I had a clear view of him and his date.

They were soaking wet, but not just from the rain. The woman in Gram's arms had blood streaming from a cut on her forehead, and the way she was slumping made me wonder if she was bleeding from anywhere else.

I gasped, then rushed out.

It looked like Gram was struggling to keep her from sliding to the ground. She was tall, so I scooted around her side, propping my shoulder under her armpit, and making myself into a human crutch.

"What happened?" I asked.

"May we come in?" asked Gram. His face was strained, and his attention was focused on the woman.

"She's bleeding! Like I'm gonna say no," I said.

Between the two of us, we helped her up the porch steps and into the house. Bayley shut the door behind us, then lit up the hallway as we made our way to the kitchen at the back. Fuzzy trailed along behind us.

"What's going on? What happened?" I asked.

"Please Finn. Just let me get her settled."

He said please. Again.

Oh this is bad, was all I could think.

Gram and I deposited her in a chair at the kitchen table. He knelt beside her while I surveyed the situation. The woman looked terrible. She was still bleeding from her head wound. She also had a cut lip and some bruising on her face. I could see one of her hands, and she had some nasty abrasions on her knuckles. My best guess was that she'd been in some kind of fight.

She slumped over the table, shivering, eyes glazed. She had deeply caramel skin, like Gram, but it had taken on a gray undertone, and I couldn't tell if it was from blood loss, pain, or something else.

Fuzzy hopped up on a chair near the woman and watched her and Gram, tail swishing back and forth.

I wanted to know what was going on and why Gram thought he should bring her here of all places, but first things first. I was pretty sure she was in shock.

"We need to get you warmed up and get that bleeding stopped," I said.

Gram nodded, but the woman didn't react.

I had to get supplies to treat her, but no way was I going to leave Gram alone in the house, so I asked Bayley for help. In my mind, I visualized the upstairs linen closet, picturing the towels and then the blankets.

Bayley, bring those to me please, I asked.

I could hear rumbling and thumping moving toward us, then the ceiling over me opened and a slab of wood lowered to the floor with the towels and blankets stacked on it. I took the pile off, and the slab returned to the ceiling, which closed back up again.

Gram stared at me. "Handy."

No reaction from the woman. She looked almost catatonic.

"Sure is," I said, stacking the pile on the table. I unfolded a blanket and tried to put it around her, but when I reached toward her, she flinched.

I looked at Gram. His face was pinched, and he looked like someone had just kicked his puppy. I handed him the blanket and said, "Here, you wrap her up. Help yourself to the towels too. Do we need to call a doctor?"

I barely finished the word "doctor" before Gram cut me off, shaking his head as he said, "No, no doctor."

"Okay..." I walked to a kitchen cabinet, pulled down the first aid kit, and brought it back to the table. "What's her name?"

Gram hesitated.

"Gram, you show up here in the middle of the night, dripping and bleeding, the least you can do is tell me her name," I said as I pulled out some gauze pads.

He ran a hand through his hair, pushing a few dripping clumps back out of his face. "Yes. Of course. Sadie. Her name is Sadie."

"Hi Sadie," I said. She didn't move. I adopted the voice my dad used on frightened strays. "My name is Finn. Sadie, it's going to be okay. You're safe now. You're here in my nice warm kitchen, and I'm going to make you a nice cup of tea. Or coffee. Or both. Maybe with some whiskey in it. But first, that's a nasty cut you've got there. Can I have a look?"

I leaned forward slowly and reached to push her hair away from the cut on her forehead, but she roused herself enough to wave me away.

I stepped back immediately. "It's okay. Not ready to trust me yet? No worries. How about Gram? Can Gram help you?"

I handed the gauze pad to Gram. "Here. See if you can get the bleeding stopped while I make some tea. Or coffee. What do you guys want? We need to get you both warmed up."

"Either. Both. It's fine." He was so distracted, his attention riveted on Sadie, that I could probably have offered him worms *à la mode,* and he'd have said yes.

He leaned forward until he was in her direct eyeline, then slowly reached up to dab at the cut on her head. She didn't move away from him, so I left him to it and went to make coffee and tea.

I brought the coffeepot and the kettle to the sink and turned on the water. Nothing came out. I stood blinking and frowning for a few seconds before I remembered that the same thing had happened the last time Gram was here.

Bayley, is there some reason you don't want Gram to drink the water?

The cups in the cupboard rattled and I heard a clear *ding*, which was Bayley's way of saying "Yes!"

Now that I'd been Housekeeper for nearly two months, I knew to trust Bayley, even if I didn't understand what he was doing. So, I went to the pantry, hauled out some bottled water, and used that to get the coffee and tea started.

I also poured two glasses of water and brought them over to the table. "Here's some water while we're waiting for the hot stuff," I said.

Gram had managed to get the bleeding slowed down and was placing a bandage over the cut.

I said, "Sadie, would you like some ice for your lip? If we get some ice on there, it won't ache so much, and I bet we can keep the swelling down." I walked to the freezer and hauled out a bag of frozen peas, wrapped it in a towel, and brought it to Gram as I talked.

Sadie still didn't move. Gram finished bandaging her head and took the bag of peas from me. With one finger, he gently stroked her long, dark hair off her face and tucked it behind her ear, then held the bag to her lip.

Her eyes fluttered closed. A single tear rolled down her face.

"Don't," said Gram, his voice cracking. "It'll be alright. I swear."

"Liar." Her voice came out low, a bit slurred and muffled, whether from the peas or the swelling, it was hard to tell. I thought she might have an accent of some sort, maybe British. But what struck me most was how utterly hopeless she sounded.

Gram folded his free hand over hers, and she leaned forward, turning her head to the side so she rested the unbruised bit on his shoulder. He put the peas on the table and wrapped his arms around her as another of those silent tears escaped down her face.

I felt like I was intruding on something intensely personal. I slipped over to the counter to give them some privacy.

The tea kettle started to whistle.

Sadie yelped, jerking out of Gram's arms, staring wild-eyed around her. She had her arms up, as though to ward off someone's blows.

Gram grabbed her arms. "Sadie, no. It's alright."

"Sorry! It's the tea kettle," I said, as I hurried over to the stove and took the kettle off the burner.

It took Sadie a moment to register what Gram and I were saying, and another moment to lower her arms.

Then she started shaking.

"Gram," I said, "I know you guys love the water and all, but she's freezing. If we don't want her to go into shock any more than she already is, we've got to warm her up. I don't know how we're going to do that with her clothes so wet."

Sadie blinked and for the first time really focused on me. "You're right." She blinked again, pulled away from Gram, and raised her hands.

Gram looked alarmed. "Sadie, I don't know if that's a good—"

Brow furrowed, Sadie made a swirling motion with one hand. All the water from their clothes floated up into the air, forming a floating puddle. She looked at me and made the same gesture. All the water that had sunk into my clothes while I was supporting her joined the floating puddle. With another hand motion, Sadie sent the puddle flying across the kitchen. It splashed into the sink.

"Well that's cool," I said, as I watched the water disappear down the drain.

Sadie groaned, and I looked over to see her swaying.

Gram caught her as she pitched forward. "Goddamn it, I told you that wasn't a good idea."

"Is she okay?" I asked, rushing forward to help.

"She's unconscious. Magic drain." Then he muttered, "Stupid. She was already drained. She knows better." He looked up at me. "Got anywhere I can lay her down?"

"Sure. There's a couple of really comfortable couches in the sitting room down the hall. There's a fireplace, too, so it'll be nice and warm."

Gram cradled Sadie in his arms as Fuzzy and I led him back down the hall toward the front of the house and into the room to the right of the front door. Inside, two large couches faced each other in front of the fireplace.

While Gram got Sadie settled on the couch on the left, I started a fire.

I stood up to see Gram staring down at Sadie, expression troubled.

Fuzzy hopped up onto the couch across from Sadie and settled down, gazing steadily at her.

I sent him a smile. I felt better knowing Fuzzy would keep an eye on her.

I looked at Gram's drawn face and felt some sympathy for him, despite myself. I asked, "Do you still want some tea?"

"Please."

He looked so worried that I added, "Don't worry, your girlfriend's safe here. I'm sure she'll be fine."

The ghost of the arrogant Gram grin that I was so familiar with made a brief appearance. "Do I detect a note of jealousy?"

I didn't have a chance to retort. Sadie whimpered in her sleep, and Gram's grin tightened into a grimace, the shadows in his eyes drowning the brief light that had been there.

He said, "You know what? Forget the tea. If the offer's still open, I could use some of that whiskey now."

"Sure."

As he followed me out the door he added, "And Finn? She's not my girlfriend. She's my sister."

Chapter Two

Back in the kitchen, I snagged the bottle of whiskey from the pantry. I brought it and a glass to the table for Gram, who slumped into a chair. I fixed myself some coffee and sat down with him.

I said, "When she wakes up, I have something that'll help with the magic hangover."

"I'm sure she'll appreciate it. Although, you'll be amazed at what she can do with a power nap," he shook his head, looking both annoyed and impressed. "I swear, she can rally like no one else."

I waggled the whiskey bottle at him. "How do you want it? Straight? Splash of water? Irish coffee?"

"Neat. Please."

There it was. That "please" again. Every time he said it, I got more disconcerted. I recalled a conversation I'd had with him in this very kitchen where I'd had to badger him to get him to say please and thank you. I didn't know what to do with this polite version of Gram. More to the point, I didn't trust it, and I didn't expect it to last. Eventually, he'd return to the usual Gram that got on my last nerve, and no way was I going to let this false civility lull me.

I poured him a generous amount of whiskey and nudged it toward him. I didn't even get a chance to sip my coffee before he'd tossed the whole thing back and clinked the empty glass on the table.

I raised an eyebrow but didn't say anything as I poured him another glass, setting the bottle closer to him on the table this time. I also nudged his glass of water toward him. The last thing I needed was a drunk Gram stumbling around Bayley.

Gram turned the glass of whiskey around and around in his hands, staring into it like he was divining the future in its amber depths.

Wrapping my hands around my mug, I said, "Okay. Let's have it."

Gram looked up, searched my face, and sighed. He leaned back in his chair, whiskey still clasped in his hands.

"It's complicated."

"Well, duh. You brought your bleeding and battered sister here. At three in the morning. Given how fond you are of me, you must be desperate. What'd you do, rob a bank or something?"

The corner of his mouth crooked up. "If only it were that simple."

He thought robbing a bank was simple? Then again, he was a puddle jumper. He could transport himself anywhere he wanted by stepping in and out of the rain—rain that he could summon—so, on second thought, maybe robbing a bank would be easy for him.

He interrupted my musings when he said, "She's in trouble with our family Council."

I'd been having all sorts of fun battling my own family Council, which he knew, since he'd helped bail me out when a faction had attacked me. Was that why he was here? He was hoping to play on my sympathy?

Out loud I said, "The Murphys have a problem with Sadie? Why?"

"It's her magic. It's…"

"Don't say complicated again."

He gave me a look that told me that was exactly what he was about to do. With a pained sigh, he said instead, "Fine. But it is. She has all the main Murphy water wielding abilities, but then there's her…other skill. Like any magic, it has its pros and cons. Hers is just, well, it's…unusual."

He was dancing around so much I felt like he should be wearing tap shoes. I tried to read between the lines. "Unusual.

As in scary? As in dangerous?" His face tightened, and I sat up straighter. "How dangerous?"

My mind went to Bayley. I could feel him monitoring Sadie, but he wasn't worried at all. If anything, he seemed happy to help her out.

I focused back on Gram, who was fidgeting with his glass again, avoiding eye contact. I huffed out a breath. "Gram, you came to me. Either tell me what's going on or hit the road, Jack."

I would never evict someone in Sadie's shape, but he didn't know that. And my threat worked.

His shoulders slumped, and he said, "She's a desiccant."

From the way he said it, I got the general gist that he thought this desiccant thing was, if not the end of the world, approaching the apocalypse.

I'd learned a little in the last couple of months, but my training so far had been focused on Foster magic. I hadn't learned much about the Murphys yet, except a few odds and ends in passing. And none of those odds or ends had been about a desiccant.

This was one of those situations where I wished Nor or Carmine was around. Besides being dear friends, both were experienced Fosters, and they'd know what was going on and could give me a sense of the gravity of the situation. But they weren't here, so I hiked up my big girl boots and waded in on my own.

"What's a desiccant? And before you look at me like I'm an idiot, keep in mind that I had no idea magic even existed two months ago."

He shook his head. "This is high-level Murphy stuff. Even if you'd been raised a real Foster, you likely wouldn't have heard of this."

I let the "raised a real Foster" jab go and stayed focused on what I wanted to know. "Okay, fine, so what is it?"

"It's rare."

"Like you being a puddle jumper is rare?"

He nodded. "We're both products of generations of top-level talents creating more top-level talents. Except, when our parents had Sadie, they didn't get the talent they expected."

Gross, I thought.

Nor had explained the whole eugenics thing the five magical families had going on, and I still found the whole thing horrifying. Rewarding people with stronger magical talents and discriminating against people who had mixed lineages? I had really strong feelings about how wrong the whole thing was. But I managed to hold my tongue and just nod. I couldn't help frowning, though.

Gram mistook my frown. "Hey, I know it's not the best thing when the genetics go awry, but it happens. And look, my parents got the powerful top-level magic user they wanted. But they got a talent that, like mine, no one's had in over a hundred years."

"Stop pussyfooting around. And this talent is?"

"She can suck the water out of anything."

That didn't sound that bad. In fact, given how she'd dried us all off, it sounded downright handy.

He said, "I can see the wheels spinning in your head. Let me cut to the chase for you. It's a great combat magic for use against the Fosters because your earth magic can't grow anything if there's no water." I frowned at him harder, but he plowed on. "But you know who else needs water?"

"Um, every living creature on the planet?"

Gram blinked at me and shook his head. "Yes. Granted. But who needs water to make their spells work?"

"Oh. The Murphys."

He nodded, "Now you're getting it."

Okay, sure, that wasn't great for the Murphys. But as the scope of Sadie's powers sunk in, I was having a hard time getting past the fact that she could basically kill anyone she wanted by sucking the water out of them until they turned into people croutons.

Instead of pointing that out, I tried for diplomacy and said, "I can see where that might seem like a problem."

A bitter laugh escaped him. "Seem? It is a problem. Certain factions on our Council think Sadie should be locked up. Others favor more extreme measures."

I was pretty sure he was saying they wanted to kill her. The fact that I didn't find that surprising was disturbing to me.

"What happened tonight?" I asked.

"There was a power shift. A new group took over ruling the Council—"

"Let me guess. It was the 'Sadie's gotta go' group."

"They didn't even wait till the meeting was over to send people after her. I was at the meeting, and by the time I realized...I was almost too late." He stopped and took a deep drink of the whiskey. His hand shook as he brought the glass to his mouth.

After downing half the glass, his voice was whiskey-hoarse when he said, "Sadie's an offensive wizard. A really good one. She can hold her own. But it was a five-man team. Even so, she neutralized their magic."

I winced as I thought of the kind of magic drain that would cause. "Ouch."

"I'm amazed she was still standing, never mind fighting. When I arrived, three of them were down, but two of them were still on their feet, engaging her in hand-to-hand combat. Like I said, she's good, but she was already drained. If I hadn't jumped in when I did..." he shook his head and slammed back the rest of the whiskey. "We took care of them, but they had a backup team that pulled up just as they went down. Even with both me and Sadie, there was no way we were going to win. I grabbed her and took her to the one place I knew they couldn't go without permission."

"Ah."

"I need to go check on her."

"Sure."

We got up and headed to the sitting room. As we walked, I mulled over what he'd said.

I had to give it to him. He'd made a smart, ballsy decision. Smart because no one could enter Bayley's property without Bayley and me allowing it. That meant she was safe here. Ballsy because Gram knew I'd only grudgingly allowed him any access to the property at all because I hadn't had a choice. I'd been left holding the bag when my predecessor, Meg, made a deal with him, and I was stuck making the best of it. He knew I didn't like having him in the house, so showing up with someone else in tow took a brass pair. But it wasn't like Gram was particularly worried about my feelings. He had tried to pelt me to death with hail once.

I sighed. Just because I wasn't a fan of his, that didn't mean I should take it out on his sister.

As we approached the sitting room, I said, "Okay, now that you're here, do you have a plan about what to do next?"

"What I need is time," he said as we walked into the room.

"Time's not going to fix this." Sadie opened her eyes and stared at Gram. She still looked exhausted, but there was some fire in her eyes now as she said, "They're only going to stop when I'm dead."

Chapter Three

Sadie inched herself upright and looked around the room.

"Where am I?" She looked at Gram and then her gaze shifted to me.

I wasn't sure she remembered anything that happened in the kitchen, so I reintroduced myself. "Hi Sadie. I'm Finn. Finn Foster. Welcome to Bayley House. How are you feeling?"

She looked confused for a few seconds, then her gaze narrowed and swung back to Gram. "You didn't."

"I was short on options."

Sadie's gaze darted around the room again, this time assessing. "This is it? This is the…house? *The* house?"

I looked at Gram, who ignored me, staying focused on his sister. "Yes."

"Why? No wait," she held up a hand, and Gram closed his mouth on whatever it was he was about to say.

I couldn't help it. I was impressed. I wished I could just hold up a hand and make Gram shut up.

Sadie definitely had an accent. It reminded me of British, but it was slightly different. And while she still looked like she'd gone a few rounds with Rocky, as I watched, her whole demeanor changed. I could see her pulling herself together, making a visible effort to look more in command. I didn't know if it was for Gram's benefit or mine, but as messed up as she was, I was kind of amazed that she made the effort.

"Hang on, let me get you some water," I said. I dashed down the hall and back, then handed her the water glass.

Sadie swallowed the whole glass down. She tipped her head

back and closed her eyes. "Let me think this through." She swallowed hard then said, "We were fighting."

"Yes," Gram said.

Her sentences came out slowly, like it was taking her some effort to put things together. "We were outnumbered. And I was drained. You arrived when I was finishing off the second wave—"

"The second? They were the second?"

Sadie cracked open her eyes and gave Gram a look. "You always underestimate me." She closed her eyes again. "Yes. They were the second. I took out the first group, but I didn't manage to get far before those idiots came at me. Wussies. As soon as they realized I still had enough juice to neutralize their magic, they called for backup. Then you showed up." She frowned, winced, then raised a hand to her lip, feeling at the edges of the cut there. Sighing, she dropped her hand, looked at Gram and said, "And now we're here. Where no Murphys have permission to come. Well, except you." She looked at me and a hint of a grin appeared. "Which I'm guessing from the look on Finn's face isn't something she's exactly thrilled about. It's okay, don't look so guilty, Finn. He's my brother. I know what a pain in the ass he is."

Gram looked put out. "Excuse me, that'd be the pain in the ass who just saved your sorry wreck."

Sadie flinched when he called her a "sorry wreck," and she looked away. Gram looked like he wanted to kick himself. I gave him a look that said I'd be happy to do it and save him the trouble.

"All things considered, you look pretty good to me," I said. "But, how are you feeling?"

She shrugged a little, and it looked like it hurt. But she hid it quickly and said, "Could be worse. Although, do I remember something about coffee? I was a bit out of it. Well, if the offer's still good, I could use some."

"You're welcome to it, but I actually have something better—well, okay, not better, because let's be honest, nothing's actually *better* than coffee—but, I do have something special for a magical hangover. I call it the Shake-It-Off. Trust me, I've been in far worse shape than you, and I swear that it's awesome."

She looked a little dazed by my verbal barrage. I was just about to repeat myself, slowly this time, when she said, "Why not. Thank you."

I mentally asked Bayley to keep an eye on them while I went to the kitchen. Fuzzy opted to stay and stand guard, so I felt okay leaving them alone for a few minutes. I'd gotten in the habit of keeping the ingredients for the Shake-It-Off fully stocked, so I whipped it up in no time.

As I headed back to the sitting room, I could hear them arguing in low voices. I stepped into the sitting room, and they both froze. Gram stopped mid-sentence, arms frozen in mid-air, where they'd been waving around.

Sadie looked more tired, tense, and drawn.

"Jeez Louise, Gram, could you do the overbearing brother thing later? Can't you see she's exhausted?" I said. "Here Sadie, drink this," I added as I handed her the shake. I rounded on Gram and said, "Seriously. You think you could maybe take it down a notch?"

Gram growled in frustration and stomped over to the window, pulling aside the curtain so he could look outside.

I turned back to Sadie, who was trying to hide a grin.

"Go on, take a sip," I said.

She took a tentative taste. "That's not awful," she said.

"Give it a minute. It'll be your new best friend." I sat down on the couch opposite Sadie, next to Fuzzy. As she dutifully swallowed a few more mouthfuls of the Shake-It-Off, I said, "Okay, so what's the plan?"

Gram swung around to face me. Whatever Sadie saw in his face, she didn't like it, because she started shaking her head, and said, "No—"

Gram talked right over her. "Finn, we need you to let Sadie stay here. Just until I can find another viable option. Or find some way out of this mess."

Sadie huffed. "There is no way out of this mess. You're delusional. You should have just let me go down fighting."

Gram said, "Don't start that again."

"It's my life! I should get to live what's left of it the way I want. If you hadn't interfered, at least I would've gone out on my own terms."

"Oh don't be so dramatic. You're not going to die. You're going to live to be a hundred, if only to drive me insane for the rest of my life."

Fuzzy and I sat watching them argue for a minute, our heads swinging back and forth like we were at Wimbledon. I wasn't sure if it was the shake, the power nap, or being angry at Gram, but Sadie definitely had more energy. And she was unleashing it on Gram. I had to give her points—she was going toe-to-toe, despite her condition.

Watching them, I couldn't help but notice the family resemblance. Both were tall and dark-haired, with the same caramel complexions and deep, brown eyes. They had the same brooding energy about them, the same aggravated expression on their faces, and both were using the same hand gestures as they yelled at each other. Plus, the longer Sadie argued with him, the more Gram seemed to be slipping into her accent. He hadn't noticed, but I thought it was funny.

Finally, Sadie snarled something that sounded like, "Go home, Dinesha," then abruptly turned to me. "You don't need to put me up. There's no reason for you to get involved in this. I just need a minute to patch myself up, and I'll be good to go."

"Go where?" Gram said, hands on his hips. "Because this is the only place I know of where they can't get at you. You have no options. There is water every-damn-where and, therefore, no matter where you go, they can attack you. You know I'm right. There's no place on Earth with no water."

Sadie and I both said, "The desert," at the same time.

Gram pinched his nose and said, "There's still water in the desert, you morons. Just not much of it."

"Gram, this is ridiculous. Listen to me—" Sadie tried to stand up, sucked in a breath, and sat back down, huddled over, with an arm around her middle.

Gram strode across the room, anger gone, replaced by

something that looked a little like panic.

"Sadie—"

"I'm fine," she said, a little breathless. "I'm pretty sure I cracked a rib, is all."

I jumped in before they started arguing again. "Are you hurt anywhere else? The Shake-It-Off will help with the magic drain, but it won't help with your physical injuries."

Sadie flicked a glance at Gram, then looked back at me. "I'm fine. A few cuts and bruises here and there, is all."

If she was fine then I was a tea lover. But I figured she was trying to put on a brave face for Gram, so I didn't challenge her.

"Well, I have bandages aplenty. After you have some more of the shake, I'll show you where you can wash up. You have to drink the whole thing. Just taking a couple of sips isn't going to do the trick."

She dutifully drank down some more of the concoction, then said, "Thank you for your help, Finn. Gram, thank Finn for putting up with us."

I had to stifle a grin.

Gram muttered, "Thank you, Finn."

Sadie said, "Although I appreciate your help, the more I think about it, the more the desert sounds like a viable option. It's a good place to get lost for a while, maybe buy some time. Make it hard on them at the very least."

Gram said, "Dammit, haven't you heard a thing—"

Sadie said, "You're not the boss of me—"

I listened to them yell at each other for a minute. I'd always thought it might be nice to have a sibling. Watching the two of them made me see my only-child status in a new, increasingly positive light.

I thought they might simmer down, but they just got louder. I looked at Fuzzy. He looked back at me in a way that seemed to ask "What are you going to do about this?"

I checked in with Bayley. He still wasn't a fan of Gram, but he seemed...concerned about Sadie. So was I. Well, that settled it.

I raised my hand and waved it at them.

"— too stupid to realize—" yelled Gram.

"—stubborn jackass—" Sadie hollered over him.

"—for God's sake, what Finn?" asked Gram, as they both stopped abruptly and turned to look at me.

"If I could say something?"

Gram paced away. "By all means. Maybe you can talk some sense into her."

Sadie muttered, "Yeah, cuz I'm the macho idiot in this scenario."

"Um, guys? So here's the thing. Sadie, you're welcome to stay here. And in fact, I think you should." Sadie looked exasperated. Gram just looked smug. I turned to him. "You can stuff that superior attitude of yours in a sock, mister. In fact, you should apologize to your sister for being so overbearing. What's wrong with you? Picking on your sister when she's wounded, for Pete's sake! Maybe if you'd talk to her instead of bossing her around, you wouldn't be having this argument." I turned to Sadie, "And Sadie, I know he's a jerk, but you have to admit, this is a safe place to hole up temporarily." I raised my hand to stop her objection. "If your Council has already gone after you once, I don't see them backing down now. My guess is they will escalate."

Sadie snorted. "Escalate? They already tried to kill me. What are they going to do? Sic more Murphys on me? If I'm in the desert, there's not a lot they can do."

"What about the other families?" I watched the color drain from both of their faces. I nodded. "Sadie, it's not that I think your desert idea is bad. I mean, the desert might help. Against the Murphys. But they're not the only talents you have to consider."

"Shit, she's right," said Gram. He sank into the armchair.

I looked at Sadie. "I'm guessing you hadn't gotten that far in your thinking yet. I don't blame you—you guys are in crisis mode and haven't really had time to think of the big picture. But Sadie, I can tell you from personal experience that if your family Council really wants you gone, they may start with in-house talent, but they won't hesitate to outsource. When Sarah was the head of my family Council, she used members from all the families to try to stop me from getting to the Housekeeper trials." Not to mention that she and Meg had colluded with Gram, but it was best not to go down that road, or I'd be tempted to throw Gram out.

Bayley heard my thoughts and gave the floorboard near Gram a grumble to let me know he was ready and willing to eject Gram at any time.

Gram heard the grumble and raised an eyebrow at the floor.

I shook my head at Gram. "Whatever comment you're about to fling at my house, I wouldn't if I were you. Unless, that is, you want to spend some quality time hanging by your ankles in the freezing cold."

Gram kept his mouth shut.

I turned back to Sadie. "Look. I get that this is a lot. I really do. How about we start with you just hanging out here for today? You can have a hot shower, and we can get you bandaged and fed. You can even take a nap if you want—I've got comfy guest rooms upstairs where you can crash. A little rest and a little food will go a long way toward helping you feel better so you can plan ahead."

Sadie thought for a minute and then she nodded. "Thank you, Finn. I'd appreciate the chance to regroup." She glowered at Gram. "But that does not mean I'm hiding out here indefinitely."

Gram opened his mouth to argue, but I cut him off. "One thing at a time. Let's just start with today and go from there."

Gram heaved out a breath, and some of the tension went out of him. "Great. Thanks. That'll give me some time to assess our options."

"Terrific. You do that." I turned to Sadie. "How do you feel about pancakes?"

Chapter Four

Gram called up another rainstorm. One moment he was complaining that he didn't get to have any pancakes, and the next he stepped into the rain and was gone.

I took Sadie upstairs and installed her in a guest room. With Gram gone, she finally admitted to being tired, despite the rejuvenating effects of the Shake-It-Off.

When I asked Bayley, I was surprised to find that he was fine with letting Sadie use our water. Apparently, whatever was going on was limited to Gram. So I suggested that Sadie have a hot shower or bath and then take a nap. I told her I'd fix breakfast whenever she got up. Then I lent her some clean sweats to wear and left her to do her thing.

Back in the kitchen, I glanced at the clock. It was almost five. The sun wouldn't be up for a while yet, but I was too wired to go back to sleep, so I made some more coffee and sat down to talk with Bayley.

"What's up with you not letting Gram have any water? And how come it's fine for Sadie to have some? Not that I'm not grateful—it'd be really hard for her to stay here if she didn't have access to our running water."

My communication with Bayley kept improving, but I still wasn't totally fluent in Bayley-speak. I had to parse what the images he sent me meant. When I asked him about the water, there was a pause and then I got an image of the pool in the basement.

I thought for a moment and said, "Okay, you're showing me the pool. That's where Sibeta and her people hang out. Oh, you want me to ask Sibeta? It's awfully early. I don't want to wake them up."

Bayley showed me the pool again.

"Okay, I'm going."

I topped off my mug, and then I made a second cup and loaded it with even more cream and sugar than I'd put in mine. As I stirred, I checked in on Sadie. The last thing I needed was for her to catch me slipping into the basement. My mental map of the house showed a blue dot where she was located in her room. The dot wasn't moving.

"Hey Bayley, is she asleep?"

Ding.

"Oh, that's good. Okay, when she wakes up, will you just give me a heads-up? In case I don't notice on my own."

Ding.

"Thanks."

Mugs in hand, I walked across the hallway, into the mudroom, and over to the basement door. As soon as I opened it, Fuzzy darted ahead of me, trotting down the stairs. I'd only made it halfway down before I heard the splash that let me know he'd jumped straight into the pool.

Sure enough, when I reached the bottom of the stairs, I found Fuzzy paddling around in the water. I couldn't help but laugh.

"You're adorable. Weird, but adorable."

I still didn't know exactly what his deal was. I'd figured out that he wasn't an ordinary cat. He was crazy smart, loved the water, and grew a lot faster than a normal cat. But I hadn't figured out what that all added up to. My mysterious neighbor Zo and the equally mysterious Boots seemed to know something about him, but they hadn't seen fit to tell me. I kept telling myself it didn't matter what Fuzzy was, so long as he was healthy and happy, but I sure was curious.

I was enjoying Fuzzy's antics when Sibeta's head popped out of the water. Although I managed not to yelp or drop either mug, I did gasp a bit. I'd sort of gotten used to her green "hair." But there was always a moment of adjustment when I first looked at her.

She was the same brown as the water from the main pond that she lived in, which was connected to the pool by an underground aquifer. But her body wasn't remotely human. Made of some kind of watery blobbish material, her body could change shape to suit Sibeta's needs. And though she had a gaunt, humanish face, it was just *not*-human enough to make me want to do a double-take whenever I saw her. I still hadn't gotten her to tell me what, exactly, she or her people were, or how they'd wound up in my pond.

"Hello, Housekeeper," she said. She smiled when Fuzzy paddled up to her, and she patted him. "Hello, Travis-Fuzzy." I still didn't know why she insisted on calling him Travis, but before I could ask again, she sidetracked me by saying, "I am sorry for the startling you. You need to talk at…no…with! You need to talk with me?"

Sibeta and her group had magically waterproofed a TV and remote so they could watch Netflix from the pool. All that TV was helping them to learn English. The rest of her clan were learning slowly, but in the space of a couple of months, Sibeta had learned the language astonishingly well. She'd gone from speaking a few words to conversational English.

"Sibeta, your English is getting really good. I've been told it's a hard language to learn. How are you learning it so fast?" I knew I shouldn't be surprised. The more time I spent with Sibeta, the more I realized how incredibly smart she was.

Sibeta rose out of the water until she was standing on it. As usual, she'd adorned herself in a cloak made out of water. It swayed and rippled as she moved, like some kind of exquisite, magical silk.

"I am the…" she watched Fuzzy play in the water as she searched for the word.

Along with learning a new language, she'd been learning how to mimic human facial expressions. She frowned and smiled regularly in conversation now and was experimenting with more nuanced expressions. The frown she currently wore clearly telegraphed her frustration as she struggled to find the word she wanted.

"I am...the one who talks the different languages and talks to the different kinds of peoples." She made a clicking sound, which I'd learned was her speaking in her native tongue. "What is the word?"

"Um...an interpreter?"

"Yes. That. But more. I will find the word and tell you."

"Okay, thanks."

"This is what you wanted to talk to me?"

"Oh, sorry, no. I wanted to know why Bayley won't let Gram drink the water here, and Bayley told me to come talk to you. Uh, Gram Murphy, the, er, puddle jumper?"

Sibeta let out a quiet hiss and a series of those clicking sounds. She'd run into him once before. Actually, she'd sensed him coming, gotten angry, and hidden before he could see her. Sure, he was a pill, but as far as I knew, she'd never met him, so I was pretty sure she was objecting to his presence on principle. I just didn't know why.

"Uh, speaking of which, I have some news—oh, here, I brought you some coffee, if you want it. I know it's early to be bothering you, so I figured it's the least I could do."

I actually had no idea when or how long she slept, but I knew she liked coffee, so I'd decided to err on the side of politeness. I walked over to the edge of the pool and handed her the mug.

She smiled and said, "Thank you," then downed the whole thing in one swallow.

"Uh, you're welcome," I said, taking back the mug she handed to me.

I knew I was staring, but I couldn't help it. When Sibeta swallowed the coffee, I could see it sloshing around her mouth through the semi-transparency of her head. She didn't swallow right away, instead holding the liquid in her mouth for a full thirty seconds. I had no idea why, but I was fascinated. As I watched, the coffee flowed through her mouth and down her throat, where it disappeared from sight under the more opaque water cloak she wore. I wasn't sure if I should be grateful or disappointed that I couldn't see the rest of her digestive process.

I blinked, reminded myself to concentrate, and said, "Okay,

do you mind if I sit down and talk?"

Sibeta swept a hand toward the lounge chair next to the pool. Bayley had built it for me so I could hang out more comfortably with Sibeta and her people. That was the plan, at least. They'd been extremely shy, so I'd only managed to spend time with the whole group twice in the past couple of months.

I plunked myself down. Fuzzy hauled himself out of the water and came to sit on the ground beside me, as Sibeta drifted closer.

I said, "Sibeta, I know you're not a fan of Gram's, so you might find what I'm about to tell you upsetting. Gram was here earlier. He brought his sister, Sadie. She's hurt, Sibeta. There was a battle tonight. The Murphys, the water magic family, have a new Council, and they are trying to kill Sadie because they don't like her magical ability. Uh, am I making sense to you so far?"

Sibeta nodded.

When she didn't comment any further, I continued on. "Okay. So. There's no place for her to be safe. Anywhere she goes, the Murphys can get to her."

"Not here. They cannot get to her here."

I nodded, once again impressed by how fast she grasped things. "Exactly. Gram left to try to figure a way out of this mess. But she's staying here—for a little bit. For today, at least. I'm not really sure how long, to be honest. Right now she's upstairs sleeping."

Sibeta still didn't say anything.

"So, um, I wanted to let you guys know that she's here. I will, of course, keep her out of the basement. And away from your pond and that whole area of the woods. Unless you tell me otherwise. But telling you about Sadie is only part of the reason I'm here. Bayley sent me. He told me that I should ask you about the water thing. He's fine letting Sadie drink the water here and shower in it, but every time I try to give Gram water from the sink, Bayley won't let me. If you know why, could you please explain?"

Sibeta tilted her head. "Gram is the puddle jumper. Bayley protects us."

I felt my face crinkling in confusion as I looked at her. "Okay...I mean, good. It's good that Bayley wants to protect you. So do I. We both do. I hope you know that."

Sibeta gave a shallow bow and nodded her head in a way that I'd come to learn meant a combo of "yes" and "thank you."

I bow/nodded back and then said, "But I don't understand what protecting you has to do with the water thing."

Sibeta looked at me like I was weird for not knowing. Since I'd become Housekeeper, I'd been getting that look a lot. From everyone.

I sighed and tried again. "Sibeta, could you please explain? I don't understand."

Sibeta bowed her deep, formal bow and said, "Of course, Housekeeper." She straightened and said, "Puddle jumper..." Just saying the term, she looked like I did when my mom made me eat slimy steamed spinach. "It is...not just walk through the rains. It is...talk with the waters."

"Talk with the waters?"

Sibeta said, "Yes. Know where the water goes. What the water touches. Then can puddle jump and be safe."

"By water, do you mean the rain that Gram calls up?"

"All the water. He is the puddle jumper."

I sipped my coffee as I thought it through. If I understood her correctly, Gram could walk through the water safely because he could communicate with it. It made sense, sort of. If he sent the rain ahead, he could tell who and what was on the other side of the water he walked through, then he couldn't be ambushed or accidentally materialize in the middle of a freeway. But he wasn't limited to only the rain that he called. She was saying he could use tracking magic in any kind of water. One thing I'd learned so far was that every family had its own kind of tracking abilities. But this kind of tracking had never even occurred to me.

"This is not good news," I said, as I looked at her.

She nodded and gave me the "now you're getting it" look that I'd also been seeing a lot. From everyone.

"It's bad enough he can just, you know, show up anywhere he feels like. But now he has tracking magic, too?" I stared into my mug and muttered, "I need more coffee to deal with this kind of news." Looking up at her again, I thought out loud, "So, let me see if I get this right. Let's say Gram drinks the water here. The water comes from the aquifer under the house. You guys use the aquifer to get from your pond outside to this pool. In fact, your pond feeds the aquifer. When Bayley brings aquifer water into the house, he does something to the water to make it safe to drink. But that's not going to block magic, is it? So, if Gram drinks, he'll know you're here?"

"Yes, Housekeeper."

"Well, crap. No water for Gram then, that's for damn sure."

"Thank you, Housekeeper. That is...appreciated."

My mind raced. "I wonder if there's some kind of booster magic I could do to, you know, block Gram's tracking ability. Some kind of ward. I'm part Murphy, as you know. Maybe that can actually be something useful." Of course, to learn to use the Murphy side of my magic, I'd need a Murphy to tutor me. Only a handful of people knew that the Murphys were part of my bloodline, and I kind of wanted to keep it that way. So getting a Murphy tutor seemed unlikely.

"Ugh, what a mess. Well, I'm glad I know. And for the moment, we're safe. Gram's gone, and Bayley's okay with Sadie being here, so she must not have the same tracking abilities."

"Puddle jumper...this happens not often. Very not often."

"Thank goodness for small favors."

"This...Sadie. What is she?"

"What is she? You mean what's her ability?" I winced. "I don't think you're going to like this much better than the puddle jumper thing."

Sibeta floated and stared, waiting me out.

I sighed. "Fine. She's a desiccant."

"I do not know this word."

I cringed as I said, "She can suck the water out of anything."

Sibeta froze. One second she was drifting on top of the water, her robes rippling, and the next she was so still she might have been made of glass.

I jumped up, "Sibeta, are you okay?"

A moment passed before a wave passed through her, and she resumed her movement. "You are correct. I do not like this much better than the puddle jumper thing. I must go."

"Sibeta, I'm so sorry. I didn't mean to alarm you, but, well, you asked! You know Bayley and I would never put you in harm's way."

"Thank you for telling me. It is good I know."

Sibeta started to sink into the pool.

"Thank you for explaining to me about the water," I called after her. "And don't worry about Sadie."

And then she was gone.

I looked at Fuzzy and said, "Well, that wasn't good."

But I didn't have time to worry about it because Bayley alerted me that Sadie was awake.

Chapter Five

Fuzzy and I made it up the stairs and out of the basement just as Sadie was approaching the top of the staircase that came down into the mudroom. I heard Bayley lock the basement door behind me and gave the wall a pat while I told Bayley, *Good thinking.*

As Sadie neared the bottom of the stairs, I said, "Hey there. How are you feeling?"

She moved stiffly as she entered the mudroom but said, "Better, thanks."

I looked her up and down. The gray pallor had disappeared from her face, but she still had a drawn look to her that told me she was achy and tired. I could tell from the way she was standing that her ribs must be hurting. But when my eyes snagged on her sweatpants, I couldn't help grinning.

"Uh, sorry about the fit."

I wasn't short, but Sadie had to be close to six feet, and my sweatpants only reached to mid-calf on her.

She looked down then back up at me, amusement flickering in her eyes. "I don't know what you mean. 'Ready for a flood' is the hot look right now."

Laughing, I led her to the kitchen. "Well, I appreciate your patience. Okay, I've got fresh coffee, if you want it. And I have all kinds of tea. Are you hungry? I feel like after the night you had, you deserve some pancakes for breakfast. If that still sounds good to you."

"That all sounds good—the coffee and the pancakes. But I don't want you to go to any trouble."

"No trouble. I like cooking." I poured Sadie a mug of coffee, showed her where the sugar and milk were and set about mixing up the pancake batter.

As I measured ingredients, she hovered behind me. Her gaze was darting all over the kitchen, and she was shifting her weight constantly as she sipped her coffee.

"Should you be sitting down?" I asked.

"No. Well, maybe. But I don't feel like sitting." And with that Sadie started pacing.

I gave her a minute to settle, but she just seemed to be getting more agitated, so I said, "Are you walking off the aches? Or is this a stress pace?"

"What? Oh, sorry. I didn't realize I was doing it. I pace when I think." She started to run a hand through her hair, winced as she pulled at the cut on her forehead, and then growled in aggravation. "I can't believe I'm in this mess. I mean, I can. It's been a long time coming. It wasn't completely unexpected or anything. But this—" she waved a hand around her to indicate the house, "and you—no offense—I never would have thought this would be part of the equation. What am I supposed to do with you, with all this?"

Amused, I gave her a wry grin. "Uh, since you're the guest in my house, isn't that supposed to be my line?"

She gave me a small smile. "You're right. What a bloody mess, though."

"If you don't mind me asking, what kind of accent is that? Where are you from?"

"Here and there. But the accent is part British, part Indian. I've lived in both places."

"Cool! Oh, does that have something to do with why you called Gram 'Dinesha'?"

"Dinesha?" Sadie looked confused, then started to laugh. "Oh God. I did, didn't I. I said 'Po mone, Dinesha.' It's a quote from an Indian movie, but it's used to mean something along the lines of 'I'll make you regret it if you don't stop being an ass.'"

"Hah. Like that'll happen—have you met your brother?" popped out of my mouth before I could stop myself. I winced and followed quickly with, "Sorry."

"Believe me, I get it."

"Wait, Gram's your brother, so how come he doesn't have an accent?"

"He does. It slips out if he gets angry enough. Or really drunk." She paced another few steps then stopped again. "I can't believe he dumped me here. No offense. It's just, I'm used to having a plan. And a backup plan for that when it goes wrong. And then a backup for the backup. This was not part of the plan."

I nodded. "I can see where that would be disconcerting. What was the plan, if you don't mind my asking?"

She shrugged, "Dodge as long as I can. Go out in a blaze of glory. That sort of thing."

"If you don't mind my saying, a plan that ends up with you dead doesn't seem like a great plan."

"It's realistic. And at least with my plan, I get to pick how I go out." She looked into her coffee as she muttered, "And then this would all finally be over."

"There is that." She reminded me of how my friend and sometime booty-buddy Reese acted when he first showed up at Bayley House.

I said, "You know, I have a friend who was in a similar situation. Yeah, I can see you don't believe me, but it's true. I don't think it's my place to say exactly what his talents are, but I can say, in terms of people going after him because of his gifts, he can give you a run for your money. Anyway, he thought his situation was hopeless, and he wasn't exactly excited to get dumped on my doorstep, either. But, he holed up here for a little while and guess what? They figured something out. Now he's back out in the world with a whole new thing going on, happy as a desert flower after a rainstorm."

"That's nice for your friend. But I don't see that working for me."

"Look, I don't expect you to believe everything's going to be all unicorns and rainbows from now on. But who knows what we can come up with, given a little time."

When she looked at me dubiously, I said, "Hey, I'm just

saying that it's not the worst thing in the world to hang out here and take a breath."

She stared into her coffee and didn't say anything.

I'd just poured my first batch of pancakes onto the skillet when I heard a rustling sound. A red dot appeared on my mental map and began moving down the driveway.

I swung around to look at the clock and said, "Oh crap. Eagan's here. What day is it? It's Monday, isn't it? Oh man. I totally forgot."

"Who's Eagan?"

"A friend. On the plus side, he's a member of the Smith family, so it's not like you have to worry about your watery brethren messing with you. On the minus, I didn't mean for you to have to deal with company so soon. Do you want to avoid him? You could grab a bowl of cereal and hangout upstairs if you like."

The driveway was really long, winding through the woods for a long while, but even so, Eagan was rapidly approaching the house. Whatever we were going to do with Sadie, we needed to do it quick.

Sadie sat up straight and raised her chin in an arrogant way that reminded me of her brother. "Hide from a Smith? Not likely."

I wondered if this was going to be a mistake. I said, "Okay, well, he's pulling up now, so last chance."

She settled into her chair. "I'm good."

"Okay then. Keep an eye on the pancakes for me, will you, while I go get him?"

She nodded, and I took off down the hallway for the front door, Fuzzy at my heels.

Eagan was already halfway up the porch steps when I opened the door.

When I'd first met him, I'd dubbed Eagan "Cute Guy" before I learned his actual name. Just slightly taller than I was, he was a red-headed, amber-eyed genuinely nice guy. And I'd discovered that behind his quick wit and friendly smile, Eagan was a really smart guy.

That's why I'd decided to ask him for help with my greenhouse. When I'd first gotten it set up, I'd worried about having a backup plan to make sure that the greenhouse stayed consistently warm, even if anything went wrong. It had finally occurred to me that I could kill two birds with one stone by asking Eagan for help. I could make sure there was a spell in place to keep the greenhouse warm no matter what. And, I could get Eagan to show me how he used his magic.

Of course, Eagan had no idea I was part Smith. I hadn't told Eagan or anyone else that Reese had discovered that I was a balance: my genetics were an exact balance of each of the five magical families. Reese seemed to think it was a big deal, so I'd kept it to myself.

Despite thinking I was a Foster, when I'd asked Eagan, he'd been happy to help me. In fact, he'd been tickled that I wanted to learn how the Smiths did magic in addition to learning my own Foster magic.

"Hey, Eagan."

"Morning, Finn. You ready to work? It's a little while to sunrise still, so I figured we could do some planning before we get to work." He paused, then added, "Uh…you gonna let me in?"

I was standing in the middle of the doorway, which kept him standing on the porch. "Erm, about that. I have company."

Eagan peered over my shoulder down the hallway, then looked at me with a mischievous grin. "Oh? Am I about to bear witness to a walk of shame?" he asked, waggling his eyebrows.

I laughed, I couldn't help it. "Not that kind of company. And for the record, if it were, there would be no shame involved."

"Well, in that case, how about you let me in before I get so frozen I'm completely useless to you? Freezing the fire guy is not the best way to get his magic to work."

"Oh, sorry." I stepped aside so he could come in, then closed the door behind him.

Eagan looked around the hallway, brows furrowed. "Did you redecorate again? I swear the last time I was here, it was darker."

"Maybe it's the lighting," I said.

Bayley rumbled the floorboards in a way that sounded distinctly like a harrumph. I shushed him in my mind. I didn't want to get into a discussion of Bayley with Eagan right now, given who else I had in the house.

"So, who's your company?" asked Eagan.

Sadie appeared in the doorway to the kitchen at the end of the hall. "I am," she said.

This should be interesting, I thought.

Eagan and I walked down the hallway to the kitchen. As we walked, I said, "Eagan Smith, meet Sadie Murphy."

By using their last names, I let each of them know what kind of magic the other had, without me having to go into any explanations. Fire and water. Nothing could possibly go wrong there.

While I went to the stove to flip the pancakes, Eagan and Sadie nodded at each other. I looked over to see Eagan assessing the various bruises and cuts decorating Sadie's face.

"Rough night?" he said.

"I've had worse," she said.

His gaze snagged on where my too-short pants left her legs bare and said, "Did it involve a flood?"

Sadie gave him a bland stare. "No. Coffee?"

"Sure. I'll get it," he added, when she made a move toward the counter.

She shrugged and sat at the table.

I said to Eagan, "Did you eat? I'm making pancakes, and there's plenty."

"I never turn down pancakes." Eagan draped his coat over the back of a chair and took a seat across from Sadie. "So, I'd ask what brings you to Bayley House, but—"

"—it's none of your business?"

Eagan blinked at her and then a slow smile bloomed. "—but being that you're a Murphy, it's unlikely that I'll get a straight answer out of you, so why bother."

I turned from the stove to find them having a staring contest. I waved my spatula at them. "Children. Play nice, or no one gets any pancakes."

Both of them sipped their coffee, but the staring contest continued.

"Okay you two. It's too early for family politics. Let's see if we can all get along." I realized I needed to give them something to distract them, so I asked the question circling around the back of my mind. "Hey, do I have to worry about you two accidentally blowing up my kitchen or anything?"

That did it. They stopped staring each other down and turned incredulous looks on me.

I said, "What? You're fire," I said pointing my spatula at Eagan. Then I shifted to point at Sadie, "And you're water. That makes you opposites, kind of. Right? Is it, you know, okay for you guys to be in the same room for a while?"

Sadie looked between me and Eagan, settled on Eagan, and said, "She's serious?"

Eagan nodded. "Finn's new at the magic thing. She was raised in a magic-free home."

Sadie looked horrified.

Eagan said, "I know, I know. Not optimal. Especially for the Housekeeper." He turned to me and said, "But you're doing really well, Finn. Surprisingly well."

I smiled and said, "Well of course you'd think so. You're the first Smith to visit Bayley in who knows how long."

Sadie glared at me. "You've been making my brother jump through hoops to visit, and you just let this Smith—"

"—Eagan, my name's Eagan—"

"Fine. Eagan. You just let Eagan, a Smith, in here with no problem?"

I said, "It has nothing to do with your brother being a Murphy. It has to do with him being, well, a total dick—no offense—and oh yeah, there's that one time where he tried to kill me."

Eagan said, "Who's your brother?"

Sadie and I said, "Gram Murphy" at the same time, though she said it with less attitude than I did.

Eagan's posture changed, and he suddenly looked very tense and alert. Sadie reacted to that by mirroring his posture. When

I looked over they were both on the edges of the seats, facing off, shoulders stiff. The air in the kitchen felt charged.

"Hey, hey, hey. What just happened? Cut it out, you two. I mean it. I don't know what's going on, but no battles before breakfast. It's a rule here at Bayley House."

Eagan relaxed a little, though it looked like an effort. After a beat, Sadie followed suit. Eagan gave me an amused look. "It's a rule, is it?"

"It is now," I muttered. "Eagan, it's not Sadie's fault her brother's an ass."

"An ass who recently helped you," said Sadie.

"True," I said with a sigh.

Eagan said, "Fair enough. But Finn, given your, er, current learning curve, I don't know if you know just who you have here in your kitchen. Meet Sadie Murphy, second in line to run one of the most powerful branches in the Murphy family. By reputation, an extremely deadly Offensive Wizard."

Sadie gave him a smile that made me run cold. "Scared, Smith?"

Eagan gave her a cheery grin in return. "That a little old Murphy's going to rain on my day? Not on your life, Sweet Pea."

"Who are you calling little, short stop?"

Eagan's grin widened.

"Pancakes!" I called and thunked a loaded platter between the two of them. That broke the tension that was building, and the two of them sat back a little.

I shifted a gaze to Sadie. I was worried that bickering with Eagan wasn't going to be helping with her recovery, but I was surprised to see the little spark in her eyes had chased away the resignation I'd seen earlier. I smiled. Maybe sparring with Eagan was good for her.

I set the table quickly and sat down with them to eat.

"So," I said. "About that blowing up my kitchen thing...."

Sadie said, "No it's not something you need to worry about, Finn. First, fire and water cancel each other out, more or less."

That was true in general, but I knew what Sadie's talent was, so it was "less" not "more." If she sucked the water away, then everything would be more flammable. That didn't sound like canceling anything out to me.

"Second, we're adults. It's not like we're going to lose control of our magic or anything."

"Lose control? A Murphy? God forbid," said Eagan.

"Exercise restraint? A Smith? I know it's a stretch, but I have to believe that at your age, even you can exert basic control."

"Careful who you're calling old. I'm pretty sure I see some crow's feet to go along with that raven hair of yours."

I wanted to laugh, but I figured it was my duty as host to settle things down. I waved my fork in the air. "No insults during meals."

Eagan smiled. "Another rule?"

"Sure, why not. Here's another one: next one to call anyone a name does the dishes."

Sadie said, "I'm sure I can manage that. Can you?"

Eagan grinned and said, "Sure thing, Princess."

Chapter Six

While Eagan did the dishes, I pulled Sadie aside.

"I need to do some work with Eagan. What do you want to do while we're at it?"

She looked over my shoulder at Eagan. He was humming as he washed, periodically looking out the window over the sink and watching the backyard come into view as the sky lightened.

Sadie said, "Can I watch?"

Startled, I said, "You want to watch?"

"Yes."

I chewed on my lip while I considered. I didn't know if this was a good idea. If breakfast was any indication, those two were going to snipe at each other nonstop, which was going to make it hard to get anything done.

"Um, let me ask Eagan if he minds an audience," I said.

Sadie leaned against the hallway wall, watching as I walked to Eagan.

"Eagan."

"What's up?"

"Sadie wants to watch you do your thing. Uh, you okay with that?"

Eagan shrugged and said, "It's fine." Raising his voice, he added, "She might learn something."

"Great. Thanks."

"No problem. Since you're curious about how we Smiths do things, if you want to bring a pen and paper and take notes, that's fine." He turned to Sadie, "You're welcome to take notes, too."

"Oh can I, really? Thanks, I'll pass."

Eagan grinned and shrugged. "Suit yourself."

I said, "Well, I'd love to take some notes, let me just grab a notebook."

I dashed down the hallway to the sitting room and grabbed a notebook and pen I had stashed there. By the time I got back to the kitchen, Eagan had finished the dishes and was drying his hands.

"Ready?" he asked.

"You bet. I'm really looking forward to this."

Eagan grabbed his coat off the back of the chair, and he and Sadie followed me into the mudroom where I also snagged my coat. Frowning, I turned to Sadie, "You didn't have a coat when you arrived, and I don't have an extra coat for you. Do you want me to loan you a sweatshirt?"

Bayley mumbled the floorboards under me and hit me with a gust of heat.

I laughed. "Oh, right. Thanks. Bayley says that he can keep the porch warm enough if you want to hang out there."

Sadie was looking from the floor to me and back again.

Eagan said, "Don't worry. You get used to it. I give you an hour before you're talking to the house without even thinking twice about it."

Sadie gave him a look of disbelief but didn't say anything.

"And besides, if you need someone to help with your frigidness, I'd be happy to lend Bayley a hand."

Sadie gave him a bland look while I resisted the urge to do a facepalm.

We all trooped out the back door and onto the porch. The sun had begun painting the sky with lighter shades of blue, but it hadn't cleared the treetops yet. Still, it was bright enough to see my breath creating little clouds in the air.

"I see you went straight for the McMansion version," said Eagan, looking at the large greenhouse behind and to the right of the garden shed. He shook his head, a half-grin quirking the corner of his lip. "Not a big believer in starting off small, are we?"

I couldn't exactly tell him—or Sadie—that I was worried about feeding an entire flock of water creatures who were hanging out in my basement, so I grinned and said, "Go big or go home. Besides, it's big enough that it'll give me plenty of room to, well, grow. I can always start in one corner and spread out from there. This just gives me options."

Sadie drawled, "Aw, what's the matter? Too big for you to handle?"

Eagan winked at her and said, "Turns out I like 'em big."

Before Sadie could retort, Eagan turned and walked over to the greenhouse. Sadie stayed on the porch, which Bayley immediately heated to a comfortable temperature.

"You okay hanging out here?" I asked.

She nodded.

"Bayley?" I asked. "A place to sit, please?"

As the porch planks rumbled and then flowed upward, Sadie jumped back a little, then stood watching, a bit wide-eyed.

I grinned as I watched. Bayley could have just popped up a basic chair, but as usual, he chose to get creative about it. The wood twisted and bent, weaving together to form an intricate lattice-work pattern on the back and seat. It looked like waves crashing across the back and flowing down the arms and legs.

"Jeez, that's pretty. Thanks, Bayley!" I said.

The porch boards squeaked happily at me.

Smiling at Sadie, I said, "Please feel free to make yourself comfortable."

She looked back and forth between the chair and me. "You guys do this all the time?"

"What, make chairs? Bayley is great that way. If I need something, he helps out if he can."

Sadie looked thoughtful but didn't say anything else, so I trotted down the porch stairs to where Eagan was standing by the greenhouse.

"You ready to stand back and watch me work?" he asked. In a quieter voice he added, "Don't worry, I'll explain as I go."

"Yup. Thanks."

Eagan opened the door to the greenhouse and stood in the doorway. He whistled, long and low. "Damn, I've had apartments smaller than this thing."

I shrugged. "Room to grow, remember."

"You're the boss. Let's light this fire."

Eagan stood in the doorway of the greenhouse and cupped his hands in front of him.

"Wait," I said, tuning into the rustling leaves sound that alerted me to a visitor. Sure enough, a blue dot had appeared at the edge of my mental map and was making its way down the driveway.

Eagan was looking at me questioningly.

I said, "We've got company." I turned toward Sadie and called, "There's a Murphy headed down the driveway toward the house."

Chapter Seven

"Does anyone else know you're here?" I asked Sadie.

She frowned and shook her head. "Not that I know of."

Her posture had gone rigid, and she'd shifted into what looked like a fighting stance, so she expected this to be trouble.

Me too.

I turned back to Eagan. "The lesson is going to have to wait. This might be a thing."

Eagan shrugged. "Need a hand?"

"I'm not sure yet. Maybe. How about you come with me, and we'll see," I said as I strode toward the back door. Eagan followed in my wake. As I walked up the porch steps, I said, "Eagan, no one can know Sadie's here for now, okay?"

To his credit, Eagan didn't ask questions. He said, "Okay," and kept following me.

I said, "Sadie, no sense revealing your location if we don't need to. You can hang out in the front sitting room and listen in. I'll holler if I need you."

She looked as tense as a coiled spring, but she nodded and fell into step behind us.

Bayley opened the back door for us. Fuzzy joined me as I hurried down the hallway and out the front door onto the porch. Eagan ducked into the kitchen, then dashed after us, carrying two mugs. He came out onto the porch with me and Fuzzy while Sadie scooted into the front parlor. Bayley cracked open a window so she could hear what was happening.

I shut the front door just as I sighted a car approaching the grove where the house lived.

Eagan shoved a mug into my hand, gave me a big smile, and said, "Nothing happening here. Just a regular day with two friends sharing coffee."

I smiled and turned to watch the approaching car.

It drove down the left side of the circular driveway, passed the little parking area, and pulled to a stop in front of the porch steps.

Eagan was leaning against the porch railing, the picture of casualness, but I saw him stiffen slightly as he caught sight of the driver. From my angle, the sun was bouncing off the window, so I couldn't see who was in there.

Smile in place, he mumbled, "Yup, trouble."

The driver-side door opened, and I had to stifle a groan when I saw who climbed out. I didn't know her name—in my head I referred to her as Not-Meg. She'd been working with Gram when I first arrived at the house. She was with him when he'd confronted me, Eagan, and our group in the diner downtown, and I was pretty sure she'd been helping Gram when he attacked me with that hailstorm. She'd also been with Gram and Meg when they partially opened the magical door in the house.

For all of these reasons, she was firmly in the "Icky People" column in my book. And from the way she was currently frowning at me, I bet I was occupying the same spot on her internal ledger. Unlike Gram, she'd made no attempts to explain her actions or to make any kind of peace with me. Given the dislike dripping from her frown, I didn't think any such overtures would be forthcoming in the near future.

Instead of telling her what she could do with her frowny pants, I gave her a cheery wave. "Good morning! This is a surprise."

That was a loaded statement. She knew that she shouldn't just show up here. She didn't have permission to be on the property. In fact, until I became Housekeeper, no one but the Fosters was allowed here. I'd only recently opened Bayley up to more visitors, but I got to choose who those visitors were. And people always asked first. So her just showing up was a huge faux pas, and she knew it.

Not-Meg didn't look like she cared what rules she was breaking. She strode around the car, studying the area around us like she owned the place. But when she approached the porch stairs, Bayley growled at her.

Bayley didn't like her either.

She pulled up short and, gaze darting between the steps and house, carefully backed up a few paces until she was standing in the driveway with her car at her back. She swept her gaze over Eagan and then settled back on me.

With a nod, she said, "Housekeeper. I'm here to take custody of Sadafea. I have a warrant."

I didn't have to fake the look of confusion on my face. Aloud, I said, "Custody? What now?" But in my mind, I was thinking, *Sadafea?*

Not-Meg crossed her arms and gave me a pained look. "Are you really going to go this route?"

My confusion deepened. "What route?"

She sighed. "The playing dumb route."

I looked at Eagan, who shrugged, then I looked back at her. "I honestly don't know what you're talking about. What's this about a warrant? And also, can we just back up a second? Do you want to start by introducing yourself?"

She looked insulted. "We've met before."

Maybe not the brightest thing she could have said, given how we'd met before. But I let it slide and said, "Yes, but we haven't been introduced. I'm Finn."

"I know that."

"And you are…?"

Another sigh. "Kate. Murphy."

"Hi Kate. Nice to meet you. This is Eagan Smith."

Eagan gave her a little finger wave.

She looked at me like I might have a few screws loose. "I know. He was at the diner with you."

Definitely not a diplomat, this one. I held onto my smile and said, "Okay, well, now that introductions have been made, let's talk about this custody thing you mentioned.

Would you like some coffee while we talk? Eagan, would you mind grabbing Kate a cup of coffee?"

Eagan straightened. "No problem."

Kate said, "I don't want any coffee."

Another point against her. No coffee. And no manners. Okay, that was two points. What was it with the Murphys, anyway, that they didn't say basic "pleases" and "thank yous"? Maybe it was just Gram's friends who were like that?

Well, just because she didn't have any manners didn't mean I'd forgotten mine. I asked, "Would you like tea instead?"

"No." She must have seen something in my face because this time she added, "Thank you."

"Suit yourself. Now, what's this about custody?"

Eagan asked, "Did you guys lose a kid or something?"

Kate looked like she wanted to charge up the stairs and whack Eagan. I saw her eye the steps and think better of it. She settled for glaring at Eagan and saying, "Of course we didn't lose a child. The *Murphys* are careful with our kids. It's not like we're Smiths."

I said, "Whoa now," but I guess I didn't need to worry about Eagan's feelings because he burst out laughing.

Kate didn't like being laughed at and took a step forward.

Bayley made the steps growl at the same time as I said, "Okay, let's just simmer down."

Kate stopped where she was, but she kept glaring at Eagan. He laughed harder, which made her glare harder.

I scrubbed my hand across my face while I mentally muttered to Bayley, *Freaking family politics. Hey, do you think if they get into it, the fire and water will create steam? Maybe I'll get a nice facial out of it?*

Bayley creaked the porch's floorboards under me in a way that made it obvious he was laughing. Hearing him chuckle made me smile.

I realized Eagan had stopped laughing and looked up to see them both staring at me.

"Uh, Bayley and I would appreciate it if you two would quit it with the family politics for the moment."

Eagan said, "What did I do?"

I ignored him and looked at Kate. "Okay, look. There's no one here for you to take custody of—I don't have any children here. Well, I mean, Fuzzy is a kitten. But I don't think he's what you're looking for. I mean, he likes water, but I'm pretty sure he's not a Murphy."

When Kate looked at Fuzzy, he let loose a low growl, which managed to be both adorable and fierce at the same time.

I said, "Yeah, see. He's not going with you. So, no kids here for you, sorry. But if you have a picture of who you're looking for, I'll be happy to keep an eye out for you."

Kate stared at me for a moment. Then a cold, hard smile crept across her face. "I see what you're doing, Housekeeper. I won't be distracted. Let me be perfectly clear here. I've come to collect Sadafea Carsey Murphy. Under the terms of the extradition agreement between the Fosters and the Murphys, you have to turn her over to me. Immediately."

When Kate said Sadie's full name, all the humor drained from Eagan's face. He moved to stand next to me.

I said, "I take it this is serious?"

He said, "Very. Whatever is going on, she's not messing around."

"Kate, Eagan here says that whatever is going on, it's really serious. Since I'm really new at all this family politics stuff, and he isn't, I'm going to just assume he's right. And given that I have no idea what the hell is happening, I'm not doing anything legal until I call my lawyer, Nor."

Eagan shook his head, and he and Kate said, "You don't have time," at the same time.

I looked at Eagan, who said, "It's part of the treaty terms. It's the same for all the families. You can get into legal options after extradition. But you have to submit to extradition—immediately—as soon as the person to be extradited is identified to you."

I frowned. I was sure if I could get ahold of Nor, she'd have some way to keep me from having to turn over Sadie. And I suddenly realized, I really didn't want to turn Sadie over to

Kate if I didn't have to. It wasn't like Sadie and I had bonded or anything, but I felt sympathy for her. Also, I really disliked Kate, and I didn't trust her.

I wished for Nor again, then sighed. Well, I'd just have to bluff it for now and hope she could fix any mess I made.

"Well that's a stupid system." I shrugged and looked at Kate. "And, this is all very interesting, but I've never even heard that name before. So all this is a moot point."

Eagan tilted his head, "You sure?"

I nodded. "Believe me, if I'd heard a name like that, I'd remember it. Kate, what makes you think he's here?"

"She. And I know she's here. I tracked Gram's cell phone here."

Goddammit Gram! You idiot! I yelled in my head. Out loud, I said, "Gram's not here."

Kate gave me a smug smile. "But he was. Last night."

Mentally, I continued cursing Gram for not being more careful. But I nodded at Kate and said, "You're right. He was here."

Her smug smile widened.

"But I still don't know who that Sad…er, Sad Sack…?"

"Sadafea," Eagan supplied.

"Sorry. Sadafea. As far as I know, I still don't know anyone with that name."

For the first time, Kate looked a little unsure.

I asked, "Well, look. You know as Housekeeper that I can't leave the property. Also, I know when people show up here. I can tell you that no one's snuck onto the property recently. How long has she been missing?"

Kate ignored me. "You admit Gram was here?"

"Yes. Though there's nothing to admit. He did, in fact, show up here. In the middle of the damn night, to tell you the truth."

Sharp-eyed, Kate said, "Alone?"

I felt Bayley nudge my mind. I had the strong sense that he wanted me to be careful.

So I channeled my annoyance at Gram into the look I was giving Kate. "I don't know what kind of relationship you think I have with Gram, but I can tell you that we're not exactly friends.

I don't even want *him* here, never mind him bringing along any friends. And to answer your question, yes, I spent some time alone with Gram—in my kitchen, so don't get any ideas. Being Gram, he danced around what the hell he was doing here. He eventually admitted that he was dealing with a family issue, needed a place to hide out for a minute, and oh hey, let's just wake Finn up! That man is such a ginormous pain in the patootie, I don't know how you work with him. Anyway, I got aggravated, and he left. I haven't heard from him since."

All of this was true, as far as it went. I had been alone with Gram in the kitchen. For part of the time. The rest of the time Sadie had been around. And it was true she hadn't been introduced to me as Sadafea. She was Gram's sister Sadie. Could I draw a conclusion that Sadie and Sadafea were the same person? Well, yes. But that would just be an assumption, not a proven fact, until someone confirmed it. Was I walking a logic tightrope here? You betcha. But for now, I was going to hang out in this very shaky gray area and hope for the best.

Kate studied me for a long moment, then said, "I don't believe you."

I choked back the "I don't care" and squashed the urge to have Bayley drag her off the property. Grasping at straws, I said, "Was this the only place Gram stopped last night?"

She hesitated and then said, "No."

Again, I saw uncertainty slide through her eyes. I pounced on it. "So he might have deposited that Sad lady someplace else?"

"Sadafea. And he was here the longest."

"Lucky me," I muttered.

Eagan said, "Look, I've been here since early this morning."

Kate frowned at him. "So what?"

Eagan beamed at her. "Damn, I know you Murphys are slow, but honey, you sure you don't need some coffee?"

While I gaped at Eagan, Kate turned her frown into a glower. When she said, "I beg your pardon?" I was pretty sure the temperature dropped ten degrees.

Eagan said, "Well, you know I'm a Smith, right?"

She said, "Yes."

"Like I said, sweetheart, I've been here for a while. What friend of Gram's would lower themselves to slumming with a Smith all morning?"

Eagan pushed the right button. I saw the moment she bought what he was selling.

I tried not to look relieved as she nodded and said, "Mmph." After a last, long look, Kate headed back around her car to the driver's side.

"I may be back," she said, as she climbed into her car.

"Can't wait," said Eagan, and he gave her an outrageously flirty wink.

"Have a nice day!" I called.

She didn't respond. She didn't flip us the bird, either, so I guess that was something.

Eagan and I watched her drive away. When she was out of the house's grove, I turned to Eagan.

"How much trouble am I in?"

"You need to get Nor over here. Now."

Chapter Eight

I sent Eagan to the kitchen and called Nor using the encrypted phone that her girlfriend, Mila, had given me. Mila ran some kind of super-secret espionage-ish organization that, among other things, spied on the magical families—the kind of organization you didn't ask too much about. Mila was part Scrounger from *The Great Escape,* part Black Widow, and all badass. Given her vocation, she had access to all kinds of neat gadgets, including my new phone, which was not only high-tech, but also charmed six ways from Sunday so that no one could eavesdrop on my calls.

She'd also set up Nor's system, so I didn't hold back on any of the details when I called Nor and filled her in on what was going on.

Nor listened silently until I wound down, sighed almost imperceptibly, and said, "Don't do anything until you hear back from me," and hung up.

I walked back into the kitchen to find Fuzzy babysitting Eagan and Sadie. His tail flicked back and forth as he watched them sitting in silence, eyeballing each other.

Eagan broke the staring contest to look at me and asked, "What did Nor say?"

I shrugged. "I'm supposed to stay tuned. And to try not to muck up anything in the meantime."

Eagan grinned, "Good luck with that."

"You know I can have Bayley drag you out of here by your ears, right?" I said mildly, as I loaded up on some more coffee.

Eagan gave me a mock wounded look. "And risk bruising

all this?" he asked, gesturing to his face. "You wouldn't want to do that, now would you?"

Sadie said, "I would."

"I wasn't asking you."

Before they could start bickering again, I jumped in, "I won't drag anyone out who doesn't deserve it." I swept them both with a stern look which somehow just made them both grin. So much for being the boss lady. I suppressed my sigh and leaned back against the counter, coffee cup in hand. "But actually Eagan, you should probably go soon."

Was that a look of disappointment I saw flit through Sadie's eyes? It was there and gone so quickly, I couldn't be sure.

I held up my hand as Eagan started to squawk at me. "You didn't do anything wrong, in fact you've been a huge help, but something tells me we're not going to get any work done today, so you might as well pack it in. Can you do something temporary, to maintain the temperature for now, and we'll do a longer-term solution later?"

In a flash, Eagan simmered down from outrage to agreement. He scrubbed his hand over his face. "Sure. I can whip up something quick. I've got to be heading off to work soon anyway. Want to try putting something more permanent in place tomorrow?" He slid a glance toward Sadie.

She said, "Don't let me stop you. I don't plan on being here."

We'll see, I thought, but aloud I said, "Sure thing. If anything changes, I'll give you a call, and we can re-reschedule."

Eagan nodded and stood, heading out the back door. Sadie and I stood at the kitchen window and watched him walk into the greenhouse. He was only in there for a few minutes before he came back into the house.

"That was quick," I said.

"That'll hold you for now," he said.

"Thanks Eagan."

"No problem." He hesitated just a second, then stepped over to Sadie and held out his hand. "It was nice meeting you."

Sadie looked disconcerted for a moment, then squashed her face into the arrogant, snarky look that I was coming to think was the hallmark of her family. She shook his hand. "And you as well."

Before she could pull away, Eagan brought her hand to his lips, gave it a quick kiss, and with a smile said, "See you around Princess."

I thought for sure she was gonna slug him and had already transferred the weight to the balls of my feet to jump forward and intervene when Sadie stepped back and gave Eagan a slow sexy grin that rendered him mute. She leaned forward, and my eyebrows shot up as it looked like she was going to kiss him.

She stopped an inch from his face, booped him on the nose, stepped back and said, "Not if I see you first," then strutted out of the kitchen, booty swinging.

Eagan gave a low whistle as Sadie disappeared up the back stairs to the second floor.

"I might have to marry that woman," he said.

I barked out a laugh. Eagan and Sadie. Well, they'd certainly have the love gods putting in overtime.

Shaking my head at him, I said, "Easy there, Romeo. Let me walk you out."

Eagan earned major brownie points with me as he took both his and Sadie's mugs to the sink and rinsed them. Someone had raised that boy right.

As we walked to the front of the house, Eagan shot a glance at the second floor and said, "All joking aside, you've got yourself into a bit of a pickle here, Finn. Holler if you need anything."

"Hopefully things will be okay till tomorrow," I said. But given my luck, I added, "I will absolutely call if I need you though."

Eagan gave me a hug and headed off to work. As I stood on the porch and watched him drive away, Libby and Todd, the two ancient oaks at the entrance to the grove, bobbed their branches at me from across the lawn. Fuzzy came dashing up behind me and went scampering off toward Libby.

Fuzzy paused near Libby's base and looked back at me. I did a quick mental check and found that Sadie was in her room. Fuzzy meowed impatiently at me, bringing my attention back to him pacing back and forth in front of Libby.

I laughed. "Okay, I'm coming," I called. I dashed back inside, grabbed my coat, hat, and gloves, then headed out across the lawn to Libby.

Fuzzy had scrambled up the tree and was halfway to the treehouse by the time I reached Libby's trunk. She leaned a large branch down for me, so I could climb up easily.

"Thank you, Libby," I said, patting her branch before climbing aboard. "How are you? Looks like it's going to be a lovely day." Libby swayed gently, and somehow gave me the sense that she was feeling very content. Libby and Todd's branches were entwined over the road, so as I climbed, I came near some of Todd's limbs. He reached out with one and gently tugged at my hair, teasing me. I giggled. "And good morning to you, too, Todd. I see you're in a playful mood." To that, the branch gave my hair another little tug, making me giggle again. I gave the branch a gentle tug back, it waved at me, then withdrew.

Bayley could make steps appear that led up to the treehouse, but he never needed to. Libby took care of it. She always dipped and rearranged her branches for me so I'd have an easy climb. It was a little like watching a ballerina executing intricate arm movements, all grace and awe and "how on earth did she get her arms to do that!"

With Libby offering helpful stepping branches, I quickly finished my ascent to the treehouse. Fuzzy was already there.

The treehouse, like everything Bayley built, was a work of art.

The inside of the treehouse was a single, open room, with walls and floors made of a rich, grainy wood the exact shades of Libby's bark. The front of the treehouse had a walled balcony, the railing intricately woven to look like tree branches.

Fuzzy was perched on the balcony. He was looking toward the horizon, tail swinging back and forth. The treehouse faced east, like the house, and on a clear day like today, we could see a tiny sliver of ocean glinting in the distance.

I sighed. "Do you miss the ocean, Fuzzy? I sure do." We'd only been that one time, but it had been as soul-searingly beautiful as I'd dreamed. And now I could never go back. Could never leave this property. It was the bargain I'd made to become Housekeeper, and I'd just barely begun to adjust to the consequences of that choice. Winter loomed, and I was more than a little worried about how I would weather the long, frigid days alone in the house.

As I looked at the ocean and felt swamped with longing to visit it again, I felt an answering nudge from Bayley at the back of my mind. When I tuned into him more closely, I could feel his concern and compassion.

"It's alright, Bayley. I'm still okay with the choice I made. It's just to be expected, I guess, that there are things I'm going to miss."

Fuzzy jumped down and headbutted my shins, so I plopped down next to him to pet him. He climbed into my lap and started purring.

"Hey buddy. Quite a morning we're having. How are you doing?"

Fuzzy said, "Meow."

He nuzzled my chin and then started kneading my leg.

"I'm happy to hang out with you too." And I realized I was, despite the chill in the air. Fuzzy's purr disintegrated the wistfulness I'd been feeling, and I found myself surrounded by affection from both him and Bayley.

Leaning against the balcony wall, I enjoyed the gentle swaying of the treehouse and let my mind wander. While I petted Fuzzy, I mulled over the situation with Sadie. I tried to put myself in her shoes. It must truly suck to have such a powerful magic and to have everyone be afraid of you. I was so accustomed to the pity I received at my utter lack of magical prowess that I had to work at it to imagine what it'd be like to be so powerful that people wanted to kill you.

On second thought, I could totally relate to the people wanting to kill me part. That was becoming a disturbingly regular occurrence since I came to the house.

I wasn't sure how I felt about Sadie yet, but I thought I might like her, despite her being Gram's sister. Although given that relationship, and the fact that they were obviously close, that meant I couldn't really trust her. But still. She seemed like someone I could be friends with.

The thing was, she really needed help, whether she wanted to admit it or not. And I was in a position to give it to her. Even with the Gram factor to consider, I'd have to be a complete ass not to at least offer her some time to recoup and plan. The problem was getting her to accept the helping hand.

Fuzzy interrupted my train of thought by abandoning my lap and hopping back up onto the balcony railing.

"Meow."

"Hey Fuzzy, what's up?" I asked, climbing to my feet and moving to stand next to him.

It took me a moment to realize he was laser-focused on a bird in a neighboring tree. It looked like a sparrow.

He looked at the bird, then looked back at me.

"I see him. But look at him, he's so little, he doesn't mean any harm. How about you leave the poor little guy alone?"

Fuzzy gave me a look that told me what I could do with my bird-loving sentiments. Then he turned to the bird and started making odd, sort of chirping sounds at it, like he was doing his best to imitate sparrow speak.

I laughed. "Nice try, sweetie, but I don't think you can talk the bird into flying into your mouth."

Fuzzy shot me another look followed by another "Meow!" He turned back to face the sparrow and kept chirping. Then, he squished down, hunkering into a low crouch.

I realized a fraction of a second too late what he was up to and yelled, "No!" as he sprang off the railing. It was at least a thirty-foot drop, and nine lives or no, there was no way he would survive that kind of fall.

I reached for him, trying to catch him as he launched into the air, but I was too slow and too clumsy. My hands grabbed empty air as Fuzzy flew off the railing.

It took me a heartrending moment to realize that he wasn't falling, he was...soaring. Sailing, really.

He was freaking air gliding.

He looked for all the world like a weird, feline version of a flying squirrel, sailing on the wind, arms and legs stretched out to the four corners with flaps of skin connecting them on each side. I held Fuzzy all the time, and I'd never realized that his skin could stretch like that.

As I stood gaping, he glided over to the next tree, landing on a limb seconds after the sparrow that had been sitting there vacated the space.

Fuzzy watched the bird take off, let loose a disgruntled "Meow," and then squished himself down again, gathering himself in another crouch. With a butt wiggle and a mighty surge, he was off. He glided to the next branch where the bird had landed. Once again, his prey escaped him. Fuzzy made little growling noises that sounded like he was muttering in disgust. Then he did it again.

I stood squeezing the railing of the treehouse in a death grip as I watched him glide from tree to tree, chasing the sparrow.

Once I realized he wasn't going to kill himself, my brain kicked into gear, and I started to think about what I was seeing.

What the hell?

I knew that Fuzzy wasn't what you'd call "normal," but this was so far outside the norm that I couldn't even wrap my brain around it. My cat was flying. Well gliding, but it was nearly the same thing.

As my brain churned, I realized he'd done something similar once before when he'd hopscotched his way along the tops of some saguaro cacti to get to me. At the time, I'd thought it was super weird, but there'd been so much other even crazier weirdness happening that it sort of just blended in. But watching him now, I couldn't deny that he was actually sort of flying from tree to tree.

That was just nuts.

All along I'd been saying that I didn't care what Fuzzy's deal was, so long as he was healthy and happy. Not anymore. As my heart leapt into my throat every time he leapt into the air, I admitted that I really did want to know what was going on with him. At least maybe then I wouldn't have a total heart attack when stuff like this happened.

I realized that Fuzzy was starting to make his way back to me. The closer he got, the more he looked odd to me. Something was off with the shape of his face.

I figured it out just as he landed on the railing in front of me and dropped the dead bird at my feet. Fuzzy had caught his prey.

"Meow," he said proudly, flicking his tail.

I scooped him into my arms and hugged him hard. "Oh thank the flying squirrel gods. Really, Fuzzy? Are you kidding me?"

Running my hands over him, I searched for signs of injury. He seemed fine. In fact, he seemed totally normal. Just like a flying squirrel, his skin had contracted back to his body. He looked like a regular kitten.

I hugged him close until he started to squirm. I looked at him, and he looked back with an expression of disgust that would've done any teen proud. I couldn't help but laugh. "Oh Fuzzy, what am I gonna do with you? Are you totally mental?" He squirmed more, so I put him down. He looked at the bird and then looked at me. He even nudged it toward me and said, "Meow."

I laughed again. "Okay, okay." I petted him on the head. "Thanks for sharing your snack."

Fuzzy meowed again and pushed the bird toward me some more.

"Thanks for trying to feed me, bud. I appreciate it. You're an excellent hunter," I said. I felt really bad for the bird population though. It seemed that now that Fuzzy was a little bigger, he'd be hunting more, and given his flying squirrel routine, the birds wouldn't have their usual safety in the trees.

My thoughts were interrupted when a voice from the ground called up, "Why are you up in a tree?"

Chapter Nine

I leaned over the side of the treehouse to find Zo glaring up at me. She was dressed in her usual baggy sweater, half her dreadlocks piled in a messy bun. No jacket, though, despite the chill.

My neighbor Zo was the only one who simply appeared on the property. One second, no Zo. Next second, there she was.

Granted, Bayley and I'd given her open access to come visit any time she liked. I just never had any idea how she got here. It was one of the many things she'd thus far refused to tell me. However, I kept chipping away at her gruff exterior, hoping she'd eventually spill the secrets she was keeping.

Her arrival, though unexpected, was excellent timing because, after what I just saw, I really needed to get her to tell me what she knew about Fuzzy.

Out loud, I called, "Hey, Zo," and gave her a little wave.

"I'm not climbing up there."

"I'll be right down." I turned to Fuzzy. "I don't suppose you want to come down with me?"

Fuzzy picked up his bird and bounded off down the tree.

"I'm sure Zo will love seeing your conquest," I called after him, grinning as I pictured the look on Zo's face.

I followed him down the tree, albeit at a much slower pace.

"Hey Zo," I called, as I neared the ground. "I think it's time we had a real talk about Fuzzy. You'll never believe what he just—"

On my way down the tree, I'd been watching where I was going so I didn't really focus on Zo until I hopped down to the ground—the ground where Zo was squatting next to Fuzzy, poking the bird he'd just killed. With her bare hands.

"Uh…." I made a strangled sound when Zo stood up, still holding the bird, and started…molesting it. She was really digging in there with her fingers, like she was giving the bird a deep-tissue massage.

"What are you doing to that poor bird?" I choked out.

Zo glanced up at me. "Looks like it's dead," she said. A calculating look flitted through her eyes as she stared hard at the bird.

I opened my mouth to question her but before I could say anything she shook her head at me. Frowning, she raised a finger in front of her lips in a "shh, don't talk" motion.

Dumbfounded, I nodded and shut up.

Zo went back to poking the bird. She was totally focused on what she was doing, and I was totally at a loss as to why. Fuzzy was stalking back and forth at Zo's feet, agitated, looking ready to fight.

What's happening? I wondered.

As though she heard me, Zo looked up and said, "We'd better put this poor thing to rest," made the "shh" motion to me again, and took off toward the house.

I had to jog to keep up with her as she strode across the lawn. Fuzzy dashed ahead of us, waiting on the porch for us to catch up to him.

My thoughts raced, trying to figure out what was happening. I checked in with Bayley and stumbled a little when I felt how tense he was. Whatever was happening here, he was really concerned. My own sense of confusion gained a sharp edge of anxiety.

As soon as Zo and I neared the house, Bayley opened the door. Zo marched on in without pausing, and Fuzzy and I followed her inside all the way to the kitchen.

I did a quick mental check, and thankfully Sadie hadn't moved at all, so I was guessing she was still asleep. I had Bayley lock her door, reminded him to let me know if she woke up, and then returned my attention to Zo.

She went straight into the pantry and emerged a moment later with the canister of salt. When she went to stand at the kitchen island, I moved to stand on the other side. Fuzzy hopped up on a chair at the kitchen table behind us, so he also had a clear view of what she was doing.

Zo held onto the sparrow with one hand and used the other to dump the entire canister onto the kitchen island.

I made a mental note: add salt to the grocery list.

Shaking out the last of the salt, she put the canister aside.

As she flattened the salt hill into a wide, inch-thick circle, Zo said, "Bayley, are you able to…light up…the whole kitchen?"

A vibration went through the room in a buzzing wave that passed through the floor, walls, and ceiling. It left the whole room with a subtle sort of tingly feel to it.

Zo nodded, so it must've been what she'd wanted Bayley to do. She put the bird on top of the salt, then strode over to the counter and grabbed a cleaver from the knife block.

I blanched as she approached with the knife. A wave of relief passed through me when she walked past the bird and headed out of the kitchen. As she walked, she called, "Don't eat it," and I realized she was talking to Fuzzy, who twitched his tail in response.

"Stay here," she added to us both.

Just before she left the kitchen, I felt the vibrating by the door drop, then pick right back up as soon as Zo walked through and continued out the back door.

Jumping from the table to the kitchen island, Fuzzy positioned himself so he was standing guard over the bird.

He seemed to have no interest in actually touching the bird, so I went to the kitchen window over the sink to watch Zo.

Zo stomped through the section of the garden Carmine and I had finished weeding and planting and made her way to the part that was still running wild. She kept on going until she reached a clump of dried flowers. With a few quick strikes, she sliced off a bunch of the flowers and headed back for the house. At the edge of the garden, she stopped again and hacked branches off the behemoth rosemary bush, and then came back to the house.

When Zo returned to the kitchen, I felt the vibrations by the door drop and then rise again as she entered.

Returning to the kitchen island, Zo slapped the knife onto the counter, and dumped the flowers in one pile, the rosemary in another. She rapidly wove the branches of rosemary together to form a circle. "Probably overkill, but…" she mumbled, then placed the rosemary circlet around the salt circle.

I still wasn't sure what she was up to, but at least the kitchen smelled nice.

She stripped some rosemary leaves off an extra branch, cupped them in her hands, and whispered to them. Then she piled them on top of the bird.

A long, tense moment passed while Zo, Fuzzy, and I stared at the rosemary-topped bird.

Nothing happened.

Zo let out a breath on a "Hmph. Good. I was pretty sure the spell died along with the sparrow, but better to be safe."

"Wait what? What spell?"

"That's not a bird."

"What do you mean it's not a bird?"

"Well obviously it's a bird, but it's not a regular bird. It's been spelled."

"Wait. Someone spelled a sparrow and somehow snuck it past Bayley?"

Zo nodded.

The floorboards under us made an ominous, growling noise.

I didn't need a magical bond to know that Bayley was pissed.

If people could sneak stuff onto the property without Bayley noticing… "Oh this is bad," I said out loud.

"You think?" Zo said.

Bayley growled louder.

I looked toward the wall and said, "It's okay, pal. I'm sure this is probably my fault somehow. Don't worry, we'll get better as we go."

Zo said, "Well if you can postpone your pity party long enough to pay attention, then maybe we can learn something."

That seemed a little harsh, but I nodded and focused on what she was doing. "So, um, what's the salt for?"

Zo looked at me like I was stupid. "Neutralizes any residual magic."

"And the rosemary?"

She sighed. "Extra protection."

"If the spell is dead, why do we need protection?"

"We don't know who did this or why. Better to be safe than sorry. Rule one with magic: assume the worst. You might not die from stupidity that way." Zo looked around at the walls and said, "That's why I had Bayley circle the kitchen. I need to interact with the bird, but I didn't want to take the chance that there are any nasty surprises, particularly since the original spell was able to sneak past Bayley."

"Wait, circle the kitchen? That's what the vibrating is?"

"Yes."

"Oh! It's, what, some kind of protective circle?"

Zo looked exasperated as she nodded.

"Bayley can do that?"

Exasperation turned to disgust as Zo said, "How do you not know this? You've been here for nearly two months."

Stung, I said, "I've learned a few things. Carmine is teaching me, but he's been busy lately. And circles haven't come up yet."

Zo muttered something under her breath, shaking her head as she rapidly crumbled the dried flowers into a pile.

"Is that goldenrod?" I guessed.

She nodded. "You should harvest some before you clear it all. Very useful."

"Why? For what?"

Glaring at me, she said, "You can read, right?"

I blinked at her. "Well, yeah."

"Then get a book and look it up."

I felt like I'd been slapped. I must have looked like it, too, because she said, "Oh don't look so stunned. It's high time you got off your ass and took charge. Yes, it would be helpful if you had an official tutor. So what? You're not stupid. Figure something out. In the meantime, stop asking me so many questions and be happy I'm letting you watch."

For once, I was speechless, so I just nodded. She sounded even angrier than usual and I couldn't figure out what I'd said to get her back up. Bayley seemed as shocked as I was.

As Zo finished shredding the goldenrod, she commanded, "Quickly. Run me through the colors you see on your mental map."

"Green for the Fosters, red for the Smiths, blue for the

Murphys, purple for the Guthries, and tan for the Bests."

Grabbing a handful of the dried flower bits, Zo cupped her hands and whispered to them. Then she blew into the flowers, at the same time spreading her hands, so that the pieces flew out into the air over the sparrow. But instead of dispersing and falling, they stayed grouped together, hovering in a dust cloud. It began to whirl slowly, picking up speed until it was spinning. The flower cloud swirled and dipped, like a tiny murmuration.

Fuzzy watched it closely, tail swishing. He raised a paw and reached to poke at it but it flocked out of his reach.

Without looking at him, Zo said, "Fuzzy," in a tone that had him putting his paw down immediately.

Zo stayed laser-focused on the cloud as it dove and dashed around the sparrow, then came to hover above it. The flower bits kept shifting and rearranging themselves as the cloud moved. The way she was staring reminded me of how she'd looked when she read my tea leaves the first time I met her. Was she reading the particles somehow? If so, what were they saying?

All at once the cloud turned purple, the individual bits and pieces glowing and pulsing. The flower bits slowly drifted to settle over the sparrow, where they pulsed purple once more and then disintegrated.

Zo straightened, looking thoughtful. "Interesting. Guthrie. Air magic. Well Finn, someone in the Guthrie family is spying on you. Know anyone who fits that bill?"

"The only Guthries that I know are Lou and Pete. And I can't think of a reason they'd spy on me."

"Mmm. Interesting."

"You said that already."

Zo gave me a look. Then she picked up the bird. With a few quick movements, she wrapped the bird in the rosemary, somehow weaving the rosemary together around the bird, encasing it. Then, she put the whole thing in her pocket.

Now it was my turn to give her a look.

"What? It's not like you've got any use for it."

I wasn't sure I wanted to know what Zo thought a dead spelled bird was good for. Bayley didn't seem to know or care.

He was still miffed that someone had snuck the bird by him.

My concern for Bayley's wellbeing overwhelmed my fear of Zo, and I blurted out, "Zo, how come Bayley couldn't sense the spell?"

"They used a…I'm trying to think of how to explain it to you…it's like a camouflage spell. Oh stop looking so worried. Now that he's seen it once, they won't be able to sneak the same spell by him again. Right, Bayley?"

Bayley grumbled the floorboards beneath us, managing to sound both disgusted and determined.

"Well good," I said. "But how did you know there was a sparrow spying on me, if even Bayley didn't know?"

"I didn't."

"Oh. Then why are you here now? Was your Spidey-sense tingling?"

Zo gave me a flat look at the Spidey-sense remark, then said, "I came to find out who's here."

I threw up my hands. "How do you do that? You knew when Carmine was here the first time, too. How can you tell?"

As usual, Zo ignored me and repeated, "Who's here?"

I was still stinging from her earlier rebuke, and I suddenly wasn't willing to be bossed around anymore, particularly when I had someone in my care to protect.

I crossed my arms over my chest. "Uh uh. You know that I don't mind answering your questions usually, Zo, but this is important. I told her she'd be safe here, but if people can tell she's here, then we're in for some trouble."

Zo looked like she was thinking something over. After a moment she said carefully, "Bayley and I have an…agreement— it predates you. No one else can sense what goes on here—that's why they have to resort to things like that sparrow." With an irritated look, she repeated, "Now. Who. Is. Here?"

Well, despite her surliness, she had answered my question. And even though her answer brought up a whole boatload of other things I wanted to know, since she'd given me an explanation, the least I could do was to tell her the truth. "Gram's sister Sadie is here."

Zo's eyebrows shot up into her hairline. "You don't say." I

could see her connecting the dots. "You realize he's playing on your sympathies because he's counting on you feeling like you owe him—which you don't, by the way. But you being you, of course you'd take her in." She thought for a moment. "You told Sibeta?"

I nodded.

"Of course you did." She frowned. "I bet that was fun." Zo stared off into the distance for a minute then looked at me and said, "Well, this should be interesting."

"There's that word again."

"Well, you said you wanted not to be bored. Careful what you wish for."

"Mmm."

Now that the excitement was over, Fuzzy hopped down and started to groom himself.

Which reminded me, "Hey Zo, about Fuzzy. We need to talk."

Zo's face went carefully blank as she said, "Oh?"

"I think it's time you tell me what his deal is. I know you know."

Zo's eyes gleamed. "I do."

"Well?"

Zo pursed her lips and studied me. "He's not a cat."

I'd known that on some level, but having it confirmed so baldly made my heart speed up. "Okay."

Tensing for whatever came next, I asked, "Well? What is he?

A calculating look crept into her eyes. She looked around the kitchen, as she considered. Her gaze snagged on the hallway, and I could see the thoughts darting behind her eyes as she stared into the hallway. "Once you figure out the door situation, we can talk about the rest."

I blinked at her. "But—"

Before I could finish, she turned around and headed out of the kitchen, calling, "You need some motivation to get on with things. Consider this your kick in the pants. Time to learn, Finn. Top of the list is that," she thumbed toward DeeDee. "That damn door has you spooked. Get over it."

Conflicting thoughts whirled in my brain. She was right. I was building myself up to a full-on phobia. But clashing with that thought was the fact that she was withholding information that kept me from properly caring for Fuzzy. Neither my fear nor my protective instincts were able to battle the other into submission, so I wound up stomping my feet and sputtering as I watched her leave.

Lot of good that did.

She waved as she reached the back door. "We'll talk soon."

Before I could ask anything else, Zo was out the door. She crossed the lawn and stepped into the forest. A few seconds later, her silvery blip was gone from my mental map.

Pacing around the kitchen, I vented at Bayley. "Are you kidding me? Who does she think she is to give me an ultimatum like that? She's not the boss of me."

Bayley made a sympathetic squeaking sound.

"And what the hell was that earlier with all the snapping at me? I mean, Zo's always kind of crotchety, but that was bordering on mean. We didn't do anything to deserve that. Hell, we didn't even invite her here, she just showed up! Of course I'm going to have questions when she starts doing magic."

This time Bayley made a supportive noise that I interpreted as "uh huh" or "damn straight."

I ran my hands through my hair, growled in frustration, pacing back and forth some more, muttering, until I felt a little calmer.

I looked down at Fuzzy, who was looking up at me expectantly.

"So you're not a cat, huh?"

He swished his tail.

"Any chance you can tell me what you are?"

"Meow," he said, then strutted over to his food bowl. I took my cue and followed after him.

"Lemme guess, you didn't get to eat your sparrow, so you're hungry." I shook my head at him. "You may not be a cat, but you sure do a good impression."

Chapter Ten

After I fed Fuzzy, I made myself some coffee, and checked on Sadie. My mental map said she still hadn't moved an inch. Given how drained and bruised she'd been, she probably needed as much rest as she could get. She was going to be super sore when she woke up. With that in mind, I whipped up another batch of the Shake-It-Off. While I was at it, I decided to make some chicken soup. Nothing like some homemade soup to cure what ails you.

I was in the middle of dicing celery when a Foster blipped onto my mental map. From the rate the green dot was sailing down the driveway, whoever it was was driving. I found myself grinning in hopes that Nor had decided to come deal with my current mess in person. I strode to the front door and stepped out onto the porch in time to see Wil parking his car.

My heart sank, and my stomach clenched a little. Immediately, I gave myself a mental scolding. Wil wasn't a bad guy, per se, he was just heavily aligned with the Council. The Council that kept trying to get rid of me. Sometimes by trying to kill me.

I sighed. Well, he'd made no secret of his ambitions to be a part of the Council. He'd told me from the get-go that was his goal. I just hadn't realized at the time that it'd mean I'd wind up saddled with this discomfort around him. I didn't genuinely distrust him, but I wasn't sure if I could fully trust him, either.

Fuzzy came over to sit by my feet, wrapping his tail around his legs. We watched as Wil climbed out of his car and hauled out his ever-present messenger bag, which for some reason looked like it weighed a ton today. He gave me a quick wave as he walked over to me.

While Wil wasn't a full-time professor anymore, he still gave off a hip-professor vibe. Between his just-worn-enough-to-be-super-stylish jeans, his button down, his blazer, and his glasses, his overall look all but screamed, "Hi, I'm an intellectual." Not for the first time, I thought some of his students must've had crushes on him. With his coffee-colored skin, big brown eyes, and engaging smile, he could be a real charmer.

As he climbed the porch steps, he tried turning some of that charm on me as he said, "Hi Finn. Hope you don't mind me dropping in unannounced."

"No problem," I said. Wil's charm bounced right off me as I prayed that Sadie remained asleep. I gave Bayley a fast mental nudge, reminding him to let me know the second Sadie woke up and got a quick acknowledgment back.

Out loud, I said to Wil, "How are you?"

"No complaints."

"Is everything okay?"

"Why don't we go inside and chat."

Well, that was a big fat "no." I traded a look with Fuzzy. He gave me the look he gets when he knows he's in trouble. I wondered if I had the same look on my face.

We filed into the kitchen. "Coffee? Tea? Have you eaten?" I asked Wil.

"Sure, I'll have some coffee." At my raised eyebrow he laughed and said, "I know I usually drink tea, but I like to switch it up." His gaze took in my pile of veggies on the kitchen island. "Looks like I'm interrupting. Why don't you continue and let me get my coffee. You want me to top you off?"

Wil was already moving toward the cupboard, so I let him help himself and replied, "Sure. Thanks."

Fuzzy hopped up on a chair and sat watching us. Wil brought me my coffee, then propped his hip against the kitchen table across from the kitchen island and stood sipping and watching me as I resumed chopping.

"What are you making?"

"Soup. It's getting cold so I figured it's a good time to stock up, have some in the freezer." That wasn't entirely a lie. I did plan on freezing the leftovers. If there were any. But most of the soup was for Sadie, which he didn't need to know.

Wil nodded and sipped his coffee.

"So, what brings you by?"

"I heard you had a little run-in with the Murphys this morning."

I shot him a quick look as I kept chopping. "That didn't take long."

"If the way you're going after those veggies with that knife is any indication, I'm guessing it wasn't a great way to start your morning."

I wasn't about to tell him that I was already several hours into my day by the time Kate showed up. Instead I said, "Kate isn't my favorite person, that's for sure. What is it with the Murphys, anyway? Or is it just Gram's friends? Are they all born cranky or something? They're, what, in the water family so they all have a perpetual case of diaper rash?"

Wil chuckled. "Given your limited exposure, I can see why it'd seem like all Murphys are that way. But no. I can promise you there are some more…level-headed…members of the family. Actually, that's one of the reasons I came in person."

"Oh?"

"My purpose is threefold. First, to hear from you what happened with Kate, so I can run interference for you—she filed an official petition with our Council. That's how I heard about her surprise visit."

"Of course she did."

"It's the kind of petition that's a political headache, so I'd like to get your version of events on record before the Council makes any moves. And second…well, today's run-in just highlighted your lack of protocol training again."

I was still feeling sensitive from the talking to I'd just gotten from Zo, so Wil's comment smarted more than usual. I started to protest but Wil talked over me. "I know, I know. It's totally not your fault. Which brings me to point number three. Your tutor. This is taking too long, and I've about had it with the Council dragging their feet."

"Preaching to the choir." Of course, he didn't know that Carmine had been secretly tutoring me a little.

"I know. So I had an epiphany this morning. I really don't know why I didn't think of it sooner. It's the perfect solution, really. I'll be your tutor."

I stopped chopping and stared at him. "You?"

Wil held up his hands in a placating motion. "Will you just hear me out?"

I went back to chopping so he couldn't see how uneasy I was and said, "Sure."

He started counting points off on his hand. "First, you're getting access to a world-class education. I'm a professor, remember? An exceedingly good one, if I'm being totally honest. Not only that, but my specialty is the history of our family."

Nor had said on more than one occasion that Wil probably knew as much or more about the Foster family than anyone living. He also knew a frightening amount about the other families.

I nodded at him, and he continued.

"So I've got the knowledge and teaching background you need. You'll be getting a blue-chip education that people usually pay thousands of dollars for, and instead of sitting in a classroom, you're getting one-on-one attention."

Despite my attempt to hide my expression, I must have looked as unconvinced as I felt because he continued, "Second, and as importantly, it'll give us a chance to get to know each other much better."

He fidgeted with his coffee cup. "I know things haven't gone smoothly since I became liaison. I've apologized—and you've been kind enough to accept—but I don't feel that I've done enough to earn your trust. I'm asking for this chance to be of real service to you, so you can size me up firsthand. At the very least, I'm hoping that we'll forge a good working relationship, but I'm really hoping we can be better friends."

I didn't know how to react to what he was saying. On the

one hand, Wil knew more about the Fosters than most of the Council. And, as he'd said, he was a professor—not just good, but so good that he'd taught at prestigious places all over the world. Nor said he was crazy brilliant.

But since he'd gotten his seat on the Council—a position he'd won by being my liaison—he'd been siding more with them than with me. He hadn't managed to stop that homicidal nut job who'd come after me—hell, he hadn't even warned me.

But I felt bad, which I'm sure he knew—the whole point of the "let's be friends" part of his little speech was to play on my emotions. Smart of him, really, but also a red flag to me because it seemed so calculating. Maybe he was sincere. Part of me wanted to believe he really meant it, but another part was highly skeptical. Unbidden, scenes from my recent battle with the head of the Council flitted through my brain.

I realized I was staring at my knife frowning when Wil pulled out his last point. "And third, of course, if you have me as your tutor, I can tell you about the door."

Chapter Eleven

I quirked my eyebrows at him. "Way to save the big guns for last," I said. But he knew he had me. He could've been taking lessons from Nor, the way he waited to hammer home his deal with that doozie.

My gaze drifted to the hallway and the innocent-looking door that led to the closet under the stairs. Except it didn't really. Well, not always. Sometimes, with Bayley's help and if you could get the magic right, it led somewhere else. I'd labeled it DeeDee—for Demon Door—because the two times I'd been able to crack it open, I'd wound up unconscious and half-dead. I still hadn't figured out exactly what was on the other side. Well, okay, at the very least, I knew that when magic was used to open the door, on the other side there were trees that had some kind of seed pods.

The thing was, I had no idea how to open the door safely. And opening the door was a major part of being the Housekeeper. Those seed pods on the trees were valuable, apparently. The Council wanted them and wanted them bad. I'd deduced that they had some kind of medicinal value, but I didn't know the specifics.

I really needed to know the specifics.

"Well?" asked Wil.

"I'm thinking," I said, as I returned to chopping.

"Take your time," Wil said. He sounded amused. Probably because he knew he had me.

I held back a sigh. After this morning's conversation with Zo, I had more motivation than ever to know what the hell was going on with the door. I really needed to know what was going on with Fuzzy. I glanced to where Fuzzy was sitting in a chair at the table. He looked back at me, and my heart melted the way it always did when I looked at him.

I'd do just about anything for that little guy.

"Okay, I'm in," I said.

Wil grinned and bounced a little on his toes. "Excellent choice! You won't regret it!" He went to where his bulging messenger bag lay on the table. As he opened it, he said, "I was hoping you'd agree, so I took the liberty of bringing some materials to get you started."

"Wait, wait, wait...I thought you were going to tell me about the door."

"I need you to do a little reading first, get a little background."

I frowned at him. "Sounds like stalling to me."

Wil winked at me. "Dinner before dessert, Finn. Trust me, this is the way to do things."

As he started to haul out a pile of books, I realized why his messenger bag had looked so heavy. It had a whole freaking library in it!

"Jeez, Wil, did you leave any books on the shelves?" I said.

He just laughed.

I put my knife down as the stack on the table continued to grow. "That's way more books than you've got bag there. How did you do that?"

Wil reached his arm into the bag all the way up to his shoulder and dug around. "It's an extension charm. Really useful. One of things I'll be teaching you, in fact. It expands the interior space of a given object."

I was already familiar with this kind of spell, though I had no idea how you went about creating it. Bayley had done something similar to our shed out back, though on a much grander scale.

I could feel Bayley's sense of pride as I thought of his awesome shed, and I sent him a mental, *Good job*.

"So, it's a TARDIS spell?" I asked.

Wil fished out the last book he was looking for and turned to me. "TARDIS spell?"

"You know, like in *Doctor Who*. Bigger on the inside..." I said.

He smiled. "Yes, exactly."

"Well that'll come in handy," I said.

Wil patted the top of the nearest pile of books. There were five stacks of books in all, and there had to be at least thirty books in total.

Wil said, "I hope you don't mind, but I took the liberty of getting you a starter library. Since you've got Council resources at your disposal, I was able to get everything you need to get going. Of course, this is just the tip of the iceberg. I'll bring more as we go along."

I eyed the stacks dubiously. "Uh, thanks?"

Wil laughed. "You look like my students on the first day of class when I hand out the first assignment. Don't worry it'll be fun."

"Sure. Fun."

Wil searched through the piles and pulled out three books. The one on top had a cracked leather cover, worn thin in spots. The pages were brown with age, and the binding was crumbling at the edges. "Start with the one on top, then read the other two if you have time. If you can finish them in the next couple of days, that'd be great, but at the very least, get through the first five chapters in each. Do you think you can manage that?"

"I have no idea. I've never tried to read books on magic before. I'll give it a try, though." My parents had homeschooled me, so I was used to diving into a stack of books and discussing what I'd learned. Still, I felt like the tomes on the table were staring at me in challenge. It felt daunting.

Wil said, "I'm taking a holistic approach. Since you're utterly lacking in any background on magic, I'm incorporating a good deal of general history as well as texts that delve into the backgrounds of all the major families. There will, of course, also be instruction on magic, both theoretical and practical. I'm approaching that more like a science class—in addition to the reading, we'll have hands-on practice time."

That sounded like home, too. My mind flashed back to the time my dad and I built a volcano in the kitchen. While Dad went to answer a phone call, I doubled the amount of baking soda in the middle of the volcano.

Dad came back and said, "Where were we? Oh yeah. The fun part!"

"Can I pour the vinegar in?"

Dad smiled. "Sure you can. But *slowly*."

I started off slow. I did.

The volcano started bubbling up, and Dad said, "Good job, Finn. You can see how the baking soda and the vinegar react to—you can stop pouring now, Finn. Finn. Finn!"

I cackled with glee as the volcano bubbled harder. My glee turned to a weird sort of delighted horror as the bubbling kept going, over the top and sides of the volcano, merrily spreading out all over the table, and cascading onto the floor.

"Oops," I said.

Dad looked at the ceiling, shaking his head, then looked at me and laughed.

The picture of the two of us mopping the kitchen and laughing had me smiling now.

Wil saw my smile and said, "Glad you like my plan. I really think this will do wonders for you."

I snapped back to the present and focused on Wil. I lowered my eyes so he couldn't see the hurt and disappointment I was feeling. My mom and dad should have taught me this stuff. I shouldn't have needed Wil or anyone else to tutor me. Why had they kept me in the dark? The question had been nagging me since I'd had my magical eye-opening. I didn't see how I'd get any answers, though, given that they were dead.

"Is there a way to talk to the dead?" popped out of my mouth.

Wil shook his head slowly. "That's not a Foster talent, I'm sorry. Who are you thinking of contacting—oh, your parents. Of course. I'm sorry, Finn. That's not a magic that's going to be on our agenda."

I nodded. "Just thought I'd ask."

Bayley moaned and sighed around us, responding to the sadness that swamped me.

Wil looked alarmed. "There's plenty else to learn, though, Finn. Don't worry. You won't be bored."

"Of course I won't. Thanks, Wil. I appreciate the assist. Really."

Wil shrugged. "I was thinking that you were planning on going to college, before," he swept his hand around the kitchen, "all this. This will be as close as you can get from your current position. Think of it as the homeschool version of college."

I barely kept from wincing. The whole point of going off to college for me was to get out of the house, away from homeschooling, and get to see the world a little while I learned. I knew Wil meant well, but he hit a sore spot. Not that I regretted becoming Housekeeper. But I was still worried about becoming claustrophobic.

Out loud, I said, "Sounds great, Wil," but him mentioning homeschooling made my gut tighten.

Bayley creaked the floorboards near my feet, an acoustic rendering of my anxiety. I nudged the floor with my toe, while in my head I told Bayley, *Don't worry. If I do start feeling boxed in, you and I will figure it out.*

Fuzzy hopped down from his chair and came over to rub against my legs. He plunked down beside me, leaning into me.

"Looks like Fuzzy approves," said Wil with a laugh.

"Sure he does," I said, leaning down to pet Fuzzy. His purr lowered what was left of my anxiety.

As I relaxed, I felt Bayley relax, too. But a second later, the house crackled and popped around us as I felt Bayley go on alert.

Wil looked around. "Is Bayley okay?"

"Just settling," I said, while I tried to have a conversation with Bayley at the same time. He was showing me Sadie's room, and her little blue dot was moving around.

Chapter Twelve

My mind spun as I tried to figure out a way to deal with this. Without making Wil suspicious. Without pissing Sadie off. And without giving her an excuse to bail. My mind locked up in panic. Why oh why hadn't I made a "what to do if people show up" plan with Sadie earlier? People were always showing up. What the hell was I thinking?

I wanted to bang my head on the cutting board.

I had an image of me doing just that and coming up with my forehead covered in mashed veggies. The image made me grin, which snapped me out of my panic.

Wil mistook my grin. "I'm glad to finally do something that makes you smile."

I took the out and said, "Of course I'm smiling. You know I love to learn new stuff. Not to mention I've been dying to learn magic. So yeah, I'm psyched." I grinned wider then toned it down a bit when Wil looked a little alarmed.

As Wil began explaining my first assignment to me, I nodded and half-paid attention to him while I talked to Bayley at the same time.

Bayley, don't let her out of her room.

I glanced down at Fuzzy.

Bayley, can you tell Fuzzy to go to her room and keep her company? Maybe if I send Fuzzy, she'll figure out something is up and won't freak out.

Fuzzy looked up at me, blinked once, then trotted out of the kitchen.

Bayley had somehow relayed my message. I knew they

communicated. I just hadn't figured out how.

I realized that Wil had stopped talking and struggled to remember anything he'd just been saying.

"You look confused," he said.

"Sorry, it's just a little overwhelming. Don't get me wrong, I'm eager to learn. I guess I'm just rusty."

Wil laughed. "You really do look just like my students on the first day of the first semester. I know it's hard getting back into the swing of things academically. Don't worry. It'll all come back. How about if I write some of this down?"

"Thanks, that'd be great." I didn't have to fake the relief I felt. That'd keep him busy for a few minutes while I monitored Sadie.

As Wil sat down and hauled out his laptop, I checked my mental map, and Sadie had stopped moving. She was still in her room too. Maybe she had heard Wil's voice?

Wil cut short my mental meanderings. He kept his eyes on what he was typing and said in a very casual voice, "So, what happened with Kate this morning?"

I heaved a long sigh before I could help myself.

Wil busted out laughing. "Yeah, she does have that effect on people. What happened?"

I shrugged, then busied myself gathering the veggies I'd chopped so far and putting them in the pot. "She showed up here, all grumpy and cocky—you know, the usual Murphy bad attitude."

Wil waved a hand, "I swear, it's not all of them. You've just had a very…specific…introduction to a select corner of the family."

"It's Gram, isn't it. I knew it. That man has 'jerk magnet' tattooed on his forehead."

Wil grinned and kept typing his instructions. "I can see where you might think that. What about Kate?"

"I don't know what crawled up her butt. Something about her looking for a Murphy. And I was like 'Here? You're looking for a Murphy *here*?' And she got all snooty and said something about some rules. Then Eagan got involved—"

Wil stopped typing to glance at me. "Eagan was here?"

"Don't you give me that look, Wil Foster," I said, pointing

an unchopped celery stick at him. "I know you're not prejudiced against the other families the way the rest of the Council is, so don't be making Council faces at me. Eagan's a friend, and I have every right to have my friends visit."

Wil raised an eyebrow. "At that hour of the morning?"

It dawned on me that Wil thought Eagan got caught doing the walk of shame. No wonder he was making a face. The Council would probably go nuclear if they found me dating someone from one of the other families. I wondered if they'd found out about my fun fling with Reese. I shook my head and focused on Wil.

"You can get your mind out of the gutter. He dropped by on the way to work. But, even if he was enjoying 'special friend' status, that's my business."

He raised his hands in surrender. "No judgment here. So…Kate?"

"Right, Kate. She seemed to think that since Gram was here—"

"Gram was here?"

"Like I told her, yeah he was here—the jerk woke me up."

Wil turned his full attention to me. "That's…odd."

I recognized the intense curiosity Wil was beaming my way and knew that if I didn't diffuse it, he'd keep digging until I wound up in even more hot water. So I told him the same half-truth I'd told Kate. "No kidding. It's not like we're friends. But he insisted on coming inside for a few minutes. I was trying to follow protocol," Wil gave me an approving nod, "so I let him in, gave him a drink, and then he left again."

"Strange."

"Right? When I asked him what the hell, he muttered something about needing a break from family, so I think something's going on with the Murphys. But why Gram felt like he had to drag me into it is beyond me." I frowned at Wil. "Just because he negotiated access to the property doesn't mean he gets to use this as his personal getaway spot. And certainly not at all hours."

Wil nodded and said, "Very true. I'll bring that up when I'm dealing with the Murphys later."

"Thanks."

"Anyway, I told all this to Kate. But she went on acting like she was conducting an inquisition or something, so of course, Eagan couldn't resist jumping in and teasing her. She and Eagan bantered, and then she took off. But not before citing some kinds of regulations. I dunno. It sounded like legalese to me, so I called Nor, and she'll deal with it."

Wil surprised me when he nodded and said, "Good idea."

I guessed my explanation satisfied him because, to my surprise, he dropped the subject and turned his focus back to his laptop. Wil typed away for a couple of minutes, then closed it up, saying, "Okay, I've emailed you instructions." He stood up, stuffing his laptop in his bag.

I asked, "Is that it? We're done?"

Wil smiled. "For now. Glad to see you're so eager. Sorry I can't stay longer, but I've got a bunch of meetings today. If it's okay with you, I'll come by tomorrow—"

"Tomorrow? How fast of a reader do you think I am?"

Wil gave me one of his professor looks. "Well, I figured you'd want to get a jump on things. If you get through that," he pointed to the ancient book on top of the stack, "we can talk about the door. I didn't think you'd want me making you wait."

Wil's knowing smile had me gritting my teeth. It was a carrot I couldn't resist, and he knew it. It sucked being such an easy mark. I was really starting to hate that door. Freaking DeeDee. If everyone was going to use it for leverage against me, then I had to get a grip on the situation.

Also, unspoken in Wil's statement was the "and it's not like you've got a ton going on right now." He had no idea about half the stuff I was doing behind the Council's back so of course he thought I was sitting on my ass all day eating bon bons, bored out of my mind.

"Okay," I said. "But I reserve the right to reschedule if I can't get through enough by tomorrow."

"Deal," he said. "Anything else I can do for you before I go? Need me to bring anything back with me tomorrow?"

"Not that I can think of, but I'll text you if something

comes to mind."

While Wil and I walked to the front door, I checked my mental map, and Sadie's blue dot was going back and forth from end to end of her room. It took me a minute to realize she was pacing. Not a good sign.

I focused back on Wil as we got to the door and stepped outside. I hugged my arms around me. The temperature had dropped instead of warming up.

Wil nodded, his breath frosting the air as he said, "Yeah, it's getting cold. Temperature is going to drop all day. No snow in the forecast, but it's going to be in the twenties tonight. Good excuse to hunker down with a book and blanket," he said with a wink, then bounded down the steps.

I watched him walk to his car as I mentally monitored the pacing dot that was Sadie.

Somehow I got the feeling that curling up quietly with a book wasn't going to be on the menu just yet.

Chapter Thirteen

As soon as Wil's car disappeared down the driveway, I dashed up the stairs to Sadie's room. I kept one eye on Wil's green dot, making sure it left the property, and another on Sadie's blue dot. The speed with which she was pacing back and forth across the room had increased since last I checked. I felt like I was watching a game of Pong.

I reached her door and knocked, calling out, "Sadie? Can I come in?"

"Sure, if you can open the door."

Of course, Bayley let me in with no problem. I swung the door open to see Sadie standing in the middle of her room, arms crossed over her chest, glaring at me.

Fuzzy was sitting on the bed watching her. He glanced at me and said, "Meow."

"Uh, sorry about that," I said, gesturing to the door. "We had company—Wil, he's my liaison with the Foster Council—and I didn't want you to wander downstairs at an inopportune moment."

"And the cat? What's he doing here?" she gestured to Fuzzy.

It occurred to me that I couldn't say "I sent him" without tipping her off that there was something special about Fuzzy. I went with, "Oh, he's really friendly. He probably just stopped in to keep you company. You know how cats are. Always doing their own thing. Bayley seems to like him and lets him in and out, so I never know where he's going to turn up."

Fuzzy gave me a look. I flashed him a quick, apologetic glance then focused on Sadie.

"Uh, so how was your nap?"

"Fine. I'm feeling much better," she said.

She didn't look better. The bruise was continuing to bloom across her forehead, and I had the feeling she was hugging herself not just because she was annoyed. From the way she was standing, I was willing to bet a pot of my favorite coffee that her ribs were killing her.

"Well, that's excellent news," I said carefully, "but how about I give you some more of my Shake-It-Off concoction, just in case."

She shrugged and almost managed to hide the wince that went with it. I pretended not to notice and headed for the kitchen.

Fuzzy tagged along at my side. I whispered, "Thanks for looking after her," and he swerved to brush against me, then darted ahead to the kitchen.

When we reached the kitchen, I said, "I'm making some soup," pointing to the soup pot and the remains of the veggies on the butcher block. While I went to the fridge and fetched the Shake-It-Off I'd made earlier, I grabbed some painkiller to go with it.

I said, "I was thinking a nice, thick chicken soup might hit the spot." She looked like I'd just offered her Fuzzy's dead sparrow, so I added, "Do you like soup? Because I can make something else. Oh, are you vegetarian? Because I can do a vegetarian stew. It's really quite tasty—"

"Not all Indians are vegetarians."

I refrained from saying the "Don't you take that tone with me, Miss Thing" that nearly leapt off my tongue, but didn't manage to keep my eyebrows from hiking up. "I didn't say they were. I'm just offering dinner options. You're my guest, so you get a vote."

"There's no need to go to any trouble for me. I'm not staying."

I poured the Shake-It-Off into a glass and tried to think of how to handle her. When I turned to hand her the glass and painkillers, Sadie was pacing around the kitchen.

"Sadie, why don't you have a seat."

"I don't need to sit down. I'm fine standing," she said, snagging her cup then beginning to pace again.

I went back to chopping the remainder of my veggies and let her sip and pace for a few minutes. She reminded me of a Ping-Pong ball, blipping back and forth.

A few seconds after I had the thought, I noticed that when she reached one end of her pacing, the floorboard there made a hollow, clicking sound. When she reached the other end, the floorboard did a similar thing. As I chopped and listened, I kept hearing the click-clock sound. It took a couple of rounds before I realized what Bayley was doing.

I gigglesnorted. I couldn't help it.

That arrested Sadie mid-pace. "What?"

"You didn't notice it?"

"What?"

"Do another couple of rounds of pacing and tell me what you hear."

She did, then stopped, brows beetled. "There's a…sort of a…clicking and thonking noise? When I walk."

I mimicked the sound. "Click-clock. Click-clock. Remind you of anything?"

"Yes…" she paced some more, frowning in concentration, then stopped. She looked at me uncertainly. "For all the world, it reminds me of a—"

"Ping-Pong game," we said in unison.

I grinned. "I was thinking you reminded me of a Ping-Pong ball. Then Bayley decided to have some fun by adding the sound effects."

She spun around, looking at the floor, then the walls and ceiling. "It, uh, he has a sense of humor?"

"Sure does."

"Huh." And then, miracle of miracles, I saw a small grin tug at her lips. "I guess I do look a bit like a Ping-Pong ball."

The floorboards beneath her made a series of creaking sounds.

"Is he…it sounds like he…is he laughing?" she asked.

I giggled. "Yup."

Sadie burst into giggles. "This is the craziest thing."

"Yup. Fun, isn't it?"

She nodded. But then she must have moved the wrong way because she flinched and her laughter died. Her usual grim look replaced her smile. I figured she must be hurting even more than I suspected when she chugged the entire Shake-It-Off in one go.

I watched her sit at the table, struggle to find a comfortable seated position, give it up, and start pacing again. It hadn't occurred to me until then that she was acting like a caged tiger because it hurt too much to hold still.

That decided me. While I finished chopping the last of my veggies, I tried to work out how to get through to her. I felt a mental tug and tuned into Bayley. He wanted her to stay too. I couldn't work out why, but it was clear he was down with having Sadie stick around.

After a few minutes of internal debate, I decided to go with blunt. "You're staying," I said as I added chopped veggies into the soup pot.

"What?" That got her to stop pacing.

"You're staying," I said, lugging the pot to the stove.

"Oh? Am I?" she asked.

"Yes. You are. Want to know why?"

"Do tell." She crossed her arms over her chest and fixed me with the same stubborn, angry look she'd given Gram last night.

I ignored the look and said, "You like Bayley. Bayley likes you. When else are you going to get a chance to make friends with a house?"

She blinked at me. Whatever she'd expected me to say, that wasn't it.

I hid my grin as I fussed with the soup. I knew she had a whole load of counterarguments lined up when it came to talking about her situation with the Murphy family. I'd heard a bunch of them last night when she was fighting with Gram. Not only were they good arguments, but she was also really dug into her position. So if I wasn't going to be able to out-argue her on that front, I decided to take a page from my mom's book. Fairly often, the truckers in our diner would get into heated discussions, which was a lot of fun until the two sides got testy because they refused to budge on an issue. My mom would waltz by with her coffeepot in hand and say something really out there about whatever the topic was. Not only would it make the guys laugh, but it would also make them look at the issue from a different angle they never would have considered.

Sadie was going to be stubborn? Fine. I'd go at the issue of making her stay from a completely different angle.

She finally rallied enough to say, "That's ridiculous."

"Why? Is there some kind of Murphy family rule that says you guys aren't allowed to have fun?" I muttered, "Having met your brother, that'd explain a lot."

She started to smile, caught herself, and glared at me instead. "Of course we have fun. But there's a time and a place—"

"Don't you guys take time off?"

"Again there's a time—"

"What better time than now?" I ticked things off on my fingers as I puttered around the kitchen, adding things to the soup. "You're exhausted. You're aching and bruised. And, pardon me saying this, but it's not like you have anywhere you have to be. See. Perfect time for a well-earned rest." She looked like she was going to argue, so I said, "Right Bayley?"

Bayley rattled the glasses in the cupboard until they made a clear "Ding!"

Sadie looked in the direction of the sound, and I said, "See, Bayley agrees." I noticed that Fuzzy had circled around to sit next to Sadie. "What about you Fuzzy? What do you think?"

"Meow," said Fuzzy.

"See he agrees too."

Sadie frowned down at Fuzzy, then switched her frown to me. "This is crazy. I can't believe you're using a cat and a house to try and talk me into staying here. You know this is crazy, right?"

"Depends. Is it working?"

Sadie looked like she was struggling to come up with a good counterargument. After a minute, her shoulders sagged, and she ducked her head, shaking it as she muttered, "How do you argue with a house? And everyone knows you can't win an argument with a cat." She sighed, lifted her head and said, "Maybe."

"That's not a no!" I said, flashing her a cheery smile.

"Mmm," Sadie said.

I swung around, holding the soup pot lid in my hand, and said, "Now, about dinner—"

Bayley rang an alarm in my head and flashed a picture of the greenhouse in my mind.

Three things happened at once.

Sadie said, "Dinner. Yes. You should probably pay attention to that. It smells like it's burning."

Bayley swung open the back door.

And Fuzzy darted outside.

I said, "That's not dinner!" and charged into action.

I dropped the lid on the pot, ran into the pantry, grabbed the fire extinguisher, and rushed after Fuzzy.

As soon as I stepped onto the porch, I saw the problem.

The greenhouse was smoking.

Chapter Fourteen

I ran to the greenhouse, skidding to a stop on the damp grass in front of the door. I didn't see any flames inside.

In fact, on closer inspection, it looked like the smoke was coming from just one small area toward the back.

I peeked inside and looked around.

The plants for Sibeta's clan were near the door and didn't seem to be in any immediate danger. I heaved a quick sigh of relief as I scanned the rest of the greenhouse.

In the far, back corner, smoke swirled. Not a lot of smoke, but enough to be alarming. I wrinkled my nose as the acrid smell of burning rubber attacked me.

I stepped inside. I expected it to be overly warm inside, but it felt the same as usual. I walked to the far end of the greenhouse and approached the smoke, holding the fire extinguisher in front of me at the ready.

The closer I got to the back corner, the hotter it got. But when I sighted the corner through the smoke, there were no flames.

The more I looked, the more confused I got.

The fire had apparently burned itself out already. But the area where the greenhouse met the ground looked…melted. All the rubber seals connecting the aluminum framework to the glass had melted near the ground. That's what was emitting the smoke and the lovely burnt-rubber smell. Weirder, there was a bunch of loose dirt in little mounds, and the ground under the melted spot had collapsed, forming a hole to the outside.

I sprayed the melted spot with the fire extinguisher until it stopped smoking.

I walked back outside to find Sadie standing on the porch, arms crossed, shaking her head. "Stupid Smiths and their fire spells. Now look what he's done. Everything all right, then?"

I nodded. "I think so. The fire seems to have gone out already. Now there's just a lot of smoke. I think something got overheated somehow. I need to check around the back."

I walked around the greenhouse until I was standing outside the back corner that had been smoking. Fuzzy was already there, stalking back and forth, flipping his tail in an agitated manner.

"It's okay, Fuzzy," I said. "No need to worry. We've got it under control now."

The greenhouse had stopped smoking, so I put the fire extinguisher down and knelt next to the wall. It was melted on the outside, too, and I could see the hole leading under the edge of the greenhouse to the inside.

Fuzzy circled back and forth around me, nose to the ground, then looked at the greenhouse and growled.

"I don't blame you, pal. Burnt rubber is not my favorite smell either. What are you—no!"

I scrambled back just in time as Fuzzy stomped over and peed all over the hole and the melted area.

I rubbed my hand over my face and shook my head. "Uh, thanks for the assist, but that *really* wasn't necessary. Can't you see it already stopped smoking?"

Fuzzy shook himself all over and padded away to the porch.

My eyes started to water. If I thought the burnt-rubber smell was bad, adding *eau de Fuzzy* on top was not helping matters.

I stood and backed up a few paces, then took another look at the hole. Inside the greenhouse, I'd thought the ground had collapsed, but now looking at it from the outside, it looked like something had been digging.

Had an animal been trying to get into the greenhouse? Not that I could blame it. The greenhouse was nice and warm. Had it disturbed Eagan's spell somehow? Or worse, had it gotten into the greenhouse, then the spell went wrong? The poor thing would've been terrified. I looked around me, searching the ground for signs of a wounded critter, but I didn't see any prints leading away or anything else that gave me any clues. Nothing to see but my usual backyard view of a rocky brown lawn, big overgrown garden, and autumn-colored trees.

I checked in with Bayley. He seemed worried, which wasn't surprising. What was surprising was the fact that his attention was focused near the tree line, not on the greenhouse.

I jogged over to the tree line, my concern about a wounded animal growing. On my way across the lawn, I still didn't see any obvious signs of an animal passing this way. No blood or chunks of fur, thank the animal gods, and still no paw prints. By the time I got to the tree line, Fuzzy had dashed over to join me. I looked where Bayley seemed to be focusing, but all I saw was the autumn landscape: lots of trees losing their leaves and a forest floor covered with the usual rocks, stumps, and fallen leaves. If an animal had come through there, I couldn't tell. Whatever instincts I had as a member of the Best family, they weren't helping me at the moment. Or maybe they were, by telling me that there was nothing to see. How did I know? For the millionth time, I kicked myself for not knowing more about my magic. I resolved to read everything Wil had assigned me for tomorrow, even if I had to stay up half the night to do it.

Fuzzy stalked back and forth in front of the tree line. I watched him in case he went chasing after something, but he stayed near me, pacing between me and the forest.

The wind gusted, reminding me just how cold it was getting and that I'd run outside with no coat on. I shivered, checking in with Bayley. Now he seemed more worried about me than whatever had caught his attention in the woods, and I felt him urging me to come closer to the house so he could warm me up.

Another gust of wind decided me. There was nothing further I could do outside.

Striding across the lawn at a brisk pace, I stopped at the greenhouse. It seemed fine now, so I grabbed the fire extinguisher, and headed back for the porch. Speaking of no coat, I was surprised to see Sadie still standing there, waiting for me.

"You didn't need to wait for me," I said, climbing the stairs to the porch. My shoulders sagged in relief as Bayley blasted me with warm air.

"I'm perfectly comfortable here on the porch," said Sadie. "How bad is the damage?"

"Not bad, fortunately."

"You're lucky. Those Smiths," she shook her head.

"Sadie, I'm not sure this is even Eagan's fault," I said.

"Really? Because I didn't see anyone running around the yard with a blowtorch."

Truth be told, it seemed like the most likely scenario, but I didn't want to encourage her picking on Eagan. "Even if it does turn out to be a problem with his spell, I'm guessing these kinds of issues happen fairly frequently. Can you tell me that every spell you cast works out the way you planned?"

Sadie harrumphed and stared at her feet, so I guessed I was right.

"Besides," I said, "If he did make a mistake, mistakes are a great teacher, and maybe I can learn something from it. As a beginner, pretty much everything is a lesson to me at this point. Not only that, but it's not like I'm not already making a ton of mistakes myself, so who am I to make a fuss." I snorted. "With my luck, if I tried to do something like heat a greenhouse, I'd be happy if I didn't manage to burn the whole thing down."

Sadie shook her head at me. "You're a Foster. You could possibly make the greenhouse explode by growing too many plants inside. But you're not going to set it on fire with magic. You know that, right?"

I spent a few seconds kicking myself while I said, "Of course. Duh. Sorry. I'm just a little frazzled with this whole thing. I've got plants in there I've been working hard to raise, and I'm going to be super bummed out if they're damaged."

Sadie looked at me like the smoke might have clouded my thinking. "Finn, you're a Foster." She said "Foster" slowly, like it was a word I had trouble understanding. "You can fix plants." The "duh" was left unsaid but was so loud she might as well have said it.

"Good point," I said. "C'mon, let's go inside, and I'll call Eagan."

"Great. Just what I need. More time with fire boy." But I caught the gleam in Sadie's eye before she squashed it.

Sadie went into the house, and I started to follow her until I realized that Fuzzy hadn't gone ahead with her.

When I turned to call him, he was sitting in cat pose on the edge of the porch, his unblinking stare fixed on the tree line.

"Fuzzy? You coming inside?"

He turned to look at me, then went back to staring off into the woods.

With a sigh, I left him to his vigil and followed Sadie inside.

Chapter Fifteen

"It wasn't my spell," Eagan said.

I paced around the kitchen as I spoke to him on the phone. Sadie lurked behind me, leaning on a counter, sipping a cup of tea, and shamelessly eavesdropping on my half of the conversation.

"Okaaaaay," I said. "Let's say you're right—"

"I am."

"—why is my greenhouse melted and smoking?"

"No idea. But I'm telling you it wasn't my spell." The sounds of clanging, men's voices, and general commotion leaked in from the background behind him. "Look, why don't I swing by after work and have a look?"

I flicked a gaze at Sadie. "I'd appreciate it if you'd come take a peek," I said to Eagan, then mouthed to her, "Okay?"

"Fine by me," she said.

Eagan heard her and said, "Well, if the princess approves, I'm definitely coming."

I shook my head at the phone. "You're incorrigible. Text me a heads up when you're on your way."

I hung up in time to catch Sadie wincing as she moved the wrong way. Frowning, I took in her color, which was edging toward gray again. The fact that dashing toward the fire took so much out of her just confirmed my suspicion that she was in much worse shape than she was letting on.

I was trying to think of a good way to convince her to go lie down some more when she volunteered.

"If that Smith is coming later, I'm going to take a nap.

Maybe then I'll be less tempted to turn him into a pile of sand."

"You can do that?"

She smirked but didn't answer.

I tried not to look worried. It had never occurred to me that "No making sandcastles out of the other guests" was a rule I needed.

I said, "Uh, let's not turn Eagan into sand or anything else."

Sadie shrugged, snagged a bottle of water and an apple, and disappeared upstairs.

The moment she was safely in her room, I slumped into a chair. I felt like I deserved a nap too.

I heard the back door open and close, and a few seconds later, Fuzzy hopped onto my lap. I petted him while I thought about the damage to the greenhouse. The more I thought about it, the harder I frowned.

How much heat would the hole cause the greenhouse to lose? I wasn't sure how much cold the plants could stand, and I pondered whether I should bring them inside temporarily. Then, I worried about whether that horrible-smelling smoke had any negative impact.

That would be bad. Really bad. Sadie had assumed I could easily fix any harm to the plants, but that wasn't the case, at least not yet.

I chewed on my lip as I worried. Sibeta and her people were counting on those plants as a primary food source. Sure, Carmine had already made sure they had enough to eat for now. But the greenhouse plants were supposed to be their future food.

I decided to call the expert. Grabbing my phone, I dialed Carmine. There was no one better with plants than he was—he'd been the Master Gardener of the entire Foster family.

I glanced at Sprout, the lavender plant currently residing on the windowsill above the kitchen sink. Sprout was my first successful attempt at seed magic. With Carmine's patient guidance, I'd woken the plant from the seed and helped it grow. If things continued to work as they should, Sprout would bloom near the end of the year.

But while I listened to the phone ringing and waited for

Carmine to pick up, I had second thoughts. Lately Carmine had been super busy. I'd barely seen him for the last few weeks. He'd only had enough time to pop in for a couple of quick checks on the plants before he had to leave again. There'd been no time for our usual long chats, not to mention that our off-the-books magic lessons had been on hold.

If I told him about the smoke, he might feel obligated to come and check the plants out. Not only would I feel bad about dragging him away from his crazy-busy life, but if he showed up, I'd likely have to tell him about Sadie.

The result of my second-guessing was that when Carmine answered, I hesitated.

"Finn? You there? Is this a…what did you call it? A butt dial. Is this a butt dial?"

I laughed. "No, it's not a butt dial. Sorry. I was just thinking."

"Oh?"

I sighed. "I have an, er, I have a situation, I guess."

Carmine's wry chuckle was laced with a sigh. "Of course you do."

"I know, I know. I'm like the disaster magnet over here."

I could hear the amusement in his voice as he said, "How can I help?"

"Well, that's the thing. It's…complicated. I don't want to drag you into anything that could get you into trouble. Anything else, I mean."

Carmine said, "Mmm." There was a pause, then he said slowly, "I appreciate your concern…but a little trouble is good for me. Now and then. Keeps me strong."

"Well, the second part of this story is why I called you." And I told Carmine about the plants and the greenhouse.

I could hear Carmine frowning when he said, "That is concerning. I can come and take a look. It will be a good opportunity to show you how to ask the plant how it's feeling."

My brain boggled at that for a moment, my heartbeat kicking up with excitement. "Ask the plant? As in it'll speak to me?"

"Mmm. Maybe. Probably not talk. Per se. But you'll be able to get a sense…an understanding. It's easier if I show you."

"Cool!" With an effort, I reigned in my enthusiasm to add, "But are you sure you're okay coming by? I know you've been swamped lately."

"It's fine. I…I'm sorry I've been so…" he said, then paused, and I could picture him finishing the sentence by gesturing with his hands. He started again with, "It's just been, well, difficult…" but he couldn't seem to finish that sentence either and ended it with a sigh.

"Carmine, it's fine. Really. I know you're busy!"

Another sigh. "Well. I've…got things…it's worked out now." He cleared his throat, changed his tone, and said, "What's the first part of the story?"

Bayley tugged at my mind, nudging me to go ahead and tell Carmine, so I did.

"Gram showed up last night."

"Oh dear. Is anyone hurt?"

I laughed. "No. Well, yes. But not in the way you mean. I didn't, you know, kick him out on his ass."

"Admirable restraint."

"No kidding," I muttered. "But here's the thing. He brought his sister. Sadie." And I told him the whole story. I wound down with, "So, in conclusion, she's hiding here."

"Hmm."

I waited quietly while Carmine processed.

After a minute, he said, "I have a salve that should help."

I blinked a few times and finally came out with, "Oh. That's a good idea."

"In fact, I have a few things that might help." I could hear him rummaging around, muttering under his breath. "Let me just make a few notes here. Yes, that would probably help…and we'll need some…mmm. I think I've got some…Finn, if you can give me a couple of hours, I can wrap some things up here, get some things together, and head over there."

"Oh, jeez. Wow Carmine." I'd only meant to have him advise me on the plants, but being Carmine, of course he was all in on using his skills to help in whatever ways he could. "Thanks. I really appreciate it."

"Happy to help." There was another pause and then, "Clothes," he said.

"What?"

"Clothes. Does she need clothes? I was just thinking, if she showed up in such rough shape, she probably didn't have time to plan, pack a...what does Mila call it? A go bag?"

My eyebrows shot up. Carmine knew what a go bag was? "Yeah, that's what she calls it. Uh, when did you and Mila talk about go bags?"

Carmine sounded distracted when he said, "Oh, she drops by now and then."

Before I had a chance to follow up on that little tidbit, he rerouted my attention to the subject at hand when he said, "So, clothes? Or can she borrow some of yours?"

"Yes. I mean she could borrow mine except they're too short. She's really tall."

"How tall?"

"About six feet, I'd say. To be honest, I haven't gotten around to thinking about clothes because I've only just convinced her to stay put. But she'll need a whole kit and kaboodle, really. She has nothing."

"Hmm. I'll bring some things." I could hear him scribbling.

"Thank you, Carmine. I'll be happy to reimburse you."

He grunted, unconcerned. While he was making notes, I thought about it and realized that he was doing me a huge favor. With Kate lurking about, I couldn't order clothes for Sadie or have someone local, like Eagan, go buy stuff without running the risk that one of the Murphys would notice.

He muttered, "Probably could use a disposable cell, too. I'm assuming she ditched hers?"

I crinkled my forehead so hard it hurt. Just how much time had Carmine been spending with Mila? And what on earth had they been doing together?

"She did. Gram didn't. That's how Kate realized he'd been here. She tracked his phone."

Carmine grunted again, but this one sounded annoyed. I loved that I was getting to know Carmine well enough that I could tell the differences between his grunts.

Carmine interrupted my thoughts when he said, "Looking at my list here, I think our best bet is to call Mila. She has the resources for this type of thing."

"It is kind of her superpower." Mila was a mustela. The Bests named their magical talents after animals who had similar traits. Mustela was the Latin classification for "weasel," and it basically meant that, like ferrets and other members of the weasel family, Mila was frighteningly good at getting her hands on whatever she wanted—information, goods, people, you name it. She was also outstanding at distributing and/or stashing her loot with no one the wiser.

"Unless you don't want to loop her in. Which I understand," Carmine said.

I was willing to bet that Mila already knew that Kate had visited the house this morning and why. "No. It's fine. Trying to get information out of her is like trying to break into Fort Knox—she won't let anything slip if we tell her."

"I'm using that fancy secure phone she gave me," Carmine said. "I'm assuming you are too. So we don't have to worry about being spied on while I talk with her."

"I'll call her. Better she hears it from the horse's mouth."

"Okay. I'll wait to hear from her about next steps. How about I text you when I'm ready?"

"Sounds like a plan." My eyes snagged on the soup pot bubbling on the stove. "I have a big pot of chicken soup on for dinner—there's plenty, and you're welcome to join."

I heard the warmth in his voice as Carmine said, "Always trying to feed me. Sounds like just the thing for a chilly fall night."

We wrapped up the call, and I hung up with Carmine, then dialed Mila. I had to wait for her to stop laughing when I told her about Gram and Sadie.

"Smart to have Carmine bring stuff in," said Mila, when she'd simmered down to business mode. "Kate almost certainly has people monitoring your every move, so if bags of clothes and whatnot arrive at the house, she'll know Sadie's there. And she'll know that you were lying. Which, by the way, is a potential problem. I assume you called Nor?"

"Yep."

"Right. Note to self: bring vodka instead of wine tonight."

I winced. "Sorry."

I could picture Mila's shrug as she said, "Eh. The bigger the headache, the more she gets to show off her Nor-ness."

I grinned, but before I could add anything, she said, "Okay. I'll circle back with Carmine and get you set. Talk soon." And she hung up.

Bayley squeaked his floorboards in a cheery way. It took me a second to realize he was excited that Carmine was coming over.

I grinned at him and said, "So glad you're happy, buddy. Looks like we're having a bunch of company."

Bayley squeaked some more, and I couldn't help but laugh.

"Okay. Since we've got company, we want them to feel welcome. What do you say we whip up something yummy?"

Chapter Sixteen

Rustling up dinner put me in diner mode, and I found myself humming as I worked.

I already had the big pot of soup simmering, so I mixed up some quick bread, popped it in the oven, and then set about making cookies.

Rolling out the cookie dough sent my mind drifting back to making cookies with my parents.

My mom's voice echoed in my head as I pictured her looping my apron over my head as she grinned and said, "Who doesn't love warm cookies?" I remembered how it felt to clamber up on my special stool so I could reach the counter, proudly wearing my very own apron, just like my parents did when they cooked.

Looking down at the flour decorating my current, apron-less shirt, I felt a tidal wave of nostalgia and longing surge through me. I was too old for my mom to tie an apron on me now—I certainly was more than capable of doing it myself—but in that moment, I'd have given just about anything to feel her placing the apron around my neck and tugging at the strings as she tied them in the back.

Bayley and I sighed at the same time.

I said to him, "I loved cookie night, and not just because I got to sample the cookie dough and sneak warm cookies. Cookie night was family time, where my parents would decompress and talk about the day and what was happening with the business. They'd design new items for the menu and know what? They actually listened to my input. We'd talk about anything and everything." I fussed with the cookie dough for a minute before

I let slip the thought that had been plaguing me. "So then why didn't we ever discuss magic?"

Bayley murmured soothingly.

I stared at my flour-covered hands, and for the zillionth time I wondered what my parents had been thinking—and then for the zillionth time, I had to acknowledge that it didn't matter how hard I stared or how long I thought, no answers were forthcoming. The truth was that it was likely no answers ever would be. My parents were both dead now, and the best I could do was guess at their reasoning.

I took a deep breath and shook my head against the feeling of despair that was slithering through my chest. I'd been thinking about cookie nights a lot lately, replaying conversations in hopes of gleaning some understanding of my parents' motives. Several sleepless nights later, I was all too aware that if I dove down this rabbit hole, I'd end up frustrated, angry, and anxious.

Shaking my head to clear it, I said, "Alright. Enough meandering down memory lane. I've got cookies to make."

I carefully kept my mind blank, and within a few minutes the tightness in my chest eased. I let the repetition of rolling and cutting out the dough soothe me and slide me into a daydreamy, meditative state.

I'd been drifting along daydreaming for a bit when a bunch of images from random memories flashed through my mind super fast, totally out of my control. It was like my brain was flipping through memories, sifting and searching.

But I wasn't the one shuffling the memories about.

Bayley was.

Bayley was controlling my mind.

I clutched the kitchen block, trying to balance against the disorientation that swamped me as Bayley commandeered my brain. I was on the verge of panicking when a memory jerked to the surface. Cookie night, but a different cookie night than I'd been remembering earlier.

I yanked my mind away from the memory and forced myself to focus on the kitchen. Bayley didn't fight me, and I was able to regain control of my brain as soon as I tried. Still, my heart raced while I balked at the invasion. I realized I was hyperventilating and forced my breathing to slow down as I tried to grapple with what was happening.

"Bayley...did you just, er, pull up a memory?"

Ding.

"Since when can you rifle through my memories?" I squeaked.

He wiggled the floorboards under me like he was excited.

That made one of us. It was hard enough adjusting to the amount of contact I already had with Bayley.

This...this was a whole other level.

"Um...why? Why are you digging through my memories?" I asked, a little more sharply than I intended.

Bayley gave me the kind of sigh that let me know he was being patient with my dimwitted self. In my head, he showed me the image of cookie night again.

"Bayley, I see that you're interested in this memory. I don't get why. Is it supposed to be triggering some kind of recognition in me? Because it's not."

So far, Bayley had only spoken words to me in a dream and only written a few words when he was really desperate. Sometimes, like now, our lack of clear, easy communication made me want to gnash my teeth.

Bayley groaned and muttered.

"Don't take that tone with me, pal. You're the one who refuses to use people words so I can actually understand you."

This time I got an aggravated sigh from him. Then the image in my head from cookie night started blinking on and off, flashing at me like a neon sign.

Well now I couldn't help but look at it. I frowned. Maybe that was the point.

"You want me to pay attention to that memory?"

Ding.

"Why?"

Bayley didn't answer. I could feel him waiting and watching, perched in my mind.

Some contrary part of me hesitated. Even though I'd just

been willingly strolling down memory lane on my own, now I didn't want to. It was just going to make me sad again.

But Bayley knew how I felt, so if he was asking me to think about this, he probably had a good reason.

I sighed heavily and said, "Fine."

I closed my eyes and let the cookie night memory play. Bayley must have done something to jog my memory because I was able to play it back as easily as if I was remembering something that happened yesterday.

"Look Mom, Dad! It's snowing!" I giggled, sprinkling flour to make it "snow" on the kitchen counter.

Mom and Dad were carrying the last of a series of wilted-looking plants into the kitchen and setting them on the far counter.

I thought about the memory for a minute, my mind scurrying for context. Eventually I realized that I was wearing a bright red scarf in it.

To Bayley, I said, "I remember now. This was after we had a surprise cold snap. A whole bunch of Mom's herbs got damaged. Why are you showing me this, Bayley? Why do you want me to remember it?"

Bayley nudged my mind and started the memory blinking again.

I threw up my hands and said, "Fine!" and dove back into the memory.

"Look Mom, Dad! It's snowing!" I was standing on my special stool as I played with the flour.

Mom and Dad stopped talking mid-sentence to turn and watch my snow-making antics.

"It's cold enough to snow, but it's not wet enough," said Dad, regret lacing his voice. "Sorry, Finn."

Mom said, "You're doing a pretty good job making your own snow though. Just try to keep the snowstorm on the counter and not get your 'snow' all over the floor."

Dad added, "Too much snow on the floor, and you'll need a snow shovel."

I laughed and turned back to the counter. Humming to

myself now, I continued to artfully sprinkle flour, making my own winter wonderland.

I tuned into what my parents were saying when I heard Dad say, "You could let her help."

I looked over to see Mom shaking her head so hard her hair was flying around her face. "Not an option. You know that. We agreed. It's for her own safety."

Dad sighed and scrubbed a hand over his face. "I hate this," he said very quietly—so quietly that I wouldn't have heard him if I hadn't been paying such close attention.

Mom looked heartbroken as she said, "Me too. But it's too dangerous."

Dad reached for her hand and squeezed it.

"Mom, don't be sad. I can help! I'm a big girl now."

Mom and Dad turned to me, still holding hands.

Mom said, "You *are* a big girl now. And you're right. How about you help me make special snow cookies?"

"Snow cookies!" I crooned with delight. "What are snow cookies?"

Dad walked forward, rubbing his hands together. "Wait'll you see! We're going to make snowballs and sleighs and snowmen—"

"With red scarfs?"

"Sure with red scarfs, just like yours. That's a great idea!"

Behind him, I saw my mother touching the damaged plants. But then my dad snagged my attention when he asked, "What's happening here in Snow Land?" and I turned away from Mom to show him.

Bayley snapped me back to the present by wiggling the floorboards under my feet.

I blinked rapidly, refocusing on the cookie dough in front of me, as I tried to sort through what I'd just remembered. I could feel Bayley watching my reactions, waiting.

Something was nagging me. Something about the way Mom touched those plants.

What did it remind me of...? Carmine.

Oh. Oh wow.

I called up the memory again. Whatever Bayley was doing to enhance my recall was working incredibly well because I was able to dive back in and replay the part of the memory that I wanted to with no problem.

I watched the last bit again, focusing on my mom.

Holy flocking sheep.

The plants started to perk up just as my dad redirected my attention away from her.

She was doing magic.

The rest of their conversation fell into context.

They were talking about magic.

And me.

At the time, the conversation seemed innocuous. But now that I knew about magic, I saw the memory through a different lens.

For weeks I'd been trying to find a memory like this with no success. But Bayley had been able to.

I folded my arms and looked around me at Bayley. "I have questions." I waited, but Bayley didn't say anything, so I continued. "I...okay. How did you even know that memory was there? And how did you make me remember it?"

Bayley continued to give me the sense that he was waiting patiently.

"Maybe I should start with why." What had I been doing when Bayley started this? I walked my mind back and tried to reconstruct my thoughts. I'd been thinking about cookie night, wondering why my parents never told me about magic.

"Oh."

In my memory, they'd said it wasn't safe.

"Dangerous. They said it was too dangerous."

But why was it dangerous? In what way? What did they mean it wasn't safe? The memory did give me an answer, but that answer just brought up more questions.

I looked at the wall and said to Bayley, "I wanted to know what my parents were thinking. You found me an answer. That's why you did this."

Ding.

"How? How did you know the memory was there?"

An image of me pacing around my room popped up in my brain, followed by an image of me tossing and turning, then one of me finally sleeping.

I nodded. "That's the other night when I couldn't sleep. When I was obsessing over Mom and Dad."

Ding.

Next, Bayley sent an image of me sitting in a movie theater seat with a glowing bowl of popcorn.

The movie theater thing was from when Bayley and I had dream-linked while I was unconscious from a magic overload.

I concentrated, trying to put together what Bayley was showing me.

Boots and Zo seemed to think that dream-linking was a huge deal. I got the sense that it was an unusual degree and type of connection between the Housekeeper and Bayley.

"We dream-linked, so…what? Now you have access to more of mind?" I guessed.

Ding. Bayley flashed the picture of me sleeping again.

"Particularly when I'm sleeping?"

Ding.

My mind raced. So Bayley had been rifling through my brain while I slept? Indexing my thoughts and memories?

I felt a little queasy.

"Bayley, that's…" Invasive? Creepy? A huge boundary fail?

I clutched the kitchen butcher block with one hand, the other hand on my stomach as I tried not to freak out.

If I were being logical about it, I had to admit that we were already bonded and a part of Bayley's consciousness was always in my mind. So was it really any more invasive than what was already happening?

Not to mention that I'd known that as we spent more time together our bonding would evolve and increase.

I really shouldn't have been surprised.

But I was.

I started to pace. The idea that Bayley could just rifle through my mind and yank out whatever thoughts, memories, or feelings were in there made me feel panicked. And the fact that he knew more about what my memories held than I did terrified me a little.

I checked in with Bayley and the feeling I got back from him was that he'd totally expected me to flip my lid and was just waiting me out.

"I'm going to need a little time with this," I said.

Ding. Then the house made a soft cooing sound. The combined effect was "of course you do," along with an unsarcastic "there, there."

It took me a few more minutes of pacing, my brain scrambling to think through the consequences, before I could calm down enough to stop. With a concerted effort, I shut my whirling brain off.

When in doubt—or in this case, full-on panic—cook something.

I faced the kitchen block and the partially cut-out cookies.

"For now, no more memories. I have cookies to make."

Ding.

"We'll talk more about this later."

Ding.

I tried to focus on the dough, but one thought was stuck on repeat.

My parents warned me about all kinds of dangerous things as I was growing up. Why didn't they ever talk about magic?

Chapter Seventeen

Once I got some cookies in the oven, I dove into cleaning up the mess I'd made.

Normally, bopping around the kitchen would put me in my happy place, but not this time. The best I'd managed to do was to move from deer-in-the-headlights panicked to uncomfortably numb.

I stared blankly out the kitchen window over the sink as I washed up. Usually, I'd have been talking to Bayley while I bustled about, but I just couldn't bring myself to chat like everything was normal. I was still too wigged out.

He didn't seem offended by my reaction at all. Well, I wasn't his first Housekeeper, so he'd probably handled freaked-out Housekeepers a bunch of times before.

My train of thought was interrupted as something by the greenhouse caught my eye. I squinted, trying to figure out what I was seeing. It looked like there was a lump on the ground by the greenhouse. I frowned.

What *was* that? A downed tree branch? An animal?

It was late afternoon, and the sun was setting earlier these days, so the shadows had already lengthened across the yard, making it hard to see clearly. And, of course, the lump was sitting right where the shadows pooled in the lee of the greenhouse.

I switched to my mental map of the property and frowned harder. The area by the greenhouse where the lump was had a foggy spot. Normally, foggy spots occurred on parts of the property where I hadn't visited yet. I spent tons of time in the area around the greenhouse, so why was it suddenly foggy?

Instead of consulting Bayley like I normally would, I decided to investigate on my own. A part of me scolded myself for acting petulant, but that part quickly got squashed by the section of my brain that was still feeling vulnerable and, if I were honest, a little bit violated.

Of course, Bayley knew I was ignoring him, but he continued to seem unbothered.

I dried my hands and headed for the mudroom to grab my coat. Fuzzy appeared by my feet and followed me as I went out on the porch.

Bayley helpfully turned the porch light on, but there was enough daylight left that it didn't really illuminate much.

I walked nearer to the steps, shifting so I could see the lump by the greenhouse. Yup, it was still there. If anything, from this angle, it looked even closer to the greenhouse than it had from the kitchen window.

A low, menacing growl rumbled from Fuzzy, who stalked over to stand in front of me. If he hadn't been growling, he'd have done a great impression of a furry statue. His whole body had gone stiff, muscles coiled tightly, his unblinking eyes riveted on the lump.

My alarm level went up. Whatever was up with the lump, Fuzzy really didn't like it.

I looked down at him. "Fuzzy, I'm guessing you think that's some kind of animal. How about we don't get in a fight, okay?" The last thing I needed was for him to get into it with something like a raccoon. One or both of them could get seriously hurt.

Fuzzy didn't move and he didn't stop growling.

"How about this. Let me get a closer look and see what's what. Stay. Fuzzy? Stay!"

I moved to step around Fuzzy, and he countered me, walking down to the next porch step and blocking my path.

I stopped short. "Okay. I can see that you don't want me to go over there." Fuzzy had excellent instincts. If he wanted me to stay on the porch, there was probably a good reason.

The smart thing to do would be to stop being stubborn and talk to Bayley. I checked in with him. Unlike Fuzzy, he wasn't worried. He was, however, very interested in what I was going to do next.

"Do you know what's going on, Bayley?" I asked.

Bayley didn't answer.

That shocked me almost as much as the scary growling that Fuzzy was doing.

Aggravated, I said, "Look Bayley, you're already on thin ice with me right now. You really want to give me the silent treatment?"

The porch grumbled around me, then trailed off into a long-suffering sigh—the equivalent of "I'm not giving you the silent treatment" followed by an exasperated "ugh, Housekeepers."

"Yeah, not helpful Bayley."

Fuzzy was still rumbling his warning with no signs of letting up any time soon. Whatever the lump was, it didn't seem to care, or at least it wasn't running away.

"Fuzzy, will you stop already? I appreciate you trying to protect me, but chill a minute."

Fuzzy stopped growling long enough to glare at me over his shoulder. Then he resumed growling, though this time in intermittent bursts. I supposed that was an improvement of sorts.

It suddenly occurred to me that if it actually was a tree branch—or any other kind of plant—I should be able to tell. One of the first magics Carmine had shown me was how to reach out and "ping" a plant with my magic.

I focused on the lump and reached toward it with my thoughts, the same way I did when I was working on plants with Carmine.

Hey there. I'm Finn, I mentally crooned to the lump.

The lump didn't respond.

It occurred to me that if it was a dead plant, it wouldn't respond because it was, well, dead.

Frowning, I tried again, extending a tendril of my magic to reach out and touch the lump. If I could make contact with it, I could look for the little glowing spark that told me the plant was alive.

I felt the moment my magic made contact, then everything

seemed to happen at once.

Instead of finding a spark, I found a blowtorch.

Something slapped my magic tendril out of the way.

And the lump jumped back a foot.

I yanked my magic back with a gasp and took an involuntary step back. My heart started pounding.

That wasn't a plant.

Some of my Best magic must've chimed in because I was pretty sure it wasn't any kind of animal I recognized either.

Fuzzy's growl got louder. He paced back and forth in front of me once, then sat directly in front of me again.

"Bayley! What is that?"

Bayley's attention was keenly focused on what was happening. But instead of responding in my head, he tipped the floorboards that I was standing on so that I slid forward toward the steps.

I yelped and stepped down next to Fuzzy.

Hooking one clawed paw into my pant leg, Fuzzy turned his head so he was facing the porch and let out a string of kitty chatter. Despite my Best magic, I couldn't speak Fuzzy yet. But I knew that he and Bayley could communicate, and right now, I was pretty sure Fuzzy was chewing Bayley out.

Bayley grumbled back at Fuzzy in a way that sounded disgruntled with a hint of aggravation.

The two of them went back and forth like that for a couple of rounds before Bayley got louder and made some thumping sounds.

Fuzzy growled then turned to look at me. With the kind of disgusted look that only a cat can manage, he removed his claws from my pant leg. He took a moment to groom his paw, then looked up at me like he was surprised I was still standing there.

Bayley made more disgruntled noises then wiggled the step we were standing on. Fuzzy dug his claws into the step until it stopped wiggling. Then he turned to me and gently headbutted me toward the next step.

I looked down at him. "You want me to go over there now? You sure about this?"

Fuzzy looked distinctly put out, but he headbutted me again.

I walked down the stairs and a few feet onto the lawn. Fuzzy paced me, keeping a short distance to my left.

The sun had continued to sink, and the shadows were lengthening. I could see even less now than I could a few minutes before.

"Uh, hello?" I called softly.

The lump didn't respond.

I took a few more steps and stopped again. I suddenly realized that it was much warmer. I glanced to my right, but thankfully the greenhouse wasn't smoking again.

I took a few more steps forward, stopping again, as a wave of heat blasted me. I looked to my left to see Fuzzy standing stock still, tail swinging, ears slightly back.

Five more steps, and I had a clear view of the lump. Unfortunately, I wasn't sure it helped.

The lump still looked like a lump, even though I was only about ten feet away from it now. Except it had gone from looking like a shadowy formless lump to looking like a lumpy craggy rock. From what I could see, parts of it had smooth planes, while other parts had crevices.

The closer I got to the "rock," the hotter it got. I could see the air around the lump shimmering, reminding me of the heat mirages in the desert. I was willing to bet that whatever I was staring at had caused the damage to the greenhouse, a suspicion supported by the fact that I'd just caught the lump a few feet from said greenhouse.

I was hot enough now that sweat was beading at my hairline. I looked at the grass under the lump and gasped a little when I realized that it looked extra brown.

"Oh geez. Please don't set my lawn on fire. Bayley!" I yelped. "Can you keep the grass from catching on fire?"

Bayley gave me a *ding* but I didn't have time to respond because my attention jerked back to the lump. I guess the lump didn't like me raising my voice because I heard a rustling sound and turned to see that it had scooted back halfway to the tree line.

I blinked a few times.

"Can someone please tell me what's going on?" I asked Fuzzy, Bayley, and the lump. Since no one answered, I looked at the lump and asked a little more gently, "Hey. What are you? Also, could you please not set my lawn on fire? Or the trees? Especially the trees."

"Finn?"

As Sadie hollered for me, I realized that Sadie's blue dot on my mental map was walking down the back stairs and had nearly reached the mud room.

She strode out onto the back porch just as the lump zinged toward the tree line, sticking to the darkest shadows so that it was hard to track its movement.

"Finn? Are you alright? I thought I heard you yell."

I tore my gaze away from looking for the lump and turned to Sadie. I tried to figure out how to respond to her when I heard a buzzing sound from the kitchen.

"Oh no, those are the cookies," I called, dashing back to the porch, past Sadie and into the house.

Saved by the bell. Temporarily.

Chapter Eighteen

While I rotated another batch of cookies into the oven, Sadie asked again, "So who were you yelling at?"

I decided keeping the lump to myself was probably wise for the moment.

"Fuzzy," I said, grateful that fussing with the cookie sheets gave me an excuse to avoid meeting her eyes.

Fuzzy looked at me but refrained from comment.

"Sorry if I woke you," I added. Before she could inquire further, I waved one of the cookie sheets filled with warm cookies in her direction. "Cookie?"

"Sure," Sadie said.

I got a plate and slid a couple of warm cookies onto it and handed it to her.

"Aren't you going to have some?" she asked.

"Good idea." I was so distracted by what I'd just seen that it hadn't even occurred to me to join her. "I'm going to make some coffee to go with them. Want some?"

At her nod, I busied myself setting the coffee to brew before I joined her at the kitchen table. Sadie scanned the remaining cookie sheets that were waiting to go in the oven.

"Don't get me wrong," she said, a small smile playing around her lips, "I like cookies as much as the next person. But don't you think that's a lot for just the two of us?"

"And Eagan—don't forget he's coming by later." I realized this was a good time to tell her about Carmine. "And we'll have one more person joining us."

She stiffened immediately, the tiny smile collapsed into a

flat line. "Oh? Am I spending the night in my room then?"

I shook my head. "Carmine is a friend. You can trust him." At her skeptical look I added, "He's very nice. You'll see."

"I thought the whole idea was that no one knew that I was here. Isn't that the point of me staying here?"

"Well, yes, but Carmine's not just anybody."

She opened her mouth to argue when my phone chimed.

"Excuse me," I said. I hopped up and grabbed my phone off the counter. It was Carmine.

His text read, "I'll be all set in 15 minutes."

I texted back, "Okay, I'll text you when I'm ready."

I turned back to Sadie, "Speak of the devil, that was Carmine."

Sadie pushed her cookies around her plate and finally said, "It sounds like you're really busy. Eagan this morning, Wil this afternoon, now this Carmine guy. Maybe this isn't a good idea. Me staying here, I mean. You've obviously got a lot going on, and really, it's probably better if I'm on my way anyway."

I shook my head at her. "Oh no. We decided you were going to stay a few days."

The mutinous look she'd had earlier returned as Sadie huffed out a breath.

I wanted to bang my head on the counter. I'd just convinced her to stay, and she was already trying to back out. The cranky part of me wondered if I should even bother—she was Gram's sister after all and if I were honest, I knew that having her here would be a ginormous headache.

But then Sadie shifted in her chair and sucked in a breath so sharp that it gave away how much pain she was in.

Who was I kidding? No way was I going to send her out there to deal with the stupid Murphys, or anyone else, in the shape she was in.

Time for me to change tactics again.

Sadie's stubborn streak reminded me of a coffee klatch of old guys that used to visit the diner once a week. Each was astoundingly stubborn in his own way. Yet they managed to goad each other into doing things. No matter how much one of them dug his heels in, somebody else in the group could get him to budge. I quickly scanned my memory for their favorite techniques and latched onto the one that usually did the trick.

In an understanding voice, I said, "I mean, I get it if you're a little nervous staying in a living house. No one can blame you for feeling scared."

Mutiny morphed into outrage as Sadie glared at me. "I'm not scared," she growled.

I turned to get two mugs and to hide my grin. "Sure you're not," I said.

I heard a long, pained sigh as I poured coffee into the mugs and had to stifle the urge to full-on giggle. I plastered my best concerned look on my face as I turned around and brought the coffee to the table.

Sadie was aggressively chewing a cookie as I handed her a mug. "I know what you're doing," she said around a mouthful of cookie.

I helped myself to some milk and said, "Trying to cheer you up with delicious, warm, sugary goodness?" I waved a cookie at her. "There's two other flavors coming. You're welcome to try them all."

She pointed a cookie at me. "You're trying to embarrass me into staying."

"By feeding you cookies?"

Frustration crinkled her face. "Not cookies. With the being scared thing. I'm not twelve, you know. It won't work. Plus, I'm not actually scared."

Bayley picked that moment to groan. Already wound super tight, Sadie jumped so hard that her chair squeaked back. Then she winced, pressing a hand to ribs.

She saw me notice and glared.

"Of course you're not scared," I said in my best patronizing "poor little camper" voice.

For a moment, I thought she might wing the cookie at my head but at the last second she decided to take her feelings out on the cookie with a vicious bite.

"So since you're not scared, I guess that means you're

staying," I said.

The buzzer went off, and I took the finished cookies out and put the last trays in.

Ignoring her death glare, I asked Sadie, "More cookies?"

"Why not," she said. From her tone, you'd have thought that I was feeding her Brussels sprouts.

I placed another couple of cookies on her plate. A quick glance at the clock told me it was almost time to fetch Carmine. As I cooled the remaining cookies, I tried to figure out the best way to get him without tipping Sadie off to how he actually got here. No way was I going to show her my magic necklace.

It looked like the antique it was. Made of some kind of metal, the necklace was sort of a locket, with a front cover that was engraved with a five-petaled flower. The top petal held a seed, which made the whole design remind me of the cross-section of an apple.

The necklace hid some interesting features. As a child, I'd learned that a pair of folding scissors were tucked behind the lovely flower cover. My mom had used them all the time to cut herbs and other things, and since I'd inherited the necklace, I'd done the same.

But when I'd become Housekeeper, I learned that wasn't the only thing tucked in the necklace. It also had some kind of entity living in there. The whatchamacallit could use the necklace to open a door to other places. That was how I was going to fetch Carmine all the way from Seattle: the thing in the necklace would open my pantry door, but instead of opening into my pantry, the door would open into Carmine's house.

I didn't want Sadie to know I had that kind of capability because then Gram would know, and that was a hard "no" in my book. I'd only told a few people, and I wanted to keep it mostly secret, for now at least.

So how was I going to get rid of Sadie?

I decided to go with the most straightforward solution.

"Hey Sadie, would you mind going upstairs again for a minute?"

Sadie gave me an irritated, "Why?"

"Because there's a car coming down the driveway, and while I think it's Carmine, I can only tell that a Foster is coming. Better to be safe than sorry."

Sadie glared at me.

"Look, I'm only trying to keep you safe. Speaking of which, I think we need a system. How about this: if you can open your door, the coast is clear. If you can't, then I'm trying to protect you, and you should stay put for the time being."

"Do I have a choice?"

"Do you have a better idea?"

Without a word, Sadie grabbed her coffee and cookies and disappeared upstairs. I watched her blue dot, but it turned out that I didn't really need to, because I could hear her door slam all the way in the kitchen.

Okay then.

I texted Carmine. "Ready?"

Chapter Nineteen

Once I got confirmation Carmine was standing by, I pulled out my necklace and gave it a little shake. "Hey you."

No response.

I swallowed my aggravated sigh and tried for patience. Shaking it some more, I asked, "Are you paying attention?"

There was a pause and then I heard, "Not really."

I couldn't tell if I was relieved the thing wasn't eavesdropping or annoyed because I had to goad him into opening a door every time I needed one. Probably a little of both.

"Could you please open a door to Carmine's house?"

"Can I? One would think that was obvious by now."

It had been a long day, and I so wasn't in the mood for the thing's bad attitude.

"Look you…" I halted. It was totally ridiculous that I still didn't have a name for the thing. "You know it'd be a lot easier to talk to you if you'd just tell me your name." I'd been trying to get the thing to tell me its name for the last couple of months. Each time I asked, I was met with silence.

Like now.

I waited another thirty seconds before I burst out, "If you don't tell me, then I'm going to give you a name."

Still nothing.

I heaved an aggravated sigh. Why did the thing have to be such a… "What about Dick?"

"No."

I thought about it. "Johnson?"

Bayley started snickering.

"No."

"John Thomas?"

"Certainly not."

"Peter?"

"No."

I ran through the rest of the Monty Python song that had started playing in my head. Well, "Willy" was out. I already had a Wil. "Percy?"

There was a pause, then the thing said, "Like the poet?"

It knew about Percy the poet? I shook my head. "Sure. Like the poet." The poet was not at all what I had in mind, but the thing didn't need to know that.

"Acceptable."

Bayley had moved onto a full chortle at this point. Well, at least someone got my sense of humor.

"Okay Percy, open the door to Carmine's. Please." Just because the necklace was ornery didn't mean I also had to have no manners.

"Fine."

I unfolded the scissors, and pressed them, point down, against the pantry door. The seed in the flower sprouted glowing blue tendrils. I jerked my hand out of the way as the tendrils stretched down along the scissor blades, then across the top and bottom. The tendrils anchored themselves into the pantry door, forming a glowing capital *I*. The vertical tendril popped out a bit, forming a handle. The edges around the door flared blue, I pulled, and the hinge side of the door swung open.

Instead of looking into my pantry, I was looking into Carmine's bedroom.

Carmine stood waiting and smiling. "That never gets old," he said, eyes twinkling with delight. The smile deepened the creases in his face.

Dressed in his usual plaid shirt and khaki pants, Carmine's browned, leathered skin hinted at how much time he spent outside in the sun. In his former position of Master Gardener, he'd spent nearly all his time with plants. Even now, though he was retired, he still spent a lot of time outdoors.

I noticed the satchel and a couple of duffel bags at his feet. I felt a pang of regret that I couldn't offer to carry things for him. He was in his sixties and still very energetic and spry, but his arthritis could really bug him. However, we both knew that leaving Bayley was a death sentence for me, so I didn't offer to come grab the bags, and Carmine didn't ask.

One at a time, Carmine transferred the bags over the threshold into the kitchen, where I grabbed them and lugged them to the table. They were heavy, and I was grateful to be able to help out at least a little.

When the last bag was in the kitchen, Carmine grabbed his satchel and stepped over the threshold himself. I closed the door behind him.

The blue light flared once then disappeared. The tendrils retracted into the seed in the necklace, and I caught the necklace before it could fall to the floor.

"Thank you," I said to Percy, who, per usual, didn't bother to respond.

I quickly folded the scissors back behind the cover, and put the necklace on, tucking it into my shirt. Then I spun and said, "Hi, Carmine! Thanks for coming!"

I stepped forward to hug him. When I first met him, he'd been stiff when I hugged him, like he was out of practice. I'd been giving him lots of hugs, so he definitely wasn't out of practice anymore. Still, once in a while, like now, he seemed startled and not sure how to respond.

After a moment, he squeezed me back.

I released him to take a look at the stack of duffel bags. Quirking my eyebrows at him as I said, "Planning on staying a few days?"

Carmine gave me a small grin and a slightly guilty shrug. "Better to have it and not need it."

"Fair enough. And thank you. What all is in there?"

"Those two," he pointed to the two gray duffel bags, "are for your Sadie. The blue one has my things. Those two," he pointed to the army green ones, "are some things I thought might be useful, including some books."

That explained why they weighed a ton.

"And this," Carmine hoisted the satchel, saw that the butcher block was full of cookies, and changed direction to place it on the counter near the sink, "has that salve I told you about. And some other medicinals. In case we need to mix something else on the spot." He pointed to the green army duffels again, "The books in there have some excellent remedy recipes."

"Regular recipes or spells?"

He gave me a patient look as he said, "Spells. Good learning opportunity for you."

"Wait, we can spell medicine?" I probably looked like a dog that had just sighted a squirrel as I perked right up at the idea of learning new magic from Carmine.

"We can spell plants that are used as medicine."

Seemed like the same thing to me, but I nodded and rubbed my hands together eagerly. "Sounds fun."

Carmine gave me another small smile and said, "I thought you might think so." He hauled a tin out of his bag and looked around the kitchen. "Where's your Sadie?"

"Trust me, she's not my Sadie. And she's upstairs, locked in her room. Don't look at me like that, it's for her own safety. Well, okay, and mine. No way was I going to show her what the necklace can do. And I need to make sure no one sees her. Random people keep showing up here—first Kate, and then Wil showed up unannounced earlier."

"Wil?"

"Yeah I was as surprised as you are. Turns out he's going to be my new Foster tutor."

"Mmm." Carmine thought about it for a moment. "Makes sense. He's very knowledgeable. And a real professor, like you deserve." A shadow passed over his face and something like guilt or shame flitted through Carmine's eyes.

Did Carmine think I was replacing him because he wasn't good enough? I scrambled to explain. "Of course he's no replacement for you—you're not off the hook! If you want to still be on it, of course. The hook, I mean. Teaching me. Because I'd really love it if you'd still teach me. But only if you want to, of course. Schedule permitting and all that."

Oh geez. I was doing it again. I clamped my mouth shut in an attempt to get myself to stop babbling.

Carmine shook his head. "I should have been around more—"

"Are you kidding?!? You're around. You're helping all the time! I don't even have to ask and you help. If anything, you're here too much for your own good because I'm greedy and like having you around! And if I ever actually need something," I waved my hand around at the flock of duffel bags, "you deliver. If you were an actual delivery service, I'd give you five stars!"

I sounded like an idiot.

The buzzer dinged saving me from making any bigger of a fool of myself. I retrieved the warm peanut butter cookies from the oven and waved a cookie sheet in Carmine's direction.

"I have cookies!"

"What did I do to earn cookies?"

"You're here, which is always reason for cookies. Plus, Eagan's coming for dinner. And I have Sadie to feed." Which reminded me, "Excuse me, Bayley? Would you please unlock Sadie's door and open it so she knows she's free to come down?"

Ding.

"Thank you."

Carmine was looking at me funny.

"What?"

He studied me as he said, "I've never heard you talk to Bayley like that."

"Like what?" I said, sounding more defensive than I would have liked.

"Like you're not happy with him."

"What? I was perfectly polite. I said both 'please' and 'thank you.'"

"That's true." Carmine was still studying me.

I avoided his gaze by dealing with cooling and transferring the last batches of cookies. When I realized that I was banging the cookie sheets around way more than was strictly necessary, I stopped and my shoulders slumped.

"We had a—it's not that I'm mad—this...thing... happened..." I said shaking my head. I mumbled, "I apologize, Bayley, if I sounded mad."

"Not mad, just...distant," said Carmine. "Do you want to talk about it?"

"Maybe." I heard footsteps on the back stairs. "But not now."

We both turned to the kitchen doorway as Sadie stormed in.

Chapter Twenty

As Sadie leaned on the door frame, arms crossed, she reminded me of her brother—all broody thunderclouds just waiting to let loose on us.

"You wanted me?" she said, sweeping Carmine with an assessing gaze before settling on me.

"Oh, sorry, I didn't mean to make you come downstairs if you weren't ready—I just had Bayley open the door so you'd know you were welcome." Which I now realized wasn't part of the plan I outlined and probably seemed like an invasion of her privacy. "I'm sorry if it seemed impolite."

Sadie nodded but didn't make a move to come into the kitchen.

I put on my best hostess smile and said, "Actually, it's great that you came down anyway because I wanted to introduce you two. Carmine, this is Sadie. Sadie, this is Carmine. He brought you presents."

Sadie raised an eyebrow, pushed off the door frame, and crossed to Carmine. She extended a hand and said, "Hello sir. Nice to meet you."

My eyebrows shot up. Sir? I didn't think I'd ever seen a Murphy be polite.

Carmine chuckled and shook her hand. "No sirs are necessary. Call me Carmine." He dropped her hand and waggled the tin he was holding in his other hand, extending it toward her. "Finn said you're a little banged up." His eyes shifted focus, taking in the bruises on her face. "I have this salve that should really help. It's particularly good for deep tissue bruises. If you also have any of those."

Sadie looked suspicious. "Is it magicked?"

"Yes."

"And you're a Foster?"

"I am." At Sadie's frown, Carmine gave her a little wink. "But I promise not to turn you into a tree or a fungus. You have my word."

I bit back the urge to ask Carmine if that was really a thing we could do. I'd ask him later.

Sadie looked like she was trying to suppress a smile. "What about a slime mold?"

Carmine's eyes twinkled with mischief. "No slime mold either."

Sadie took the tin and said, "Thank you," and I let out a breath I didn't know I'd been holding.

"Early birthday isn't over yet," I said. I pointed to the two gray duffel bags. "Since you didn't have the opportunity to pack for your, er, spa getaway here at Chez Bayley, we got you some stuff. Hopefully, it'll fit better than my sweatpants," I said, shooting her a cheeky grin.

She walked toward the two duffel bags, but I snagged them off the floor and put them on the kitchen table before she had to bend and carry them.

Sadie stepped over to the table and unzipped the bags and looked inside. I caught sight of a pile of clothes with a bunch of toiletries on top in one bag. From the other bag, Sadie pulled out a phone, still in its unopened package, and a laptop. There was more in the bag, but she just stared at it.

Sadie's face had gone carefully blank as she repacked the duffel. She looked up and glanced between me and Carmine, settling on him as she said in a cold voice, "What are you?"

I wasn't sure what she meant, but Carmine must've known because he said, "I'm retired."

Oh. Of course she was asking him about his magic.

She said, "Hmm. Good dodge. I'm guessing you're with one of the Foster spy groups? You're attached to the Housekeeper, so one of the elite units. Nice job with the salve. Smooth way to make inroads with your target." She looked him up and down. "Also smart to send someone your age. Play on my cultural preference to be deferential to your generation."

I could feel my eyes bugging out of my head. What had just happened? How did we get from a bag full of goodies that would make me weep with joy in her situation to thinking Carmine was a spy?

I knew she wouldn't explain so I turned my confusion on Carmine and said, "I don't get it."

I'd said that so often since entering this new magical world that I'd started feeling like I should have it tattooed on my forehead.

In his shoes, I would probably be aggravated if not full-on peeved by Sadie's little speech. He'd gone to all that effort to help her, and she was attacking him. In fact, underneath my confusion I was feeling a little peeved myself. But Carmine just looked tired.

He said, "She thinks I'm a spy because I brought her a go bag."

I said, "Oh." I could kind of see her point. It was a really well-equipped go bag. Personally, I would maybe ask a few questions instead of skipping straight to the conclusion that he was a spy, and we were colluding to screw her over somehow. But given her life with the Murphys, it made a disturbing kind of sense that she was suspicious.

Sadie said, "The fact that you even know what a go bag is helps make my point."

I said, "Anyone who has seen a spy show or read a spy novel knows what a go bag is."

Sadie said, "Said the woman helping the spy. I bet the laptop and cell phone are bugged."

I groaned, "Sadie, if you could dial down your paranoia for just a sec—"

Sadie glared at me. "It's not paranoia if they're actually out to kill you." She jabbed a figure toward Carmine, "And if this sneaky son of a bitch thinks I'm going to fall for his false kindness—"

Nope. That was it. She could be cranky with me all she

wanted, but she didn't get to pick on Carmine.

I said, "One, you don't get to call him names. Two, he didn't put that together. A friend of ours did. He just delivered it. And three, how many times do I have to prove to you that I'm trying to help you?"

Carmine said, "Finn, it's fine."

I said, "No it's not. Look, lady. I get that you're bruised and tired and scared, not to mention you have head trauma, so you're probably not thinking straight. So let me just spell this out for you. In case you hadn't noticed, I have nothing to gain from having you here. I'm not trying to work some kind of deal or take advantage of you in some way. I am trying to be a decent human being and give you a hand because, newsflash, you need one."

Sadie pointed at a duffel and said, "The laptop—"

"Is not bugged!" I saw Carmine wince out of the corner of my eye, and decided I should probably drop my volume back down from shouting-at-kids-across-a-playground to aggravated-mom-delivering-a-lecture.

Carmine said, "It really isn't. I'm sorry if it's distressing you. I just thought you might be bored or feeling cooped up and a laptop might help, so I asked them to include one."

I said to Sadie, "You see that? You've got Carmine apologizing for being a good guy and trying to help." I turned to Carmine and said, "You have nothing to be sorry for."

I turned back to Sadie and crossed my arms. I used an exaggeratedly slow, calm voice like I was a nursery-school teacher talking to a room full of four-year-olds. "Carmine is one of the nicest, most genuine, most honorable people on the planet."

I thought I saw Carmine wince a little out of the corner of my eye, but I ignored offending his modesty to focus on Sadie.

"He is so nice that he hadn't even met you, and he realized you might need some things and tried to help. Not only that, but he's so nice that he brought you a salve—a salve he made himself, by the way—to help you heal, which p.s., you really need. So, in conclusion, just stop it."

Both Sadie and Carmine were staring at me. Sadie looked really startled, and Carmine looked worried.

I spun to Carmine and said, "Carmine, please make yourself at home." Staring at the ceiling I said, "Bayley, would you please put their bags in their rooms?"

I heard a *ding*.

"Thank you, Bayley." I saw them both start to object and shook my head. "Neither of you should be lugging that much stuff upstairs. Don't even think about it. Now if you'll both excuse me, I need to go for a walk," I said, and I stomped out of the kitchen.

Chapter Twenty-One

I grabbed my coat from the mudroom and stepped outside.

Fuzzy slinked along behind me.

The temperature had continued to drop, and the cold bit at me, demanding my attention. As I focused on my surroundings, my anger dissipated, and I was left feeling tired and frustrated.

Fuzzy brushed against my legs, winding back and forth around them until I picked him up.

"Oof, you're getting heavy," I said as I pulled him to me. "And big!" Snuggling him, I buried my face in his fur and was rewarded with a loud purring. "I wonder how big you're going to get. Of course figuring that out would necessitate knowing what you really are."

I sighed. The events of the day came crashing back to me, from arguing with Gram to fighting with Zo to negotiating with Wil to falling out with Bayley to yelling at Sadie. I decided my day sucked and groaned when I realized it was nowhere near over yet.

Lifting my head, my gaze fell on the greenhouse. Oh yeah. I could add that to the list. The greenhouse got melted, and I had a mysterious moving lump running around.

I buried my head back in Fuzzy's fur and murmured, "I'm so ready to be done with today."

Fuzzy purred louder and rubbed his cheek against my chin. I smiled at him and nuzzled him back.

It occurred to me that I wasn't nearly as cold as I should have been, and I realized that Bayley had warmed the porch. I sighed again. He was taking care of me, even though I was totally freaked out still.

"Thanks Bayley," I mumbled.

The back door swung open and Carmine joined me on the porch.

He walked over and stood next to me, looking out into the night. The sun had set so there wasn't much to see, but he stood quietly contemplating the darkness with me.

When he didn't say anything, I asked, "Did you want to look at the greenhouse?"

He shrugged. "We can. Or we can wait for Eagan to get here. What would make things easier for you?"

I snorted. "Moving to Bermuda?"

Carmine nodded. "I hear Bermuda is lovely."

"Or maybe Hawaii. I bet Hawaii is nice."

"Hawaii is beautiful. I had the good fortune of visiting there several times. Leilani had family on a couple of the islands."

I winced. "Sorry. I wasn't thinking."

Leilani was Carmine's dead wife, and he still mourned her. I hadn't gotten the whole story about how she died yet, but I got the feeling that it was extra grim.

Carmine shook his head and smiled wistfully. "Nothing to be sorry for. She's gone, and all I have now are memories—it's good to remember her. Even if it hurts."

"I feel the same way about my parents."

We stood for a few moments, united in our battles against our grief demons.

Carmine looked like he was about to say something. He kept opening his mouth then closing it again. Finally he shook his head and looked at his hands and said, "Seems like there's a lot on your plate right now."

Given I'd just blown my top at Sadie, I supposed I looked like a grumpasaurus rex. I shrugged at him. "Just another fun day in magical paradise."

"Mmm." We stood in silence for a few seconds. Then Carmine added, "If you want to talk, I'd be happy to listen."

"I don't even know where to start." Fuzzy wiggled for me to put him down, so I did and leaned against the porch railing.

"Can you tell me what's going on with you and Bayley?"

Carmine asked.

I opened my mouth to demur, and instead it all came pouring out of me. I was so anxious recounting how Bayley had been rifling through my memories that I stared at the ground the entire time I was talking, twisting my hands and scuffing my feet like a little kid.

When I finished, I glanced up to see Carmine's eyebrows were raised. "That could be very useful," he said, sounding as though he were choosing his words carefully. "But I can see where that would feel extremely invasive."

I pushed away from the railing and paced the porch. "I haven't really gotten around to thinking of any advantages. I'm still stuck on 'Bayley's rummaging in my brain.' It feels…" I stopped pacing, waving my arms as I searched for the right word. I couldn't find what I was looking for and wound up dropping my arms in defeat as I said, "Icky. I feel icky. So icky I want to crawl out of my own skin to get away from myself. Away from my own mind."

I cringed, waiting for Carmine to chastise me for being un-Housekeepery, but instead he said in his calm way, "Understandable. The bonding is a lot to process."

"Yeah, yeah. I know. I get it—it's the whole 'Finn's new at this' thing." I was back to scuffing my feet.

Carmine chuckled, "For once this has nothing to do with you being new. Even seasoned magic users struggle with the Housekeeper position." He nodded when I looked at him questioningly. "Really. The cognitive strain of melding two different magics is immense. And this is one area where you're way ahead of the curve. You seem to be bonding with Bayley in ways that are more complex than what's usual."

"Do you think it's because of my Best magic?" I asked.

"Could be. Or it could just be you, Finn. Regardless, this is a new phase of your evolving partnership with Bayley, and it's perfectly reasonable that you'd need some time to become more comfortable with it."

"How do I do that with him in my brain constantly? Uh, no offense Bayley."

Bayley didn't say anything, but I didn't get the sense that he was offended. I was still getting that "I'm being patient" feeling from him.

"Have you tried asking him for some space?" asked Carmine.

Startled, I said, "I can do that?"

"I don't see why not. In a healthy relationship, couples give each other space to do their own thing. And what are you and Bayley if not a couple, of sorts, albeit with a special type of relationship."

I turned to look at the house. "Bayley, is that true? You can give me some space? Without harming yourself? Or me? If you can't it's okay."

There was a pause. Then the house gave a long, resigned sigh, and I heard a *ding*.

I swallowed hard against the feeling of relief that swarmed through me. Just a little bit of space would make me feel like I had some breathing room and would help me to feel less panicked.

"Okay then. Yes please. A little space would be nice. Let's start with just for tonight."

In the back of my mind, the pressure that was Bayley suddenly felt...less. He felt somehow farther away.

A feeling of fatigue washed over me, and I swayed a little.

Carmine grabbed my arm and steadied me. "Finn? Are you alright?"

"Yeah, I'm just really tired all of a sudden."

Carmine looked like he was thinking hard, then he nodded once. "You and Bayley share energy. My guess is that when he pulled back a bit, you lost some of his energy feed, and he lost some of yours."

"Great. So now we're both tired?"

Bayley said *ding* loudly.

I closed my eyes for a second, shaking my head. Why couldn't anything be easy? Opening them, I said, "Well it's only for tonight. It should be fine." I mustered a smile and said to Carmine, "Of course you know what this calls for then? More coffee!"

Carmine raised an eyebrow and said, "Is there anything that doesn't call for more coffee?"

"For the love of caffeine, I hope not!"

Chapter Twenty-Two

I was just about to suggest that we go take a peek at the greenhouse before we went inside, when I heard a soft rustle and a dot appeared on my mental map. I noticed that my map wasn't as bright as usual—it was like I'd dropped from HD back to a more pixely resolution—a side effect of distancing myself from Bayley, I supposed. But I could still see the map, so I wasn't alarmed.

"We've got company."

"Eagan?" Carmine asked.

I frowned. "No. It's a regular person—not somebody from one of the magical families. Someone with a death wish, given the way they're driving."

The driveway leading from the main road to Bayley was more of a long, dark road winding a good quarter mile through the woods. Taking those turns that fast was a little nuts.

Carmine's eyebrows hiked up. "Were you expecting someone?"

"No."

He and I headed inside. Carmine peeled off into the mudroom, took off his jacket, and headed upstairs. He tried to stay out of sight when he visited so no one asked questions about how he was coming and going so often when he lived outside Seattle and I lived in New England.

As I hung my coat and headed to the front of the house, I did a quick check of my mental map and saw that Sadie was in her room.

When I reached the sitting room, Fuzzy trotted up and sat himself by my feet. I peered through the curtains to see a car speed into the grove, whip around the driveway, and screech to a stop in front of the house, motor still running. Music was blaring so loudly from the car that I could hear it in the house.

It was a pizza delivery car from a big fast-food chain.

I looked down at Fuzzy. "I didn't order any pizza. Did you?"

Fuzzy gave me a look, which I took to be a "no."

Carmine was with me the whole time, and he hadn't ordered anything, and I was fairly certain Sadie hadn't ordered, so I was stumped. Plus, I always ordered from the local pizzeria, not this mega chain, which made this doubly weird.

Gently tapping at my consciousness first, Bayley peeked out of the back of my mind to let me know that he was monitoring things, even from the background. He flipped on the porch lights so I could sort of see what was happening.

The light extended just enough that I could see someone who was wearing the bright shirt and hat of the fast-food chain get out of the car, haul out a pizza-warmer bag, and then climb the porch stairs.

When they knocked on the door, I opened it.

I relaxed slightly at the sight of the delivery guy who greeted me. He looked like he'd just started college, which explained the driving.

I said, "Hello."

"Hey. Got your order." He held up the pizza-warmer bag.

"I didn't order any food."

He frowned and looked confused. "This is number 55 right?"

"Yes."

He looked at the delivery slip. "It says number 55 for Foster. One extra-large sausage with extra cheese. You Foster?"

I nodded, but I must've looked as confused as I felt because he offered, "It's already paid for. You want it?" He shoved the pizza-warmer bag toward me.

"Um, sure? Does it say who paid for it?"

He looked at the slip again and said, "Nope sorry."

He reached into the bag, slid a pizza box out, handed it to me, and said, "Here you go."

Normally, the smell of melted cheese and garlic makes my stomach growl, but when he held the pizza out, it had a fake, over-processed smell that, if anything, made me less hungry. It made me even gladder I'd been patronizing the local shop.

Fuzzy, on the other hand, thought the cheese smelled just great. As Delivery Guy tried to hand the pizza over to me, Fuzzy popped up on his hind legs and batted at it.

I snagged the box, swinging it out of Fuzzy's reach with a, "I know you smell the meat and cheese, but this is not for you pal." To Delivery Guy I said, "Thanks," realized I should probably tip and added, "Oh hey, wait here."

I handed him back the pizza, shut the door, dashed down the hallway, and fished some cash out of my purse. The whole time I was thinking how strange this was. A Foster always delivered my food. Who'd send a normal delivery guy to Bayley House? For that matter, who'd send me an order from a crappy fast-food place, no less? And why? I ran back to the front door and found Fuzzy pacing back and forth.

"Jeez, Fuzzy. Didn't I just feed you?" I said as I stepped around him and opened the door again.

Keeping one foot in front of Fuzzy to hold him back, I said to Delivery Guy, "Sorry for the delay. Here's your tip."

He traded me the cash for the pizza.

"Thanks. See ya," he said. He got back in his car and tore down the driveway.

I closed the door and said to Fuzzy, "Well this is strange."

Fuzzy ran beside me, eyes on the pizza, as I went back to the kitchen. He chatter-meowed at me all the way down the hallway.

Bayley started growling back at him rather ominously, and though our connection was dimmed, I thought I felt some tension leaking from Bayley.

"Don't worry, Bayley, I'm not letting him eat any of this. I know better. Both of you, chill," I said, as I took a detour to the back stairs and hollered up, "The coast is clear." I heard footsteps moving upstairs as I entered the kitchen.

"Fuzzy, seriously?" Fuzzy had jumped up on the counter, from which vantage point he was the perfect height to paw at the pizza lid.

Jerking the box to the side I said, "No cheese for you, pal.

Get down please." I nudged him off the counter, but he just stood on his hind legs and tried to bat at the box from there.

I shook my head at him and laughed. "Well you get points for persistence."

Then, I put the pizza on the counter.

The second it touched the surface, Bayley went nuts.

He rocked the floor so hard that I stumbled back. At the same time, he yanked a vibrating field into place around the counter. To top things off, he jumped forward in my consciousness so fast that disorientation swamped me.

When Carmine entered the kitchen a moment later, he found me clinging to the kitchen island, with Fuzzy stalking back and forth in front of me.

Carmine stopped short. "What's wrong?"

I managed to squeeze the word "Pizza," out past the nausea and dizziness the disorientation had caused.

Carmine eyed it. "Okay."

I swallowed and tried again. "I didn't order it. Someone ordered me an extra-large with sausage. They even paid for it."

Carmine nodded. "That's why there's a protective circle. Good idea."

"It wasn't me, it was Bayley. And you can tell there's a circle?"

"Yes." Carmine turned a grave face to me. "I wouldn't eat that."

I hadn't given a lot of thought as to what to do with the pizza yet, but given that Bayley had just snapped a protective circle around it, I didn't think eating it was an option. "Why?"

Carmine sighed. "Because you have a lot of enemies. And you don't know if anything special has been done to it."

"Special? Carmine, are you saying someone poisoned my pizza?"

Sadie slipped into the kitchen. "Doesn't have to be poison. There are a variety of food-borne spells that can do all sorts of damage. You can really pack some extra power in there because the spell is ingested by the target."

I inched farther away, putting the kitchen island between me and the counter.

The second I backed away, Fuzzy stopped prowling and sat quietly, watching.

It finally dawned on me that Fuzzy hadn't been trying to eat the pizza. He'd been trying to warn me. And the growing tension I'd sensed from Bayley was because Fuzzy was warning him something was off.

"Oh no. This is so not good," I said. "The last thing I need is to get…uh…Spellmonella poisoning!"

Sadie looked confused. "Spellmonella?"

"Uh, yeah, you know…like Salmonella, but with spells."

Sadie looked at me like I was a little wackadoodle, but Carmine gave me a broad smile. "That's a clever way to think about it."

I said, "I'm not feeling real smart right now. Should I have been checking all my food for Spellmonella this whole time? Do I need to worry about everything that's being delivered?"

"No," said Carmine.

"Why not?"

"The Housekeeper is off limits," said Sadie and Carmine at the same time, in the same sort of monotone that made me think it was an oft-repeated rule.

Carmine added, "Well, you're supposed to be."

"Really?" Given the number of people who'd had it in for me so far, that rule wasn't ironclad. "Uh, it's looking like maybe somebody didn't get the memo. What do I do with this?" I pointed to the pizza.

Carmine said, "There are a number of ways—"

"I'll do it," Sadie interrupted, stepping forward.

Carmine and I both looked at her in surprise.

"What? It's not like it's hard," Sadie sniffed.

I said, "Uh, are you okay to do magic? You spent a lot of energy yesterday."

"Oh please. I got some sleep. For this? I'm fine."

Sadie forestalled any more arguing by stalking over to the pizza. She studied it for a moment. "Can you drop the circle, and I'll replace it with one of my own? Or expand the circle to include me?"

Bayley apparently didn't like the idea of dropping the circle because before I could answer, he expanded it to include Sadie.

I felt the vibrations shift.

"And the sink, please," Sadie said.

Bayley obliged and shifted the circle again.

She turned on the water faucet and made a circling motion with her hand. Part of the water stream split off and formed a bar about a foot long. Sadie pointed and the water bar arrowed over to the pizza box. When she pointed again and jerked her hand up, the water bar acted like a lever and flipped the lid open.

We all looked inside.

It looked like a sausage and cheese pizza.

Next, Sadie stuck her hand under the water faucet, wetting her hand and flicking handfuls of droplets over the pizza so that the water "rained" onto it. When she was satisfied, she shut the water off.

Carmine looked just as interested as I felt. We both scooted closer to get a better look.

Fuzzy hopped up on the counter, outside the circle, but close enough that he could maintain his vigil.

Sadie waved a hand over the pizza in a complicated whirling pattern and muttered some words under her breath. With a sharp, upward flick of her hand, all the water droplets she'd just added rose up from the pizza and hung above it. Then they joined together in a clump.

Flattening itself into a pizza shape, the water clump began to change color. After a few seconds, the bottom and middle turned clear, but the top turned muddy with an iridescent overlay, reminding me of an oil slick in a polluted puddle.

Sadie motioned with her hands until the water turned clear, then jerked her hand to the right. The water clump flew through the air and flowed into the sink, where it went down the drain.

I nearly clapped, but my hands froze in mid-air when Sadie turned and said, "There's an illusion spell on this."

Chapter Twenty-Three

My brief delight at Sadie's magic skills fizzled.

Another illusion spell?

Bayley growled so angrily that both Carmine and Sadie looked a little worried.

I sighed and said, "It's alright Bayley. We'll figure it out."

Sadie was studying me closely. "You don't look that surprised."

"It's the second illusion spell we've seen today," I said.

She and Carmine raised their eyebrows at me at the same time. It would've been funny under other circumstances.

"It's a really complex illusion. I don't think I've ever seen one this seamless—I wouldn't have noticed it either, so don't feel bad. The good news is that the illusion is limited to the top of the pizza. There's nothing spelled inside, under, or around it." Sadie eyed me. "Pissed off any Guthries lately?"

I shook my head. "Not that I know of." Eying the pizza, I asked, "Is there a way to break the spell?" I looked at Carmine. "What do illusion spells even do?"

Sadie used her patient voice to say, "Illusion magic is a type of air magic. As with any magic talent, there's a whole range of things they can do—"

"They generally hide things," said Carmine.

"I was getting to that," groused Sadie.

I rubbed my forehead. "So there's a spell that's hiding something." Like the sparrow spell this morning had been hiding the fact that it was spying. "Bayley, do you think this is the same person who did the spell this morning?"

Bayley grumbled a *ding*.

I asked him in my mind, *Fuzzy could tell something was wrong. Am I right to guess that you thought something was up too?*

I heard a *ding* in my head.

Why didn't you warn me?

I got a sense of resignation, and then he gave me the sensation of pulling back into the corner of my head.

Okay, yes, I did ask you to give me some space. I thought for a few seconds and then I asked him, *Were you giving me a chance to figure it out?*

Ding.

Okay. I sighed and rubbed the ache forming in my forehead. *You were able to detect the spell this time though right, so that's an improvement.*

Bayley sent me a mental image of the pizza touching the counter.

You were only sure when you touched the pizza? I asked.

Ding.

Oh boy. Well, they still snuck it by us again, but on the plus side you kept it from doing any damage.

Bayley sent me a wave of aggravation so strong that I flinched.

I know. This really isn't good.

I looked up to find Carmine and Sadie staring at me.

I sighed. "So what's the procedure here? What's the spell disposal protocol?"

Carmine said, "Bayley already isolated it, so now all that's left is to dismantle it."

A red dot blipped onto my map. "Uh, hold that thought. Eagan's here," I said and headed for the front hall.

When I opened the door, Eagan was climbing the stairs, hauling a big gym bag.

"Uh, hi," I said, waving him inside. "We have a bit of a situation," I explained as I led him to the kitchen.

"Another one?"

"I know. At this rate, we're going to have to get me a t-shirt that says 'Danger-prone Daphne.' Also, my friend Carmine is here."

Eagan said, "He knows about Sadie?"

"Yeah. He even brought her a change of clothes and some stuff."

Eagan looked down at the bag he was carrying. "Well, she might not need these then."

When we reached the kitchen, Sadie and Carmine were studying the pizza, talking in low voices.

"Carmine, Eagan. Eagan, Carmine."

They shook hands.

Eagan looked at Sadie, who was still standing inside the protective circle, and held up the bag he was holding. "I brought you some things to get you by."

Surprised, Sadie said, "Thanks."

As he set the bag on the kitchen table, Eagan asked, "Someone want to tell me what the current disaster is?"

I explained to Eagan about the pizza.

Sadie said, "I was about to disassemble the spell when you interrupted."

Eagan looked concerned. "Are you sure you're up for this?"

She curled her lip at him. "I'm fine. I'm not some shrinking violet, you know."

"Shrinking violet? Really Grandma?" Eagan asked with a teasing grin.

I held up my hands. "Guys, now is not the time. Can we focus please?"

Sadie sniffed, "I can. I don't know about him," and turned her back on Eagan to focus on the pizza.

Carmine, Eagan, and I arranged ourselves so we could watch what she was doing. Fuzzy continued to stand guard on the counter, just outside the protective circle. I would've told him to get down, but I had the feeling that he wasn't going anywhere until he was sure the threat was neutralized.

Sadie stood up a little straighter. I got the sense that she enjoyed showing off her skills.

Turning slightly, she adjusted her stance so that her feet were braced shoulder-width apart, and she was squared off with the pizza.

She turned on the water faucet with her right hand, circling with her left hand, causing the water to flow up into the air and form a big, round, floating pool. When it reached the size of a water balloon, she shut the faucet off.

With a swish of her hands, the water shot over and hovered above the pizza, shifting and sliding until it formed a puddle the exact size of the pizza. While keeping up a steady murmur, Sadie reached up with both hands and pressed down, like she was pushing on a plunger. As she pressed, the puddle lowered.

When it made contact with the pizza, the puddle shuddered. Sadie squinted, murmured faster, her arms straining as she pushed down harder.

The puddle shimmered and little ripples rocked back and forth across its surface. The ripples became waves, turning the puddle into a small ocean.

A hum of triumph escaped Sadie. The puddle, waves and all, sank into the pizza, then expanded all the way through and around it, forcing it to float up into the middle, effectively bubbling it. Waves churned inside the bubble, rolling over the pizza again and again.

It looked to me like the puddle was washing the pizza.

After a few minutes, there was a shimmer, and suddenly the toppings looked really weird. I squeaked as I recognized the one in the middle.

"Is that—"

"A snake head?" Eagan finished. "Looks like it."

Sadie made a motion with her hand and jerked the puddle up and off the pizza, which landed with a squelch back in the box.

The water in the puddle had turned a sick greenish brown that reminded me of swamp water.

Pointing to the muddy puddle hanging in the air, Sadie asked, "How would you like to dispose of this? I've got a couple of different things I can do."

"I've got this," said Eagan. "If that's okay."

Sadie shrugged. "Sure."

"Fine by me," I added.

As Eagan stepped toward Sadie, Bayley dropped the circle

for a second to let him in.

Eagan took up a position to Sadie's right. He raised his hands, widening them so he was roughly framing the puddle in front of him. As he whispered something, a ring of fire appeared around the puddle.

"Please don't fry Bayley," I said to Eagan.

He chuckled. "As if. Don't worry, Bayley. You're perfectly safe."

Bayley mumbled at him in response, sounding more encouraging than worried.

The fire expanded to form a bubble around the murky puddle. Eagan looked at Sadie and said, "You can let go. I've got it now."

Sadie looked at him, speculation making her eyes glint. "It's surprisingly concentrated. You sure?"

Eagan smirked at her. "Are you impugning my manhood?"

"Guys! Could we get rid of the scary puddle now and snark later?"

Sadie said, "Eagan, if you could focus for a moment, we can get this done quickly. Here, I'll give you an assist."

She turned back to the fire-and-water bubbles. "Unless you want me to punch through your magic, make a hole, Eagan."

Eagan shifted into business mode. The laughter in his eyes was replaced by focus as he opened a small window in his fire bubble.

Eyes narrowed, Sadie held out one hand. "Get ready to close it fast," she said.

At Eagan's nod, Sadie gestured toward the bubble. Sadie must've used her desiccant powers because one second there was a puddle, and the next the water disappeared as Sadie snapped, "Now."

The window in the fire bubble snapped shut. Inside, now that all the water was gone, only a swirling murky cloud remained.

"Did you just dry all the water out?" Eagan asked.

Sadie nodded.

"Nice. I mean, I could have dealt with the water, but nice."

Sadie shrugged nonchalantly but there was a proud gleam in her eye.

Eagan said, "Okay, let's finish this." The fire expanded inward to fill the entire circle, incinerating the murky cloud within. When there was nothing left but fire, Eagan waved his hands, and the fireball disappeared.

"Wow, thanks you guys!" I said.

Bayley dropped the protective circle. A foul stench oozed from the pizza's surface.

"What the—what is that?" I stepped back, waving a hand back and forth in front of my face. "Bayley, please open the window." The window over the sink flew open. Without my asking, Bayley got a breeze going, blowing the stink outside.

We all stepped closer and looked to see what the illusion had been hiding.

That was, indeed, a snake's head ornamenting the center.

A generous helping of sausages also dotted the surface, but something seemed off about them.

I blinked and looked closer. "Are those—?"

"Turds? Yeah," said Eagan.

"Oh gross! No wonder it smells," I said.

"Let me take care of this," Eagan said.

"Wait," I said. I grabbed my phone and snapped a couple of pictures. "Okay," I said.

Eagan slammed the lid down on the pizza box and took it outside. From the kitchen window, we saw him quickly incinerate the whole thing.

As Eagan came back inside, I looked at my guests, shaking my head. "What the hell? To recap, someone sent me a pizza covered in poop and a dead snake? But covered it in an illusion spell, in hopes I'd take a bite."

Eagan said, "They probably expected you to discover the spell—you're the Housekeeper. Although I suppose it would have been a bonus if you'd bitten into it."

I just looked at him.

Sadie said, "It looks to me as though someone is sending you a message."

"What message? Also, again, what the hell? Is this something you people do?"

Eagan said, "If by 'you people' you're referring to the magical community, then no. This is the first I've heard of something like this. Although I suppose it could be a Guthrie thing. Other than Lou and Pete, I only know a few Guthries." He looked to Carmine and Sadie, who were both shaking their heads.

Carmine said, "You seem to have someone's attention."

We stood there, contemplating, when Eagan jerked, looking like a lightbulb had gone off in his head. "Shitty snake. I got it. That's what that pizza was saying. Someone is calling you a shitty snake."

Sadie said, "Not just someone. A Guthrie."

I looked at Carmine. "Do we think this is just me, or is this a Housekeeper thing?"

"I don't know," Carmine said.

"Is there a difference?" Eagan asked.

He had a point. But someone targeting just plain ole me rather than Finn the Housekeeper somehow made things a lot more personal.

Either way, I had the feeling I was gonna need some help.

Chapter Twenty-Four

I was pondering whether I wanted to call Lou and/or Pete about the Guthrie situation when Eagan sidetracked me.

"I don't know about you guys, but the poop pizza took the edge off my appetite," he said. "Want to go check out the greenhouse before we eat dinner?"

Carmine nodded. "Good idea. I can have a quick look at the plants."

My mind raced. What if the lump had come back? I had no problem sharing the mystery of the lump with Carmine, but I wasn't as sure about Eagan, and I certainly didn't want Sadie involved.

A look at her told me the magic drain had taken more out of Sadie than she was willing to admit. Maybe I could get her to stay inside. I said, "It's cold out. You're welcome to hang here if you'd like. We won't be long."

Sadie shrugged and said, "I don't mind tagging along."

I shifted back and forth, trying to figure out a way to wiggle out of this.

"Finn, what's the matter? You look like my three-year-old cousin right before we make a mad dash for the restroom," said Eagan.

"It's just, you know, it really is cold out. And dark. Maybe we should wait?"

Eagan laughed at me. "I hate to tell you this, but this is nothing. It's only going to get worse. Might as well get used to it now."

They were all staring at me with varying degrees of "Would

you suck it up, buttercup?" on their faces. I sighed and caved with an, "Okay fine."

While Carmine and I grabbed our coats from the mudroom, Eagan reached into the bag he brought and hauled out a coat. Thrusting it at Sadie, he said, "It's not fancy, and it'll be big on you, but it'll keep you warm for now."

Sadie took the gray wool peacoat and bundled herself into it with a surprisingly sincere, "Thank you."

The other three of us grabbed our coats as well, and the whole group, followed by Fuzzy, trooped outside.

Bayley flooded the porch with light, enough of which spilled across the lawn so that we could make our way to the greenhouse without tripping.

I stared hard at the spot where I'd seen the lump before, but I didn't see anything lurking in the shadows. As far as I could tell, we were currently lump-free. Still, as we walked across the lawn, my head swiveled this way and that, looking for the lump.

Fuzzy wasn't taking any chances either. He zipped past us, trotting behind the greenhouse, then circling back to me. He brushed my leg, and then headed back into the house, tossing me a last, "Meow," which I took to be the equivalent of "the coast is clear."

I let out a breath.

Carmine had helped me pick out good lighting for inside the greenhouse, and when he flicked the switch the place went from night to day in an instant.

I pointed to the back corner and said, "The melted section is back there. The plants were far enough away that they didn't get scorched, but I'm not sure if there was any damage."

Carmine headed straight for Sibeta's plants, while Eagan beelined for the hole in the back of the greenhouse. I wasn't sure who to follow and wound up following Sadie as she drifted over by Carmine.

Carmine ran his hands gently over the plants and nodded once. "They're fine. They weren't too fond of the smoke, but there's no damage done. What's Eagan doing?"

I followed his eyeline to see that Eagan had knelt next to the hole at the corner of the greenhouse.

He whistled. "Well, I've got good news and bad news. The good news is this wasn't my spell. The bad news is I have no idea how this happened."

I did. I suspected it had to do with the lump, but I didn't want to tell Eagan that.

He pointed to the melted frame. "See that? That's melted aluminum. You need something hot—really hot—as a heat source to melt aluminum. Way hotter than my spell. I put limits on the upper reaches of the spell I'm using so that the spell disintegrates if it reaches a certain temperature."

"You can do that?" I said. "That's really neat."

Sadie was looking impressed despite herself.

Eagan shrugged. "When you're working with fire, safety is important." He waved a hand through the air and nodded once. "The spell is still running, by the way. That's why the temperature in here hasn't plummeted with all the cold air the hole is letting in."

I whacked myself in the head. "Duh. I should cover the hole. I didn't even think of it—it was still so hot earlier that I didn't want to mess with it and then I forgot about it."

Carmine said, "You've been a little busy."

That was an understatement. With all the people coming and going, the weird magic, and whatever was going on with that lump, today had edged over the line from busy to slightly insane. Add to that my discomfort with Bayley, and I was ready to crawl into bed and pull the covers over my head.

But I had guests to feed so that wasn't an option.

With a small sigh, I trudged over to where Eagan was studying the hole. He pointed at it and said, "See how the metal flowed into the greenhouse? Whatever melted this happened from the outside." He looked at me and said, "Are you sure you aren't punking me and that you didn't take a blowtorch to the outside?"

I shook my head, "Sorry. I left my blowtorch back in the desert."

He ran his hands along the ground.

Carmine came over and said, "Looks like something was digging."

Eagan lifted his head to look at Carmine, who was peering at the ground. "Do you recognize the tracks?"

Carmine shook his head. "No, but spend enough time gardening, and you see a bunch of digging just like this. Critters are clever."

Eagan shook his head. "Well, Finn, I think you've got two problems here. One, you've got something that wants to get into the greenhouse really bad."

Carmine said, "We'll have to figure out what sort of animal it is so we can gently discourage it."

Eagan nodded then said, "And two, you've got a fire of unknown origin. I have no idea what happened, but it looks fine now. I guess keep an eye on it, and call me if anything else happens."

I nodded, "Okay thanks. And thank you again for the spell—turns out it was a really good backup plan to have in place."

Eagan smiled. "No problem."

Eagan and Carmine volunteered to patch the hole, and Sadie lingered to watch, so I went inside and set the table for dinner.

Bayley, I said.

He'd retreated again after the pizza incident, giving me the space I'd asked for. I felt his consciousness come forward from the back of my mind. A wave of shame washed through me. I felt like I was treating him like a little kid and leaving him in his timeout corner. He'd only been trying to help me.

You don't have to stay in the background anymore. I'm sorry. I just—we're going to have to talk about this at some point. Not right now, but soon.

Bayley made crooning sounds with the floorboards, trying to soothe me. It made me feel like a heel.

Hey, while we have a moment, can you tell me if the lump is what caused the greenhouse to melt?

Ding.

Was that a "yes, you can tell me," or a "yes, the lump did it"?

Ding.
The lump did it?
Ding.
Do you know what the lump is?
Ding.
Can you tell me?

There was a pause and then the image of the lump floated up in my mind.

I know what it looks like. What is it?

Bayley kept showing me a picture of the lump.

That's not helping.

Another pause, then Bayley showed me a picture of Sibeta.

The lump has to do with Sibeta?

A slow *ding ding* sounded in my head. Usually that was more of a "no, not exactly" than a straight "no."

I thought for a second then tried, *You want me to ask Sibeta about the lump?*

Ding.
Okay.

Curiouser and curiouser. I had the feeling that I wasn't Sibeta's favorite person right now because I was harboring Sadie. I didn't know how happy she was going to be to talk to me. Well, I supposed it could've been worse. Bayley could've told me to talk to Zo. Then I'd never get any answers.

I'd finished setting the table when Sadie, Carmine, and Eagan trooped inside. Carmine and Eagan were chatting while Sadie looked on.

"Ready for dinner?" I asked.

"I don't know about these two, but now I'm starving," said Eagan.

Everyone piled around the table, and though they offered to help, I insisted on serving them. Slipping into diner mode felt comfortable, comfort that was really welcome as I was feeling rather frayed around the edges.

Thanks to Eagan's boisterous personality, dinner was lively, with Eagan making friends with Carmine, teasing Sadie, and joking with me and Bayley. When Eagan first addressed Bayley,

Sadie looked so startled I thought she might choke on her food. But Carmine and I included Bayley too, and before long she seemed to get used to it.

The food was a big hit, and after dessert, I packed up some extra cookies for Eagan to take with him. When Eagan left, Carmine and Sadie headed upstairs to their rooms.

Before I went to see Sibeta, I decided to wait a bit to make sure Carmine and Sadie were settled in for the night. After I'd tidied up the kitchen, I sat down at the table to take a quick look at the assignment Wil had left me. I started reading and within a minute I got totally sucked in.

Chapter Twenty-Five

Bayley tugged on my attention just as Fuzzy appeared by my feet.

I dragged my mind out of the history book with an effort, then was startled to realize that a half hour had sped by. "Oops. Sorry Bayley! I'm guessing this is your reminder that I need to go talk to Sibeta?"

Ding.

I got up and followed Fuzzy to find him sitting in front of the basement door, which Bayley swung open as I approached.

Fuzzy took off down the stairs to the basement. A quick check of my mental map showed me that Carmine and Sadie were both in their rooms, so I followed Fuzzy, closing the door behind me.

"Bayley, will you lock this please?"

I heard a click as I continued down the stairs.

When I reached the bottom, Fuzzy was in the pool, paddling toward a bobbing object, while Sibeta stood on the water, watching him.

Fuzzy reached it and batted it, then swam after it as it sped away. I squinted and realized that it was a ball made of solid water.

"Did you make Fuzzy a ball?" I asked Sibeta.

She nodded. "Yes."

"Thank you."

"You are welcome."

We both watched Fuzzy play for a few moments, and I was pretty sure that the smile on her face was meant to convey delight. She really liked Fuzzy. Hopefully her good mood from playing with him would stay intact as she talked with me.

I enjoyed Fuzzy for a few more minutes before I turned to Sibeta and said, "Uh, Bayley and Fuzzy told me to come see you."

"Bayley called to me. I came."

"Thank you. If you have time, I would like to speak with you."

She bowed her head and swept her arm in a gesture that I took to mean "go on."

I explained about the lump.

"When I asked Bayley to explain what it is, he told me to talk to you. What is it?"

Sibeta looked me up and down. Her face showed no expression, but it was clear she was assessing me.

"Sit, Housekeeper," she said.

Oh boy. It was never good when they told you to sit down before they delivered the news. I dragged a pool chair over to the side of pool and sat facing her. Maybe I should have waited till tomorrow to have this conversation. I was already tired, and the day had been a real tornado of crazy already.

But, I reminded myself that I couldn't take the chance that the lump could burn down the greenhouse. I plopped myself into the chair and said, "Lay it on me."

Sibeta stared at me, unblinking.

I said, "Please go ahead and give me the bad news."

"Why do you think the news is bad?"

"You made me sit down."

"Ah," Sibeta drifted closer. "You appear tired. That is all. I apologize if I have worried you, Housekeeper."

"Thank you for thinking of my comfort, Sibeta. I do appreciate it. It's been a very long day." I tried to shrug some of the tension out of my shoulders, then squared them as I faced Sibeta and asked, "So, about the lump?"

"It is not a lump."

"I figured. What is it?"

"She is," and then she said a word I couldn't understand. It was a weird combination of clacking and grinding sounds, with some groaning thrown in.

My brain latched onto the part of the sentence it could grasp. "She?"

Sibeta nodded once.

"Uh," was all I could manage as my brain jammed with all the questions bubbling up. I was really glad Sibeta had told me to sit down.

Sibeta gently swayed on top of the water as she waited for me to sort myself out.

Fuzzy stopped playing with the ball, swam over, and climbed out of the pool. After shaking water off himself like a dog, he came to sit by me.

I gave him a quick pat on the head and then returned my attention to Sibeta.

"What, um, what is she? I mean, is she some kind of animal?"

Sibeta frowned. "How do you define animal?"

I blinked. "Uh, well, I guess…animals are…alive, but not people." That was not a great definition, but it's what I could come up with at the moment.

Sibeta said, "Is Fuzzy an animal?"

I said slowly, "I'm not sure. I thought he was a cat, but I don't think that's true anymore. I'm not sure what he is, to be honest. I'm waiting for Zo to explain that to me. Unless you'd like to?"

Sibeta shook her head once. "If Zo has taken that responsibility, so be it."

Because that didn't sound ominous at all.

"Okay, well then, I can't really say what Fuzzy is. Heck you still haven't told me what you are. Would you like to do that now?"

She just looked at me.

When she continued not to say anything, I plowed on with, "Okay if Fuzzy were a regular kitten, he would be an animal. Does that help?"

"What is the difference between people and animals? How do you tell the difference?"

This was a weird discussion. I rubbed at the kink in my neck as I tried to figure out what she was trying to get at. "I think what we're talking about," I said slowly, "is intelligence and sentience. You know what intelligence is, right?"

She nodded.

"Do you know the word 'sentience'?"

Sibeta said, "No."

"How about 'consciousness'?"

"No."

"Okay. Side note, I'll add some documentaries on the brain to your list." I sighed. "Um, so, one of the ways that we, that is, humans, categorize living things is by how they think—how complex their thought process is. We call it the ability to reason. So, a kitten, for example is alive, it has a personality, but it can only reason a little. A person, like me, has much more ability to reason."

Allegedly.

I wasn't feeling like my reasoning skills were anything to write home about as I stumbled through this explanation. I was pretty sure scientists everywhere were cringing.

"Does this make sense?" I asked a little desperately.

"Yes."

"Okay, so anything that is aware of its own existence is considered sentient. For example, everyone is this room is sentient, and I know that you, Bayley, and I can reason, and I'm guessing Fuzzy can, too. An animal would be less able to reason the way we do. Does that help?"

Sibeta cocked her head, "Bayley, Fuzzy, and I are people, not animal."

"Well, there's a whole species thing, but yes, for the purposes of this conversation, I think of all of you as more like people than animals."

Sibeta said, "By this definition, the," she said the unpronounceable word again, "is people."

"The lump is a person?"

"Not lump," and she said the word again.

"Whatever it is you're saying, I can't pronounce it. Can you say it slowly?"

Sibeta did as I asked. The first syllable was kind of a growling "grr" sound followed by a snapping that sounded like "ack."

"How about I call her a Grack?"

Sibeta thought about it for a moment, nodded once, and said, "An acceptable solution, Housekeeper."

"Um, thanks. So if the, er, Grack is a, um, person, then does that mean it's possible to talk to her?"

"Yes, Housekeeper."

"Any chance she speaks English?"

"No, Housekeeper."

"How do you know so much about her? Does that mean you can speak to her?"

"Of course, Housekeeper. That is my responsibility," she said and bowed deeply.

"Your responsibility?"

"I found a better word than interpreter. I am somewhat like what you call a liaison." Again, she bowed.

A liaison? That brought up a whole host of other questions.

"Sibeta, who do you liaise between?"

At her blank look I explained, "A liaison liaises, or goes between and communicates with, different groups. Who are the groups you are helping to communicate with each other?"

"My people and the others."

"Others? What others?"

She said, "Like you. And Bayley. And the Travis-Fuzzy."

A sneaking suspicion grew in the back of my mind as I asked, "Sibeta, how many others are there?"

The perpetual undulating motion of Sibeta's water cloak stopped. When it resumed, her posture shifted so she somehow seemed to be standing more stiffly.

She said, "I am sorry, Housekeeper Finn Foster. It is not my place to say." And she did the formal bowing thing.

Uh oh. She used my full name. I couldn't remember her ever doing that before. It was like when your parents called you by your full name—you knew things were serious.

My mind was racing. "Is the lum—er, the Grack—one of the others?"

"Yes."

"Sibeta, where are the others?"

"I am sorry, Housekeeper. It is not my place to say."

"Can you tell me what the others are?"

"I am sorry, Housekeeper. It is—"

"Not your place to say. Yeah, I get it." Except I didn't. I had no idea what was going on. As usual.

"Okay, let's stick to the current 'other' at hand and talk about the Grack. Do you know why she melted my greenhouse?"

"Yes."

I waited but when nothing else was forthcoming, I prodded, "Can you please tell me why?"

"No."

"Why not?"

"It is not my place to say."

I was really getting to hate that phrase.

"Okay Sibeta, how about this. You can communicate with the Grack right?"

"Yes."

"Would you be willing to do your liaison thing so I can talk with the Grack?"

She bowed. "Of course, Housekeeper. It is my responsibility."

"Great. Thank you." It was too late to have a meeting right then, but I figured I should try to set it up sooner rather than later if I wanted to keep the greenhouse and Sibeta's plants safe. "Can you set up a meeting for tomorrow? And in the meantime, ask her to please stay away from the greenhouse? Your food is in there, and I don't want her to damage it."

Sibeta's cloak rippled faster, which I took to be a sign of alarm. I held up a hand. "Don't worry, she didn't cause any damage to your plants today—Carmine checked and they're fine. But if she causes another fire, that might not be the case, and I'd rather be safe than sorry."

"I will speak with her. Yes."

I had no idea how I was going to be able to coordinate a meeting while I dodged Sadie, but maybe I could get Carmine to help. He already knew about Sibeta, so I supposed it didn't matter if he knew about the Grack. In for a penny, in for a pound.

"Thank you for your help Sibeta. Is there anything I can do for you in return? Anything you need?"

Sibeta looked at the ceiling. "The...Sadie. She is still here?"

"Yes."

"It would be...better...if she were not."

"I understand," I said. "If it's any comfort, she wants to leave as much as you want her gone. But," I shook my head, trying to figure out how to explain. Finally, I just went for honesty. "Sibeta, I'm sorry, but Sadie needs help—she needs time to heal and figure a way out of her situation—and I can't in good conscience throw her out in the cold. I know that's unlike how the other Housekeepers did things, but frankly, they seem like they were," *a bunch of asshats,* "er, short-sighted. I know I'm different, but this is the way I roll."

Sibeta studied me for a long moment, and I had the sense that she was evaluating me again. I thought I was going to have to explain more, but then she said, "The way you roll. This is important."

And with those cryptic words she started to sink into the pool. Just before her head disappeared she said, "I will call to you tomorrow," then disappeared below the surface.

I looked down at Fuzzy. "Why do I get the feeling that tomorrow is going to be even more messed up than today?"

Chapter Twenty-Six

I tried to study, I really did. But exhaustion swamped me and, after reading the same sentence five times, I gave it up and went to bed.

I had no idea how long I was unconscious before I became aware that I was sitting in a movie theater chair looking at a blank screen.

I looked around and yup, I wasn't actually in a movie theater. I'd seen this place before—I was in a mental space that Bayley had created. It looked sort of like I was in a secret room between the walls of the house, except as far as I knew, the real walls didn't hide a movie theater.

I sat in the middle of several rows of movie-theater style seats, complete with worn red velvet, facing the inside of a wall, which was adorned with a huge movie screen.

Out of the corner of my left eye, I could sort of see a guy. Like the last time this happened, when I turned around to look directly at him, he disappeared.

Facing front again, I asked, "Bayley, is that you behind me?"
He said, "Yes."
Not a *ding*. A warm, baritone "yes."
"You can talk—" I turned around as I was talking, and he disappeared again. With a frustrated hiss, I faced front. "Dammit Bayley. How come I can't see you when I look at you? And hey, how come I'm aware of what's going on?"

When I'd been here before, I'd been in a coma, and I'd had no idea that I was dream-linking with Bayley. This time I knew what was happening.

Bayley said, "It's a little like that thing where you know you're dreaming, and you can control how you act in the dream."

"That sounds like lucid dreaming."

"This isn't exactly a dream—I'm holding us in a liminal space—but the concept is similar."

I was curious about the liminal space, but I had more pressing questions. "Okay, but how come I can't look at you?"

"It isn't time yet."

"What does that mean?"

Bayley repeated, "It isn't time yet."

"Bayley—"

"I'm sorry Finn. It isn't time yet."

I growled in frustration. "Hey, how come you have a British accent?"

"I'm...foreign. Your brain is interpreting it as a British accent." He sounded amused. "If you prefer, I can be Scottish," he said in a Scottish accent, and then continued to switch accents as he said, "Irish, Russian, Australian—"

"Okay, okay. I get it. You know what, you pick the accent you like best and go with that."

I could feel his surprise followed by his delight. "I'll try British. For now." He paused and then said a bit shyly, "Thank you."

"For what?"

"For allowing me to choose."

My heart broke a little bit. "Of course, Bayley. I'd like to think that with me as your Housekeeper, you'll always have choices."

I swallowed hard to get rid of the lump that was trying to form in my throat. "Bayley, you can talk any way you like. Speaking of which, why are you suddenly able to talk like this," I gestured back and forth between us, "I mean, have a conversation?"

"I have more energy."

That was true. Bayley reminded me of a run-down battery when we first met. In the last two months, he seemed to be slowly recharging.

He sounded ashamed as he added, "But I am so lacking. Not nearly...my full self. I had to touch that illusion spell before I could sense it. I should be able to sense any spell as soon as it crosses onto the property, even the ones that hide. I am sorry Finn."

"It's not your fault, Bayley, that the Fosters have let you get so run down. And if we're being honest, I'm not helping the situation with my lack of knowledge. But like I said when Zo was here, we'll figure it out."

Bayley said in a determined voice, "I will get stronger, in time."

"I believe you. I mean, look at how much stronger you are already. You're talking to me and everything. Hey, does this mean that now you'll talk to me like this when I'm awake?"

"It's not time yet."

Aggravation stomped out the sympathy I'd just been feeling. "Seriously? You have to do better than that."

I could feel him thinking. At length he said, "There's an order that things happen in. When it's time, I'll be able to speak with you more easily. Until then, we have the liminal space." He must've heard me grinding my teeth because he added, "If it helps, this is much farther than any Housekeeper has come in a long while. You are the first I've spoken with like this in some time."

"How long?"

"Centuries," he said and his voice was filled with a cold emptiness that stabbed at me.

"Well, um, are you going to be able to talk to me in the real world? Preferably sooner rather than later? Because in case you hadn't noticed, there's a bunch of stuff happening, and it's getting nuts out there," I gestured toward the movie screen, which previously had given me a window into what was happening in the real world while I was unconscious. At the moment, it remained blank.

He perked up, physically and vocally. In a much more cheery voice, he said, "I have every confidence that things will continue to move apace."

Apace? Which century did he pick that up in?

"Great," I said grumpily. "Speaking of moving apace, what am I doing here?"

"You said you needed to talk." I saw Bayley stiffen out of the corner of my eye. "I angered you earlier. And you said," he switched to an imitation of my voice, " 'we're going to have to talk about this at some point—not right now, but soon'." Switching back to his regular voice, he added, "Given how upset you've been, I thought it best that we expedite the process."

Oh great. Just what I needed after such a long day. I mean, I did ask to talk to him. And I did actually want to talk to him. I just...I hadn't really thought it through yet. And thinking back to earlier in the day got me all freaked out again.

I sighed heavily and rubbed my eyes, which somehow felt gritty even though I knew I was asleep.

"I don't know what to say."

Bayley waited while I tried to sort my thoughts and feelings out.

"Can you explain what you did to me?" I asked. I winced. It came out a lot harsher, a lot more raw than I intended.

I felt Bayley's confusion and, I thought, a tinge of fear. The fear made me feel bad. I didn't want him to be afraid of me.

"Bayley," I said, doing my best to keep my tone comforting, "you never need to be afraid of me. While I might, heaven forbid, hurt you accidentally, I would never do it on purpose."

I saw him nodding vigorously out of the corner of my eye. "Yes. I would never hurt *you* on purpose as well."

I heaved out a breath and slouched back in my chair, staring up at the ceiling. Surprisingly, the image of him in the corner of my vision resolved a little more, became a little sharper, a little more solid. Huh. I'd have to try to remember to slouch if we did this again.

I smothered a grin when I saw him slump down in his seat, mirroring my posture.

I knew I was letting my mind wander so I wouldn't have to deal with the uncomfortable subject at hand. With a soft sigh, I forced myself to focus.

"Okay, I concede that you weren't trying to hurt me. I do,

honestly, believe that. But Bayley, can you see how you just rifling through my mind without my permission might upset me? Look at it from my point of view, if you can. My thoughts… well they're *mine*. They're *private*. And very personal. Hell, I don't even know what's in there, and the fact that you are looking at stuff…ugh stuff I may not even remember…that's, that's…" I shuddered.

"I feel your discomfort. You do not need to find the words."

We sat quietly for a few moments while I tried to corral my rioting feelings and think about this logically.

"It would help me if you'd explain exactly what you did," I said.

Bayley nodded. "Of course. When we spoke here before—"

"When I was in the coma and we dream-linked like this?"

"Yes. It made our connection…different…more. One result is I can see your memories, access them, in a way you cannot."

"Oh." I thought for a moment. "Since we can talk like this now, does that mean we can dream-link regularly? It makes things a lot easier when I can have a conversation with you."

"I am sorry Finn. But no."

"Why not? Do not say it's not time yet."

There was a pause. "I'm…not able. This takes a great deal of energy. I'm sorry, Finn. I can only do this rarely."

"Great."

I didn't sound particularly happy, but Bayley plowed on. "The other night you were wondering about your parents again. Memories were flashing through your mind, some seen, some just under the surface. When you went to sleep, those memories were still right there in a way they usually are not. I made a note of where a helpful memory was. And today, when you were making cookies, wondering about your parents again, I knew where there was a memory that might help you understand, so I showed you."

He paused, then added, "You were so upset. When you think of your parents, you're so sad, Finn. I only want to make it easier for you, in the ways that I am able to at this time."

In the ways that he was able to at this time? I figured it had to do with our evolving bond.

And that was the thing, our bond was evolving. It would continue to evolve.

"Our bond is different," Bayley said.

"Don't. Do. That!" I said jumping out of my chair. Of course, when I spun around to confront him, he disappeared. I didn't care, I yelled at the empty chair where he'd been.

"I get that you're in my head. But it freaks me out when you…you just…you pluck things right out of my head," I said, throwing my hands up in the air. I paced back and forth as much as I could, given the confined space.

Bayley waited until I flopped back into my chair before saying, "But Finn. I always share your mind."

"This is different."

"How?"

I struggled to figure out how to explain something to him that I didn't quite understand myself. Then I latched onto something we'd said earlier.

"Choice, Bayley. It's about choice. It's one thing if you ask me if you can invade my memories. I mean, I get that we're bonded and that means our minds our linked. I get that." And that was a weird enough adjustment. "But so far, I've felt like you, I don't know, hang out, but not like you're…reading my mind. I mean, I know you're monitoring my mind, but it's not the same as *reading* my mind." I wasn't making any sense and I wanted to pull my hair in frustration.

"If I may?" he said.

"Sure, why not."

"What you describe is the difference between engaging and watching. You have become accustomed to my presence but you only interact with me directly when you choose."

"Well, it sounds kind of mean when you put it like that."

With an amused warmth he said, "That is not how I meant it. As you should realize by now, you interact with me more than any Housekeeper—"

"—in many centuries. I know Bayley. I am so sorry."

"No Finn. More than any Housekeeper."

That shocked me so much that I froze. "That can't be true."

Bayley didn't argue. He didn't say anything. He was just quiet. I reached for him in my mind and felt the weariness and loneliness that had been crippling him when I arrived.

Bayley said, "As much as you feel like this is a huge learning curve for you, it also is for me. Things with you are...different."

I didn't know how to feel about that. I'd been counting on Bayley being the experienced one.

"Wait, does this have to do with the balance thing?"

"It isn't time yet."

I wanted to bang my head on the chair in front of me. Did he and Sibeta get together and come up with a list of ways to drive me out of my ever-loving mind?

I grabbed hold of my temper and ground out, "Ugh. Fine. Well, until it is time, how do you suggest we proceed?" I almost said "and keep you from creeping me out" but that would've been petty and not really an entirely accurate representation of how I felt.

Bayley leaned forward, not enough that I could see him clearly, but enough that he solidified a bit more in my peripheral vision. "I could ask."

"You could ask?"

He nodded. "Before I search your mind, I could ask first. Would that suffice for the moment?"

I chewed it over. The truth was that, although it pained me to admit it, Bayley being able to access my memory and retrieve memories that I didn't even realize I had could be incredibly useful. In my quest to figure out what the hell my parents had been thinking, Bayley could be a huge help.

Plus, when I had a chance to get past the skin-crawly invaded feeling I was fighting, I knew I'd wind up in the same place I always did. I'd realize that Bayley was doing the best he could for me. And it was my job to do the best I could for him. Not just my job, if I was being honest. He was my friend, too, and I tried to treat my friends the way I wanted to be treated.

I sighed. "I think that asking should help. I think it should help a lot. Thank you for thinking of a compromise while I've been over here being all emotional. This is all just so new to me, Bayley. I'm guessing that you of all people know just how overwhelming this is for me and how lost I feel...so much of the time," I finished softly.

I heard movement behind me and felt Bayley place a warm hand on my shoulder. "I know, Finn."

I stayed facing front, but I reached up to my shoulder and put my hand over his. It felt surprisingly real.

"We'll figure all this out," I said. "It's just going to take time."

"In the future, I will try to give you...choice."

"Thanks Bayley."

"Time, I think, for you to go."

Chapter Twenty-Seven

I opened my eyes to find Fuzzy on my chest, staring at me. The sun had already begun to rise, and I was tempted to go back to sleep since I didn't feel like I'd gotten any rest.

It took me a few seconds to realize the vibrating in the background wasn't Fuzzy purring. My phone was ringing.

I peeked at the screen, stifled a groan, and answered with a groggy, "Hi Wil."

"Good morning, Finn!"

I couldn't fault Wil for being so perky first thing in the morning. Usually I was the same way. I felt a moment's pity for every not-a-morning-person who'd ever had to deal with my morning cheer.

"What's up?" I asked.

I heard the hesitation in his voice and his cheer factor dimmed a bit. "I'm sorry. Did I wake you?"

"I'm up. Just haven't had my coffee yet. What's going on?"

"I was calling to see when might be a good time to swing by today to start our tutoring."

Wow, he really had a bee in his bonnet about tutoring me.

I peered at the clock. "Wil it's not even seven a.m."

I could hear the humor in his voice. "Yes, well I know that you're an early riser, and I wanted to catch you before your day filled up. Early bird catching the worm and all that."

There was something forced about his cheeriness that made me shift Fuzzy onto my lap and sit up.

"Uh huh. You sure there's not anything going on?"

The cheeriness slipped a little more as Wil said, "Well, I do want to update you on the Murphy situation while I'm there. But the main purpose of the visit is to start in on the tutoring."

I was guessing from the edge in his voice that whatever the Murphy update involved, I wasn't going to like it.

I sighed. "Well, I read most of my history assignment already, but I fell asleep before I read the rest. I can try to power through it before you get here. Can you come by this afternoon?"

"I have a lunch meeting—how about after that?"

"Uh, sure. Just text me when you're on the way over."

"No problem."

My gaze fell on the books beside my bed and an idea popped into my head. "Hey Wil? I noticed there aren't any books in my stack that deal with magical creatures. Do you have any?"

"Magical creatures?"

"You know, like mermaids, dragons, gryphons—all that kind of stuff."

There was a pause, then Wil said gently, "You know they're not a real thing, right?"

"I know. I think it was Mila who said if they ever existed, they don't now. And that got me thinking about whether there's a real historical basis for any of them and if so, if maybe they're like dinosaurs—they were here, but now they're extinct."

Wil sounded like I'd piqued his curiosity. "It's interesting you should mention that. There's a whole magical research branch dedicated to just that subject."

"I guess it must be my Best side coming out, but I've been curious about it ever since she mentioned it, and since you know so much about all the things, and you're going to be teaching me now, I thought I'd ask."

I heard Wil clacking away at his keyboard. "I'm making a note, and I'll adjust our tutoring schedule to include this as a subject. It's actually a really fun one. I'll bring you some books to get started on when I come by today."

Great. More homework. I held in my sigh lest I seem ungrateful and said, "Thanks, Wil."

We wound up the phone call, then I got up and got dressed. My mental map showed that Carmine was already in the kitchen, and Sadie was still in her room.

Fuzzy and I entered the kitchen to find Carmine sipping a cup of tea and staring out the kitchen window.

"Morning, Carmine," I said.

He smiled and said, "Good morning, Finn, Fuzzy." He leaned down to pet Fuzzy's head.

I set the coffee brewing and fed Fuzzy while I chatted with Carmine.

"How's it looking out there?" I asked him.

Carmine sipped his tea. "Looks good. I can see you've made real progress with the weeding. And it looks like we got those seeds planted just in time." He pointed to the cloudy sky. "I wouldn't be surprised if we had some snow today."

I perked up. "Snow? Really?" I was looking forward to the chance to put my new snow boots to use and go crunching through the fresh snow. For the first time in my life, I could make snowballs, and snow angels, and—

Carmine interrupted my snowy thoughts with, "You know, it's the strangest thing, but I swear I don't remember seeing a rock there before. Did you do some landscaping since I was here last?"

I dashed to the window and looked out. Halfway between the woods and the greenhouse, the Grack lurked in the field.

I groaned.

"What? Finn, what's wrong?"

"Sibeta must've not talked to it, uh, her, in time."

"Her?"

I did a quick mental check to make sure Sadie was still in her room where she couldn't overhear us. Then I pointed at the lump and said, "Yeah. Her. The Grack."

Carmine looked at me in confusion. However, he'd gotten used to the weird turns that conversations around me tended to take, so he waited for me to explain.

And explain I did. "Oh Carmine, yesterday was a real doozie of day. I didn't get a chance to tell you, what with everything else that was going on, and all the people around. But, that's not a rock!" I waved frantically toward the Grack.

Carmine looked at the lump then back at me. "Oh?"

"I'm not crazy."

"I didn't say you were."

"That…whatever-it-is…Sibeta didn't really explain what it—she—is…I'm calling it a Grack because that's what the first part of its name sounded like, though now that I come to think of it, that's probably its species name, so calling it a Grack is a little like naming a dog Dog—"

"Finn, try to focus."

"Yeah, sorry. So that thing there, it's a Grack. And it burned the hole in the side of the greenhouse. I think. Bayley told me to ask Sibeta about it, and Sibeta says the Grack is a she, and she's a person, not an animal."

Carmine blinked at me. "That's a lot to take in."

"Tell me about it. Sibeta can speak the Grack's language and is supposed to keep her away from the greenhouse until I can get a meeting with her." I looked out the window. "Crap!"

Carmine turned in time to see the Grack move a few inches closer to the greenhouse.

His eyes widened. "It moved."

"Yeah, she can really scoot when she wants to." I sighed. "I'll be right back." I fetched my coat and strode out the back door. Fuzzy bounded past me, down the steps, and streaked toward the Grack.

"Fuzzy, no!" I called and sprinted after him.

I guess the Grack could see us coming because she stopped inching toward the greenhouse, paused, and then sped off toward the woods again.

"Fuzzy, stop! I mean it!" I halted where I was and used my sternest voice.

Fuzzy slowed from a dash to a lope, cast a last glare at the Grack, who was crossing the tree line and disappearing into the forest, and then turned and trotted back to me.

"Thank you for trying to help, but it's not nice to chase the guests," I said, leaning down to pat him as he stalked by.

He gave me a disgusted look then trotted back into the house. I followed him.

Carmine was still at the window when I returned to the kitchen.

"Well," I said, "I'm pretty sure that didn't go well. Now she's going to think we're bent on chasing her away. Which, if I'm honest, we sort of are, until I can find out what she is and what she wants. Man, I really need some coffee."

Carmine watched me fix my coffee. I added extra milk and extra sugar. It was already that kind of morning.

He waited until I'd had my first sips, then said, "Finn, while you were running around, I had a thought."

He looked worried. I gripped my cup tighter. "Do I need to sit down for this?"

He moved toward the table with a, "Couldn't hurt."

We sat and I said, "Shoot."

"Having Sibeta here is…unusual."

I nodded. "No kidding."

"And now there's this Grack."

"Uh huh."

"I was just wondering, well…Sibeta alone could have been an anomaly. But now with the Grack…I was just wondering what else there might be?"

Well that thought had occurred to him a lot quicker than it had to me.

I sounded as frustrated as I felt when I said, "Sibeta says she's a liaison. When I asked who she was liaising between she said 'the others.'"

"What others?"

"She won't tell me."

"What about Bayley?"

"He sent me to Sibeta to get her to explain."

"I see."

We sat sipping our beverages in silence. It occurred to me that I'd asked Bayley about the Grack, but not specifically about who else Sibeta was talking to.

Hey Bayley?

I felt his attention focus on me. I was startled at the level of exhaustion I could feel radiating from him.

Alarmed, I asked, *Are you okay?*

Ding.

Is this from the dream link?
Ding.
Jeez. It felt like he needed to sleep for a week.
Was it worth it? It slipped out before I could edit myself.
I got a much stronger *Ding* in return.
I shook my head. *Well, look, are you up to answering a few more questions?*
Ding.
Who else is Sibeta talking to?
Bayley didn't respond.
I frowned and tried again. *Okay, how about this: how many "others" is Sibeta liaising with?*

My mental map appeared in my mind. As usual, parts of it were foggy. Every one of those foggy places pulsed with light, some brighter, some so dim I could barely see them. Then the lights went out, leaving just the foggy map again.

I nearly dropped my mug.

Carmine looked at me in alarm. "Finn, are you alright?"

"Oh crap. Carmine, I think I've made a big mistake." My mind raced. I'd just assumed that the foggy spots were foggy because I hadn't spent much, if any, time in those places. But I'd never actually asked Bayley why they were foggy. "Give me a minute."

Carmine nodded, concern etching his features.

Bayley, those foggy places on my map, are they foggy because those are places I haven't visited yet?

When I heard a *ding* I felt a rush of relief which was quickly squashed when a *ding ding* followed.

What do you mean by "yes" and "no"? I thought for a moment then said, *So yes, part of the reason they're foggy is because I'm not familiar with that part of the property? I can't "see" it in my head because I haven't seen it in real life, or at least haven't seen it enough to have a clear picture.*

Ding.
Okay, but also no?
Ding.
So, what you're telling me is that there's another reason for the fog?

Ding.

I swallowed hard. *Bayley, are there other…things…living in the foggy places?*

Ding. I was getting a feeling of tense anticipation from Bayley, like he was holding his breath.

I thought hard then tried again. *Are there creatures like Sibeta and the Grack in those places? And part of the reason it's foggy is because I haven't met them yet and don't know what they look like?*

Ding! sounded loudly in my head. The floorboards around me squeaked happily.

Carmine looked around and said, "Bayley is pleased about something."

"You know how I told you that I have a mental map of the property floating around in my head?" When Carmine nodded, I said, "I've been reading it wrong."

"Oh?"

"Bayley's happy because I just figured it out."

"Thus allowing him to communicate with you more clearly. No wonder he's pleased." Carmine paused and said, "I'm not sure what this has to do with your Grack, though."

"You know how you were wondering if there's more things like Sibeta and the Grack wandering around?"

Carmine nodded.

"There's more."

Carmine set his tea down with a clunk. He studied my face, which I was pretty sure looked as shocked as his did. "How many more?" he asked slowly.

"I'm not sure yet. But let me put it this way. It's a good thing we got the deluxe-size greenhouse."

Chapter Twenty-Eight

We were interrupted from further discussion when my phone rang.

I didn't recognize it but that didn't mean anything. Nor and Mila used burner phones all the time, and they both knew I was an early riser, so figuring it was one of them I answered.

"Hello?"

"Wakey wakey eggs and bakey." The voice on the other end of the phone was distorted, like they do in spy movies.

I looked at Carmine in surprise.

"Finn?" he asked quietly, concern etching his face.

As I put the phone on the table and hit the speaker button, I asked Bayley to close the kitchen door so that there was no danger we'd wake Sadie.

The voice on the other end spoke again, annoyance dripping from each word as it said, *"I said wake up. Sorry, not sorry, to interrupt your beauty rest. But time to get up and face the music."*

"Who is this?" I asked.

I heard snickering, followed by, *"Yeah sure. I went to all the trouble of using a voice distorter, but I'm just going to go ahead and to tell you my name because you asked. Wow, you really are as stupid as they say, aren't you?"*

Who said I was stupid? Carmine looked as dumbfounded as I felt.

I tried to figure out what was happening by asking, "Okay, if you aren't going to tell me who you are, then can you at least tell me what you want?"

The voice sounded smug as it said, *"How was your pizza?"*

I felt my eyes widen. I looked at Carmine, whose face had gone hard.

Since the voice already thought I was an idiot, I decided to oblige it and play dumb, "Did you send it? Sorry, I didn't eat it yet."

While I was talking, Carmine dug out his phone. He swiped a few times, then set it quietly next to mine.

I looked down to see that his phone was recording. I shot him a grateful look and a thumbs up.

The voice sounded flustered. *"You didn't eat it yet?"*

"Well, no. Sorry. Sausage isn't really my thing. Plus, I'd already made dinner. If it makes you feel any better, I might have some for breakfast. Nothing like cold pizza to start the day off right. Um, hey, is this some kind of secret admirer thing?"

The voice sounded both startled and offended. *"Secret admirer?"*

"Well, yeah, you're sending me gifts. That says secret admirer, doesn't it?"

"Go look at the pizza."

"What now?"

"Yes now!"

"Okay fine. This sure is a weird way to flirt. Um, can you at least tell me why?"

That smug humor was back. *"Things have a tendency to look a little clearer in the morning."*

"Hang on." I put the phone on mute.

I looked at Carmine who said, "There must've been a time limit on the spell. I'm just guessing, but it sounds like they expect you to see what they did and want to hear you react."

I said, "Okay, let's give them what they want and see what happens."

I took the phone off mute and threw as much outrage into my voice as I could as I said, "That's disgusting! What's wrong with you?"

Giggling rippled through the phone, the voice distorter making it extra creepy. *"Too bad you didn't take a bite, but this is almost as good."* Now the voice was sniggering. *"I can just imagine the look on your face."*

"What is this? Some kind of prank?"

All laughter was gone from the voice, and instead an edge of anger laced it as it taunted, *"Aw, what's the matter? Is the big bad Housekeeper upset?"*

Big bad Housekeeper? I looked at Carmine and he shook his head. He didn't know what was happening either.

"What do you want?" I asked again.

"What do I want? As if you give a shit what anyone wants. It's all about you and your stupid house and your stupid cat." I fought the urge to back away from the rage pouring through the phone. *"What do I want. That's awesome."*

There was a pause and a rhythmic crunching sound that made me think that maybe the owner of the voice was stomping back and forth somewhere covered in gravel.

"It's too late now, Housekeeper. There's nothing that you can give me." The crunching stopped abruptly. The speaker added, *"But I have so much I can give you. Enjoy your day."* And they hung up.

Carmine stopped recording while I stared at my phone. I looked at him, bewildered. "What just happened?"

Carmine said, "That's a really angry Guthrie."

"But I don't know any Guthries other than Lou and Pete."

"They seem to know you."

I kept shaking my head. Unfortunately no answers shook loose.

Bayley rumbled angrily around us, and I absentmindedly patted the nearest wall in a comforting motion. Bayley stopped rumbling but I could feel his anger.

"I'm going to call Lou and Pete," I said.

While I called them, Carmine and Fuzzy went outside to check that the Grack hadn't done any more damage to the greenhouse.

I couldn't reach Lou, but I got Pete on the phone. When I explained what happened with the sparrow, Pete seemed surprised but not overly worried. When I got to the part about the pizza, he went ballistic. "The Housekeeper is off limits!"

Then I told him about the phone call, and Pete sounded icily grim as he said, "Do you still have the pizza?"

"No, Eagan burned it."

"Hrmpf. I need to get a look at the spell. I'll call Zo, see if she still has the sparrow. But Finn?"

"Yeah?"

"Watch your back. It doesn't sound like this is over. I'll get back to you as soon as I can."

I was just hanging up with Pete when a red dot appeared on my mental map and came sailing down the driveway. I glanced at the clock. I'd only been up an hour and I'd already had a close encounter of the Grack kind and been taunted by a stalker. Now what?

I dragged myself to the front porch and watched Eagan park. He climbed out of the car and walked over, arms laden with bags.

He paused at the foot of the porch, eyes searching my face. "Hi. Uh, hope I'm not intruding. You look stressed."

"It's been a long day."

"It's not even eight o'clock."

"I'm aware." I eyed the bags. "What you got there?"

"Since you've got all this company, I figured these might help." He tipped one of the bags toward me and donuts peeked out. "I know how much you love the downtown diner's coffee, so there's a growler of coffee in this other one, and some pastries, too."

Genuinely touched at his thoughtfulness, I gave Eagan a one-armed hug. "Thanks, Eagan. That's super nice of you. Come on in."

As we walked down the hallway to the kitchen, Carmine and Fuzzy came in the back door.

"Hey Carmine. Eagan brought us some goodies. Would you guys mind getting things set up in the kitchen? And Carmine could you tell Eagan about our fun encounter with my stalker? I need to make a quick call."

Chapter Twenty-Nine

I grabbed my coat and stepped out on the back porch. I dialed Nor, but got her voicemail. As succinctly as I could, I told her about the Guthrie trouble yesterday and the call this morning.

I ended with, "Wil is coming back to tutor me today, and I'm not sure if I should ask him for help with this or not. I kind of want to get him out of here as quickly as possible because I'm trying to hide Sadie and Carmine from him. But if you think I should read him in, let me know. Oh, and p.s., I've got other…things…I need to discuss with you, when you get the chance. Because, you know, dealing with one thing at a time is apparently not on the table at the moment." I wanted to tell her about the Grack, and the possible other beings on the property, but it could wait.

While I was talking to Nor's voicemail, I saw Sadie's blue dot moving down the back stairs.

By the time I ended the call, Sadie and the boys had been alone in the kitchen for a few minutes. Given how Eagan and Sadie had interacted yesterday morning, I hurried inside to rescue Carmine from the crossfire.

I arrived in the kitchen in time to hear the end of Carmine's recording of my phone call with the stalker.

Watching Sadie as she listened, I took in her attire and nearly laughed. Apparently she'd decided to use both Carmine and Eagan's clothing options. From the waist down, she matched Carmine, both of them decked in identical khakis. The top half of her wardrobe consisted of a pullover men's sweater that was the same style as the one Eagan currently wore.

When the recording finished, Sadie and Eagan swiveled to

face me, similar expressions of concern on their faces.

Eagan said, "This is getting out of hand. Have you talked to Lou or Pete?"

"Pete. He's looking into it."

Sadie was shaking her head, "I can't tell if this guy has giant bollocks or if he's an idiot." At my look, she clarified, "Nobody threatens the Housekeeper. It isn't done. So either he's sporting a world class set of cojones, or he's a moron. As soon as the Guthries are notified about this, they're going to have to take care of it, and he knows it."

"Why do you think it's a he?" I asked.

Sadie shrugged, flinching a little as she did. "Something about the way he talks, that arrogant bravado. Seems like a man thing to me."

Neither Carmine nor Eagan took offense, thankfully.

Since I'd caught her flinch, I took a closer look at Sadie. She looked rough, and it wasn't just that the bruise on her forehead had bloomed overnight. There was a tautness to her face that said she was in pain, and the circles under her eyes said she hadn't slept well. She was standing a good distance from the boys, arms wrapped around herself, hunched over slightly. Her breathing kept hitching when she moved too abruptly.

Guessing by what I was seeing, Sadie felt like she'd been run over by a truck.

"Sadie, can I talk to you for a sec?" I said, heading out of the kitchen so that she had to follow me.

She drifted after me, moving at half the pace she'd been walking yesterday.

I led her into the sitting room at the front of the house, then spun around and asked, "How bad is it?"

Her shoulders hunched, and she started to bluster, "I'm fine—"

I held my hand up in a "stop" motion. "No you're not. Don't even try. How bad?"

"It's not great," she grumbled.

"Mmm. Carmine's salve didn't work?" If even Carmine's salve wasn't working, then I was calling Dr. Paige and having her do a house call, no matter what Sadie said.

She looked embarrassed and wouldn't meet my eyes. "I didn't use it."

"Why not? If this is that ridiculous 'I don't want it because it came from a Foster' thing, you've met Carmine, you know he's nice—"

"It's not that. I couldn't reach."

I couldn't decide if I wanted to comfort her or yell at her for being too stubborn to ask for help. In the end, I decided to skip both and go straight to fix-it mode.

Using a brisk, no-nonsense tone that reminded me of my mom, I said, "Where's the salve?"

"In my room. On top of the dresser."

"I'll go get it." She didn't object, which told me she was in really bad shape. I bounded up the stairs, fetched the salve, and came back to the sitting room.

I said, "Will this hurt less sitting or standing?"

"Standing."

"Standing it is then." I set the salve on the table under the window and gestured her over to stand in the warm pool of sunlight. "How's your modesty level? I'm going to need to lift your sweater—"

Sadie shrugged out of her top, hissing a little as she lifted her arms just enough to tug it off. She seemed perfectly at ease, standing there in her bra.

As soon as I got a look at Sadie's skin, I was not at ease. Not at all. I gaped and stared at her, wide-eyed. "Oh Sadie."

"Don't make a big deal of it." Bayley moaned and she added, "You either, Bayley."

I nodded and didn't say anything else as I opened the salve. Her entire torso was covered in bruises. Some of them were so dark purple as to look almost black. The skin was scraped raw in several places on her back. It looked like road rash, so I was guessing it was a result of her hitting the ground hard. I couldn't see an inch of skin on her entire torso that wasn't damaged in some way.

I heard footsteps and Eagan came striding down the hallway calling, "Hey Finn, where can I find the—"

I grabbed Sadie's sweater and held it out to her but she ignored it, making no move to cover herself as Eagan stepped around the corner into the room.

Eagan stopped short. His eyes swept Sadie. "You should be in a hospital."

I looked at Eagan. "Don't start. We've already had this conversation and that's not happening. If you want to help, please find out from Carmine if I can put his salve on broken skin."

Eagan opened his mouth to say something, thought better of it, turned and hurried back to the kitchen.

A few seconds later, I heard him running up the stairs and heard Carmine's slower footsteps coming down the hall.

He stopped outside the sitting room and knocked, "Okay to come in?"

I looked at Sadie, who looked resigned and said, "Sure why not."

Carmine stepped around the corner into the room. He sized up Sadie in a glance. "Mmph," he said, walking over to stand by me. "You'll want to apply the salve here, here, and here," he said, "and it'll work best if you can use this type of motion," he made a circular motion with his hands.

"Oh for heaven's sake, why don't you just do it," Sadie snarled at Carmine. I would've taken exception to her tone, but I was pretty sure she was so miserable it was either snarl or cry.

Carmine nodded and took the salve from me.

Eagan came bounding down the front stairs and into the sitting room, holding one of Carmine's duffels.

"This one?" he asked.

"Yes, thank you Eagan. Put it on the table there." Carmine looked up at Sadie. "How limited is your range of motion?"

"Very."

"Okay, then I won't ask you to pick up your arms. I'll work around them. I'm going to apply the salve now. It'll feel cool and you might feel some tingling."

She nodded, then clenched her jaw and both her fists, bracing herself.

As he worked, I was pretty sure Carmine was adding some extra magic to the salve. I'd seen him work on plants enough that I recognized the look of meditative focus he got when he did magic.

Carmine moved surprisingly quickly, applying the salve in record time, avoiding any areas that were abraded. It must not have hurt as much as Sadie expected because her jaw and fists gradually unclenched.

Putting the salve down, Carmine reached into his bag and pulled out a different tin. "This will work better on the cuts."

I watched carefully as Carmine covered her abrasions. It was a testament to how good a fighter Sadie was that none of them were deeper.

I glanced at Eagan and was surprised to see the raw fury there as he stared at Sadie's wounds. He looked like he was going to kill whoever had done this to Sadie.

When she looked over at him, the fury was gone, replaced by a look of admiration. "I hate to see what the other guy looked like," said Eagan.

Sadie smirked. "It wasn't pretty."

Some of the fierceness leaked back into Eagan's eyes. "Glad to hear it."

Carmine stepped back. "Done. How are your legs?"

Sadie said, "A few dings, but nothing like this. They were going for kill shots, so most of the damage is to my torso."

She said it so casually. I had to make an effort not to gape. The guys, however, didn't look surprised. Carmine nodded, a look of weary recognition in his eyes. Eagan was back to looking like he wanted to kill someone.

"How do you feel?" I asked.

Sadie looked at me, surprise widening her eyes. "Better." She looked at Carmine, "Thank you."

He nodded. "We'll need to do this twice more today. Some ice would be a good idea, too. And if Eagan's around tomorrow, you should let him apply some heat to those bruises. It'll help them heal faster."

"I'll be around," Eagan said.

I thought Sadie would argue, but she didn't. She gave him a regal nod. But when she turned to grab her sweater, I thought I saw a flash of relief in her eyes.

While Sadie gingerly put her top on I said, "Well I don't know about you guys, but I think what all this healing needs is some food. Who's hungry?"

Chapter Thirty

Breakfast was surprisingly lighthearted. I guess trying to heal Sadie was a bonding experience of sorts, because everyone relaxed and joked as we snarfed down the donuts and pastries that Eagan had brought.

Following breakfast, Eagan headed off to work. After accepting some painkiller from the pantry, Sadie excused herself and went back to her room. I briefly considered dissuading her from sitting alone and brooding. But I was unlikely to sway her, and with her gone, I'd be alone with Carmine. And I really needed some time alone with Carmine.

"Now that we've got some space, want to see if we can find the Grack?" I asked.

"Sure. And then we can check on the greenhouse."

Originally, Bayley had offered to build the greenhouse for me. But when I'd realized that it would basically drain him, and that we'd have to order the glass anyway, I decided to just use my enormous Housekeeper budget and build the whole thing like normal people do.

I wasn't sure yet if it was a good decision.

On the one hand, Bayley couldn't fix any damage for me, and I'd have to make repairs the hard, nonmagical way.

On the other hand, if he'd made the greenhouse, the support structures would have been made of wood rather than aluminum, and I shuddered to think how fast it would have burned when the Grack torched it. It made me a little queasy to think how it might affect Bayley to have one of his structures burning.

Regardless, I needed to make the current greenhouse work,

so Carmine, Fuzzy, and I traipsed outside to sort out the greenhouse and the Grack.

The cold bit at me, but I kind of enjoyed it. This much cold was a novelty for me, and I found the different moods of the cold interesting. This morning's chill definitely had some teeth to it, stinging my skin where it nipped me.

Neither Carmine nor Fuzzy seemed bothered by the cold either. Both strode outside as if it were a balmy spring morning.

We walked the area around the greenhouse and then went a little ways into the woods, but I saw no sign of the Grack. A glance at Fuzzy's calm demeanor confirmed that she wasn't in the vicinity.

With the Grack hunt a fail, Fuzzy went back inside the house. Carmine and I backtracked toward the greenhouse.

As we walked, Carmine started to say something, hesitated, then looked me over, considering. "You've already had quite a morning," he finally said.

"Just another fun day in the life of the Housekeeper," I said with false cheer.

Carmine stared at the ground pensively and remained quiet until we reached the greenhouse door.

As we walked inside the greenhouse, he studied me again, then said, "Well, things are under control here for the moment. Why don't you take some time for yourself."

He looked worried. I realized I hadn't looked in the mirror this morning, and I must be looking kind of rough—rough enough that Carmine thought I was too tired to spend time with him. True, I hadn't gotten much sleep. And I still had some more reading to do before Wil arrived. But no way was I going to squander any time I could get with Carmine. He'd been so busy lately, now that he was finally here, I was going to enjoy his company as much as I could.

"I'm good, honest Carmine. Since I've got you here, and if you're feeling up to it of course, I'd be super grateful for a quick lesson."

Carmine hesitated. "Are you sure?"

"Yes please. But only if I'm not being a pest."

His lips quirked. "Not a pest. What was it you wanted to know?"

"Yesterday, I was worried about smoke damage," I said.

Carmine nodded.

"When you're not here, how can I tell if the plants are okay? I mean, other than the usual normal-person-taking-care-of-plants way. I think by the time they show the damage, they're already in trouble, and I'd like to help earlier if I can."

Carmine said, "As a Foster, you have an innate green thumb—we all do. So you'll gravitate toward the right way to care for them by instinct. That's your latent magic kicking in."

"Okay."

"What you want to do is really just a step beyond that. How are things going with Sprout?"

I glanced back at the kitchen window where my lavender plant sat on the windowsill. "Fine. Good."

Carmine nodded. "And how do you know things are good?"

I thought about it. "Well," I answered slowly, "he looks healthy."

"And? What happens when you use your magic with him?"

"When I reach for him with my magic…it's hard to describe. It's like I can feel this, uh, energy? And when it's flowing, he's all good. If there's something, um, I guess different? Yeah, if there's something different about the flow, then I know something is up. It's taken me a few weeks—I've been practicing every day like you told me—and now I can kind of tell if he's thirsty or needs more sun. It's hard to explain, but it's like I get this…gut-instinct feeling that he's communicating to me."

Carmine grinned. "Very good. You're coming along very quickly."

I felt myself blushing at his praise.

"Let's see if we can up the ante a bit," he said and held out his hand. "As you noticed, trying to put what we do into words is unwieldy. Let's see if I can show you."

I took Carmine's hand and watched as he used his other hand to gently touch the plant. "You go ahead and touch, too," he said.

I put my other hand on a leaf of the plant.

Carmine's eyes became both more focused and more distant, like he was concentrating really hard but on something far away. I felt Carmine's magic swell around me.

The plant shifted in front of me. It took me a moment to realize that the plant hadn't actually moved, but the way I was seeing the plant had changed.

Sometimes when I looked at Sprout, I could see a faint line of light moving through him. Now, standing with Carmine, I could see hundreds of dancing light beams branching this way and that inside Sibeta's plant. All around the plant, a soft glow suffused it.

"Wow," I breathed. "I don't see this when I look at Sprout."

"You'll eventually see more, if you keep working at it. Look here," he said, pointing to a larger line of light. "See how the light looks a bit like liquid, flowing smoothly from one place to another? That's good. Also, the overall color of the glow tells you the plant is healthy—it's nice and bright. If it were dull or discolored, that would indicate a problem."

I nodded.

"Now comes the fun part. Ask the plant how it was affected by the smoke and fire. But don't use words, or don't *just* use words. Form a full sensory image. Picture how the greenhouse *felt*—how it smelled, how hot it was—get as close to exact as you can."

Carmine let go of both my hand and the plant and watched me.

As I concentrated on the plant, I was startled to feel my magic sort of perk up, which somehow also made me more aware of my connection to Bayley. He didn't interfere, but I could feel him watching closely.

My fingers tingled as energy flowed down my arm and through my hand. I sent a warm greeting to the plant. When I felt the plant acknowledge me, I let my concern flow through me into the plant. Then I called up the memory of the greenhouse. I hadn't actually seen any fire, but I'd experienced the smoke, so I thought about that and the way it made my eyes burn, my throat itch, and my nose drip.

There was a pause and then I felt a gentle push from the plant.

"Pfft, ugh, bleh. Carmine, why does my mouth suddenly taste like I licked an ashtray?"

Carmine smiled. "This is excellent."

It didn't seem excellent to me at all, but he looked so happy that I refrained from commenting.

Carmine said, "You asked it about the fire?"

"Yes."

"It's showing you how it experienced the smoke. Basically, it tasted as bad to the plant as that ashtray taste does to you. So it's telling you it didn't like it."

"I don't blame it."

"Since it's not damaged, there's nothing wrong for you to see, so it's sending you the information you asked for in the best way it knows how. If it were hurt, it would direct your attention to what was affected so you could help it heal."

"How does it know that I want to help it heal?"

"This is where building a relationship with the plant comes in. You build up trust by taking care of it and listening to it, and before you know it, the plant is willing to talk to you."

"It's just like taking care of customers at the diner," I said. "If you give them good food and you treat them with respect, they keep coming back, and over time you build up a relationship."

I mentally thanked the plant, then let go.

Carmine looked at me thoughtfully. "You know, Finn, even though your parents didn't give you any formal magical training, it seems to me like the experience they helped you get in the diner did a lot to prepare you for learning magic."

I shrugged and gave him a noncommittal "Mmm." To my mind, the opposite seemed true. All roads pointed to my parents bending over backwards to make sure I had no magical experience whatsoever. The fact that I'd gained experience that could help me learn magic was just dumb luck.

Chapter Thirty-One

Carmine decided to stay outside and putter around the greenhouse and garden, so I went back inside and spent the rest of the morning cramming for my tutoring lesson with Wil.

A couple of hours in, Sadie wandered into the kitchen, mumbled something about needing some air, grabbed her coat, then disappeared outside.

Fuzzy appeared in the doorway.

"Meow," he said, looking after Sadie.

I looked at him. "You want to go with her?"

He took a step toward the door.

"Okay. Stay out of trouble."

I heard Bayley open the back door, and Fuzzy trotted out.

I'd just finished my last bit of reading when a green dot appeared on my mental map. A quick glance at the clock told me that it wasn't even lunchtime yet.

I looked for Sadie and Carmine on the map. They were together, but they were both out in the woods, heading away from the house. I was startled to realize that I could tell Fuzzy was with them. He didn't have a dot on my map, but I knew he was there nonetheless.

I stared at their location, considering. I could warn Sadie and Carmine that someone was coming. But, thanks to Sadie's injuries or Carmine's arthritis, they were moving slowly, and given how far away they were, they'd be gone a while. I didn't want to stress them out on their walk if it wasn't necessary, so I decided to leave them alone for now. I also felt better knowing Fuzzy was with them, keeping an eye on things.

Walking out to the front door, I opened it and watched Wil pull up and park.

I crossed my arms over my chest, leaned on the door jamb, and frowned at him as he walked up. "You were supposed to call first."

Wil gave me his most charming grin. "My meeting ended early, and you were on my way, so I thought why make you wait? I know how eager you are to get started."

I had to work at keeping my frown from deepening into a scowl. There was a lot of assumption in what he'd just said. "You know I do have a life, Wil."

"I know." He started shifting back and forth in the cold, juggling his messenger bag like it was heavy. I didn't really want to let him in the house but I couldn't keep him standing outside forever.

"If you're going to be my tutor, you're going to have to be more respectful of my time. Just because I don't go running around to meetings all day doesn't mean my time isn't just as valuable as yours."

Bayley grunted in agreement.

Wil looked properly abashed. "I'm sorry, Finn. I wasn't trying to be presumptive, really. I guess I'm just excited, too."

I couldn't think of a good way to get rid of him without being obvious about it, so I let him in.

Bayley, I said as I walked Wil back to the kitchen, *I might need you to hide Carmine and Sadie. While I'm working with Wil, can you see if you can think of a good way to hide them? Hopefully we'll be done before they get back, but I want options just in case.*

Ding!

We walked into the kitchen, and Wil eyed the stack of books on the table with a satisfied smirk. "Hah. See. You are excited about getting started with tutoring."

I was getting less and less enthused by the minute, but I shrugged and said, "I told you I'd try to do my homework." And unlike some people, I did what I said.

I barely put the kibosh on that thought when an alarm rang in my head, and Bayley started grumbling.

"You've got to be kidding me," I said.

Wil said, "What?" but I ignored him and stomped to the front of the house. He hurried after me, calling, "Finn? What's the matter? What's going—oh."

I'd yanked open the front door to reveal a distinctive, narrow curtain of rain showering a section of the front lawn.

Gram stepped out of the rain then came up short when he found himself staring not just at me, but at Wil, too.

"Holy shit. He's a puddle jumper!" When I turned to look at him, Wil looked like it was Christmas morning.

I turned front again so he couldn't see my disgust, and said, "Yup."

Gram looked distinctly put out that Wil was watching him, but hey, that wasn't my fault.

Glaring, Gram stalked toward me, and I put up my hands saying, "Don't you dare look at me like that. You're the one who just showed up. This is what happens when you don't call first." I darted my dirty look at Wil, but he was too busy fanboying over Gram to notice.

"You're a puddle jumper. How did I not know you're a puddle jumper?"

"I don't advertise," said Gram, affecting a bored look.

As Gram walked toward us, Bayley sent me an image of Gram being ejected off the porch, sailing through the air, and landing in the mud puddle his rain had created.

I said *Tempting, but not yet. Could we have some heat though, so I don't have to let him in the house?*

Heat immediately began suffusing the porch.

As Gram walked up the stairs, I noticed a glinting bulge in his front pocket.

"Is your phone on you?"

"What?" Gram looked away from his staring contest with Wil to glare at me.

"Is. Your. Phone. On. You?"

"Yeah, of course." And the idiot pulled it out and waved it in front of me.

Bayley groaned loudly at the same time I yelled, "Oh my god, you are such a moron!" I was so mad I actually stomped my feet.

Gram looked at me, nonplussed.

Beside me Wil nodded, looking solemn. "That wasn't a wise move. Kate already tracked you here using your phone once. She'll assume you came back here for a reason." Wil looked at me. "She has grounds to ask for a search now."

I closed my eyes and counted to ten slowly. I opened them in time to see Gram struggling to cover his dawning horror.

I scowled at him, while I scrambled to figure out how to fill him in without tipping Wil off. I said, "Kate was already here this morning looking for, um, some sad lady—"

"Sad lady?" Gram asked.

I waved my hand. "She said a name I hadn't heard before—"

"Sadafea?"

"Yeah, that's it. She wanted to know if Sadafea was here because you were here, and I told her I'd never heard that name before, and that yes you were here, unannounced, in the middle of the night, that I talked to you alone in the kitchen, and no we weren't," I made a grossed out face, "booty buddies."

Gram blinked at me as he tried to process my verbal barrage.

I stared hard at him, trying to bore the details into his tiny idiot brain so he'd keep his story in line with mine.

"All of that is true," he said slowly. "So why would Kate come back?"

"I don't think she believed me."

Wil said, "She didn't. She filed a formal petition with our Council yesterday after she left here." He looked at me. "Nor's working on it?"

"Yes." Although I hadn't heard back from her, I wasn't worried. Nor was insanely busy—I wasn't her only client—but I knew she was on it, no matter how busy she was.

Gram focused his stare on Wil. "What are you doing here?"

"Rude much?" I asked. "It's none of your business who I have in my home or why."

I could see he was about to argue that point when Wil answered, "I'm not only Finn's liaison with the Council, which thanks to your unscheduled visits, she really needs right now, but I'm also her tutor."

Gram smirked. "Finally learning some magic? How sweet."

I wasn't sure why Gram felt the need to antagonize me, especially since I was doing him a big a favor by hiding Sadie, but it was working. I wanted to strangle him.

Bayley didn't like it either. He growled, low and long.

Both Gram and Wil looked at the porch with concern.

A blue dot appeared on my map and sped toward the house.

"Oh just perfect," I snarled. "Well boys, hang onto your socks. There's a Murphy racing down the driveway."

I saw the moment when Gram thought about puddle-jumping away and I glared at him, "Oh no you don't. You stay right here and deal with the mess you're making."

He glared back but he stayed put.

Wil's diplomat face slid into place, which meant he was ready to take on whatever happened next. Maybe his early arrival was going to be a good thing after all.

We all turned to watch as Kate's car sped into the grove and circled around to the front of the house.

Wil murmured, "She must have been watching the driveway to get here so fast."

I glanced at him, startled, and realized he must be right. I suppressed a shiver as I imagined her skulking around, watching the entrance to the property. Great, now I had two stalkers, the unknown Guthrie and Kate Murphy.

Kate stopped in front of the porch and launched herself out of the car. "You!" she pointed at Gram. "I was right. You did bring her here. Where is she?"

Gram strolled to the top of the steps, then leaned lazily against the railing, crossing his arms and smirking at Kate as he said, "Sadafea is not here."

Technically, that was sort of true. She wasn't in the house. She and Carmine were still in the woods. But I realized with a sinking feeling that their dots had changed direction and were headed back toward the house. They still had a while before they arrived, but at the rate things were going, Sadie would have a whole fan convention waiting for her.

My attention jumped back to the situation at hand when

Gram smiled at Kate and said, "Why don't you stop embarrassing yourself and leave?"

Kate strode around her car and made for Gram, her hands fisted at her sides. "Don't be an arrogant prick—"

She stopped at the foot of the stairs when Bayley let out a hissing snarl loud enough to make the hairs on the back of my arms stand up. Wil, Gram, and Kate all took an involuntary step back.

I raised my hands in a placating motion. "How about we all chill out a bit?"

Given that Bayley was only heating the porch, that should have been no problem for Kate, who was the only one of us standing in the cold. No such luck. She crossed her arms and stared up at Gram so angrily I was surprised he didn't burst into flames.

She said, "You knew this day was coming. This was always going to happen. Just give her up." Kate softened her voice slightly and said, "At least if it's me, I'll make it quick. I promise."

"No deal," Gram said, his face as hard and uncompromising as his voice.

Wil was watching them like a hawk. He said, "If I understand correctly, we're talking about a termination, not a simple extradition."

Kate broke her staring contest with Gram to say to Wil, "By the terms of the inter-family treaty, it's none of your business what happens after the extradition."

She turned back to Gram, sneering as she pointed at him, "You screwed up. I'll give it to you that bringing Sadie here in the first place was pretty smart. But coming back here to visit her was unbelievably dumb, particularly since you've still got your cell phone on you. As usual, you think you can do whatever you want, and you can weasel your way out of the consequences. Not this time."

I winced. I wasn't sure what was going on between Gram and Kate, but she sounded so bitter that I bet they'd had some kind of falling-out. She'd been the one working with Gram when they brokered a partnership with Meg. Except Meg hadn't become Housekeeper and their grand designs on Bayley fell through. But Gram had walked away from that fiasco and still finagled access to Bayley. Kate hadn't. If I were her, I'd be bitter too.

"She's. Not. Here," Gram bit out.

"I don't believe you," said Kate.

Wil looked at me. I shook my head and said, "She's not here."

Wil nodded and looked at Kate. "I suggest a possible compromise, with your permission, Housekeeper."

Wil almost never addressed me by my title, so him using it let me know he was slipping into his formal Council representative mode.

Then he dropped his bombshell.

"With the Housekeeper and Bayley's permission, I suggest you do a room-by-room search of the house."

Chapter Thirty-Two

I gaped at Wil.

He stopped me with his hand, while saying to Kate, "Your search will be accompanied of course. You'll see for yourself that your fugitive isn't here. You may have this access on the condition that you cease harassing the Housekeeper and that you take your search elsewhere. This is a one-time only proposition, and it expires in one minute. Housekeeper, are you agreed?"

My mind raced. "I need a moment to consult with Bayley."

Wil nodded, "Of course. Take any time you need."

I didn't feel comfortable closing my eyes with this group so I stared at the porch floor while I talked to Bayley.

Bayley, we're so totally hosed. We've got to find a way to let Kate walk around the house without her knowing Sadie's here. Or Carmine for that matter. Oh no, or Sibeta! Or the pond. Oh jeez.

I resisted the urge to run my hands over my face and fought to keep my expression neutral.

I don't want Kate—or Gram—or Wil, for that matter—to see anything important. On second thought, I don't want them to see anything personal, either.

I frantically tried to remember if I'd made my bed that morning and what state my room was in.

Bayley, this sucks. What are we going to do?

I could feel them all watching me, and I struggled to keep my dismay off my face as my brain scurried to come up with a plan. I could also feel Bayley waiting patiently for me to continue, so I forced myself to calm down and think.

Bayley, I need you to reconfigure some things, quickly and quietly. Can you hide all Carmine and Sadie's stuff somehow so that their rooms look empty? And if they insist on looking in the attic or basement, I need to make those areas look both innocuous and impassable. Can you help?

Ding!

I felt a wave of mischievousness from Bayley. I was startled to realize he thought this was fun. Well at least one of us was having a good time. My stomach was tying itself into knots.

Okay one more thing. I need you to talk to Fuzzy. Uh, can you reach him in the woods?

Ding!

Okay, good. Have him try to slow Carmine down.

I would've just texted Carmine, but I was sure Kate would pounce all over that and accuse me of warning someone. Which I would've been. So Fuzzy it was. I was betting on the fact that Carmine knew Fuzzy wasn't a normal cat, and I was hoping Carmine would realize I was pulling a version of "What's that Lassie? You say Timmy is in the well?"

Bayley interrupted my train of thought with an enthusiastic series of dings. It took me a moment to realize he was dinging in the rhythm and tune of the song "Eye of the Tiger." As soon as I had the thought, the music started playing in my head, and Bayley joyously dinged along with it.

It seemed Bayley was ready to get his game on.

I shook my head and a wry smile at Bayley's antics tugged at my mouth as I refocused on the people around me. They were all looking at me strangely.

Wil said, "It's so interesting watching you interface with Bayley," and I could see the professor part of his brain taking notes.

"Uh, thanks?"

"I'd love to talk to you about it later sometime."

"Later. Sometime. Sure. For now, Bayley has agreed to let you guys walk around the house." Matching looks of pure greed washed over Kate and Gram's faces at the same time, and I realized I'd just given them what they'd wanted all along: access to the house. I resisted the urge to grind my teeth.

Bayley opened the door.

"Okay everyone, let's go inside."

This time when Kate tentatively stepped onto the porch, Bayley let her, but he grumbled at her the entire way up the stairs and across the porch. I had to hide a smirk.

"Let's get this over with," I said.

Doing my best tour guide impression, I gestured, "Sitting room."

Bayley turned the lights on in any room I pointed at.

The sitting room was obviously empty. Continuing down the hall, I called out "Dining room," also empty and then, "kitchen."

After Kate checked out the kitchen and pantry, we stepped back into the hallway.

"What about in there?" Kate pointed to the door under the stairs.

"Seriously?" I knew she knew that DeeDee was a magic door. And I knew that she knew it was a normal door most of the time. She was just messing with me because she could.

She crossed her arms over her chest and said, "Seriously," with a malicious little gleam in her eyes.

"Fine." I made no attempt to activate DeeDee so it just remained a normal door. I opened it and showed Kate the closet under the stairs.

"Empty." I shut the door and resisted the urge to wipe the smirk off Kate's face.

We went into the mudroom.

"What's that?" Kate pointed to the basement door.

My stomach dropped. "The door to the basement."

"Open it."

"Seriously?"

"You can stop asking me that and just assume that yes, when I say open it, I mean it."

"Fine. I hope you like dust and spiders." I'd considered asking Bayley to disappear the door to the basement, but quickly discarded that thought because Wil knew there was a door there, and I didn't want him wondering why I was going to the trouble to hide the basement from the Murphys.

I pulled open the door, hoping they'd take my reluctance for fear of the creepy basement. Bayley sent me a pulse of reassurance through our connection. Taking a deep breath, I led my little party down the stairs.

I had to physically restrain myself from doing a double-take as the basement came into view. Instead of a huge basement containing an enormous pool, the stairs ended in a tiny, cramped room with an unfinished floor.

Wil looked around and said, "They originally used this as a root cellar. Not much to it."

Not only had Bayley reconfigured the basement, but he'd also restored it to a former version of itself, one Wil might know about.

Jeez, you're awesome, I told Bayley in my head.

I got a sense of satisfied amusement back from him.

Bayley had made it cold and damp in the basement, too, which encouraged Kate not to linger. She walked around the space, then said, "Okay," huffing out an aggravated sigh like she was disappointed.

It took me a second to realize that the impression I was getting from Bayley was that he was...giggling at Kate's aggravation. He apparently disliked Kate as much as I did and thought messing with her was hilarious. I relaxed a fraction and tried to enjoy his shenanigans.

We all traipsed back up the stairs to the mudroom. Next, we moved on to the huge empty room that took up the whole other side of the house.

Kate strode about the room, making a show of checking behind the curtains in front of the floor-to-ceiling windows. "Waste of space," she muttered into the echoing room.

I hadn't decided what to do with this space yet, so she was kind of right. But I wasn't about to tell her that.

While Kate was stomping around, I asked Bayley, *Is the second floor ready?*

Ding!

How about the attic? If she wanted to go in the basement, she'll probably want to go in the attic.

Bayley gave me a *ding* that sounded a lot like, "Duh," in my head.

I don't want her getting a good look at all the stuff that's in the attic.

There were all sorts of goodies in the attic, including the stolen star thing Mila had brought me that I was hiding up there. I didn't want any of them to look at any of it.

Can you make it hard for her to see stuff or even to dig around?

I don't know how, but somehow Bayley managed to give me a mental eye roll along with his *ding*. Bayley clearly felt that he had this in the bag, and after the great job he'd done with the basement, I decided I needed to trust him to do his thing.

Besides, he was having fun.

That made one of us.

Kate finally finished checking behind every curtain. She looked more frustrated than ever. "Next?" she asked, dusting her hands impatiently.

"That's it for downstairs," I said. I led them out of the front end of the room and up the front stairs.

We reached the main hallway. "Bayley," I called. "Please open all the doors on this floor, including the bathroom doors and closet doors.

There was a small pause, then in unison all the doors swung up. Bayley rumbled the floorboards in a distinct, "Ta dah!"

Kate and Gram looked a little disconcerted, but Wil and I smiled.

"Thanks Bayley," I said.

Kate gave me a look. "You realize you're talking to a house like it's a person."

I shrugged, "Bayley is a person."

Kate snorted in derision.

I felt my eyes ice over as I drew myself up and said, "Be very careful, Kate. You are a guest here at my invitation. Disrespect Bayley just one more time, and not only will your invitation be rescinded, but you'll be dragged out of here by your ankles."

She looked at Wil and said, "She can't—"

Wil said, "Rescinded permanently," in such a cold tone that she looked momentarily stunned.

Kate opened her mouth to say something, but Gram clamped his hand on her arm and shook his head at her. Whatever she saw in his eyes made her close her mouth.

I pointed to our left. "This is the master bedroom."

We walked inside, and Kate's head swiveled as she took in the space. "It looks like no one lives here."

"It's a guest room," not that that was any of her business.

"You don't sleep in the master?" her eyebrows hiked up.

Wil must've seen how aggravated I was because he stepped in and said, "That's outside the purview of your search."

Kate shrugged and went about searching through the room. She was thorough, even checking under the bed.

We continued the same routine in all the rooms up and down the hall. When she got to my room, she gave a derisive, "You sleep here?" but I didn't take the bait.

I was too busy applauding Bayley. Not only was my bed made, but the room was spotless. Bayley'd also hidden the family photos I'd hung. Basically, he'd effectively quashed any chance Kate had of snooping on me.

Thank you!!! I told Bayley.

Ding ding, he replied warmly.

As we approached Carmine and Sadie's rooms, I walked ahead of them, so I could see inside first. Sure enough, Bayley had disappeared all their belongings. I had no idea where he put everything he was hiding, but I was so thrilled with the result, I didn't care.

I had a moment of discomfort when I thought I smelled a hint of Sadie's salve, but Kate either didn't notice or didn't think anything of it and continued on with her search.

When we got to the end of the hall, sure enough, Kate noticed the attic door, which was the only one still closed.

"What's in here?" she asked, gesturing toward the door.

"The attic," I said.

"Let's go," she said, yanking the door open more roughly than necessary.

"You've really got a thing for dust and spiders, huh?" I muttered, following her up the stairs with the boys trailing behind me.

We reached the top of the stairs, and I held my breath to keep from gasping. Usually the attic was a treasure trove of random boxes and furniture, strewn willy-nilly about the space.

Apparently, Bayley had been playing Tetris, Attic Edition. He'd managed to arrange everything so that it was jam-packed together, floor to ceiling, on either side of the attic. I couldn't tell for sure, but I thought he'd changed the dimensions of the attic so that the available junk fit the space perfectly, with no gaps.

Fortunately, if Kate, Gram, or Wil thought it was weird the way things were stacked, no one said anything.

There was an aisle down the middle and absolutely no way to get through the mounds of stuff on either side of it. It was packed so tightly and precisely that I didn't think a mouse could squeeze in there, never mind a person.

"As you can see," I said, "there's years of stuff. I need to go through it all."

I glanced at Wil. His eyes were riveted on the stacks to my left. I couldn't figure out what he was looking at—it was just a stack of boxes with a lamp jutting out between them. Then it occurred to me that, given his obsession with Foster history, this place would look like Fort Knox to him. It was a miracle he wasn't drooling.

Wil caught me looking and shifted back into his bland Council face. But not before I caught the desire flaring in his eyes.

Kate whipped out her cell phone, then inched down the central aisle, shifting a box here, a table there, using her cell phone flashlight to peer into any nook and cranny she could.

It took forever. This was not good news because while we stood there, waiting for her to finish her fruitless poking and give it up, Carmine, Sadie, and Fuzzy reached the edge of the forest and were about to cross the backyard to the house.

I tried to keep my face blank as I frantically talked to Bayley in my head.

Bayley, can you get Fuzzy to lead Carmine and Sadie to the shed? We can hide them in there for now.

Ding.

When I realized I was holding my breath, I forced myself to breathe evenly as I watched Carmine, Sadie, and Fuzzy on my map. After a few agonizing minutes, I saw them move toward the shed. Both the boys were watching Kate, who was still inching through the attic toward the front of house.

I realized I was chanting "hurry, hurry, hurry" in my head as I watched Carmine, Sadie, and Fuzzy dart across the lawn. I let out a slow breath when they made it into the shed.

This whole thing sucked, and the stress of worrying about it was starting to wear on me. I was struggling to hold onto my temper while Kate took her sweet time.

Bayley, on the other hand, enjoyed himself. Every time Kate got really aggressive, shoving something to get it to move, I could hear Bayley snickering in my head as he sprinkled her with dust and/or spiderwebs. A few times, her hair "just happened" to catch on something, and once or twice I heard an "Ow," as she tripped over something.

Eventually, Kate reached the end of the attic and ran out of nooks to check.

I said, "See, nothing here," and didn't even try to keep the "told you so" tone out of my voice.

Kate spun to glare at me. She started to say something, looked at the three of us looking at her, and said, "What?"

A glance at the boys told me they were as impressed with her appearance as I was. Her hair was sticking up in a bunch of places, she had dirty smudges on her face and clothes, and she was trailing cobwebs from a bunch of places. It wasn't nice of me, but I wanted to laugh and applaud Bayley for a job well done.

"Nothing," we all said at the same time.

We trooped down the attic stairs, then down the back stairs, and through the mudroom. As we passed the back door on the way to the kitchen, Kate stopped and said, "What's in there?"

I backtracked and looked to where she was pointing, hoping against hope that she wasn't pointing where I thought she was. No such luck. "It's a shed. It has gardening tools."

She looked at me, and I could tell the moment she picked up on my dismay because her face lit up. "Nice try. Let's go," she said with a smug smile.

Bayley! I cried in my head, as I moved as slowly as I could getting my coat and putting it on.

After a brief pause, I got the same cheeky *Oh I got this* sense from him I'd been getting since this nightmare started.

With a sigh, I said to Kate, "You're wasting my time," and walked with her and the boys over to the shed. On the way by the greenhouse, Kate made a show of looking in the windows, but she didn't bother to go in.

As we neared the shed, I caught the tight look on Gram's face and the concerned look on Wil's face, and I realized they thought I was hiding Sadie in the shed too. Since that was indeed what I was doing, it was a real effort not to look worried as I opened the shed door.

There were a number of reasons I didn't want any of these people looking in the shed. First, I was hiding Sadie. Second, I was hiding Carmine. Third, the shed was special. It was bigger on the inside than it should be. Like way bigger. And I didn't want any of these people to know that Bayley had the capability to make something like that.

The door slid open, and my face split in a huge grin.

I love you, Bayley! I said in my head before I turned to Kate, beaming a delighted smile, and said, "Shed. Gardening tools."

The shed was as tiny inside as it should be. Where the space usually continued on, there was now a back wall, complete with shelves holding gardening gloves and other supplies. A few gardening tools leaned against the back wall, completing the effect. It was perfect.

"Did Bayley make this?" Wil asked.

"Uh huh."

He nodded. "Good job."

"Thanks." He had no idea.

Bayley vibrated the wood in the shed until it sounded like he was chortling along with my thanks.

Wil smiled, then turned to Kate, who was looking askance at the laughing shed. "As you can see, this Sadafea woman is not here."

Kate crossed her arms and looked around us, saying, "She could be anywhere on the property."

I said, "Now wait a min—"

Wil held up his hand. "Kate, the Housekeeper has been very generous with her time and extremely patient in honoring your request. You've searched this place from top to bottom. Your fugitive is not here. It's not reasonable that she'd be hanging out in the woods; it's too cold. The temperature has been dropping steadily since you got here."

At Kate's mulish look, Wil added, "I can see why you'd infer she might be here," he shot a look at Gram, "but she's not. I will be notifying the Foster and Murphy Councils that the search has been executed and our part in this complete. Officially, we will now be considering this a Murphy family problem."

Kate looked like she was going to argue.

Gram gave an exasperated sigh. "Fine. She's not here. I admit that I came here to throw the family off. I knew they'd be tracking me, and I figured, correctly, that they'd get so hung up on trying to access this place that it would give me time to hide Sadie somewhere else." He leaned forward a hair and gave Kate an arrogant smirk. "Thanks for giving me some extra time to get Sadie away."

I thought she was going to slap him. Instead, she narrowed her eyes, spun on her heel, and strode toward the house. I hastily shut the shed doors and followed after her, the boys at my heels.

She changed direction and walked around the house rather than taking a shortcut through Bayley. As she skirted his periphery, she looked up at Bayley and shook her head, lip curled in disgust. "I thought this place was supposed to be something special."

Wil placed his hand on my shoulder and murmured, "Don't," which is the only reason she didn't get dragged the rest of the way to her car, wrapped in ivy.

When she reached her car, Kate gave the house a last once-over. Her gaze landed on Gram. They shared a long look, and the expression on Kate's face told me she wasn't going to let this go.

Then she got in her car and drove away.

We all watched her car exit the grove, then Gram smiled and said, "Well that was fun."

I punched him in the arm, hard enough that I got a startled, "Ow," from him, and went inside the house.

Chapter Thirty-Three

Bayley, are Carmine and Sadie okay? I asked as I led the boys back to the kitchen.

I got a *ding* so I relaxed a hair. They'd be safe in the shed until I could get rid of my current company. I was tempted to text Carmine, but I was pretty sure Wil would think it was suspicious, so I decided to wait.

When we reached the kitchen, Wil said, "So Gram, why are you here really?"

Gram shrugged. "I've been hopscotching all over the place. This was on the list."

"Yes, but why is it on the list?" Wil asked, then turned to me with, "Finn, would you mind if I had a cup of tea?"

"No problem," I said automatically. But inside I cringed a little because if Wil was going to have tea, he was planning on settling in for a bit.

I hoped Carmine and Sadie would forgive me for leaving them in the shed. Well, at least Bayley would keep them warm. He could heat the shed.

"Hey, while you're at it, I wouldn't mind some tea," said Gram, seating himself at the kitchen table. He saw my frown and said an exaggerated, "Please."

"You're staying?" I blurted out. "No. You're not staying. Uh uh. It's bad enough that you just show up without notice. Now you've dragged me into your family drama, as if I don't have enough of my own family stuff to deal with. In no universe are you just hanging out here. Besides, I have plans with Wil."

"Are you refusing me hospitality Finn?" Gram asked.

Wil looked alarmed. "That's not what she said, Gram."

I glared at them. "It's not my job to cater to Gram's whims. Argh! Now what?"

A regular, nonmagical person was driving down the driveway. Glancing at the clock, I realized it was lunchtime. Oh no. I really hoped this wasn't going to be another pizza incident.

I looked at the two of them and said, "Stay," pointing at the table where they were sitting, then went to the front of the house to see who the newest visitor was.

Generally, I loved company, but the day was beginning to feel like a circus.

I trotted out the front and down the porch steps, immediately regretting that I didn't grab my coat. In response, Bayley blew heat down the steps, and I stayed on the bottom step to take as much advantage as I could of the warmth.

A minivan swung around the driveway and stopped in front of me. I blinked in surprise as Rose climbed out. I'd met her at the town's diner the one time I'd been there, and I'd felt like we had a lot in common. Like me, she was a diner waitress. Okay, like I had been. I had to keep reminding myself that I wasn't a waitress still, that I was the Housekeeper.

Rose spied me and broke into a huge smile. "Hey! I remember you! Finn, right?" She looked at the house behind me and whistled, "Nice digs!" as she came around the hood of the minivan. When she was standing in front of me, she lowered her voice and said, "You know people say this place is haunted right?" she waggled her eyebrows. "The local kids dare each other to come and visit here."

Great. Just what I needed. A bunch of hormonal teens prowling the property. Well, good to know I should look out for them. Last thing I needed was one of them getting caught in the crosshairs of whatever magical nightmare I was dealing with that day.

I smiled back at her and said, "No, I didn't know, but thanks for the warning. I'll keep an eye out."

Rose said, "Happy to be of service. Speaking of which," she held up a finger and trotted over to the back of the minivan.

I followed her and as she opened the hatch I got a look at the various bags and packages she had stacked in the back.

I huddled close, taking advantage of the heat pouring out of the back.

While she rummaged around, she said, "I work for Go Get That as a side gig. Have you heard of it?"

"Uh, no."

"Random people hire you through the app to go get stuff for them and to deliver it—sometimes to them, sometimes to someone else."

"Oh. Did you quit the diner?"

"Noooooooo. I just do this when I want extra cash." Her voice warmed with excitement as she confided, "I've got this awesome trip abroad planned, and I'm saving up." She paused shuffling packages to look over her shoulder and grin at me.

I smiled back, stifling the longing that swept through me.

A little more digging and she said, "Ah, here it is," and pulled a bouquet out from behind a couple of grocery bags.

She checked her phone and said, "I'm supposed to deliver this to F. Foster. I'm guessing that's you."

The bouquet looked like something Dracula would pick. There was a long stem rose in the middle, so dark red it was almost black, surrounded by deep crimson carnations, which were in turn surrounded by maroon ferns. The whole arrangement sat in a black vase.

I frowned at it as I took it from Rose.

She said, "I can't decide if I think it's romantic or creepy. Uh, no offense."

"None taken. Me either."

"I gotta tell you, this is a weird one."

"Weird how?"

"Well, usually when I pick up a delivery it's either from a store or from a person who wants me to courier something. This," she pointed at the bouquet, "was out on the front stoop of a building, waiting for me. My instructions were to go to that building, grab the bouquet out front, and deliver it to this address."

I said, "Who sent it?"

Rose said, "There wasn't a person's name on the account—it was just a username that was a whole bunch of random letters and numbers. There's a card," she said, pointing at a blood-red envelope I hadn't noticed in the bouquet.

I opened the card. It said:

For Finn. Because you deserve it.

I frowned harder.

Rose said, "No name?"

I shook my head.

"Hey, maybe it's meant to be romantic? They say red is the color of true love you know."

And blood, I thought, but out loud I said, "Yes, I've heard that." I made an effort to smile and look excited.

It must've worked because she smiled back. "Okay, I've gotta run, but you should come by the diner and hang out sometime." She glanced at the house. "No reason to stay out here all by yourself, you know."

"Sure thing," I said, but a pang of regret stabbed me. I was never going to visit her diner or go on vacation. As much as I loved Bayley, that really sucked.

Rose trotted back to the driver's side, climbed in, and drove off with a cheery wave.

As she left the grove, I took a cautious sniff of the bouquet.

I went cold.

Last night, when I'd smelled the pizza, it had smelled artificial to me.

When I smelled the flowers, I had the same sense that they were fake. They smelled like flowers…ish. But there was something slightly off about them. And unlike with the pizza, I had a sudden urge to get away from the bouquet as soon as I sniffed it.

I shoved the bouquet out, holding it as far away from me as I could get it without dropping it.

Wil and Gram must've been watching, the nosy Nellies, because the second Rose was out of sight, they came out the door.

"I'll be right back, go back inside," I growled at them.

They looked confused. Neither of them went back inside,

but they stayed where they were, so I took it as a win.

I stalked away from the house, keeping the bouquet at arms-length in front of me the whole time.

As I walked, I said *Bayley, do you sense anything wrong with the bouquet?*

Bayley sent me a mental image of me putting the bouquet down on the kitchen counter.

You want me to bring it in so you can check it out?

Ding.

I still was getting a strong urge to get away from the bouquet so I said, *I don't think bringing this inside is a good idea.*

I reached the middle of the lawn and set the bouquet down. How was I going to investigate it?

I need Fuzzy, I told Bayley, as I backed about ten feet away from the bouquet.

The sight of me fidgeting in the middle of the lawn, rubbing my arms trying to keep warm, somehow gave the guys an excuse to join me, because they both walked over.

I held up my arms, physically barring them both from going any further. "Stay there!" I barked, harsher than I intended. But it worked. They both stopped short a few feet from me.

Fuzzy came dashing around the corner of the house, sped across the lawn, and landed at my ankles.

The last thing I needed was for Wil or Gram to get curious about Fuzzy, so with my back turned so they couldn't see me, I whispered, "Fuzzy, is the bouquet okay?"

Fuzzy stalked toward the bouquet.

Loud enough that the guys could hear, I made a show of saying, "Fuzzy! Don't get too close to the bouquet! Come back here."

When he was a couple of feet away from the flowers, Fuzzy stopped.

Hissing, he spun and raced back to me.

As soon as Fuzzy hissed, Bayley started howling.

Fuzzy leapt at me, landing on my chest so hard that I stumbled back and went down on my ass.

At the same time, Bayley yanked the ground into a dirt wall

in front of me.

I squeaked, "What—"

And the bouquet exploded.

The boom vibrated through me, causing my heart to skip a few beats. I yipped, wrapping my arms around Fuzzy, and ducked my head.

Gram and Wil stumbled back but managed to stay on their feet. A quick look told me they were stunned but not hurt.

My face probably looked as stunned as theirs. I clutched Fuzzy to my chest and turned to look toward the "bouquet."

If there ever were any flowers, they were long gone. In their place, a column of fire spit sparks everywhere. It was tall enough that I could see it over the dirt wall Bayley had erected to protect me.

I staggered to my feet, clutching Fuzzy, and tried to make sense of what I was seeing.

Bayley had erected a series of walls, safely isolating the fire column. For a few seconds, the fountain of flame and sparks died back a bit so I couldn't see it behind the walls. But before I could relax, it belched up a succession of sparking fireballs. Each fireball sped into the sky and then dissipated in a shower of sparks. Then, the fountain stopped the fireball burps, and the fire column resumed.

That would have been impressive enough, but then the fire column grew, turned red, and instead of spewing out regular sparks, it started raining down what looked like—

"Jesus, is that blood?" Wil asked.

Gram looked grim. "I don't sense any water. I'm fairly certain it's an illusion."

I looked at him. "The explosion is an illusion?"

He shook his head. "No. The explosion, that column of fire, the sparks—all real." He gestured at the sky. "Raining down blood? Pretty sure it's fake."

I didn't have a chance to respond before Sadie came dashing around the corner. Carmine followed a little ways behind her, limping, as he tried to keep up.

I cringed as Wil and Gram caught sight of them both. Why

hadn't I told Bayley to lock them in the shed?

My phone rang, giving me the perfect opportunity to dodge the look Wil was about to give me.

I released my death grip on Fuzzy, pausing to kiss him on the head and mutter a heartfelt, "Thank you," before I hauled the phone out of my pocket.

I didn't recognize the number. It was different from the one this morning, but given the timing...

"Wil!"

He spun to look at me.

"I need you to record this. Now!"

To his credit, he whipped out his phone, swiped and punched a few things, then nodded, holding his phone at the ready.

I raised my voice and shouted, "Everybody shut up," and answered the phone.

"Hello?"

"Hey Housekeeper!" the stalker said. Again, his voice was disguised electronically.

I put the phone on speaker, tugging Wil with me as I walked farther away from the inferno behind me.

"Housekeeper? You there? I know you're there, I can hear the fireworks in the background."

"I take it I have you to thank for this?"

"What can I say? I like to make an impression."

I just stared at my phone.

"What's the matter Housekeeper? Cat got your tongue? Actually, that'd be an improvement. That furry little pest is smarter than you are by a mile. If he hadn't caught my sparrow, I'd be able to see the look on your face right now. I bet it's priceless."

"You're a jerk, you know that?"

"A jerk? Really? That's the best you can do?" The stalker snickered and said in a simpering voice, *"Aw, whatsa matter? Did I hoit your wittle feelings? Am I being a big ole meanie?"*

I glanced at Wil and Gram, who were both giving me the same, "What the hell" looks.

Sadie reached us, followed by Carmine, and we formed a huddle around the phone. Fuzzy crowded in, sitting on my foot, and leaning into me protectively. All of us were keeping an eye on the fountain of flame and "blood," which continued to burn in the background, safely contained by Bayley's dirt walls.

I closed my eyes and tried to calm myself. "I don't get this. Why are you doing this? Do I know you?"

Apparently that was the wrong thing to say. Even with the voice masking, I could hear the abrupt change in his tone. All the smugness left. He said coldly, *"Well, you do now, don't you. Little hard to pretend I don't exist now, isn't it."*

I looked at Wil. He shook his head. He had no idea what was happening either.

"I still don't understand. What is it that you want?"

"Too late," the stalker said and hung up.

I carefully turned my phone off and put it in my pocket.

Taking a few precious seconds for myself, I closed my eyes, took a deep breath, and wished I were someplace else.

The second I opened my eyes, it was like I rang a starter bell. Everyone started talking at once.

Chapter Thirty-Four

Carmine and Wil were talking to me, Gram and Sadie were yelling at each other, and Bayley was growling in the background.

"Stop." I held up a hand. Amazingly, everyone actually stopped.

I looked at Gram and Sadie. "Can you guys put that thing out?" I jerked a thumb at the fire fountain, which seemed to be dying back a bit on its own.

Gram nodded and he and Sadie walked toward the fountain, talking quietly.

I said to Bayley, *Thank you for the quick thinking with those dirt walls. I appreciate you keeping me and Fuzzy safe.*

Bayley was furious. The whole porch swayed with the force of his growling.

I was too stunned and horrified to be mad yet. What would have happened if I'd taken that "bouquet" inside? Bayley was made entirely of wood. I was pretty sure I was going to have nightmares about this for years.

I turned when I heard Wil say, "You're Carmine, The Master Gardener."

It wasn't a question. Wil had a look of recognition on his face as he studied Carmine.

Carmine looked resigned as he said, "I am. Nice to meet you."

Wil turned to me, his eyes glinting, and I shook my head. "I know you have questions. Just give me a minute."

He gave me a sharp nod. He looked over my shoulder, and his eyes hardened. I turned to see Sadie and Gram approaching. I sighed, both at Wil's expression and because the fire was still burning.

Gram said, "I can put it out, but if I do, I'll neutralize any magic and you won't be able to trace it."

I hadn't thought of that. I should have. Gram had used water to neutralize magic on my behalf recently—that's why he felt like I owed him.

Sadie added, "It's burning out on its own anyway."

I looked to see that she was right.

Bayley? Can you leave the walls up and keep an eye on that thing until it goes out?

Ding.

"Okay, let's leave it," I said to Gram and Sadie. "Maybe we'll get lucky, and there'll be something left to trace."

The wind blew, and my body suddenly reminded me I was standing in the cold. Other than Carmine and Sadie, none of us were wearing coats. I started to shiver violently, and a distant part of my brain wondered if it was partly due to shock.

"Everyone inside," I said, "before we all catch pneumonia."

Fuzzy and I led the way, and the rest of them trailed after me into the kitchen.

I gestured to the table and said, "Sit, please."

While everyone arranged themselves, I took drink orders, retreating to my comfort place.

As I puttered around making tea and coffee, using only bottled water since Gram was there, Wil looked at Sadie and said, "I'm guessing you're the one they're looking for?"

Sadie lifted her chin in challenge and said, "Yes."

Wil nodded. He thought for a moment and said, "So you got a closer look at that…thing. Do you think it was some kind of fireworks? Modified of course."

Sadie looked startled—that was obviously not what she was expecting Wil to ask because it took her a few seconds to switch gears and come up with an answer.

While Gram, Sadie, and Wil talked fireworks, Carmine came over to me. "Are you alright?" he asked softly, as he grabbed a few mugs from the counter.

I nodded. "Bayley and Fuzzy kept me away from the fire."

He shot a quick glance at Sadie, Gram, and Wil. "That's not entirely what I was asking."

"I know. Ask me again later."

I squared my shoulders, pasted my serving-difficult-customers smile on my face, and followed Carmine back to the table, mugs in hand.

When I'd delivered everyone's drinks, I couldn't stall anymore, so I fixed my own coffee, adding extra milk and sugar, and sat down. Fuzzy jumped up onto my lap, snuggling in for extra support.

"Where do you want to start?" I asked.

Wil said, "When we came out, you were carrying what looked like a bouquet of flowers as though you expected it to explode—"

"I didn't expect it to explode, exactly, I just suspected it might not be what it seemed."

"Why?"

"Because it's the third illusion attack in two days."

Wil's face went hard and flat. "Oh?"

I explained about the Guthrie stalker and the sparrow, the pizza, and the phone call.

Wil looked at me thoughtfully. "How did you dismantle the first two spells?"

As far as Wil knew, I didn't know how to use any magic, so of course he'd think I didn't do it by myself. "Zo helped with the first. Sadie and Eagan with the second."

Wil looked like he had a million questions, but instead he said, "Well I'm glad you had help. Looks like we need to make your training top priority so you can handle unexpected difficulties on your own."

I blinked at him in surprise. Of all the things I thought he might say, that wasn't one of them.

Before I could respond, Gram said, "Eagan? Eagan Smith?" At my nod, he swung an incredulous gaze to Sadie. "A Smith? You're working with a Smith?"

Sadie stared him down. "Don't. Start."

Gram clamped down on whatever he was about to say, but

it looked like it took a real effort. He shook his head and turned back to me saying, "Do you know who's targeting you?"

I shook my head.

Carmine cleared his throat and said, "They seem to be escalating."

Gram looked at Sadie. "You can't stay here."

Now it was Sadie's turn to look incredulous. "You're the one who insisted I come here in the first place, against my will, I might add. Now you've decided I can't stay?"

Gram said, "It's too dangerous."

A mutinous look lodged in Sadie's eyes. "It's not your decision." She looked at me. "I'm staying, if that's still okay with you. I'd like to help."

My gaze shifted to Wil. "Are you bound to tell the Council she's here?"

Wil avoided my gaze, taking off his glasses and polishing them as he said, "I am."

I cringed and swallowed the string of expletives dancing around the tip of my tongue.

Wil looked up and added, "But I don't have to tell them right now." He looked at Gram and Sadie. "Twenty-four hours? Is that enough time?"

They nodded.

Gram squinted his eyes, studying Wil. "Of course, I'll owe you a favor."

Wil smiled. "Yes. You will."

"And me?" I said. "What will I owe you?"

"An explanation," he said, turning the same ruthless smile he'd just given Gram on me. "But that, too, can wait."

Great. Just what I needed: something else hanging over my head.

Wil said, "Let's deal with the immediate problem first. Let's see if we can figure out who this Guthrie stalker is and why they're targeting you."

Chapter Thirty-Five

An hour later we still hadn't made any progress. I'd played the recording of the first stalker call, but that didn't help.

Finally, Wil looked at his watch and said, "I've got to go. I can do some research on my end and see what I can come up with." He looked at Gram and said, "You should be going too. No sense giving Kate more incentive to come back here."

Gram nodded and stood. He gave Sadie a look, and she followed him out the back door.

Shouldering his messenger bag, Wil said, "It's a pleasure to meet you Carmine. Of course your reputation precedes you. I look forward to hearing the story of how you came to know Finn."

Carmine gave Wil a bland smile and a nod, murmuring, "A pleasure."

Wil reached into his messenger bag and pulled out three huge books, handing them to me. "Here are the books we talked about. I'm sorry we didn't get to your lesson—if anything, today just highlights how necessary your lessons are."

I nearly spit out a cranky, "No kidding," and, "Like it's my fault the stupid Council keeps canceling my tutoring?" but I managed to hold my tongue.

Wil continued with, "I'm going to revise the syllabus I've been working on to encompass a more accelerated program. I'll email you later so you can get started on your next assignment."

He paused, staring at the ceiling like he was gathering his thoughts, then refocused on me. From the intense look on his face, I thought I might be in for a lecture, but then his gaze flickered to Carmine, and I could see Wil change his mind. Some of the intensity left his eyes, and he forced a small smile and said, "I think I should come back as soon as possible. Okay?"

I was too frazzled to argue with him right then so I just nodded.

"Great. Walk me out?"

I didn't feel like I had a choice.

I followed Wil outside, this time pausing to grab my coat.

As we trudged over to where his car was parked in the little parking area on the left, Wil was quiet. But when we reached his car, he chucked his messenger bag inside, then turned to face me.

I followed Wil's gaze as he took in the charred section of the lawn. Bayley had dropped the dirt walls, so the burned spot was clearly visible.

Wil's assessing gaze shifted to rove over Bayley, scanning from bottom to top. He seemed lost in thought for a few seconds then focused back on me. He studied me with the same x-ray stare he'd just used on Bayley. It made me want to squirm. I felt like a student who'd been called into his office for causing trouble.

"I don't really know you at all, do I," he said with a hint of wonder.

I opened my mouth to object but he cut me off, saying in a mild voice, "Whatever you're going to say save it. But we do need to talk." His gaze flicked up to the house then back to me as he added, "And soon."

He seemed to be waiting for some sort of acknowledgment, so I nodded.

"Good." He glanced at the lawn again and frowned. "This Guthrie thing is a priority. I'll see what I can find out from the recording I got." A hint of coldness seeped in as he added, "We Fosters do have excellent resources." Then he smiled at me, like winter hadn't been blowing through his voice three seconds earlier, gave me a bro pat on the arm, and got in his car.

He drove away without looking back.

I really needed his expertise, but I was already dreading his return.

I went back to the kitchen and found Carmine peering out the window with a worried look on his face. I joined him and got a glimpse of the Sadie and Gram show. From the way they were pacing around, and the amount of arm waving Gram was doing, it was obvious they were fighting. Again.

"Any bloodshed?" I asked Carmine.

"Not yet."

"Miracles never cease." I looked at my coffeepot. For once, it wasn't going to do the trick. "I need a beer. You want one?"

Carmine gave me a sympathetic smile. "Sure."

While I walked over to the fridge, I heard the dull thudding of heavy rain. A few seconds later, Sadie came storming in the back door.

And then there were three.

One look at her face, and I said, "Beer?" waggling one at her.

"Oh hell yes. Please." She stomped over to the table, flopped down in the chair, then promptly winced and doubled over, hissing out a breath.

Carmine said, "Salve wearing off?"

Sadie's mouth tightened and she nodded.

"Probably a little more excitement than you should've had today," Carmine said. He lumbered off to the sitting room to retrieve the salve from where we'd left it.

I handed Sadie a beer, placed one on the table for Carmine, and plunked myself into a chair.

Bayley sighed around us.

I sent Bayley a pulse of affection through our connection while out loud I said, "You said it, buddy. What a day."

Bayley seemed like he was tired from all the energy he'd been expending, but not exhausted, thankfully. I was too wired to feel tired yet, but I had the feeling I would be later.

I turned my attention to Sadie. "How'd it go with Gram?"

"The usual. He ordered me to leave. I told him to stuff it. He got pissy and left."

Sadie and I shared an eye roll and sipped our beers.

Sadie sighed. "Today has not gone the way I was expecting the day to go, to be honest. Well, okay, arguing with Gram and hiding from Kate, that was normal. But I didn't think I'd be romping around the woods and hiding in a shed—a very... unusual shed at that. I take it Bayley built it?" At my nod, she continued, "That was a real stunner. I didn't expect it to be so huge on the inside, and I really didn't expect it to sprout a wall to hide us. And then the exploding flowers—another surprise. And here I thought I'd spend the whole day having a proper brood."

Carmine returned and helped Sadie reapply the salve. It must've worked quickly because as soon as they were done, her face lost the pinched look, and she seemed to be sitting in her chair a little easier.

I said to her, "Well, we've got a little time now. We can talk about what to do with you—"

"I shouldn't be your top priority," said Sadie. She pointed her beer toward me. "You need to figure out this stalker thing."

Carmine nodded in agreement.

As if on cue, my phone rang. Caller ID told me it was Pete.

"I need to take this," I said. I left them in the kitchen and went to the sitting room, where I spent a few minutes catching Pete up on the recent fiery events.

Pete asked, "Can you give me the phone numbers the stalker called you from?"

"Sure."

After I gave them to him, Pete said, "I'll call you back," and hung up.

By the time I got back to the kitchen, Sadie and her beer had disappeared upstairs.

Carmine was looking out the window. "Uh Finn," he said.

One look at his face, and I guessed what he was looking at. "Really?" I groaned.

I joined him and sure enough, the Grack was halfway to the greenhouse. She must've felt us looking at her because she stopped moving and began doing a good imitation of an ordinary rock.

"Hey can you keep an eye on her for a minute?"

Carmine nodded.

I dashed down into the basement. Letting out a low laugh,

I said, "Jeez Bayley," as I took in the fully restored room. Gone was the wall that created the cramped, dusty room that Wil and Kate had seen. Instead, the pool lay in front of me in all its glory.

I was startled to see some of Sibeta's people hanging out in the pool, watching TV. They had the volume turned low, but even so, I'd figured that with so many other people in the house they'd all be hiding. Maybe it was a sign that they were trusting me and Bayley to make sure they'd be okay, no matter who was around.

I recognized one of them as the main healer who'd helped me a few weeks back. I wasn't sure if she could understand me yet, but I figured I'd give it a shot. "Uh, Mari? Is Sibeta around too?"

At the very least she seemed to understand the word "Sibeta" because she bowed once and then disappeared below the water. I spent a few anxious minutes shifting back and forth as I waited and wondered if I should ask Bayley to call Sibeta too.

But then Sibeta floated up to stand on the surface of the water.

"Housekeeper," she said with a small bow.

"Sibeta." I gave a small bow in return. "Have you by any chance spoken with the Grack yet?"

"No," said Sibeta.

I waited, and when it was clear no further explanation was forthcoming, I plowed ahead.

"Uh, okay. Could you help me speak to her now?"

Sibeta pondered this.

It took me a moment to realize that she was seriously hesitating. I looked at her in surprise.

"Sibeta, is there something wrong?"

I watched Sibeta's water cloak sway and ripple faster as she thought.

Finally, she said, "It is complicated, Housekeeper."

"Er…okay…is there, uh, something I can do to uncomplicate things?"

She didn't respond.

I tried explaining things more clearly. "The Grack is out there—again—halfway to the greenhouse. I tried to go out and talk to her myself earlier today, but she ran away. And every time I turn around, she's headed back for the greenhouse. I need to find out what's going on before there's an accident."

"I understand."

When she didn't say anything else, I had to resist the urge to start pacing again in frustration. I reached for Bayley. He showed me an image of the backyard, reassuring me that the Grack hadn't moved.

Then I felt Bayley nudge my mind. It felt like he was giving me a gentle shove toward Sibeta. After a second, I realized he was telling me that he wanted me to continue convincing Sibeta. Like, really really wanted me to convince her.

Huh.

I tried again. "Sibeta," I said, "Is there a problem with talking to the Grack? Can I do something to help?"

After another agonizing minute, Sibeta finally said, "We are...not certain...that now is the correct time."

Bayley made an impatient sighing sound. It echoed hollowly around us, bouncing around the pool chamber.

"Bayley does not agree," Sibeta said. "What say you, Housekeeper? Is this truly what you want?"

I felt another nudge from Bayley. He was making it very clear that it was important to him that Sibeta talked to the Grack.

My mind raced. Usually, Bayley was right about these things. But I couldn't figure out what Sibeta's hesitation was about. I decided to just ask. "Why wouldn't I want you to talk to the Grack, Sibeta?"

Sibeta thought that over for another long moment, then said, "You are still very new, Housekeeper."

Ah. It seemed like everyone I came in contact with had reservations about how new I was. Well, at least this was an objection I was accustomed to dealing with.

"I get it," I said. "But look. I am learning. Carmine is helping me—you like Carmine, and you know how talented he is. Plus, Bayley is teaching me. And now, I'm also going to be learning from Wil, who's a Foster. So I'm not as new as I was, and I'm going to be less new, soon."

Sibeta seemed unconvinced. She peered at the ceiling, then back at her family members, who were fixated on the TV at the other end of the pool, ignoring our conversation.

I took a stab in the dark and said, "Are you worried about leaving your people for a while? Sadie's in her room, and I can promise you she won't bother them. I know it's been a weird day—we just had people in the basement," the look she gave me made me think I shouldn't have brought that up, but I continued, "but we protected you. I will continue to do my best to keep you safe. So will Bayley. And part of keeping you safe is keeping the greenhouse intact so you have food. That means I've got to talk to the Grack before she burns the whole place down."

That last part seemed to do the trick because Sibeta caved. "I will come," she said.

"Thank you!" I said, trying to load as much gratitude as I could into my voice. "How do we proceed?"

"Bayley must create the conflict zone."

Because that didn't sound intimidating at all.

Chapter Thirty-Six

I hustled up the basement stairs to the mudroom, where I did a quick scan for Sadie. She hadn't moved since the last time I'd checked on her. I had Bayley lock her door, just in case, and gave him instructions to ping me when she started moving around again.

Sticking my head in the kitchen doorway, I said to Carmine, "Bayley and I are going to go make a conflict zone so Sibeta can talk to the Grack."

To his credit, he greeted that ridiculous statement with a blink and a nod.

"Eat this first," he said, handing me a sandwich. Looking at the remains of Carmine's own sandwich, it dawned on me that I hadn't fed anyone lunch. Some hostess I was.

"Thanks so much Carmine. Sorry I forgot about lunch!"

As I snarfed down the sandwich, Carmine said, "You've been a little busy. I took the liberty of dropping a sandwich off to Sadie, too."

"Thanks," I said around a mouthful of sandwich.

"Happy to help. You've got your hands full. Speaking of which, mind if I watch? I've never seen a conflict zone before."

"Me either. You're totally welcome. Having you there can only help."

Fuzzy appeared at my feet as we grabbed our coats and went outside. Before we stepped off the porch, I turned to Fuzzy and said, "Fuzzy, you can come, but you can't chase the Grack. Leave her alone for now. Okay?"

Fuzzy sat back on his haunches and gave me a slow blink.

"Thanks," I said.

A quick scan showed me that the Grack was holding her position, so I stepped down onto the lawn to approach her. But when Carmine and Fuzzy tried to follow, Bayley sprouted a short wall in front of them, enclosing the end of the stairs and cutting them off from the lawn.

Carmine and I looked at the wall in surprise.

"I think we're supposed to stay here," Carmine said.

Fuzzy hopped up onto the wall, but instead of vaulting down the other side, he settled himself on top, gaze focused on the unmoving Grack.

I faced the Grack and said, "Okay Bayley, what are we doing?"

In my mind I saw an image of the lawn, but in the middle of the grass there was a circle with a vertical line down the middle. Sort of like a yin and yang symbol, but the line was straight instead of wavy, kind of like a half-moon cookie.

You want to make a circle?

Ding.

Bayley, you're already feeling tired. Are you sure you're up to this?

When he said *ding*, I could feel the determination pouring off of him. I got the sense again that this was important to him.

I walked toward the garden, stopping when Bayley nudged me to let me know I'd reached the right spot.

Now what? I asked.

Bayley sent me an image of me kneeling, touching the ground, and the circle emerging.

I knelt on the lawn, resting my fingertips on the soil. I felt a pulling sensation as Bayley joined my magic with his, then the push as I directed our combined energy through my hands into the ground.

I said hello and told the grass I was touching what I wanted to do, sending a gentle pulse through my fingers.

I nearly fell over when I got an answering pulse back. Carmine's lessons were really working! Not only did I feel the response from the grass, but I could also get a general sense of what it was saying.

The gist I got from the ground was, "Okay. Have at it."

So I did.

I concentrated on the image of the circle in my head.

I felt the magic pour into the ground through my fingers, felt Bayley directing it, so that it spread outward into a circle. As I watched, the circle filled with a pale white light that pulsed and glowed.

I felt a tug as Bayley's magic reached out, beckoning. There was a soft rumbling, more felt than heard, as hundreds of tiny rocks came shooting across the lawn from every direction. Rocketing to the circle, they shifted and tumbled over one another, clicking, clanking, and clacking as they arranged themselves to Bayley's specifications before settling down. The shifting and arranging took extra concentrated effort from Bayley, and it was several minutes before he felt satisfied with the results.

When Bayley said the circle was complete, we pulled back the magic.

I sat back on my heels, fatigue pouring through me. As the glow dissipated, I saw what we'd done and gasped.

Bayley and I had formed a huge, perfect circle in the middle of the lawn. The circle had no grass in it, and the dirt surface was perfectly smooth and level.

But the tiny rocks were what really caught my eye.

They surrounded the circle, forming a gravelly border, and ran up the center in a straight line, dividing the circle into equal halves.

But that wasn't all.

The majority of the rocks were some shade of white. But woven through the white border were rocks in various hues, grouped by color. So all the blue-tinted rocks were in one section, then all the red-tinted rocks were in another section, and so on.

I looked more closely at the stones and blinked.

I jumped a bit as Carmine came to stand next to me. I hadn't realized Bayley had lowered the porch wall.

"Carmine? The colored stones…is it me, or do those look like—?"

"They're arranged to form symbols? Yes." Carmine was studying the rocks closely.

"Do you recognize them?"

Carmine shook his head. "But they run all the way around the border and up the middle."

"Huh."

Uh, Bayley, I asked in my head, *did you write something on the circle?*

Ding.

Can you tell me what?

There was a pause then *ding ding.*

Not now or not ever?

Bayley didn't answer and I said, *Sorry. That was two questions. Not now?*

Ding.

So later?

Ding.

I looked at Carmine. "Bayley wrote something, but he'll explain it to me later."

Carmine nodded and then stared at me a moment before asking, "How are you feeling?"

"Tired. I'm really grateful you made me eat something." Bayley nudged me, and a new image filled my mind. "And I'm not done yet. You might want to stand back a bit."

I reached over the gravel border and put my hand on the ground in the left half-circle.

Bayley's magic washed through me.

The ground under my fingers fell away, and water came rushing in to replace it. I yanked my hand up and scooted back. But I needn't have worried. The water filled the left half of the circle and stopped. The white rocks kept it contained so that it rippled softly in its half of the circle.

"Neat," I said. Another new image popped into my head.

"Seriously, Bayley? There's more?"

Bayley sent me a pulse of reassurance.

I did a mental inventory. If I'd done this a month ago, I'd have been about out of juice. But as I surveyed myself, I found that wasn't the case.

I turned to Carmine, who was watching a few feet away.

Looking concerned he said, "You alright?"

I shot him a grateful smile. "Yes, and I have you to thank for that. This whole time you've had me practicing, you've been building my magical muscles. I'm not saying my muscles are strong yet, but at least I have some now."

Carmine looked pleased.

I said, "Okay, just a bit more, I think."

The circle we'd just made was so big that Carmine, Fuzzy, and I could all lie down in one half and still have plenty of room.

The two circles we created next were smaller in comparison. Bayley had me make them below the main circle, near but not connected to it. Like the main circle, the smaller ones were bordered with white and colored stones.

It wasn't until Carmine stepped forward again that I realized I'd been zoning out on the cold ground.

"Finn? Let me help you up," he said.

I accepted Carmine's help and slowly staggered to my feet. For a few wobbly moments, I clung to Carmine.

"My magical muscles always affect my regular muscles. I feel like I just spent a day hauling boxes of canned goods at the diner."

Carmine studied me. "Those magical muscles are still very new. Stamina and strength will take time."

"Yeah, I know." I sounded winded. "But at least I'm not unconscious. I mean, look, I'm even standing."

"Which is excellent progress," said Carmine.

We both ignored the fact that I was swaying like I'd just chugged a six-pack.

Carmine said, "That was different than the last time I saw you work with Bayley, when you built the shed."

Startled, I said, "Oh wow. You're right. I was a lot more involved this time." I thought about it for a second and said, "I just sort of went with what Bayley asked, and I guess I sort of worked it in with what you've been teaching me."

Carmine said, "Mmm. I'd say you're well on your way

to developing your own style of magic. You're instinctively integrating your evolving personal skills with your work with Bayley. That's advanced conjuring, Finn. And you're doing it naturally." He gave me a proud squeeze.

I squeezed him back. A sound to our right had us both looking at the shed, which was rocking back and forth.

As we both laughed, Carmine said, "See, Bayley is doing his happy dance."

It took me a few more minutes to feel steady enough to let go of Carmine. When I finally stepped away from him, I looked at what Bayley and I had just made.

"What do you think it does?" I asked him.

Carmine shook his head. "If I had to guess, from the way it's bordered, I'd say it's a protected circle of some sort. If that's true, it doesn't seem to be active right now."

"Why the water?"

Carmine didn't have a chance to answer because Sibeta picked that moment to rise onto the surface of the water half of the circle.

Chapter Thirty-Seven

"Never mind," I murmured to Carmine. Turning, I said, "Hi Sibeta."

Sibeta bowed to me and said, "Housekeeper." Then she turned to Carmine and said with a bow, "Master Gardener."

Carmine gave a little bow back and said, "Hello Sibeta."

She said, "It is right you are here."

Carmine shot a glance at me, and I gave him a confused shrug.

Sibeta pointed to the first of the smaller circles below the main circle. "Housekeeper. You stand there." She pointed to the circle next to it. "Master Gardener."

Carmine and I exchanged a look, but we did as instructed and stepped into the circles. After a moment's hesitation, Fuzzy followed me into mine and sat at my feet.

Sibeta gave a weird sort of hissing and grunting call.

During my shenanigans with Bayley, the Grack had backed up toward the woods, but she hadn't left the clearing. At Sibeta's call, she sped forward, somehow landing in the dirt side of the circle without scattering any of the stones.

Maybe that was what the writing was for—some kind of no-scatter spell.

I knew it wasn't polite to stare, but I couldn't help myself. It was brighter outside than the last time I'd gotten close to the Grack and that just made her all the more amazing.

Where I'd thought she reminded me of a rock, I now realized she was far more complicated than that.

For one thing, she had eyes. They were a deeper gray than her skin, nearly black. What might look like a horizontal, jagged crack in the rock face when she was motionless turned out to be her mouth. Midway between her mouth and eyes, there were two more small cracks, which I thought might be nostrils.

A look at Carmine's face told me he was as fascinated as I was. We watched, rapt, as Sibeta and the Grack hissed, grunted, and clacked back and forth for a few minutes.

Eventually, Sibeta rotated her position on top of the water so that she was facing me.

"Apologies, Housekeeper," she said, bowing. "But the… Grack…asks for a point of law. Talks may not begin yet. She feels that since you have a witness," Sibeta nodded to Carmine, "that she must have one as well."

"Uh, okay, sure. Who does she want as her witness?"

"The fire man."

I looked at Carmine. "The fireman? We didn't call any firemen. I just used a fire extinguisher."

Carmine thought a moment, then said slowly, "I think she might mean Eagan."

I looked at Sibeta. "Do you mean Eagan?"

Sibeta rotated to face the Grack, spoke with her, then rotated back to me. "She says the fire maker in the warm house," and Sibeta pointed to the greenhouse.

Yup, she meant Eagan. "Sibeta, that's, um, problematic, for a number of reasons. The first and most important is that I'm not sure that anyone should know about you, er," I waved my hands back and forth between her and the Grack until I landed on, "people. If Eagan comes here, not only will he see the Grack, but he'll also see you, Sibeta, since you're translating. I thought you wanted to keep your presence secret."

A couple of large ripples flowed across Sibeta's robes, then she bowed. "As I said, Housekeeper. It is complicated."

So that's why Sibeta had been so hesitant. She knew, or at least suspected, that speaking with the Grack was going to open up a whole barrel of monkeys.

I had enough wackiness running amok in my life right then. I really didn't need to add any more monkey business.

"Can you tell me why she wants Eagan?"

Sibeta gestured to me, "You are earth." She gestured to Carmine. "You are earth." She gestured to the Grack. "She is fire. Fire maker…Eagan…is fire."

Ugh. Well, that made a certain kind of sense.

"Okayyyyyy," I said. "Would it make things easier if Carmine leaves?" I turned to Carmine. "If that's okay with you?"

"Fine," said Carmine.

"No, Housekeeper. I asked her this already."

"Why not?"

Sibeta said, "The Master Gardener is here much. His magic is here much." She gestured to the greenhouse and garden. "Your magic is—" she gestured in a wide arc.

"All over the place," I finished. Bayley's magic infused the entire property, and I was tied to Bayley.

"There is fire magic only there." She pointed to the greenhouse. Sibeta paused a moment, then added, "She searches for balance, Housekeeper, before she pleads her case. My apologies…she…does not trust you…as yet."

I tried to see things from the Grack's point of view. She probably looked at me as the jerk that had been chasing her across the back lawn. The powerful jerk who owned the land she was hiding on. If I were in her shoes, I'd want some kind of backup, too.

"Sibeta, are *you* okay with having Eagan here?" I wasn't sure I was.

"It is my job," she said. "I am the liaison." After a pause, she added. "He need see only me."

"Ah, okay. So you can live with it if he sees you, but I don't tell him about the others?"

Sibeta bowed, "As you say, Housekeeper."

"That's…that's really nice of you, Sibeta." She was taking a risk revealing herself to Eagan.

I wondered why until she said, "If the Housekeeper says the…Eagan…is acceptable, I will agree."

Ah, okay then. She was relying on my judgment of Eagan. No pressure there at all.

"So to sum, up," I said, "the Grack wants Eagan here to

kind of, uh, even the scales, I guess, so that she feels comfortable talking with me. And you're okay with that if I vouch for Eagan. Do I have it right?"

Sibeta nodded her head, "Yes, Housekeeper."

"Okay, well, Eagan isn't here. And I have to get his permission, to make sure he wants to help. Which means I can't make this happen right now. Can you ask her to keep from burning anything down while I set up a meeting with Eagan?"

Sibeta rotated and spoke with the Grack. When she rotated back to me, Sibeta said, "The matter is urgent, Housekeeper. The Grack will wait. But not long."

"Can she wait till tonight?"

After conferring, Sibeta said, "Yes Housekeeper."

"Okay, I'll see what I can do."

Sibeta said something to the Grack, who answered, then sped off into the woods so fast that she blurred.

Sibeta said to us, "Please call me when you have need of me." She bowed to Carmine then me as she said, "Master Gardener. Housekeeper." Then she sank below the surface of the circle and was gone.

I stood staring at the space where she'd been, my mind racing. The wind gusted, breaking my train of thought.

Shivering, I looked at Carmine and said, "Well, this is a mess."

The wind blew again, and I tugged my coat closer as we both headed back into the house. "On the bright side, at least if Eagan's here, we won't freeze to death."

Chapter Thirty-Eight

Carmine and I went back into the house.

A quick check told me Sadie still hadn't moved.

"She's sleeping an awful lot," I said.

Carmine said, "It's normal. Her body is trying to heal—the salve is helping it to heal faster—and that takes a lot of energy. Not to mention she's had a huge magic drain."

Speaking of which, I was feeling pretty drained myself. I whipped up a batch of the Shake-It-Off, making extra in case I needed a second dose later or Sadie wanted some.

Carmine made himself some tea, and the two of us sat at the table and had a snack while we tried to decide what to do about the Eagan situation. It looked like we had to invite him, but I wasn't sure how to enforce a confidentiality clause.

He was a friend—in fact he was on his way to becoming a good friend—but that didn't change the fact that he was a Smith, not a Foster. His first loyalty would be to his family. At best, he'd feel conflicted about not telling them that there were a bunch of weird creatures living on the property, one of which was fire-based. At worst, he'd feel obligated to spill what he'd learned. Bottom line, this tempting little tidbit was going to be tough to keep to himself. For all I knew, his family had rules about sharing vital info like that.

When things got this complicated, I did what I always did. I called Nor.

Carmine excused himself to wander off and do his own thing, which gave me a few minutes alone.

I dialed Nor and the second she said, "Finn—" some of the

tension leaked out of my shoulders.

"I'm sorry I haven't called you back yet. I'm working on it—"

"I'm not calling to harass you for not calling me back. I'm calling because I've got another issue to add to the pile." And I told her about the Grack.

"As if you didn't have enough going on with Sadie and the Guthrie stalker."

"About that—"

Nor must've picked up on something in my voice because she said, "Oh no. Did something else happen?"

"You might say that." I filled her in on the exploding bouquet. Then I had to back up and explain why Gram was there, which led to me telling her about Kate's fun visit.

Nor said, "In summary, you're still being stalked, and the stalking is escalating. Sadie is still there, but now Wil knows, though he says he'll hold off on informing the Council for 24 hours. Wil also knows that Gram is a puddle jumper and that Carmine is visiting, which he'll also be likely to inform the Council, possibly sooner than the 24 hours."

I winced. I hadn't thought about that.

Nor continued, "Plus, you've got this whole situation with the Grack and Eagan to handle. Am I missing anything?"

"Not that I can think of off the top of my head."

There was an edge of wicked glee to her voice when Nor said, "I love being your lawyer. You bring me all the fun stuff. I'll get back to you in the next couple of hours."

After I hung up with Nor, I found myself yawning despite the Shake-It-Off. I decided to put aside the questions churning in my brain for a bit and went upstairs to take a nap.

The sleep fairy must have snuck up and whacked me when I wasn't looking because I passed out so fast I didn't even remember falling asleep. When my phone woke me, I'd been dead to the world for a solid hour. But between the sleep and the Shake-It-Off, I was feeling much better.

I answered the phone with, "Hey Lou."

"Hi Finn. You busy?"

I hauled myself off the bed and headed for the kitchen.

"Nope. Please tell me you're calling about my stalker."

Lou's voice was grim. "That description is more apt than you realize. When's the last time you were out by the end of your driveway?"

"A couple of days ago." The property was several hundred acres, so getting all the way to the mailbox was a thing. I walked or drove to the end of the driveway at least a few times a week to grab the mail or take out the trash. "Why?"

Lou said, "How clearly can you picture the area around the mailbox?"

Given that I'd fought a battle there just a few weeks ago, "Really clearly. Again, why?"

"I'm standing across the street from your mailbox."

I closed my eyes and pictured the area around the driveway. On my side of the road, where the house was, the forest crept right up to the edge of the road. The driveway itself was barely visible, nestled into the woods. I imagined standing at the end of the driveway, mailbox on my right, looking at the street.

The road was only two lanes, but it was a major thoroughfare, so the lanes were wide enough to fit a truck with plenty of room to pass it. There was a dirt shoulder on the other side of the road, but no real sidewalk. Behind that, woods stretched into the distance.

When I'd fought with the Fosters, they'd rolled huge boulders out of those woods with the intent of rolling them across the street and smushing me, cartoon style. Gram had summoned rain that neutralized their magic, and the boulders had stopped near the edge of the woods.

Lacking my own personal army of magic minions, I'd made the executive decision to leave the massive boulders where they were.

Now, as I imagined the street, I could easily picture the huge boulder on the left with its jagged, triangular top—I'd spent some uncomfortable time picturing what it would have been like if I'd gotten stabbed by that top. Over to the right, its shorter, rounder buddy roosted. I called the one on the left Evil Gnome and the one on the right Evil Gnome's Wife.

"Are you next to one of the boulders?" I asked Lou.

"The one with the pointy top, yes," he said. "You know those two phone numbers you gave me? We tracked them. Easily—too easily. Finn, the stalker didn't smash them—didn't even turn them off. They just dumped them here."

"I take it from your tone of voice I'm not going to like whatever comes next."

I didn't think it was possible for Lou's voice to get more grim, but it did. "Either they assumed you couldn't find them, or they wanted you to know where they were calling from. Finn, it's likely they've been calling you from right here. Right across the street from the driveway. And from the small mountain of trash around, it looks like they've been hanging out here on and off for at least a couple of weeks. Watching the driveway."

And that meant they'd likely been watching me when I got the mail.

I went cold, and my mind sort of locked up.

"Finn?"

"Yeah."

"Pete's here with me. Can we come by?"

"Yeah, I think you'd better."

I hung up and just stood there for a few seconds until Bayley growled, snapping me out of my frozen fugue.

Bayley was a combination of angry, frustrated, and scared. Basically, all the things I was feeling.

"Don't worry. We'll get to the bottom of this." And then we'd need to do some serious rethinking about our safety.

The Housekeeper was supposed to be off limits, everyone kept telling me that. But this was the latest in a growing string of incidents that made me think the whole "off limits" thing was something they told us Housekeepers to distract us from all the people trying to mess with us. Because so far as I could tell, someone always seemed to have it out for me. On days like today, more than one someone.

After I hung up with Lou, I located Carmine in the sitting room. I explained that Lou and Pete were coming and invited him to join us if he wanted. Then I dashed up the stairs to

Sadie's room and knocked.

There was a long pause then, "What?"

"Company," I said. "Guthries, to help with the stalker."

A slightly muffled and sleepy, "Fine," came through the closed door, followed by something muttered that sounded like "freaking zoo."

The two purple dots indicating that Pete and Lou had arrived had me scurrying downstairs.

I opened the front door to find them standing on the lawn, studying the burned ground. Pete was kneeling, while Lou was looking around intently, studying the area.

"Hi guys. Come on in," I called.

They lingered where they were for a minute. Then Pete nodded and stood up, brushing his hands on his pants. He and Lou had a quiet, intense conversation as they walked over to the porch.

"Hi Finn," Pete said as he climbed the stairs.

Lou followed with a "Hi Finn" of his own.

I hugged them both and ushered them into the house.

As we clomped down the hall to the kitchen, I nearly did a double-take when I realized Carmine was in there. I hadn't really expected him to join in. He generally tended to keep his presence at the house hidden. At the same time, I was kind of relieved. The more help I could get dealing with this insanity, the better.

As soon as the men were all in the kitchen, the manly sizing-each-other-up commenced. I would've thought that, given that all the guys were over sixty, they'd have gotten over that by now. Nope. I couldn't decide if that was a good thing or not.

Lou was a good head taller than the other two. He still sported a full head of wavy salt-and-pepper hair that reached just past his ears. The combo of his thick hair, brown eyes, and swarthy skin made him look younger than his age.

Pete, on the other hand, had gone totally gray, and he kept his hair short and close-cropped. He had slightly ruddy skin and lively blue eyes.

Carmine was the least gray of all of them but had the most

lined face from all the time he spent in the sun.

All three men wore button-down shirts, but while Carmine wore his usual plaid-shirt and khaki pants combo, Lou had a denim shirt and jeans, and Pete had a white shirt and jeans.

I was about to make introductions when Lou said, "You're the Master Gardener, aren't you."

My eyebrows shot up.

Carmine shrugged. "Retired now." He glanced at me. "But helping out the new Housekeeper a little here and there." He held out his hand. "Carmine."

Lou and Pete took turns shaking his hand and introducing themselves.

Pete gave me a look and said, "Glad to see you're finally getting some help from the Fosters." The "instead of them attacking you" was left unsaid.

I could feel the bitterness in the smile I gave them. "Oh, Carmine isn't here because of the Foster Council. He's doing this on his own time."

Lou gave Carmine an appraising look, while Pete said, "I like you already."

I got everyone seated and set about getting drinks.

The men made small talk while I bustled about.

"Are you brothers?" Carmine asked, looking back and forth between Pete and Lou.

Pete chuckled. "No. We're only distantly related. But we've been friends so long, that, well, close enough."

Lou added, "We worked for the same…unit…of the Guthries."

I wasn't sure what that meant exactly, but Carmine nodded like he understood it.

I grabbed myself some coffee and joined them at the table, glad to see that they were all looking relaxed with one another.

"Okay guys. What's the deal with the stalker?" I asked. "Any idea what's going on? And why?"

"Here's what we know so far," said Lou. "We can confirm that you're dealing with a Guthrie. Pete?"

Pete said, "I went by Zo's and had a look at the sparrow. Unfortunately, any useful trace of magic was gone. I could confirm it was a Guthrie spell—"

"How?" I asked.

"Each family's magic has a very specific, er, I guess you'd say a sort of footprint to it. If you know what to look for, you can figure out the family the magic belongs to."

I filed that under "good things to know" and nodded for him to continue.

"But again, it was only a trace, so there wasn't enough left for me to track. Given the description of the spells you've seen so far, we can also tell you that we're dealing with a top tier, very rare class of talent. That helps us to narrow things down quite a bit."

Lou said, "I've been working the cell phone angle. I was able to trace the numbers you gave me, which is how I found the phones. I can tell you they were burners, cheap ones, that could have been purchased anywhere. I can also tell you we're not dealing with a pro."

"How do you know?" I asked.

"Fingerprints," Lou said. "They made a rudimentary attempt to wipe the outside, but there are partials left. And they forgot to wipe down the SIM cards." He shook his head at me. "Don't look so excited. Yes, I can run the prints. But, it'll take a while, and there's no guarantee we'll get a match."

I was about to ask how Lou had access to a fingerprint search when Carmine said, "Law enforcement or private Guthrie security?"

I looked at him. "What?"

Carmine said, "If he has the level of access that allows him to track cell phones and fingerprints, he's either in regular law enforcement or working for one of the Guthrie's private security firms."

Lou nodded his head, an appreciative look gleaming in his eyes. "The latter. Though technically I'm retired."

I looked at Pete. "You too?"

He nodded. "Also retired. But we still have access to some fun toys."

I found myself betting that these two were going to get

along well with Mila. They were in kind of the same pseudo-spy-ish businesses.

I said slowly, "Well that's...helpful. So given all your 'toys,' do you have any likely suspects?"

"Not yet," said Pete. He and Lou exchanged a look. "But now that we've had a look at your lawn—well, to put it bluntly, they screwed up. I'm guessing they assumed you'd dump water on the thing and neutralize any residual magic. There's been no attempt to camouflage the magical signature."

"It's sloppy," said Lou.

"They think I'm stupid." The guys all looked at me, and I shrugged. "They said it over and over again on the phone calls. They kept calling me an idiot. They think I'm too stupid to figure out their spell, so they didn't bother to camouflage it."

The guys all looked various degrees of outraged.

Pete said, "Well, we can use it to our advantage."

Lou's eyes glinted. "It's always an advantage when your opponent underestimates you. Let me tell you what we have in mind."

Chapter Thirty-Nine

Bayley, Carmine, and I listened to Lou and Pete's plan and agreed to give it a try.

Lou and Pete felt sure the stalker was going to try something again soon, so I invited them to hang out. All the boys retired to the sitting room and sat chatting around the fire Bayley lit for them.

I checked on Sadie and told her the Guthries were still there. Her only response was to growl "I'm sleeping!" so I left her alone.

The sun set, and I was thinking about what to do for dinner when I got a ping on my mental map.

"Uh," I said to Bayley. "Are you seeing this?"

Bayley squeaked at me.

I popped my head into the sitting room. "Game on? Maybe?"

"What are you seeing?" asked Lou.

I shook my head. "It's a whole pile of normal people. They're all crammed together—I'm having a hard time telling exactly how many there are." I frowned. "They're coming down the driveway—slowly, like they've never been here before—but too fast to be on foot. Guys, I have no idea what I'm looking at."

Pete shrugged, "No problem. Doesn't really matter. The plan stays the same."

Lou looked thoughtful. He and Carmine exchanged a look, and Lou said, "Hiding in a crowd maybe."

Pete added, "Or a distraction."

We all went to our places. For Fuzzy and me, that meant we went out the front door and onto the porch. I made sure to shut the door behind me, barring any views inside of Bayley.

Fuzzy sat next to me, body tensed, while I huddled into my coat and waited.

I could feel Bayley poised, on high alert.

A large van came into the grove and circled around the driveway to stop in front of the parking area.

The side door opened, and the sound of chattering female voices poured out followed by the females themselves.

A group of ladies, all of them looking roughly my age or younger, meandered over to stand in front of the stairs.

Bayley's lights only partially illuminated them, so I couldn't see them that clearly.

While one of them stepped forward, the rest of them jostled around until they stood in three rows in some kind of formation. One of them began handing something out.

My attention was diverted from whatever they were passing around when the one that had come forward reached the foot of the steps and started to climb up to me.

The second her foot hit the first stair, Bayley's magic whipped around her, scanning.

Normal.

Bayley was sure she was just a normal person.

Completely unaware that she was being probed, the girl jogged up the stairs, beaming a smile at me.

I glanced at Fuzzy. He was sniffing her like mad, but he wasn't growling, and his fur wasn't standing on end. He seemed to think she was fine, too.

Not what I expected.

"Hi! I'm Carla," she held out her hand, and I shook it.

"Hi. I'm Finn."

"Great! Just who I was looking for."

I must have looked wary because her smile broadened and she giggled. "I bet you weren't expecting an a cappella group to show up on your doorstep tonight. I mean, it's not like it's even caroling season yet or anything."

I blinked as I frantically tried to figure out if there could be some kind of magic afoot. Was *a caspella* a thing? Could someone in her group be magical? Out loud I said, "A cappella group?"

"Yup! We're The Becas. From Barnett Community College? Haven't heard of us? No big deal. If you're not into a cappella, you probably wouldn't. But we're pretty well known in the area. We do a lot of stuff like this."

"Like what?"

She beamed some more and said, "Someone thinks you're really special. They hired us to come and serenade you."

"Serenade?"

"Like a singing telegram. But way cooler." She lowered her voice and winked. "You've got yourself a really cool secret admirer. Someone went to a lot of effort to impress you."

Before I could respond to that, she bounded down the stairs and joined her group.

I realized that they were standing in choir formation. I recognized it from films I'd seen.

One of her group mates gave her something, and it took me a moment to realize it was a candle. Everyone was holding tiny taper candles.

Carla pulled out a lighter and used it to light the candle she was holding. Then she passed her flame to the person next to her.

They'd obviously done this before because they had a whole system for passing the flame candle to candle, quickly and efficiently.

Within moments, they all had lit candles and had turned to face me. Carla pulled a pitch pipe out of her pocket and hit a note.

She counted down, and then they began to sing. I braced for any magical shenanigans, but there were none. It was just music. And it was beautiful. They really knew their stuff.

But as I listened to the song and the lyrics sank in, it got creepier and creepier.

I recognized the song. It was about someone who had a crush but was totally invisible to the person they admired. In its original form, it was sweet. But in this context, the lyrics were creepy. The initial "you never notice me, but I'm always here in the shadows," gave me a shiver. When they reached the "I can't stop thinking about you" and "Being near you drives me crazy" on the chorus, my stomach plummeted.

I felt an odd sense of dissociation. They were singing their hearts out, creating what to them was a beautiful, candlelit moment accompanying a beautiful song.

What I heard was a taunt and a threat, all wrapped up in a bow with a large glittering "You're Doomed" on it.

Bayley was heating the porch, but I might as well have been standing on an iceberg, I felt so cold. The choice of song was bad enough. The amount of effort expended to find the song and arrange this performance, all just to taunt me—the sheer deranged malice involved—had icy fingers dancing up and down my spine.

I kept wanting to interrupt them to find out who the "secret admirer" was that had hired them, but they were putting so much effort into their performance that politeness made me hold my horses until they'd finished.

The ladies sang the final line. "But I'm never giving up," rang out, the chords creating a lovely finale of blended harmonies, the last notes fading into the night.

If it had been a romantic gesture, it would have taken my breath away.

As it was, I was speechless for an entirely different reason. I realized the ladies were waiting for some kind of reaction when a "Wow," slipped out of my mouth, and they all smiled, giggling and jostling each other.

Carla stepped forward, "Whoever your admirer is, they must think you're something really special."

I kept a smile pasted on my face as I said, "You keep saying 'admirer.' Did they give you a name?"

She shook her head. "No, but they said in the email that you'd be able to figure out who it was from the song." A look of unease passed through her eyes. "You do know who it was, right?"

I gave her a reassuring smile. "Oh I'm pretty sure, yup. I was, uh, just checking." I raised my voice and looked around the milling singers. They were chatting quietly and hugging themselves for warmth. "You all did a great job, really. That was something else. Unforgettable." I was super proud that I'd even managed to say that without sarcasm.

Carla smiled and said, "Thanks! We aim to please."

"Uh what happens now?"

"Now we have another gig."

"Oh great." A thought occurred to me. "Oh jeez, I'm so sorry. I don't know the protocol here. Would you guys like a tip?"

She waved me away. "We're all good, thanks. Your admirer took care of it all. But we should probably get going."

I thanked her profusely and watched the group meander to the van, chatting and joking, jostling each other playfully as everyone piled back in.

The van pulled away, beeping as it drove past me, around the driveway, and out of the grove.

I stood on the porch with Fuzzy, waiting. On my mental map, the van crept down the driveway, slowing here and there as it navigated the turns, and eventually came to the end, disappearing onto the main road.

Fuzzy looked up at the same time I looked down at him. Bayley hummed softly around me.

I said quietly, "I feel it too. It's like that was the preview." I looked down at Fuzzy. "I don't know about you, but I'm dreading the main attraction."

Chapter Forty

I'll say this for my admirer. They were patient.

An endless half hour crawled past, my nerves ratcheting tighter and tighter, while we waited for the next salvo.

When a single gray dot blipped onto my mental map, I was wound so tight I actually jumped, startled so hard that my heart skipped a beat.

Putting my hand on my chest, I made myself take slow deep breaths, trying to convince my heart to change tempo from pounding punk rock to more of a leisurely ballad.

While I practiced breathing, I kept an eye on the mental map. The dot was gray, and it was inching down the driveway, which told me two things. One, the person was a normal human, and two, they were on foot.

The driveway was super long—literally over-the-river-and-through-the-woods long. It generally took me a good twenty minutes to walk down to the mailbox. Whoever was walking toward the house was going to take at least that long, given how dark the driveway was. I found myself hoping they had a flashlight.

At least it gave us plenty of time to get back into position.

When the gray dot had reached the entrance to the grove nearly a half hour later, I was sitting in a rocking chair on the porch, covered in a blanket, reading a book, and sipping a hot cup of coffee. I'd positioned myself under one of the porch lights so that I was spotlighted against the house. Fuzzy was curled next to my feet, looking small, cute, and cuddly. Between the two of us, we looked like we didn't have a care in the world.

As the gray dot approached the grove, I murmured, "Here we go again." I wasn't sure what "gift" the normal person would be bearing, but there was no doubt in my mind that they'd been sent by my admirer.

Libby and Todd waved their branches at me from the entrance of the grove, giving me a heads-up as a figure emerged on the driveway between them. Instead of following the driveway around, the person cut across the lawn, beelining straight for the porch. A cell phone flashlight cut through the dark, illuminating their path.

I made a show of extricating myself from the blanket, putting down my book and coffee as I headed to the edge of the porch.

"Hello?" I called, waving to the person walking across the lawn.

As she got closer, I could see that it was Carla.

"Hi," she called waving at me and picking up her pace. "Man am I glad to see you. Your driveway is *long*. I mean, I knew it was long when we drove down it, but it's extra long when you're walking instead of driving."

She reached the driveway in front of the house, stepping into the light pooling in front of the porch, bending over, hands on her knees, trying to catch her breath as she said, "Whew. Well at least I won't need to go to the gym tomorrow."

"Are you alright?" I asked. "What are you doing here?"

She waved one hand, the other pinching her side like she had a stitch, as she stood upright and said, "Flat tires. Two of 'em." She sounded winded, pausing every few words to catch her breath. "They blew just after we turned onto the main road. We tried to get a cell signal, but none of us had any bars. And there's, like, nothing around here. It's woods everywhere." She gestured to the trees around us. "I'm the group leader, so I got volunteered to hike back here and ask to use your phone." She looked at me and smiled. "So hello again. Can I come in and use your phone please?"

She walked forward the last few feet to the porch steps.

The second her foot hit the bottom stair, I felt Bayley stiffen all around me. Fuzzy erupted into motion. In the blink of an eye he morphed from cute kitty at my feet to fierce feline leaping through the air as he launched himself at Carla.

In the same instant, the air blurred behind Carla. Dropping their own illusion spells, Lou and Pete resolved into focus as though they were stepping out of thin air.

Carla scooted back, away from Fuzzy, right into Lou and Pete.

Fuzzy chased after Carla, hissing and growling in a blur of motion that reminded me of the Tasmanian Devil cartoon. It would have been funny if I wasn't so scared. I lunged for him and yelled, "Fuzzy, stop!"

To my relief, he listened and leapt away as Lou and Pete each grabbed one of Carla's arms. They dragged her roughly backwards, and as Pete held her, Lou quickly zip-tied her hands behind her.

Lou kicked her in the back on the knees, and she went down hard, kneeling before the porch steps. Ivy sprouted from the lawn wrapping from her legs all the way up her torso, leaving only her head uncovered. By the time Bayley was finished, she looked like she'd sprouted out of the ground.

The whole thing happened in seconds.

Fuzzy stalked over to stand next to me. As he stared Carla down, she struggled against the ivy.

Wriggling frantically, she snarled, "Let. Me. Go!" Then let loose a string of swears. When none of us responded, she just struggled harder and swore louder.

None of us flinched.

I crossed my arms and stared at her. As far as I was concerned, her string of angry epithets placed her firmly in the amateur swearing league.

Lou stood stock still, clocking every move she made. He looked calm, but he was standing so that he could intervene if needed.

Pete was circling Carla, scanning her up and down, eyes squinted in concentration.

He looked at Lou, shaking his head. "It's seamless."

Carla stopped swearing and struggling to look at Pete,

smugness adding an ugly twist to her mouth.

Pete looked at me. "Most illusions have…imperfections. We call them seams. They make it easier to crack open an illusion."

Carla let out an ugly laugh. "Of course you have to explain it to her. She's too stupid to understand on her own."

I waited until Carla was looking me in the eye and said, "I'm not sure what kind of grudge you have against me, but drop your illusion and let's talk about it. You're not going anywhere unless we let you, so you might as well just play ball."

Carla swore at me for a full minute.

When she wound down, I said, "While having sex with myself might have its own entertainment value, this isn't really the time for it." I looked at Lou and Pete. "Okay, we'll do it the hard way."

Lou said, "Either one of us can crack it. It'll go faster if we work at the same time, though."

Pete said "But like we told you, if we forcibly crack an illusion, we can't guarantee the level of damage. There will be damage—the more seamless the illusion, the harder the force needed to crack it, the sharper the edges once it's cracked."

Carla was looking back and forth between Lou and Pete. "Bullshit. That's not a thing."

Lou snorted. "Now who's stupid? This is Basic Illusion Spells 101. Who taught you?"

That hit a nerve. I could see a flash of pain followed by a surge of anger flare in Carla's eyes, and she struggled to get at Lou. It was pointless. He was well out of her reach, but she struggled nonetheless.

Something about the way Carla was acting gave me pause. The waves of anger and the lack of emotional control all made her seem really young. I wondered if part of the illusion was an attempt to hide her age.

Over Carla's thrashing, I said, "Let's try the other hard way first." I turned to the house and called, "Sadie?"

When Sadie had sauntered into the sitting room, interrupting the plotting session I'd been having with Carmine, Lou, and Pete, I'd nearly banged my head on the table in frustration.

I hadn't had Bayley lock the door to her room because she knew there were people in the house and knew to hide till they left.

Instead, there she was flouncing into the open.

At the look I gave her, she said, "What? Wil already knows I'm here. The jig is up. I might as well have some fun before I leave. So, what are we doing?" And she'd sat herself on the couch, making it clear she had no intentions of moving.

Now, as she strode out onto the porch, an evil gleam in her eye, I was glad that she'd offered to help. If I could figure out what was going on without actually causing harm to Carla, I'd prefer it. Nasty as she'd been, I wanted to know why, and I was unlikely to find that out if Lou and Pete broke her.

Carla stopped struggling to eye Sadie. "What's with the Wicked Witch of the West?" she asked.

"Sadie's a Murphy," I said.

Carla looked startled.

"Gentlemen?" I said to Lou and Pete, who stepped back.

I stepped to the left. Two full pails of water sat waiting for me where I'd placed them earlier. I hefted them, careful not to slosh the water everywhere.

I marched down the stairs and placed the two pails of water in front of Carla, out of her reach, but still close by.

"Last chance to drop your illusion on your own," I said.

"Bite me."

"Okay Sadie, you're up," I said.

I walked back up onto the porch, and Carmine slipped out of the house to stand next to me. Lou stayed behind Carla and to the left, and Pete took up a position opposite him, on the right.

We all watched Sadie.

The wind teased Sadie's hair as she strode up to Carla.

Sadie said, "Cold tonight." Then she smiled. It was a mean smile. "This is going to suck for you."

Sadie made a motion with her hands, and the water in the pails flew into the air with a sharp snapping sound.

Carla's eyes went wide as the water flew at her. Cringing back, she ducked her head just as the water flowed over her. Bayley loosened the ivy just enough to make sure the water could get between the vines and thoroughly soak her.

When the water dripped off her and hit the ground, it didn't disperse and sink in. Instead, it sloshed around her, forming a puddle that rose up in a wave, washing her bottom to top.

It was just like what Sadie had done to the pizza. And it worked just as well.

The air around Carla started to warp like a heat mirage.

Sadie muttered, "Strong. But you can't hold out forever."

The water reformed in a puddle over Carla's head and washed over her from top to bottom again. It kept washing over her, top to bottom, bottom to top, scrubbing away at her magic.

On the fifth pass, Carla's magic broke.

Her angry, desperate cry echoed in the night as the air around her wavered hard then refocused, her magic neutralized by the water. Then she slumped forward.

Sadie let the water go, and it sank into the ground.

We all stood there looking for a long moment.

I tried to make sense of what I was seeing.

First of all, Carla was unconscious. She only remained upright because Bayley had her wrapped so tightly.

Second, on my mental map, now she was registering as purple, a Guthrie instead of a normal human.

And third, Carla was actually a teenage boy.

Chapter Forty-One

"Of course it's a teenage boy," muttered Sadie. At my look, she said, "What? Given the way he was talking to you, teenage boy makes total sense. You think Gram is bad now? Be happy you missed the moody teen Gram." She gave a delicate shudder.

Lou and Pete were studying the teen carefully.

"Do either of you recognize him?"

Lou shook his head, and Pete said, "No."

Sadie asked, "What do you want to do with him?"

After some consultation with Lou and Pete, we figured the kid would be out for at least a half hour. That gave us time to release him from the ivy, bring him inside, and restrain him.

Bayley wasn't thrilled about having him in the house, but given the situation, it was our best option.

As Bayley unwrapped the teen, we were able to see too that the teen was wearing a satchel that had been hidden before under his illusion.

Lou stepped forward and jerked the satchel away. He peered inside, face darkening.

Pete said, "Let's hear it."

"Fire poppers. A bunch of them."

Sadie whistled a descending note, while Carmine looked alarmed.

Pete muttered, "How'd he get his hands on those?"

Lou shook his head at Pete, then held one up for me to see. It looked like a small snow globe, sloshing with liquid, but without the snow or figures inside.

Lou said, "They're basically a magical Molotov cocktail. But instead of a regular fuse, you set them off with a spell."

My stomach plummeted. That kid had wanted to go inside Bayley with that hidden bag. Had he been planning to set the house on fire?

Why?

I stepped over to the nearest porch railing and patted Bayley, who felt just as confused and alarmed as I did.

I asked Lou and Pete, "Do we need to defuse the, uh, Magitovs?"

They shook their heads in unison. "They're inert until activated. We'll leave them out here for now."

I stared at the soaking wet teen slumped on the lawn. My horror at what he'd been about to do warred with my sense of responsibility—I couldn't just leave him out in the cold. That would make me no better than he was.

Lou and Pete hefted the kid between them, and we all went inside.

We put the kid in the sitting room in an armchair in front of the fire so he'd dry out and get warm. I could have asked Sadie to dry him off, but she'd already used a bunch of magic, and I didn't want her to overdo it any more than she already had.

Lou removed the zip tie, put the kid's hands in front of him, and placed a bracelet on each of his wrists.

Lou said, "Anti-magic charms. Want me to re-cuff him?"

I checked in with Bayley. I got the strong feeling he was ready to pounce on the kid if he twitched the wrong way.

"No need. Bayley's got it."

Lou nodded, but he and Pete stayed close to the kid.

Fuzzy hopped up on the couch, where he had a clear view of the teen and was in easy attack range.

Sadie and Carmine drifted closer, and everyone studied the teen.

Unconscious, he looked very young. I wasn't really sure, but between his height and the general gangliness of him, I'd be shocked if he was older than sixteen.

He didn't look like a psychotic arsonist stalker at all.

His brown hair flopped around his face, which looked

pale and gaunt even in the warm firelight. Dark circles drew deep shadows beneath his eyes, like he hadn't slept well in a long time.

I looked at his clothes. They were really rumpled, and although that wasn't that unusual for most of the teen boys I'd known, there was something much more...worn about his appearance.

A weird feeling came over me, like something about him was familiar. As my instincts kicked in and started poking me in the ribs, it dawned on me that this was exactly how I used to feel when my dad brought home what we called a "rough stray." They needed special handling and extra tending to. Every last one of them was angry. And every last one of them had good reason to be. We could always tell them apart from the other strays because they had a particular air about them—a bedraggled, apprehensive desperation.

The same air this kid had.

Pegging him as a rough stray shifted my feelings and, despite everything, I felt bad for him. I couldn't help it.

Bayley groaned and started muttering.

I ignored him and the looks everyone was darting between the house and me.

"I'm going to the kitchen. Can you guys keep an eye on the kid for a minute?"

"Sure thing," said Pete.

I scooted down the hall to the kitchen, Carmine and Sadie on my heels.

I started pulling chips, pretzels, and crackers out of the pantry and Sadie said, "What are you doing?"

I would've said, "The same thing we always did with rough strays to get them to calm down so we could figure out what was wrong," but that wouldn't make any sense to her, so I said, "Everyone has been working hard, and it's past dinnertime, so I figure we could all use a snack. Besides, did you see how skinny that kid is? And how pale? He looks like he hasn't eaten in a week."

Sadie snorted. "Have you been around a teenage boy?

They're like bottomless pits. He probably ate an entire pizza an hour ago, and I bet he still wakes up hungry."

I shrugged and said, "Then it won't hurt to feed him, will it?"

Sadie shot Carmine a look of disbelief. "She's serious, isn't she?"

Carmine gave her a wry smile and shook his head in a "what can you do" motion.

Sadie followed me around the kitchen as I loaded up a couple of trays with goodies. "Finn, you do realize this is the little twerp who's been messing with you, right? The one who came loaded with a bag full of trouble?"

"Right." I added a couple of cans of soda to the tray.

With an exasperated sigh, Sadie said, "Well then you shouldn't be rewarding him. Or, if you're going to insist on feeding him, give him a plate of mushrooms."

I stopped short. "Mushrooms? As in poison him, or as in try to get him high?"

"Mushrooms, as in force him to eat fungus because it's disgusting."

She looked at Carmine who said, "Don't look at me. I like mushrooms."

"Of course you do."

I handed her the lightest of the trays. "Do you mind? If your ribs are hurting—"

"I'm fine," she sniffed, snagging the tray. She disappeared down the hallway muttering, "Fosters."

Carmine took a tray without me asking, but he paused and said, "Not to gang up on you, but is this a good idea?"

I tried to find my words. "He's so young, Carmine…and… well, you told me to follow my instincts, and my instincts say something is really wrong. To be this young and this angry, and then to act on it the way he has…I want to know why." I picked up my tray. "And I don't think we'll find that out by feeding the kid mushrooms."

Carmine grabbed his tray without further comment and followed me into the sitting room.

While we were gone, Fuzzy had maintained his post, but Lou and Pete had dragged a couple of chairs over so they sat in front of the teen, with Lou closest to the fire and Pete nearest the couch where Fuzzy sat.

After I arranged all the trays on the coffee table, I dragged one of the side tables over and put it between Lou and Pete, directly in front of the teen, where they could all reach it.

"Please dig in, everyone," I said.

I went back to the kitchen for drinks, and by the time I returned, the boy was starting to come around.

I'd considered giving him some of the Shake-It-Off, but I decided against that for the moment. Maybe jacking the angry, powerful, out-of-control ball of hormones up to full strength wasn't the best idea just yet.

Everyone helped themselves to crackers, chips, and drinks. I plunked myself on the couch end, next to Pete and across from the kid, and Sadie and Carmine sat on the couch across from me, next to the teen.

Fuzzy hopped into my lap, but instead of curling into a ball, he sat upright, eying the boy.

When the teen opened his eyes, we gave him a minute to take in his surroundings. He looked lost and a little scared at first. It didn't take long before his bewilderment morphed into a scowl.

"I see how it is. Catch me and you throw a party. Nice."

"Want something to eat?" I asked.

He looked startled then quickly hid it behind more anger, shaking his head no. But then his stomach growled.

I shrugged. "Look we're gonna be here awhile. We're all eating. You might as well eat too." I tried to think of something that would appeal to him and then I said, "It's safe to eat. I mean, it's not like I can illusion something the way you can."

That did it. The smug look returned, and he shrugged. "I guess."

"Carmine?"

He was closer, so Carmine leaned over and placed a bowl of chips and a soda on the table in front of the teen.

Lou was giving me the same, "Are you kidding me" face that Sadie was, but I ignored him.

"I'm Finn," I said.

"I know." The teen looked at me like I was an idiot. Funny, that was exactly the expression I'd pictured from hearing him on the phone.

"And you are?"

I thought for a moment he wasn't going to answer, but then he got a look of challenge in his eyes. Lifting his chin, he glared at me and said, "I'm Neil. Neil Guthrie."

Chapter Forty-Two

I looked at Pete, then at Lou. They both shook their heads.

When I looked at Neil blankly, his expression turned incredulous. "As in *Trent* Guthrie?"

"I don't know who that is. Is that name supposed to mean something to me?" I asked gently.

A look of rage washed over him, and he would have leapt out of the chair at me if Bayley hadn't been ready for him. Neil had only gotten his butt an inch off the chair before wooden arms rocketed out of the floor, wrapping around Neil's chest, pinning his arms to his sides and his body to the chair.

From my vantage point, it looked like Bayley was giving him a wooden bear hug. Before Neil could start kicking his feet as he tried to wrench himself out of Bayley's restraints, Bayley sprouted two hands from the floor and clamped Neil's legs to the chair legs.

Fuzzy could see that Bayley had Neil in hand, but Fuzzy wasn't happy. As soon as Neil exploded, Fuzzy leapt onto the couch arm next to me and hunkered down into a crouch. He was one spring away from landing on Neil, claws out.

Not that Neil noticed Fuzzy. His full fury was focused on escaping Bayley to come after me. He struggled so hard that I was afraid he'd hurt himself.

As usual, Bayley was way ahead of me. When I looked more closely, I saw that Bayley had softened the restraints so that instead of being solid wood, they were more like saplings. They bent and flexed with Neil's movements, giving Neil just enough range of motion that he didn't do any real damage to himself.

It took several minutes for Neil to wear himself out enough to calm down a little. When he finally settled back in the chair panting, he gave me a look of sheer loathing and said, "I hate you."

I believed him. No one had ever beamed that much hatred at me, not even Sarah or Meg. It took my breath away. I sat back, astonished, and asked, "Why?"

Lou was typing madly on his phone. He looked up. "Trent Guthrie, age thirty-nine, died last month of cancer. He's survived by his wife, Karen, and his son, Neil."

Neil had flinched when Lou read the part about his father dying. I said, "I'm so sorry about your dad, Neil."

Neil hollered "Bullshit!" so loud that his voice cracked, and he freaked out again, straining against Bayley's hold.

He stopped struggling much sooner this time, instead choosing to blast me with the weight of his fury. "You are so full of shit I'm surprised you're not brown."

Pete leaned forward in his chair. "Neil, I'm Pete Guthrie. As a member of the family, I can advocate for you. As a Guthrie, you have a right to representation in any inter-family conflict. But I need to understand what's going on. How was Finn involved in your dad's death?"

Startled, I stared at Pete, wide-eyed. I started to sputter but Pete gave a little shake of his head and I subsided.

Neil looked back and forth between Pete and me. "Why should I believe you? Aren't you a friend of hers?"

"I am. But there are rules about these things, and the basic rule, as you should know, is family first. If I don't miss my guess, you're underage, aren't you? You're not eighteen yet?"

Neil looked away, and Pete nodded. "Thought so. Then it's doubly important that you have a family member present to help you. Since you're mother's not here—"

"Stepmom."

Pete paused then said, "Not a Guthrie?"

Neil shook his head.

Pete said, "Well then, bottom line, for now, you're stuck with me. I'll advocate for you."

Something that could have been hope glimmered in Neil's eyes before he hid it behind a cocky expression. "You can make her pay?" he said.

Pete said carefully, "Even the Housekeeper is bound by the rules. What has she done?"

Neil glared at me and snarled, "She killed my dad."

I gasped and said, "No I didn't—"

But Pete held up his hand and talked over me. "How? How did she kill your father?"

"She refused to give him a seed."

A wave of cold washed over me. Not the seeds again. How did Neil even know about the seeds? They were supposed to be top secret.

When Neil turned to me, so much anguish distorted his face that it hurt me to look at him as he said, "He suffered, you know. He tried to hide it, but he was in so much pain, he'd cry sometimes, even when he was asleep. All you had to do was give him one damn seed, and everything—" his voice cracked, and he looked like he was about to cry, but he covered it by getting angrier again and growling, "everything would've been fine now. He'd be happy and healthy and—" his voice broke again, "and he'd still be here."

"It's not the Housekeeper's fault," Carmine said.

I looked at Carmine and nearly did a double-take. His face was as grim as I'd ever seen it, and he looked like he'd aged ten years in the last few minutes.

Carmine scrubbed a hand over his face. "They haven't explained the seeds to her yet. And when they do, she'll still have no control over them—none. The Foster Council has all the control. They decide who gets them. Not the Housekeeper."

My mind whirled frantically as I grappled with what he'd just said.

And then, just like that, a whole bunch of puzzle pieces started to come together in my head.

The Foster Council's insistence on my being able to open DeeDee and retrieve seed pods from the other side. Alexander Foster's desperation to get one of the seed pods for his wife.

Boots's insistence that he knew how to put the seed pods to better use than the Council.

I'd figured the seeds had some sort of medicinal value, but Neil seemed to think they could actually cure cancer.

I looked at Carmine. The deep grief he usually took pains to hide was on full display. Another piece fell into place.

"Leilani?" I asked.

He nodded.

"But, but...you're the Master Gardener."

"I was. She wasn't. Apparently, she wasn't worthy."

No wonder he quit. The Foster Council could have saved the love of his life. After Carmine's lifetime of service, they still didn't lift a finger to help him save the person he loved most. How many other Carmines and Neils were out there?

I felt sick.

Lou, Pete, and Sadie were all staring at me.

Lou said, "The seeds come from here?"

Carmine said carefully, "I don't know their exact origin—it's a mystery. But the seeds are held on the property—temporarily—yes."

With a look of realization, Sadie said, "Ah. That's why Gram's so hung up on this place."

I said, "Wait a minute. Does everyone in this room but me know what the seeds are for?"

They all looked at each other and, one by one, nodded.

I looked at Carmine. "Why didn't you tell me?"

He shook his head. "That's a discussion for another time." He looked at Neil, who was watching us with rapt attention. "She didn't know," Carmine repeated. "If you hold anyone responsible, it should be the Foster Council. And believe me when I tell you, that'll get you nowhere."

I'm not sure if it was the looks of resignation on Lou and Pete's faces, my look of horrified dismay, or Carmine's look of commiseration that did it, but the fight went out of Neil, and he slumped in the chair.

Bayley let him go, but I could feel him hovering, ready to intervene again.

Neil continued to stare at Carmine, which gave me an idea.

"Carmine, Sadie, would you guys hang here with Neil a minute? I need a moment with Lou and Pete."

I glanced at Fuzzy, but he hunkered down further, making it clear he wasn't going to budge, so I left him on the arm of the couch, staring at Neil.

Carmine and Sadie scooted closer to Neil, and Lou and Pete followed me out of the room.

As I was walking out, I heard Carmine say to Neil, "The Foster Council refused my request, and I'm a Foster—"

Sadie interjected, "He's a *very* powerful Foster, and they wouldn't even help him. I'm sorry, kid, your dad never stood a chance."

Having it put so baldly shredded my heart even more, and I struggled to keep myself together as I led the guys to the kitchen.

I gestured to the table, and we all sat down.

"Well, this sucks," I said.

The whole time Pete and Neil had been talking, Lou had been typing away on his phone. He waved the phone at me now and said, "I was able to dig up some information—the basic facts support what the kid was saying. The kid is only sixteen. His dad Trent died of a particularly brutal form of cancer—it would've been awful for the whole family. It looks like both Neil's birth parents were Guthries, but his mother died when he was two, and Trent got remarried a few years later to Karen, who's nonmagical. He put Neil in normal school and, by all appearances, lived a mainly nonmagical life with him. Trent is rated as a top-tier magic user, though, so my guess is he trained Neil on his magic skills himself, but did it on the sly. Since Trent died, it doesn't look like anyone from the family followed up."

"Neil fell through the cracks," Pete said. "It happens."

"Can you guys tell me what you know about the seeds?" I felt a little pathetic having to ask, and I knew I wasn't supposed to be getting information from outside the Fosters, but at this point, I didn't think I cared anymore.

Lou and Pete had a silent conversation and finally, Lou

nodded. "We can tell you the basics. The Foster Council has a limited supply of magic cure-all seeds."

Pete said, "The rumor is that they always work, no matter what the illness is or how far advanced."

I asked, "How many people know about this?"

Lou said, "Very few. If too many people knew, there'd be a panic. Think of all the people like Neil who'd do anything to save a loved one."

"Well it seems to me like a whole bunch of people know. I mean, if it's this big secret, how come all you guys know?"

Lou and Pete exchanged another one of their glances, and Pete said, "Your...sample pool...from the various families is... somewhat unique."

I struggled to hold onto my patience. "Pete, with all due respect, this is not the time to pussyfoot around. What does that even mean?"

Lou said, "It means that none of us are average representatives of the families. None of the families was going to let some average person approach the Housekeeper—Neil being an obvious exception."

"But I first met you guys by accident. At the pub. You couldn't have known I'd be there, and I wasn't even Housekeeper yet."

Lou said, "Anyone positioned this close to the House is going to be upper echelon—basically close to Council level. That means we're going to be a lot more informed than the overwhelming majority of our families."

"So wait a minute, you're saying the reason you and Pete live here, in this town, is because you're top-level Guthries?"

They both nodded.

"And Eagan too, then?"

Again, they nodded.

And Sadie was Gram's sister, and Gram was a top-level Murphy who'd been trying to get access to the house before I even got there.

All the politics were making my head hurt. I decided to wade through the implications later. Right now, I wanted to focus on the stupid seeds.

"Okay, so you guys are some of the few in the know about the seeds. How did Neil find out? In fact, how did he find out about me and Bayley? Aren't we supposed to be super hush-hush too?"

Lou shook his head. "Not sure, but we'll need to figure that out."

I said, "So the Fosters have these seeds. And given what the seeds can do, I'm guessing they're in high demand?"

Lou said, "It gives the Fosters an edge over the other families. If there's something they really want, they bargain a seed for it."

Pete interrupted, "People have been trying to reproduce them for years. They've tried every method there is—through normal science as well as magical means—to either grow a plant from them that will bear more seeds, or to derive some kind of extract from them to turn into a medicine that could be distributed more widely. Nothing works."

"Okay got it. Very few magic seeds that people really want and need. And the Fosters are dicks about it." I rubbed at the headache forming in my temple. "Thank you for explaining it to me. Now," I looked back and forth between them, "what do we do about Neil?"

Chapter Forty-Three

We spent a few minutes going over the info that Lou had dug up on Neil, piecing together what we could about the kid. There wasn't a whole lot to go on, and we were left with a ton of questions.

After some intense back-and-forth, I sent Lou and Pete back to the sitting room.

Now that I'd come to an agreement with them, I needed to get Bayley on board.

"Bayley, we need to talk," I said quietly.

Fuzzy trotted into the room and hopped up on my lap.

"You want to be in on this too? Good idea, Fuzzy," I said, snuggling him. He felt tense, and when I checked in with Bayley, I could feel his lingering tension as well.

"Look," I said, "I know none of us is thrilled with Neil."

Bayley growled.

"Okay, you're mad. I get it. Me too. He could have really hurt us." I shuddered as I thought of the Magitovs. "But, he's just a kid. A kid drowning in grief. You've been around me long enough, Bayley, that you know how much I struggle with the grief thing, and I'm older than he is and have had longer to deal with it."

Bayley sighed around me.

"I'm not saying we need to make him our new best friend, or totally let him off the hook, but I'm thinking we could cut him some slack. Especially until we figure out how he got here—it's just weird that he knew about you and me, Bayley, and about the seeds. Something's really…off…here. I have this feeling there's more to this story, that we're missing something, and I want to know what it is. Bottom line is, I usually trust your assessment of people and, in this case, I'm asking you to trust mine."

Bayley mumbled and then Fuzzy kitty-chattered back at him. They went back and forth like that for a few minutes. I couldn't tell if Bayley was explaining what I'd just said to Fuzzy, or if they were complaining to each other about Neil, or what. But after a few rounds, they stopped talking and Fuzzy started grooming a paw.

I checked in with Bayley, who felt…resigned. "Does that mean you guys are willing to give Neil a little bit of a chance, at least until we figure out what's going on?"

Bayley gave me the sense that he was still on guard, but he seemed less angry.

That was good enough for the moment.

"Thanks guys," I said. Fuzzy and I headed to the sitting room.

I found Lou and Pete hanging back near the door, watching. When I saw what they were looking at, I had to stifle a smile. Carmine the Angst Whisperer had struck again.

He had scooted a chair next to Neil's. They were both hanging out in front of the fireplace, chatting quietly.

Neil's entire posture had changed. Gone was the bristling anger ball. In its place was an overwhelmed-looking teen, flopped in his chair, wolfing down a bowl of pretzels.

There was just something about the grounded steadiness of Carmine that helped people find their inner equilibrium. He was the human equivalent of chamomile tea. I'd seen him do it with Reese, and now he'd done it with Neil.

Carmine's influence didn't surprise me. But Sadie's did.

She'd pulled up a chair of her own and was leaning forward a bit, waving her hands as she talked. She said something that made Neil smile a little.

Studying him, I realized he was looking at her with a kind of awe. If I didn't miss my guess, he was a little smitten with her, and who could blame him. He'd witnessed Sadie in full magical-warrior-goddess mode when she broke through his illusion. And now here she was, giving him all her attention in his hour of need. I was sure it didn't hurt that she was beautiful.

It was obvious when Neil caught sight of me. He jerked himself upright, hands gripping the bowl so hard I was worried he was either going to shatter it or throw it at me. All the relaxation he'd displayed a moment before vanished.

While Carmine and Sadie greeted me, Neil's face flickered with emotions, worry and anger vying for control.

I suppressed a sigh. Well, we couldn't expect him to go from hating the thought of me to being thrilled to see me instantaneously. Even though by now he should realize I wasn't the problem, on some level it didn't matter. He'd been focusing his anger on me for long enough that it was going to take time to diffuse and redirect it.

Bayley didn't react by immediately restraining Neil, which was him trying to give the kid a break as I'd asked. But both he and Fuzzy were on high alert.

Neil, however, wasn't ready to be as flexible with me.

It was clear from his posture and the general Finn-is-the-devil vibe he was giving off that he wouldn't hear anything I had to say or answer any of my questions. We weren't going to make any headway with him while I was in the room.

I said, "Neil, Lou and Pete want to chat with you for a few minutes. While you guys are talking, can I get you a sandwich?"

Confusion won control of Neil's expression. "Why are you pretending to be nice to me? You keep trying to feed me." He looked at Carmine and Sadie. "Why does she keep trying to feed me?"

"It's her thing," Sadie said, shrugging. I could tell from the way she moved that she was feeling crappy again. "She feeds everyone."

Neil looked at me and I said, "Guilty. So, sandwich?"

He said, "Whatever." A look from Sadie had him adding a muttered, "Thanks, I guess."

"No problem."

Lou and Pete switched places with Sadie and Carmine, who followed me back to the kitchen.

Carmine went about making himself some tea, while I made Neil's sandwich, and Sadie leaned against a counter.

Sadie asked, "Now what happens?"

I said, "Well, Lou and Pete are going to offer to take him in, at least for tonight. He's a minor—did he tell you he's only sixteen?"

They shook their heads.

"Yeah, well, at sixteen, he doesn't have a lot of options. They have to get his stepmom involved before they can make any real plans. But the idea is to get permission to get him some official Guthrie training. I gathered they have schools for that kind of thing."

Both Carmine and Sadie nodded. Carmine said, "That's standard. The families all have various types of training programs available."

I tried, with limited success, not to be bitter about the fact that there were real versions of Hogwarts out there, and I hadn't ever had the opportunity to attend one. And now I never would.

I said, "A lot of it is going to depend on how aware the stepmom is about magic. Lou and Pete said it's possible that his dad Trent told her, or it's possible that he hid it. If the stepmom has no clue, then they'll have to be careful in how they deal with her."

Sadie asked, "Are you going to press charges?"

"Lou and Pete gave me the option to file an official grievance with the Guthries. But no. Don't get me wrong, Neil is not getting off scot-free. That kid has some serious anger management issues and a metric ton of unresolved grief. Plus, he's crazy powerful. That makes him a danger to himself and everyone else. So no, I'm not pressing charges, but Lou and Pete said they'll make sure he does a couple hundred hours of community service. Plus, I have a promise from them to get that kid a ton of counseling and some magic training. They said something about getting him a mentor."

Sadie and Carmine nodded. Sadie said, "That's a very Finn solution."

I wasn't sure how to take that so I said, "Uh, thanks?"

I didn't have to think about it any further because Pete came into the kitchen. "Hey Finn, can we borrow you?"

I'd finished with Neil's sandwich, so I plated it and took it with me as we went back to the sitting room.

Neil and Lou were still sitting by the fireplace. I walked over and handed Neil the sandwich. "Here you go," I said.

He hesitated slightly, but then he took it from me. After a glance at Lou, he muttered a "Thanks" that wasn't entirely dripping in sarcasm. I decided to take it as progress.

He must've been starving, even after the pretzels, because he devoured it in about three bites while Lou and Pete talked to me.

Lou said, "Neil has agreed to come with us. He's very grateful that you're not pressing any charges."

He glared at Neil who said a half-hearted, muffled "Mmpfhanks" around a mouthful of sandwich.

Pete jumped in, "Of course he understands that it's conditional on his compliance with community service, training, mentorship, and counseling."

If either of them caught Neil's eye roll when they said "counseling" they decided not to comment on it.

Lou said, "We'll keep you updated, as promised, but before we leave, Neil has something he'd like to say."

Neil looked like he was sucking on a sour lemon and refused to meet my eyes when he muttered, "Sorry."

No one in the room, including Bayley and Fuzzy, was particularly impressed with the "sorry." Both Fuzzy and Bayley issued similar-sounding low growls at the same time. But I decided to let it go for now. It wasn't like lecturing him was going to do any good.

Carmine and Sadie came in behind me. Neil's face lit up when he saw Sadie.

Which reminded me, "Uh guys. Before you go, we have one more piece of business to take care of." I jerked a thumb toward Sadie. "She wasn't here. It'd be better if you never mentioned seeing her at all, but please don't mention it for at least the next 24 hours."

Lou and Pete looked at Sadie with sharp interest. I had no

doubt that they'd figure out who she was and what her deal was. With Kate stomping around town, the Murphys weren't exactly keeping the search for Sadie on the down-low. Between the info coming from the Murphys and the info they had access to in their own Guthrie databases, it was just a matter of time before Lou and Pete pegged Sadie. As far as I knew, they had no reason to tip off the Murphys, but I couldn't take the chance. I needed to hold off the wolves for as long as I could.

Neil's eyes were alight with curiosity. "How come?"

I shook my head. "It's complicated." I looked at Lou and Pete. "I have your word? No mention of Sadie to anyone for at least 24 hours."

They exchanged a glance and Lou shrugged. "It's the least we can do," he said, shooting a look at Neil.

"Great, thanks."

Neil was looking like he was going to explode from questions, but a look from Pete kept him quiet.

Lou and Pete gestured to Neil, and he got to his feet. He gave me a wide berth as he shuffled past me, still refusing to meet my eyes. We all herded into the hallway.

Neil nodded to Carmine, who nodded back. Then Neil looked at Sadie and stammered out, "Sorry about the wicked witch comment." As he looked up at her, a bit of his former confidence kicked in and he added, "But you really are badass."

Lou looked at the ceiling shaking his head, then he escorted Neil outside. Pete lingered behind.

I asked quietly, "I know you didn't have long to talk to him, but were you able to find out anything about how he knew about Bayley or the seeds?"

Pete shook his head. "We need more time to work on him. I think we'll have better luck once we've left." The "and he's away from you" was left unspoken. "I promise I'll call you tomorrow with an update."

With a resigned sigh, I said, "Okay thanks."

Then Pete followed after Lou and Neil to their car.

I shut the door and leaned against it, closing my eyes against all the stuff that had happened in the last few hours.

I cracked them open again when Sadie said, "Yeah, it's been that kind of day."

I sighed. "Day's not over yet."

Fuzzy exited the sitting room, and I said, "Thanks for keeping an eye on Neil," then added, "You too, Bayley."

Bayley muttered at me, and Fuzzy gave me a dirty look. I had the distinct feeling that neither of them were thrilled I'd let Neil go so easily.

Fuzzy swished his tail once, stalked to the front door, which Bayley opened for him, and then slipped off into the night.

Bayley shut the door louder than strictly necessary, in case I hadn't gotten the message that they were both feeling cranky with me.

I thought, *He's just a kid* at Bayley, who responded with disgruntled mumbling.

I knew Bayley and Fuzzy would get over it, so I focused on the next thing on my list: dinner. Carmine, Sadie, and I trekked back to the kitchen where I decided to soothe myself by making us breakfast for dinner.

No one talked while I whipped up the eggs, bacon, and toast. Each of us was lost in our own thoughts. But I caught Carmine shooting uneasy glances my way. I needed food before I even tried to tackle why he hadn't told me about the seeds.

When I sat down with them to eat, I got a good look at Sadie. "No offense, but you look like you're going to fall over in your eggs any second now."

She just shook her head and ate her eggs. It looked like it hurt just lifting the fork to her mouth.

Carmine studied her movements. "You're going to be too uncomfortable to sleep."

She stared him down. "I'm fine."

Carmine ignored her. "You need to sleep. I have a tea that works great on the pain and will also help you sleep."

"I don't need a sedative."

"It's not really a sedative so much as a strong painkiller, anti-inflammatory, and restorative. The sedative is more of a side effect."

I chimed in, "I don't have any strong pain meds, so I'd go with what he's got. C'mon Sadie. You deserve a rest, and you need to heal."

She must've felt even worse than she looked because she said, "Fine."

Carmine quickly polished off his food and then went upstairs to grab what he needed. He came back to the kitchen with a backpack and began pulling out tins and baggies.

While I cleared the table and did dishes, Carmine made the tea. Sadie remained at the table, looking a little zombified.

Carmine cupped the herbs he selected in his hands, whispering over them. I felt the tingle of his magic and so did Sadie, because she frowned. Carmine stirred the herbs into a cup of steaming water, speaking quietly to the herbs as he stirred, his magic pooling in the cup. He clanked the spoon on the rim, and his magic dispersed.

After straining the herbs out, he handed the tea to Sadie.

She took the cup like it might bite her.

Carmine gave her a reassuring smile. "I just activated herbs. So all the good bits do their best to get you on the mend."

Sadie sniffed it then took a tentative sip. She didn't make a face, so I guess it didn't taste bad. I also guessed it didn't taste particularly good because she didn't try to drink any more.

Carmine said, "Drink the whole thing while it's hot. Don't worry, it's not hot enough to scald you."

Sadie gave a pained sigh then downed the whole cup.

Carmine nodded in approval.

She said, "How long till this kicks in?"

Carmine said, "Maybe fifteen minutes…thirty to get the full effects."

She looked back and forth between me and Carmine then said, "Right. Well then, I'm off. You two have some things you need to talk about, if I'm not mistaken," and she went upstairs to her room.

Drying my hands, I said to Carmine, "She's right. We need to talk."

He nodded, looking as tense as I felt, and said, "Why don't

we go out to the greenhouse, if that's alright. I have an easier time talking with my hands in the dirt."

"Sure, why not." Maybe I could find some comfort digging in the dirt, too. I usually did.

As we grabbed our coats and headed outside, I took a moment to suck in the cold night air. A wave of fatigue rolled over me, and I had to fight off the urge to go back inside, climb in bed, and stay there for a week.

Instead, I set my shoulders and clomped down the porch stairs after Carmine. No rest for the weary.

Speaking of which, I asked, "How strong is that tea really?"

A mischievous smile eased some of the tension around Carmine's eyes. "Strong. Stronger than I let on. A herd of buffalo traveling through her room wouldn't wake her. She'll be out for at least four hours."

I smiled and said, "Good to know. One less thing for me to worry about for a little while."

Which meant I had time to focus on him and why he hadn't told me the truth about the seeds.

Chapter Forty-Four

Halfway to the greenhouse, I stopped short and let out a yelp as Sibeta flowed out of the water half of the circle. When she was standing on the surface of the water, she bowed and said, "Housekeeper."

Carmine came to stand next me as I said, "Sibeta."

Fuzzy appeared by my feet and sat at attention.

"It is time, Housekeeper," said Sibeta.

"Time?" It was a measure of how crazy my last few hours had been that for a moment I had no idea what she was talking about.

"Did you bring the fire man?"

"Eagan? No." Truth was, I hadn't even had a chance to call him. "Uh, are you aware of what's happening on the property at all? Because we just had a big," I waved my hands around and finally settled on, "thing happen. I've been a little busy."

Sibeta just looked at me. I guessed the Grack didn't care how busy I was. I sighed.

"Hang on. Let me see what I can do."

I went back onto the porch where it was warmer, Carmine and Fuzzy trailing behind me.

I called Eagan. "Hey, are you busy?"

"What happened now?"

"Why do you assume something happened?"

"Your voice is about an octave higher than it should be, and you skipped right over the 'hi, how are you' section of the call."

I sighed. "It's too long to explain over the phone. Is there any chance at all you could come over? Like now? I'll owe you."

He whistled. "That bad, huh? Okay, I can be there in thirty minutes."

I thanked him, and we hung up.

"Stay here," I said to Carmine and Fuzzy.

I strode to Sibeta and said, "Eagan will be here in thirty minutes or so. I'll need time to explain to him what's going on and extract some kind of confidentiality agreement from him. So I'll be back in about an hour."

Sibeta bowed. "We will be ready. Housekeeper," another bow and she sunk beneath the surface. I scanned the dark lawn. I couldn't see that well or that far, but I didn't see any identifiable lumps that looked Grack-ish, so I figured I was safe from unexpected arson for the moment.

I hustled back to the house, joining Carmine and Fuzzy on the porch. I looked at Carmine. "You're off the hook for now. We still need to talk, but right now what I need more is to take a break and load up on caffeine before Eagan gets here." I glanced toward the circle. "I have the feeling it's going to be a long night."

We all trekked inside, and Carmine and Fuzzy disappeared upstairs while I went into the kitchen.

I called Nor. No answer, so I tried texting. "I need you. I need an ironclad confidentiality agreement for Eagan in the next thirty minutes." I had no idea what we could possibly put in a contract that would force Eagan to comply, but that's why I had Nor.

I was making a fresh pot of coffee when my phone sang out to me.

"Ten minutes," said the text from Nor.

While I waited for her to call me, I paced around the kitchen. I'd said I needed to take a break, but I was too keyed-up to sit still. How on earth was I going to be able to keep Eagan from blabbing about Sibeta and the Grack? And how angry was he going to be with me for silencing him? I rubbed my hands over my face.

I liked Eagan, and I'd been hoping to continue to build our friendship. Plus, who else was going to teach me how to use my fire magic? Not to mention that I'd just found out that he was a top-tier Smith, which could be helpful in all sorts of ways. Bottom line: I really didn't want to alienate Eagan if I didn't have to.

I poured my coffee, dosed it heavily with cream and sugar, and checked my mental map. Sadie hadn't budged in her room since the last time I checked. I was extra grateful she'd drunk Carmine's sleepy tea.

Still, I looked at the nearest wall and said, "Bayley, I'm going to have you lock Sadie's door, just to be safe, and is there any way we can soundproof her room? It'd be best if she just slept through the night and had no idea that anything was going on."

Ding.

Bayley showed me an image of Sadie's room. As I watched, the wood on all the walls grew thicker. It was like watching a time-lapse of a tree growing, but it only grew outward instead of up.

I heard a soft thumping noise, and said, "Great job, Bayley, but try to keep the thumping and bumping to minimum if you can. I know it's a lot to ask—"

Bayley gave me an indignant grunt from the nearest floorboard.

It took me another second to realize that the thump-thump-thumping was rapidly getting louder, and it wasn't coming from him.

"Sorry!" I said, giving the wall a quick pat.

I didn't see anything unusual on my mental map, so I walked toward the front of the house, where the noise seemed to be coming from. Carmine and Fuzzy must've heard it too because they came down the front stairs and joined me by the front door.

We went out on the front porch, by which time the sound had risen from distant drumbeat to full-on heavy metal concert. A small helicopter appeared over the grove then landed in the middle of the lawn.

Bayley was watching all this suspiciously, ready to pounce on the helicopter if I gave him the word.

It turned out I didn't need to.

The helicopter blades wound down, and two doors popped open.

Nor hopped out of the passenger side. She reached into the helicopter and dragged out a briefcase and rolling suitcase, while Mila climbed out of the pilot's side.

Of course Mila could pilot a helicopter.

I looked at Carmine who was shaking his head. "Those two," he said, a small smile playing across his lips.

Mila grabbed her own luggage, and the two of them strolled across the lawn to the house. They made quite the pair. With a nod to her Japanese roots, Nor wore an expensive-looking cream-colored suit with an Asian flare. In contrast, Mila was her usual study in monochromatic splendor, wearing an all-black outfit that set off her black hair and skin to perfection.

"Nice ride," I called.

Mila gave me her trademark cheeky grin. "You know I love to make an entrance."

When they reached the porch, each of them gave me and Carmine quick hugs, then we all went inside.

I checked on Sadie, and she hadn't moved. I sent Bayley a silent yet heartfelt *Thank you!* for the extra thick, sound-proofed walls.

Mila took her and Nor's overnight bags upstairs to their usual room, while Nor, Carmine, and I went to the kitchen.

Nor wasted no time in setting up her laptop and briefcase on the kitchen table, efficiently creating a workstation for herself. She looked fierce, concentrated, and intense. A mercenary we knew had dubbed her the Leopard, and I had to smother a grin at how apt that nickname seemed at the moment.

Nor said, "How much time till Eagan arrives?"

I looked at the clock. "Fifteen, twenty minutes?"

"It'll do."

"You have a decision to make," Nor said.

"Of course I do," I muttered. "Now what?"

"I brought Mila with me for a reason. You can decide that you want to read her in about Sibeta and the Grack or not. I haven't mentioned either of them to her, obviously, but given the possible repercussions—I'm assuming that by now you've realized that there's the possibility there are other long-term guests on the property?"

I nodded. Of course she'd figured that out.

Nor continued, "Well then, I think having an experienced Best helping you would be wise. Personal feelings aside, given Mila's skill set, I think she's an excellent option. Plus, you know you can trust her. That said, I'll have her sign the same confidentiality agreement I'm going to give Eagan. If, however, you decide that you'd prefer to keep her out of the loop, I'm fine with that and so is she. She knows something big is up, but something big is always up here, and she knows she's not privy to everything that goes on."

I looked to Carmine who was watching us closely. "Thoughts?"

Carmine looked surprised that I asked. I saw a little tension leave him and realized he was worried that I was angry with him.

Well, I wasn't exactly thrilled with him for not telling me about the seeds, but the truth was that overall, he'd been really good to me and I trusted his judgment. Plus, just then, I had too much else going on to get all huffy with him.

Carmine thought for a moment. "It's a binding contract?" he said to Nor.

She nodded.

He said to me, "Mila is trustworthy, and you'll have the confidentiality agreement as a backup. I think her…experience… might prove useful."

I looked at Nor. "Okay. But can I tell her and Eagan at the same time? It'll go quicker if I only have to explain this once."

Nor said, "Of course." She whipped out her phone and as she was typing said, "I'm texting Mila that we'll need to brief her when Eagan gets here. She already knows there's a confidentiality clause in play."

Nor's phone chimed. She looked at it and said, "Mila's in. She'll stay upstairs until Eagan arrives. Where's Sadie?"

"She's asleep in her room. We had another run-in with the

stalker—it's taken care of now, I'll explain later—but Sadie used more magic and now she's wiped."

Nor frowned. "That's not a great guarantee—"

"Carmine gave her a magic painkiller that knocked her out. Also, I had Bayley soundproof her walls and lock her door."

Nor gave me an approving look. "So she's off the board for now. Good. That gives us some room to maneuver."

We spent the next several minutes planning until I got a ping on my mental map.

"Eagan's here," I said.

Nor said, "I'm ready. Let me text Mila."

While Nor told Mila to come to the kitchen, I went to the front door.

Eagan greeted me with, "You know there's a helicopter parked on your lawn, right?"

Mila came down the stairs with, "It wouldn't fit in the parking area, so I had to improvise. Hi, I'm Mila Best. You must be Eagan Smith." She reached the bottom of the stairs and shook hands with Eagan.

"Nice to meet you." He looked around and asked, "Is this all about the stalker? Also, where's Sadie?"

"She's sleeping. She's not going to be part of this little adventure," I said.

"Okayyyyy," said Eagan.

As I led Eagan and Mila into the house and to the kitchen, I briefly explained about Neil to Eagan.

Eagan whistled. "Things are never dull around here."

Carmine was sitting next to Nor when we entered the kitchen. He stayed seated and waved at Eagan, but Nor stood up and held out her hand. "Eagan. Good to see you again."

Eagan shook Nor's hand, eyes scanning her improvised workspace. He released her hand and looked back and forth between her and me, his usual humor replaced by a sharp, focused look. "You called in the big guns. I take it this is serious."

I said, "As you said, never a dull moment. Eagan, Mila please sit down. Nor, you're on."

I puttered around the kitchen getting everyone beverages

while Nor spelled things out for them.

"Eagan, Mila, thank you for agreeing to this meeting. Carmine here has agreed to act as a witness," said Nor.

Carmine nodded.

Mila and Eagan nodded back.

Nor pulled out two sets of documents from her briefcase. "What I have here is *not* a standard confidentiality agreement. For the sake of brevity, I'll explain the intent and consequences, then give you a chance to read them over before making a decision.

"It's really quite simple. These documents are legally and magically binding. They are not standard, however, in the normal sense. They require a blood print."

Carmine set his tea down with a clunk. Eagan blanched. But I knew whatever was happening was really bad when even Mila looked stunned.

"Well damn," Eagan choked out on a half laugh. "You aren't dicking around."

"No. I am not."

I waved at them from my position by the coffeepot. "Uh, what's happening?"

In the same semi-amused, semi-choked voice, Eagan said, "Oh nothing. Just your standard death curse."

"What!?!" I said. "You said it was binding—"

Nor looked at me blandly. "Finn, you cannot take *any* chances." She turned back to Mila and Eagan. "To be perfectly clear, if you attempt to communicate to any outside parties anything about the confidential information you're about to learn, you will die."

Mila looked impressed. "And you are one of the few people who have the magic to pull this off. Well played."

I sputtered, trying to think of something to say.

Nor said, "Finn, it's the only way to be sure."

Bayley sighed around me.

Nor said, "See. Bayley agrees with me."

Mila recovered before I did. "I'm in."

We all turned to look at her.

"What? I like living dangerously. Besides, I wouldn't be here if you didn't think you could trust me. So yeah, I'm in."

A considering look sparked in Eagan's eyes. "You must be hiding something really amazing to go to these lengths." I knew we had him when the spark ignited into curiosity. "Sure, why not. I'm in."

I'd hired Nor in part for her ruthless brilliance, but this was taking things to a whole new level.

Well hell. I knew leopards could be deadly, but it was one thing to know it, and another thing to see this particular Leopard in action.

Nor said, "Finn, I need your okay."

I swallowed hard. I didn't want to be responsible for someone's death. I really didn't. But Mila was right. Neither of them would be there in the first place if I didn't trust them.

"Okay," I said.

Nor said, "Bayley, do I have your permission to proceed?"

Bayley shifted the glasses in the cupboard until they chimed a loud, clear, "Ding."

I looked at Nor. "That's a yes."

Nor nodded once. She pulled a slim rectangular box out of her briefcase. It was somewhere between the size of a jewelry box for a necklace and a case for glasses. The box was made out of a beautiful golden wood, inlaid with some kind of red stone.

Nor opened the box. On a piece of black velvet rested a long, thin pen made of the same wood and stones as the box. It looked kind of like an extra-long fountain pen. Next to the pen were what looked like two fountain-pen nibs, except that each had a terrifying-looking needle-thin silver tip.

Mila looked at the box with interest, but Eagan looked a little pale.

Nor then pulled out a second wooden box. It was a warm beige with some honey tones to it. I was pretty sure it was oak. When she opened it, there was a pen inside, made of the same oak wood as the box, but it had a normal fountain-pen nib on it.

Placing the two boxes in front of her, Nor looked at Mila then Eagan. "Read your contracts. Ask questions now if you have any," Nor instructed.

Mila and Eagan dutifully read through their contracts. When they'd finished and asked their questions, Nor slipped one of the needle nibs onto the extra-long pen and turned to Mila. She grabbed Mila's wrist with one hand, so that Mila's palm was face-up, and she held the scary pen in the other.

Nor said, "Mila, do you agree to be bound according to the covenants set forth in this contract, upon penalty of death?"

"I agree," said Mila.

"So be it," said Nor. And she stabbed Mila's index finger with the scary pen, which I immediately dubbed Mr. Stabby.

A single droplet of blood swelled on Mila's fingertip.

I noticed that Nor's lips were moving as she quietly chanted something.

Energy crackled in the air. Nor waved Mr. Stabby in a pattern and the blood drop floated up from Mila's fingertip and landed on the needle tip of Mr. Stabby.

Nor handed Mr. Stabby to Mila. "Sign."

Mila signed. In blood.

My stomach did a little flip.

Nor took Mr. Stabby back and did some more muttering. Mila's contract started to glow.

Nor handed the oak fountain pen to Carmine. "Sign please," she said.

As Carmine signed, Nor continued her under-her-breath chanting.

The energy in the kitchen ratcheted up.

Carmine finished signing and handed the contract and oak pen back to Nor.

Nor took the pen, still chanting, and signed her name, too.

Then she took one pen in each hand and held her hands above the contract. As she said, "And sealed by my word," she slammed both hands down on the contract.

The paper flashed so brightly that for a moment I thought it had caught fire.

The light faded, and everything looked normal. The contract looked like a normal pile of papers.

I looked at Nor. She looked like she hadn't slept in days.

"Are you okay?" I asked.

"Fine. One down, one to go. Eagan?"

To his credit, Eagan didn't balk at all. He just stuck out his hand and said, "Bring it on." Nor switched nibs on Mr. Stabby, then Eagan went through the same thing that Mila had.

When Nor finished with Eagan, she looked so drawn that I was afraid she was going to pass out.

"Shake-It-Off?" I offered.

"Please," she said.

While I put together the shake for her, Nor reiterated the terms of the contract. "Now that the contract is sealed, neither of you can communicate anything you experience here without Finn's express permission. Should you attempt to breach the contract, first you'll be immobilized. It will be painful. If you continue to attempt to communicate what you shouldn't, you will die."

Eagan smirked. "I assume that will, also, be painful."

"Of course," said Nor.

"Awesome. Well, I sure hope this was worth it. When do we get to the good part where we find out what all the fuss is for?" asked Eagan.

"That would be now," said Nor, as I handed her the Shake-It-Off. "Finn, would you like to do the honors?"

I sat at the table and explained about Sibeta and the Grack.

Mila looked like a little kid who'd just opened the best Christmas present ever.

Eagan took the news in a very Eagan way. "Cool. I suppose taking photos is out?"

"Yeah," I said, "I'm thinking going viral on social media is probably not worth dying over."

Eagan said, "So wait. The, er, Grack thing wanted me here. What would you have done if I refused the binding?" He gestured toward the contracts.

I shrugged. "No idea. But both of you are super curious, so I was betting that your curiosity would outweigh your caution."

Mila said, "Damn. I'd say it sucks to be taken as a given,

but in this case, I'm glad you assumed I'd play along. I have a question, though."

"Yes?" I said.

"If there's Sibeta and her people, and the Grack, what else is wandering around here?"

I exchanged a look with Nor. "That's another reason I wanted to swear you guys in, so to speak. I'm not sure what other, er, guests, exactly, are here. But I am sure that there *are* other guests."

Eagan blinked at me a few times, shaking his head in amazement.

Mila grinned and rubbed her hands together. She looked at Nor and said, "You bring me on the best dates, honey."

Chapter Forty-Five

With Eagan and Mila up to speed, it was time to face the music.

I asked Bayley to send for Sibeta, then we all bundled up and headed out to the porch. Fuzzy appeared by my ankles and shadowed me.

Nor was looking kind of peaky, despite the Shake-It-Off, which confirmed for me that she'd expended a ton of magical energy. I said, "Hey Nor, Mila, I'll check with Sibeta to make sure you guys can watch, but why don't you stay over here, where it's warm, until I get the all-clear?"

If I had any doubts, Nor confirmed she was in rough shape when she said, "Sure no problem," and plunked herself in a chair.

I must've looked as worried as I felt because Mila said, "Go on. We've got this."

While Nor, Mila, and Carmine got comfortable on the porch, Eagan, Fuzzy, and I hiked across the lawn to the circle.

Eagan let out a low whistle. "Well that's pretty cool. How'd you get the water in there?"

"Bayley did it," I said. I could see on my mental map that the water in the circle was connected to the aquifer that ran under the property. Sibeta and her people used it to travel back and forth. But I didn't explain that part to Eagan because I was already feeling weird about disclosing so much information today.

He didn't get a chance to ask any further questions because Sibeta rose up out of the water.

I guess I hadn't done an adequate job of describing her, or maybe it was just that the reality was so much more than any description, because Eagan gasped and his jaw dropped open.

"Hi Sibeta," I said. "This is Eagan, the, er, fire man that the Grack requested. Eagan this is Sibeta."

Sibeta gave Eagan a small bow. "Greetings, fire man Eagan." Then she turned to me and gave a deeper bow. "Housekeeper."

Eagan and I both bowed back.

Sibeta looked over my shoulder toward the porch, studied Nor and Mila for a moment, then looked back at me.

I said, "Uh yeah, so Nor is my friend. And she's my lawyer. You probably saw her when she came to help me that time at the pond? It's because of her that you, your people, and the Grack are protected—she made it so Eagan here and Mila," I pointed to Mila, "can't tell anyone about you guys. And Mila, well, she's a member of the Best family—you know, they're the animal magic family. She's, er, very...resourceful, and I think we may need her skills. And well, you know Carmine, he's been growing your food—you know he's a good guy, and super smart, and all kinds of helpful. So, uh, is it okay if they watch?"

Sibeta pondered for a few long moments, then said, "As you wish, Housekeeper." Then she added, "Changes must be made."

"What changes?"

"Bayley," she said. She was looking at me, but she was speaking to Bayley. I could feel him listening in my head. It was the weirdest feeling. "Please show the Housekeeper."

Bayley popped an image in my mind. Instead of just the split circle in front of me with the two smaller circles below, he added a little circle on top and two more small circles underneath.

Oh boy.

I looked at Eagan. "You might want to go wait on the porch."

To his credit, he didn't argue. He nodded and trotted back to the porch to wait with the others.

Fuzzy remained by my feet.

"You sure you want to hang out?" I asked him.

"Now the Travis Fuzzy must stay," said Sibeta.

I looked at her. "Oh. Okay. Well, I'm happy to have him here."

I knelt and touched the ground like I had when I'd created the earlier circles. Bayley came forward in my head, and I felt Bayley's magic combine with mine, directing it.

First, Bayley and I created a small circle above the main circle. Bayley had me make it so that it connected tangentially to the rim of the first circle.

When we finished, the new, smaller circle was centered over the middle of the top rim of the main circle. It reminded me of the little ring on top of a pendant—the one the necklace chain runs through. This new circle was small enough that a single person could sit in it, but not lie down.

Next, two more smaller circles sprouted below the main circle, joining the two circles I'd made earlier to form an arc mirroring the bottom curve of the main circle. Like the small circle that sat atop the main circle, the small circles arcing underneath were big enough that a single person could comfortably sit inside them. They were a few feet away from the main circle, so that there was a strip of grass separating the main circle from the smaller ones.

To complete the circles, stones came tumbling from around the property, ringing each of the new circles the way the original circles were ringed, complete with the odd symbols I couldn't read. I could see that stones on the top small circle touched the stones on the top rim of the main circle, so they were connected now.

Then, Bayley nudged my attention to the small circle that sat on top of the big one. I walked over and knelt down to touch it. Bayley collapsed and compressed the ground under the circle until a tunnel formed to the aquifer, and the circle filled with water.

There was a splashing sound. I looked up to see that Sibeta had disappeared from the water half of the main circle. A few seconds later, she popped out of the water in the top circle, so that she stood overlooking the main circle.

Finally, Bayley directed me to close off the tunnel that was letting water into the left half of the circle and helped me drain off the water. When we were done, both sides of the main circle looked the same.

Bayley gave me a mental nudge that felt like "Good work!" and then gently withdrew his magic from mine.

I slumped onto the ground as fatigue swamped me.

"Housekeeper?"

I waved a hand at Sibeta. "S'ok. Just give me a minute. Building this," I waved a hand at all the circles, "whatever it is, really takes it out of me."

Fuzzy nuzzled me and purred while I pulled myself together. I surveyed my work. The main circle was completely dry now while the smaller, top circle was filled with water. The four circles arcing along the bottom completed the picture, looking like a big smile.

Fuzzy stiffened next to me. I followed his gaze to see that the Grack was approaching from the woods.

"Game time, huh?" I said. Groaning, I got to my feet. To my relief, I was deeply tired, but not dizzy or headachy.

I turned to Sibeta. "Now what?"

She gestured to the left half of the circle where she had been standing before. "Housekeeper. Travis Fuzzy."

I went and stood in the left half of the circle. Fuzzy sat himself by my feet.

The Grack reached the circle, and Sibeta said something to her, then gestured to the right side of the circle. The Grack entered.

It immediately got a lot warmer, for which I was really grateful. "Sibeta, please thank the Grack for me for warming up the air. I was getting cold."

Sibeta spoke to the Grack who responded. Sibeta said, "The Grack is happy her warmth pleases the Housekeeper. The Grack offers to extend her warmth to the witnesses if it would please the Housekeeper for her to do so."

"Yes please. And thank you," I said. "Uh, is it time to get the, um, witnesses then?"

"Yes Housekeeper."

I turned toward the house and waved them over. Eagan, Mila, Carmine, and Nor immediately strode across the lawn to us.

I turned to Sibeta. "Oh. Do they stand in the circles?"

"Yes Housekeeper."

"Does it matter who goes in which circle?"

Sibeta said, "Fire man Eagan must be there." She pointed to the bottom circle nearest the Grack's side of the main circle.

She didn't give me any other instructions, so I turned back

to the four of them and said, "You heard the lady. Eagan goes there. Everyone else pick a circle."

They arranged themselves with Nor on the left end, then Carmine, then Mila, and finally Eagan on the right end.

I suppressed a grin as I realized they'd arranged themselves girl-boy-girl-boy. You can take the adult out of elementary school, but you never really get the elementary school out of the adult.

Mila said, "It's nice and warm."

I said, "The Grack offered to keep everyone toasty during the proceedings."

"My fingers and toes are definitely relieved."

I turned to Sibeta. "Okay, now what?"

Sibeta did that thing where she talked at me but to Bayley again. "Bayley, the circles."

I felt Bayley's magic surge. The lighter-colored stones lining all the circles began to glow with a flash of white energy. It made the symbols formed by the darker stones stand out extra clearly. Then the light faded. I could feel energy pulsing from the stones.

"Do not cross the boundary," Sibeta said, then spoke to the Grack, saying the same thing I guessed.

Sibeta turned to me. "Now, it is my time. With your permission Housekeeper?"

I wasn't at all sure what I was giving permission for, but I said, "Uh, sure."

Sibeta raised her arms above her head and began to move. It looked like she was dancing. She bent and swayed, turning in slow circles, gradually gaining speed. I realized she was repeating a specific pattern of movement, picking up speed as she moved faster and faster. Her semi-liquid state made her impossibly graceful, flowing from one position to another. It was like someone had combined ballet with tai chi and come up with this stunning result.

As she danced, I felt the air begin to crackle, and I realized she was doing some kind of magic. Before I had a chance to figure out what it was, Sibeta stopped and flung her arms to the side.

I felt a wave of energy roll past me.

Sibeta pointed her arms to the ground and a wall of mist rose around us. It formed a wide ring, circling around all of us standing in our individual circles. As Sibeta raised her arms, the mist grew then arched overhead, forming a dome over us.

When I looked around, I realized the whole area of circles I'd made was encased in a sphere made of mist. I could see it around and above us, and I could feel it extend under and below us.

Sibeta had put us all in a magic mist bubble.

Eagan let out a low whistle, eyes wide as he took in the bubble around us. I thought I heard him mutter, "Yup, it was totally worth it."

Mila was studying everything closely with a kind of child-like glee. It looked like she was taking mental notes.

I looked at Carmine who said, shaking his head with a look of wonderment, "Protection and concealment bubble, I'm guessing. But not one I've seen before."

When I looked at Nor, she was studying Sibeta, deep in thought.

The Grack made some sounds, and Sibeta nodded to her. "No thanks are needed."

Sibeta turned to me and said, "And so it begins."

Chapter Forty-Six

Sibeta said, "Now is the time of the," and she said a word I didn't understand. She turned to me and said, "Apologies, Housekeeper. I do not have the word in your language yet."

"Okay," I said.

"It is like 'negotiation'," she added.

I nodded.

"Do you, Housekeeper, agree to act in truth?"

"Yes." Of course I did, why wouldn't I?

Sibeta turned to the Grack. My guess was she asked the same question because the Grack gave a short response, and Sibeta turned and said, "The parties are in agreement."

She turned to the Grack and asked something.

The Grack started to change color, her gray skin turning a deep orange and emanating a glow. With all the heat she was radiating and all the glowing she was doing, she reminded me of a hot piece of coal.

As she turned orange, I could see her even more clearly. I was astonished to realize she was covered in tiny scales. When her skin had been gray, it had looked solid. But now that she was glowing, I could make out the thousands of tiny scales that covered her.

I scanned down and my eyes snagged on her legs. It suddenly made sense that she could scoot so fast—she had at least six of them. They were stubby in a way that looked muscular rather than flabby. They ended in flat feet with no toes that I could see, but the front pair were sporting three long claws each.

My attention jerked upward as she moved. I had to work to

keep my mouth from popping open. What I'd taken as lumpy bits turned out to be appendages. She had four, two on each side. The rocky lumps lifted away, revealing coiled "arms" that unrolled and waved about, kind of like the fringe on a sea anemone. The lumpy bits looked like armor protecting the arms.

The arms on one side gestured toward me, then the Grack spun to Eagan, all four arms gesturing to him.

Sibeta and the Grack went back and forth. My best guess was that Sibeta was asking questions, and the Grack was answering, still waving between me and Eagan, with an occasional gesture thrown toward the greenhouse or Bayley.

At one point, Fuzzy made a grumbling noise, but a look from Sibeta silenced him.

I looked down at him. Did he understand the Grack?

He looked up at me, blinked once, and went back to staring at the Grack.

I guessed the Grack must've finished, because she coiled her arms back up and stopped talking.

Sibeta turned to me, and I looked at her expectantly.

"In summary," she said, "fire man Eagan woke the Grack."

Eagan sputtered, "How?"

Sibeta looked at him, "You are a fire man."

I was still puzzling that over when Mila said, "Your magic. You used your magic here, and she sensed it." She looked at Sibeta. "Is that right?"

Sibeta said, "Yes."

Mila looked at Eagan. "Think about it. You doing fire magic is a big deal. How long has it been since a Smith did magic here?"

I nodded slowly. "It has to have been centuries, if ever." But that brought up another question. "How long has she been sleeping?!?" I asked Sibeta.

Sibeta went still for a second, then resumed her regular rippling. "That is a question. Not for now."

"Got it. Stay focused." But I made a mental note to ask again later. Not only how long she was sleeping, but where. And why. And why here. And how did she get here in the first place?

Sibeta was right, this was a rabbit hole, and I had to focus on what was happening now.

"Okay, I'm paying attention. So Eagan woke up the Grack. Now she's awake, and she needs…what, exactly?"

"I believe it is called a nursery."

I blinked. "Er," was all I managed. I tried again. "The Grack is pregnant? That was fast. She just woke up. Oh dear. Where's the baby daddy?" I turned around, looking into the shadows staring hard at anything that qualified as "rocky lump," looking for movement.

Sibeta said quietly, "Gone."

And the way she said it made me ask, "Dead?"

"Yes, Housekeeper."

I winced. "Please convey my condolences to the Grack. Being a mom is hard enough, but being a single mom is even harder. Does she have any help? Are there any others like her, are any of her people around here to help her?"

"No, Housekeeper," Sibeta said in the same quiet voice.

"Well crap. That sucks." I snapped into rescued-animal problem-solving mode. "Okay, how can we help? She needs a nursery? What kind of nursery? What else does she need?"

Sibeta gestured toward the greenhouse. "The warm place."

"The greenhouse?"

Sibeta said, "Yes."

I frowned. "Why the greenhouse, specifically? Bayley is warm. We could give her a room in the house. We'd have to figure it out so she doesn't burn down the place, but we could come up with something." I checked with Bayley. He wasn't objecting so I took that as confirmation we could make it work.

Sibeta spoke with the Grack, who again waved some appendages in Eagan's direction.

Sibeta turned to me and said, "Fire man Eagan's magic."

I looked at her. "What about it?"

"That is why the greenhouse. Though the Grack is honored by your offer of a room. She gives her thanks for the offer…and for your condolences."

I nodded, thinking. "Can you please explain to me what it

is about Eagan's magic that she needs?"

Sibeta said, "She is...fire hungry."

I blinked. Fire hungry? Was that some kind of hangry? "Er, okay. And Eagan's magic...what? Feeds her?"

Sibeta said, "It gives her fire. More fire. She needs more fire. For her and her young."

I frowned. "But there's no fire in the greenhouse. Well, except for the one she made. And fire in the greenhouse is not an option, or we won't have any food for you and your people."

Carmine said, "Sibeta? If I may?"

Sibeta nodded.

Carmine said, "She's not eating actual fire, if my guess is correct. I think she's getting a boost from Eagan's magic."

He looked at Sibeta, who said, "Correct." She looked at Eagan. "The Grack requests a pact with fire man Eagan, that he may aid her in this time of need."

We all turned to Eagan. He was blinking rapidly, but he shrugged and said, "Happy to help if I can. What does she need?"

Sibeta looked at me and said, "If the Housekeeper is in agreement, then the fire man will do his magic and allow the Grack to use it. Then there will be children. Then they will use it too."

I frowned again. "Sibeta, Eagan is willing to help, but he can't be at the Grack's beck and call 24/7. He has a life. How much of his time and energy will she need?"

Sibeta said, "A thoughtful question, Housekeeper." She looked at Eagan. "I propose a...there is no word in your language. I propose a...connect...with the Grack and you, fire man Eagan. That she may explain to you herself. Yes?"

Eagan swallowed nervously. "Uh, what does the connect involve?"

Sibeta said, "Step forward. Join the Grack. I will connect you. Fire to fire."

Eagan looked at me, and I shook my head. "I have no idea."

He looked at the Grack, then at Sibeta, and said, "Sure, why not?"

Sibeta nodded. I felt Bayley stir in my mind, then the glow in the rocks in Eagan's circle faded at the same time that glow in stones around the Grack's half of my circle faded.

Eagan stepped gingerly out of his circle and into the Grack's half.

With a nudge from Bayley, the stones resumed glowing. But he wasn't done yet. He focused his magic and the section of stones that bordered both Sibeta's and the Grack's spaces stopped glowing. Bayley had turned off a narrow section of boundary so that now Sibeta's circle was joined with the Grack's, with a ring of glowing stones forming a boundary around both.

Eagan was too focused on the Grack to notice or care about the boundaries. He stood a few paces away from the Grack, studying her with an expression of curiosity mixed with nervousness. "Hi," he said, and gave her a little wave.

There was a slight pause, then she waved an appendage back, mirroring his motion.

He smiled. So did I.

Sibeta said, "I will begin the connect." She said something to the Grack, who reached her appendage toward Eagan then stopped, holding it in mid-air. Then she looked at Eagan. "Touch the Grack."

Eagan looked a little nervous, but he dutifully inched closer until he could reach out and touch the appendage with his fingers. The Grack only came to knee height on him, so she was reaching up while he reached down.

The moment he touched her, Eagan's face transformed, radiating wonder.

Sibeta said, "It is now."

She waved her arms in another beautiful pattern and an iridescent light appeared around the place where Eagan's fingers touched the Grack. The light spread up both their arms until it was encompassing them both.

Eagan's eyes widened, then he squinted them shut, swaying a little. His face crinkled in concentration. He stayed like that for a few long minutes, long enough that I was starting to get worried.

But then Sibeta said, "It is done." And the iridescent light winked out.

Eagan and the Grack pulled away at the same time, and

Eagan opened his eyes, a smile blooming on his face. "That's something you don't see every day."

He looked back and forth between Sibeta and me. "I'll help. And she's right, the greenhouse is the best place for her and the kiddos." He grinned at me. "You said you got the extra-large greenhouse so you'd have room to grow. I know this isn't exactly what you had in mind, but trust me, it'll be a good thing."

"Can she keep from burning the place down?"

"Oh yeah. And I can help."

I looked at Sibeta. "Alright then. I think we have an agreement. The Grack and her babies are welcome in the greenhouse. And Eagan here will help them. So will Bayley and I."

Nor spoke up, "She and her children are welcome on the following conditions."

I spun to look at Nor, but she gave me her "trust me" look, so I kept quiet.

She continued, "They don't harm the greenhouse or any of the plants. They don't cause harm to Eagan, including through draining too much of his magic or making him overextend. The Grack agrees to set up a way to communicate with the Housekeeper, so that future misunderstandings can be avoided."

Sibeta stared at Nor with something that might have been respect and then translated for the Grack.

The Grack rapidly agreed to our terms.

Sibeta said, "Then all are in agreement. You," she pointed to Nor, Mila, and Carmine, "stand as witness. So it shall be."

And with that, Sibeta waved her arms and the mist bubble disintegrated. As it dispersed, Bayley made all the circles stop glowing.

Eagan motioned to the Grack in a "follow me" gesture. "Come on. I'll show you how to get inside without melting a hole in the wall."

Chapter Forty-Seven

Eagan took off across the lawn toward the greenhouse, the Grack following at his heels.

I was ready to go inside. Not only was I starting to notice the exhaustion dragging at me, but the cold came pouring back in now that the Grack wasn't keeping us warm anymore. But Nor turned in the opposite direction, toward Sibeta.

She said, "You guys go on in. I need a word with Sibeta."

She turned away, striding toward Sibeta, a hand raised, signaling Sibeta to wait.

I debated following her for about half a second, but the wind blew an icy breath down the back of my neck, convincing me to follow Carmine and Mila as they headed inside.

Stepping into the warm house took away the chill that had been helping to keep me awake. It was after midnight, and the day's events all slammed into me in the form of a giant wave of fatigue.

Mila eyed me and said, "You look like crap. Go to bed."

I shook my head and gestured to the backyard, "I need to talk to Nor about what's going on with Sibeta. And Eagan—"

"Eagan's a big boy. He's fine. I'll debrief him. In fact, if it helps, I promise to make him come back tomorrow and fill you in on the details." She glanced out the window in the back door. "I have a feeling he's going to be out there for a while anyways." At my questioning look, she shrugged and said, "You ever met a mom who wasn't fussy about her nursery? I haven't."

I was going to argue but she deftly played her winning card when she said, "Aw c'mon Finn. Can't you see how tired

Carmine is? He's going to hang out and check the greenhouse if you do. Go on to bed, both of you. I'll hold the fort." And for extra guilt, she added, "What's the point of going to all the trouble of a blood oath if you're not going to trust me?"

I looked at Carmine and saw how tired he looked. It had been a long day for both of us. I did a quick check on Sadie, and she still hadn't moved. We'd have to deal with her situation in the morning and I was going to need some rest if I wanted to be useful.

"Okay," I said. "Thanks. You know where everything is. Just, you know, help yourself."

"Got it," Mila said and shooed me and Carmine upstairs.

As we headed up the back stairs, Carmine said quietly, "I trust Eagan to make sure the greenhouse is secure and that no harm comes to the plants. We're both early risers anyway, so we can go out in the morning and check on things, just to be sure. It'll give you a chance to practice your plant listening skills. And, we can talk."

I nodded, and we both went to our rooms.

Fuzzy came with me to mine, hopping up on the bed to wait for me while I got ready. When I finally climbed under the covers, Fuzzy padded over to me.

I petted his head and said, "What a day, huh? I haven't even had a chance to properly thank you for looking out for me. I'm really glad neither of us got hurt," I added hugging him to me.

Fuzzy gave me a nuzzle then tipped his head so I could scratch his favorite spot by his ear.

I obliged and added, "And what was that, with you and the Grack, huh? It looked like you could understand her."

Fuzzy pulled back from me and stared me straight in the eye.

I felt Bayley go very still. It was as if the house around me was holding its breath.

Slowly, I said, "You...could you understand her?" I swallowed and said more softly, "Do you understand me?"

Fuzzy gave a little huff and said, "Meow."

My brain locked up, and I just stared at him. After a few seconds, I remembered to breathe and managed to force some words out of my mouth. "Is that a single 'meow' for 'yes'?"

"Meow."

I knew that Fuzzy wasn't a cat, and I'd known for a while that he and Bayley talked, but I'd never been sure how much Fuzzy understood of what I said.

Well, I had a science brain. I could use it. Time for some experimenting.

"If you really understand me," I said slowly, "can you, um, I don't know, turn around in a circle and meow twice?"

With a very cat-like look of exasperation, Fuzzy turned in a circle and meowed twice. He followed that with a long stare that looked a lot like "Happy now, human?" and then commenced grooming his paw.

My heart galloped as I looked at him. "Holy crap. You can really understand me?"

Fuzzy put his paw down and looked at the nearest wall. The look must have translated to something along the lines of "a little help with the human, please" because at the same time that Fuzzy said, "Meow," Bayley said *Ding*.

"Um," was all I could say because my brain locked up again. After a minute, I squeaked out, "Bayley, is Fuzzy really understanding me and talking back?"

Ding.

This time the "Um" didn't even make it out of my mouth. It was too busy hanging open to form words.

Bayley wiggled the floorboards, his quiet chortling reflecting the delight I was feeling from him.

Fuzzy patted my leg in what I could have sworn was a "there, there you simple human" motion, gave me a gentle head butt, and curled himself up in a ball.

"Wait, that's it? You're gonna drop that on me, and you're just going to go to sleep now?"

Fuzzy blinked at me and yawned. Apparently my question wasn't worthy of more of a response.

"Bayley, have you got anything to add? Like an explanation of what the hell?"

Bayley switched his happy chortling for contented sighing.

I spent a few seconds glancing back and forth between Bayley's walls and Fuzzy's head, but neither of them seemed inclined to discuss the matter further.

With a huff, I burrowed down under the covers next to Fuzzy. "How am I supposed to go to sleep now? I have too many questions. Oh man, now I've really gotta get Wil to explain DeeDee to me so that I can get Zo to tell me what you are. Argh!"

With a sigh, Fuzzy scooched over a bit until he was leaning against my side. Then he started purring loudly.

Despite my racing thoughts, the purr had its usual effect, and I relaxed enough to feel how tired I was.

The fatigue got hold of the questions circling my brain and weighed them down until they were quieter.

As I started to drift off to sleep, I said, "Why do I get the feeling there's more to this?"

I'm not sure if I imagined it, but I thought I heard Fuzzy mutter, "Meow," just as I fell asleep.

Chapter Forty-Eight

I'm not sure if Bayley was as tired as I was, or if he decided I needed some rest, but my sleep was deep and dreamless. I woke up just as the first bits of sunlight were peeping over the horizon.

Dressing quickly, I headed for the kitchen, realizing halfway down the stairs that Sadie was already there.

I had a moment's uneasiness so I asked, *Bayley, has she been wandering around the house while I was asleep?*

Bayley showed me images of Sadie's blue dot exiting her bedroom and traveling straight to the kitchen.

I felt my tension ease and said, *Thanks, Bayley. And sorry. I trust you to keep an eye on things when I can't.*

Bayley sent me a pulse of affection, which had me smiling when I entered the kitchen. Sadie was standing at the window, staring out into the blue dawn shadows.

"Morning," I said. "Coffee? Tea?"

She gestured to her mug, sitting untouched on the table. "I helped myself." After a pause, she added, "Hope that's okay."

I said, "Of course," right as Bayley squeaked his approval. I added, "See, Bayley's glad, too, that you're making yourself at home."

Sadie returned to looking out the window, emotions flickering across her face. "That's just it, though. This isn't my home."

Oh boy. Someone hadn't woken up as refreshed as I had. I went about making some coffee as I said, "Rough night?"

She shrugged, the movement stiff. "Carmine's tea worked. I slept like the dead." And then she muttered, "I should be so lucky."

I decided not to touch that one and instead asked, "Did the sleep help at all? Are you feeling any better?"

She turned to face me fully, and I winced at the bruise decorating her hairline liked some kind of warped barrette. She gave me a wry smile. "Well, let's see. I'm still homeless, hunted, and hurt. So, you know, everything's great."

I needed coffee before I could volley that serving of snark. I took the simple route and said, "How about I lather you up with some of that salve before everyone gets up?"

Sadie shrugged again but pulled a tin of the salve from her pocket. She handed it to me and hiked up her shirt.

I ducked my head so she couldn't see my wince. Her bruises looked even worse than yesterday.

As I applied the salve, she asked, "Everyone? Who's everyone?"

"Ah, yeah, about that. I, uh, called in reinforcements. The cat's kind of out of the bag about you being here, now that Wil knows, so the big guns are here to help out." I briefly described Nor and Mila to her.

She kept her face stoic, whether to avoid showing me how much her bruises hurt or to keep her reaction to Nor and Mila to herself, I wasn't sure.

I finished with the salve, and she tugged her shirt back down, then settled at the table.

I said, "I know it's more people than you were expecting—"

"I wasn't expecting anything. I wasn't expecting to be here at all. So…whatever."

My coffeepot cleared its throat, claiming my attention. As I poured myself an extra-large cup, I tried to think of what to say to Sadie to lift her mood.

Mila saved me when she came bounding down the front steps and strode down the hallway into the kitchen.

"Heya," Mila said, making a beeline for the fridge. She waved at Sadie on her way by. "I'm Mila. You must be Sadie. Nice to meet you." She yanked open the fridge, snagged a can of soda, cracked it open and chugged half of it. "Oh thank the universe for sugar," she moaned. She grabbed a second can, hip-bumped the fridge closed, and chugged the remainder of the first on her way to the table.

She selected one of the chairs a few seats down from Sadie, flipping it around so she could straddle it. As she cracked open the second can, she said, "Nor's catching a few extra z's. She was up, but I told her to stay put until she's a little more rested. She was really drained when she finally crashed last night."

"I think we all were," I said, looking from Mila to Sadie, then back again. "I know I was. I slept like a log."

Mila made a face. "Like a log. I never got that expression. I mean, do logs sleep? How does that make sense? Anyways, I'm here, reporting for duty, but unless it's dire, I'd appreciate it if you'd let Nor sleep."

I waved a hand, gesturing to the room around me. "Well, nothing's on fire, for the moment. And of course we'll leave Nor in peace."

"Thanks," said Mila. She took a swig of her soda and turned her attention to Sadie. "Now, let's talk about you."

I knew that tone of voice, so I said, "Mila, have a heart. Sadie hasn't even had breakfast yet."

Sadie stiffened and said, "I'm fine" at the same time Mila said, "She's fine."

While I stared at the ceiling and shook my head, Mila added, "See, we're in agreement. She's good to go, despite those excellent battle colors she's rocking." Mila studied the bruise along Sadie's hairline. "You know, you could get a whole Bowie vibe going if you turned that into a lightning bolt that went all the way down your face."

To my surprise and relief, Sadie cracked a smile. It was a small smile, but a smile nonetheless.

Sadie said, "I'll give it some thought."

"I'm going to make us some breakfast," I said. Eying Mila, I added, "Since you're in need of sugar, how about French toast today? Sadie, does that work for you?"

Mila whooped and rubbed her hands together in glee, while Sadie gave me a nod. Leaving them at the table, I slipped into breakfast mode.

Mila slugged back some more soda, let out a burp, and looked at Sadie. "So about you."

Sadie said, "What about me?"

"What's the deal with you and the Murphys?"

For a moment, I thought Sadie wouldn't answer. But she surprised me again when she said, "It's not complicated. It's an old story, really. They don't like my magic. There's a kill order out for me." She said it in an emotionless voice, like she was at the deli counter blandly ordering cold cuts rather than announcing her imminent doom.

Mila nodded. "Yup, pretty common."

Whatever response Sadie expected, that wasn't it. She looked at Mila, eyebrow raised.

Mila added in a conciliatory tone, "It still sucks to be you, don't get me wrong. But, you know, given the weird shit that usually gets winged my way, this is pretty ordinary." At the look Sadie gave her, she added, "No offense."

I didn't know whether to laugh or be outraged on Sadie's behalf. But as usual, Mila knew what she was doing. The lack of sympathy seemed to appeal to Sadie because for the first time that morning, her shoulders relaxed a little.

Sadie nodded, leaning toward Mila a bit. "See this is what I keep telling them." She tipped her head toward me. "This is the way things work. It's not like it's unexpected—it's been a long time coming. They should just let me get on with things."

I was about to remind Sadie that I could hear her, but Mila shot me a look that had me keeping my mouth closed.

Mila nodded along with Sadie and said, "I hear you. I'm sure the second your parents discovered your talent, the family threats started. Let me guess, the usual right? Lie about your talents, hide you away as much as possible…then when your talent got noticed, maybe pimp you out to some unit within the family where you could prove your worth—what is it you do?"

Sadie hesitated, then shrugged and said, "I'm a desiccant."

Sadie looked a little confused when Mila didn't react and instead continued with her list, "Right. So definitely pimp you out for your talent—to some security outfit, I'd guess. Combat?"

Sadie, now looking a little bewildered, nodded.

Mila continued, "Uh huh. So the usual. Put you into service—in a highly dangerous job—and use you until you get killed defending the family. Except you didn't get killed did you? And that made you even more dangerous."

Sadie shrugged.

Mila paused to chug the rest of her soda then said, "So I'm guessing something happened to make them realize just what kind of dynamite they've been playing with. Let me guess. You did something epic to protect the family, and they got freaked out?"

Sadie was now looking at Mila with something like wary appreciation.

I had to pay extra attention to the French toast I was adding to the skillet, so I didn't laugh. Gotta love Mila.

Sadie said, "You had me investigated."

"Well, yeah. I'm not stupid. But just the basics. I haven't had time to do any real digging. But like you said, this is a fairly typical story. So, am I right? You did something that showed just how 'extra' you are?"

Sadie said slowly, "Yes."

When Mila gave Sadie a little nod to continue, Sadie added, "It was a…there was a flood situation. I took care of it."

There was a lot unsaid there, and I would have had a ton of follow-up questions, but Mila simply said, "Of course you did. Lemme guess, you saved a whole bunch of people's bacon, right?"

Sadie gave the barest of nods.

Mila said, "So you do your job, save all the bacon. But then there's a council shake-up and like that," Mila snapped, "you've gone from helpful to harmful." Mila stood, shaking her head. "Yup, sucks to be you." As she walked to the fridge, she said, "Hey, all this talk of bacon…Finn, any chance you're making some?"

"Sure, could you grab it while you're over there?"

Mila snagged herself another soda and brought me the bacon. I eyeballed the soda. "That's your third soda."

Mila said, "And how many cups of coffee is that?" I'd been refilling as I cooked, so I didn't know. Mila probably did—she noticed everything. I was betting it was at least three.

"Point made," I said.

Mila sauntered back to the table with a smirk. She cracked open her soda and restraddled her chair. Catching Sadie's eyes, she said, "So how's it feel to be a dead woman? Any bucket list items you got planned, or are you just going to," she gestured outward with her soda can, "sail off into the sunset?"

"Mila!" I waved my spatula at her.

"What? I'm just asking."

"Show some sensitivity. Jeesh. Sorry Sadie."

But Sadie didn't look in the least offended. If anything she looked…comfortable. It took me a moment to recognize it because I hadn't seen her look truly comfortable since she'd gotten to the house. Mila's brand of in-your-face honesty seemed to be really working for her.

"That second thing," said Sadie with a smirk.

"Pity," said Mila. She took a swig of her soda. "Seems like an opportunity to have some fun. Okay, I'm officially starving. How soon can we eat Finn?"

Mila hopped up to set the table, keeping up a steady stream of casual conversation with me.

Sadie didn't join in. She stared into her mug of tea, deep in thought.

Chapter Forty-Nine

Carmine made it downstairs in time to join us for breakfast. Watching him and Mila interact made me smile. Watching him, Mila, and Bayley interact made my heart light up so much I was surprised there wasn't a sunbeam pouring out of my chest.

My phone went off. As I texted back, I said, "Hey Mila, would you mind setting another place?"

"Eagan?"

I looked up at her. "What are you psychic now?"

"Nah. Just smart," she said, grabbing stuff for Eagan. She must've noticed, too, that Sadie perked up at Eagan's name because she set Eagan's place next to Sadie's.

By the time Eagan arrived, I'd finished putting all the food and fixings on the table.

I greeted Eagan at the front door.

"Thanks for letting me come by so early," he said. Despite the circles under his eyes, he radiated energy. "I wanted to check on the, uh," he sent a worried glance toward the voices coming from the back of the house, "er, 'greenhouse,' if you know what I mean."

I thought it was sweet that Eagan was concerned about the Grack. "You're welcome to check on the 'greenhouse,'" I did finger quotes, "as much as you like," I said, walking with him back toward the kitchen.

Bayley murmured and I added, "And both Bayley and I thank you for taking such good care of her."

Eagan and I walked into the kitchen, where Carmine had joined Mila and Sadie. As the others welcomed Eagan with a chorus of hellos, an alarm bell went off in my head.

Bayley growled, causing everyone to stop greeting Eagan and turn to stare at me.

"Oh for the love of all that's rainy," I said, rubbing a hand over my face. "Gram's about to show up." I gestured to Sadie to stay seated and said to Eagan, "Go on and have a seat and help yourself. I'll be right back."

I stalked back down the hallway to the front door where Fuzzy materialized at my feet. When I reached the door, I could hear the sound of rain pattering against the porch.

I looked down at Fuzzy. "I see you're as thrilled at him popping in as I am."

Fuzzy looked up at me and blinked.

I opened the door just in time to see Gram step out of the rain shower and onto the driveway. The rain petered out as he walked to the porch and up the steps.

"You really need to learn to text first," I said.

He stopped in front of me. "Noted. You going to let me in?"

I took in the drawn, haunted look on his face, stepped aside and said, "Sure."

He shouldered past me and headed straight for the kitchen. No hello. No thanks. Just clomped down the hall like he owned the place.

I muttered to Fuzzy, "Someone's not a morning person," closed the door and followed after Gram, with Fuzzy trailing along with me.

As I glared at Gram's back, I realized that he was wearing the same clothes I'd seen him in yesterday. Not only did he look rumpled, but if I wasn't mistaken, he was trying to hide a limp.

When we reached the kitchen, Gram seated himself at the table across from Eagan and next to Mila, who was giving him a wide berth, nearly rubbing shoulders with Carmine as she leaned away from Gram.

"Don't drip on me," she said pointing her fork at Gram.

With a disproving shake of her head, Sadie gestured at Gram. All the water flew off of him, across the room, and into the sink.

Mila lit up. "That's useful! Man, I really coulda used you last week."

I could only imagine what shenanigans Mila was involved with that resulted in her being soaked. I let that go before I got too distracted.

Fuzzy hunkered down near his kibble bowl where he could have breakfast with us while still keeping an eye on Gram.

Sadie said to Gram, "We're eating."

Gram said, "I can see that."

Sadie said, "Call first next time. You're interrupting. It's rude," and forked a piece of French toast into her mouth.

Gram crossed his arms over his chest and glared at her, but I smiled a thank you at her.

As much as it pained me, politeness won out over my strong desire to just let him sit there, particularly since everyone else was helping themselves. I said, "Did you want something to eat?"

"Coffee," he said. At a look from Sadie, he added, "Please."

"I'll make a fresh pot," I said. I grabbed some bottled water from the pantry and dumped the rest of the old pot into my mug. I made the new pot using the bottled water and set it to brew. When I returned to the table, both Carmine and Mila were side-eying me, but neither of them said anything.

Helping myself to the dwindling French toast, I said, "So what brings you by so early, Gram?"

He looked so tense, I wasn't sure giving him coffee was a good idea.

"They know you're here," he said, staring at Sadie.

Everyone stopped eating, except Mila who said around a mouthful of food, "Well, sure. It was just a matter time. Wil probably had to spill the news to the Council earlier than he'd hoped. So?" and shoveled more food into her mouth.

It was like she stuck a pin in the tension bubble that Gram had blown. She was so casual that the rest of us exhaled and went back to our own breakfasts.

Everyone but Gram, that is, who clenched his teeth so hard that a muscle in his jaw twitched. "So," said Gram, "I need to get Sadie out of here before they show up."

"No."

Gram looked at Sadie and blinked. "What?"

"No," she said again, taking another bite of French toast.

"What do you mean no?" Gram said, voice rising.

"No," she said again, but this time she added a shrug and a smile. She turned to Mila and said, "Can you pass the syrup?"

Gram looked like his head was going to explode. A vein was standing out on his forehead, pulsing in time with his ticking jaw.

He took a breath and opened his mouth to say something, but Sadie raised her fork and said, "Count to ten. Whatever you're going to say, you're going to regret it. Count to ten."

To my shock and amusement, Gram closed his mouth and did just that. He looked totally frustrated, rubbing at his forehead while he sat in silence.

The coffeepot gurgled. I got up to get Gram a mug, and Sadie tossed over her shoulder, "You might want to put some whiskey in that. He's going to need it."

I raised my eyebrows and looked between Sadie and Gram. They had a staring contest for a minute and whatever he saw there made his shoulders slump in defeat.

He said, "It's still yesterday for me. Sure, why not."

"It's a new day for me, but can I have whiskey too?" Mila asked. When I shot her an amused look, she added, "Wouldn't want to force anyone to drink alone," with a wink.

I set Gram's coffee, a glass for Mila, and the bottle of whiskey between Gram and Mila and sat back down next to Eagan, who was watching Gram and Sadie closely.

I looked to my left at Carmine, who'd also been silently watching the interplay between Sadie and Gram as he methodically finished his breakfast. I'd learned that Carmine liked to focus on one thing at time. Now that he was done eating, he pushed his empty plate a few inches away, folded his hands in the space he'd created, and dove into the conversation with, "You might as well tell us, Gram."

We all looked at Carmine. He sighed and said, "It's written

all over his face. He came with bad news—worse than them knowing Sadie's here. Best just to get it over with."

Everyone swiveled to look at Gram who was looking at the whiskey in a way that made me think he was considering just swigging out of the bottle. Instead, he forced his shoulders back, sat up straighter and stared levelly at Sadie.

In a flat tone, he said, "The family filed for extradition with extreme prejudice." He added, "Officially," which made Eagan wince, and Carmine sigh heavily.

Mila looked at me and said, "This is the fun rule where they skip over the 'extradite' part and go straight to the 'dead' part. They show up, confirm that they've got the right person, and eliminate them on the spot. Basically, you're required to hold onto her until somebody shows up and takes her off your hands...by killing her."

The room went silent. I swallowed hard a few times as my French toast threatened to come back up. Appalled, I grappled with the fact that Sadie's own family would do this. Even though I'd been dealing with the homicidal tendencies of my own family, that somehow didn't make this any less shocking to me.

But while I was struggling, Sadie didn't look dismayed at all.

At Gram's news, Sadie's shoulders drooped for half a second, but then she turned it into a shrug and said, "Okay," and helped herself to the last piece of French toast.

"Okay?" Gram said, blinking.

Sadie shrugged again. "Okay," and recommenced demolishing her food.

Gram opened his mouth and closed it a couple of times, but no sounds came out. He reminded me of a fish.

When Gram finally managed to say "Sadie," Mila elbowed him. He looked at her, she shook her head. He stopped trying to speak and sat with his jaw clenched. She patted his shoulder in a "there, there" motion and poured a generous amount of whiskey in his coffee, nudged it toward him, then poured herself some too.

Gram ignored the whiskey and glared at his sister until she looked up.

She smiled at him and said, "Oh lighten up. It was inevitable. Admit it: it's a bit of a relief. Now we can just get it over with. You can finally move on, get some sleep," she looked him up and down, "take a shower."

Gram looked apoplectic. He started sputtering, but Mila elbowed him again—hard. He whipped his head toward her and lifted a hand, but she shoved his mug into it before he could start gesturing at her. Reflexively, he grabbed hold of the mug, and Mila lifted her whiskey glass and clinked it to his.

Mila held her whiskey glass aloft. "Here's to Sadie." She sucked back some of her whiskey and after a moment's hesitation, Gram took a few healthy swallows from his own mug.

Mila said to the table, "Sorry everyone but Sadie's right. She has to die." She turned to Sadie and said, "Sorry, Sadie. But hey, any requests on how you'd like to get bumped off?"

Chapter Fifty

Sadie didn't get to answer right away because Gram choked so hard on his whiskey-laced coffee that it took Mila a few minutes of whacking him on the back before he could breathe properly again.

Then he started shouting so loudly that I wondered if we should have let him keep choking a little longer.

He started with, "No one is going to touch my sister," and then listed the reasons why that wasn't going to happen.

I tried to interrupt him to calm him a bit, but he just talked over me and got even louder. Then Sadie tried to shout him down and that didn't work, either, as he got louder still.

When he started in on the threats of what he would do to anyone involved—including us—Eagan started to get out of his chair with a, "Now wait a minute..." but Mila motioned him to sit back down, saying, "I got this."

She pointed her index finger and poked Gram's stomach with it. Bayley and I went on alert as we felt the stir of magic.

One second Gram was hollering, and the next all the air whooshed out of him. His yelling cut off and was replaced by the sound of him gasping to get his breath back.

"Much better," Mila said. We were all staring at her, and she grinned at us.

"Uh," I said. "Is he okay?"

"Fine. Just knocked the wind out of him."

Eagan looked impressed. "Nice trick."

Mila's grin broadened. "I know, right? Same effect as a kick to the solar plexus, but it doesn't hurt."

Sadie looked wistful. "You have to teach me how to do that."

"Sure thing. We'll add it to your bucket list."

Carmine said, "I wouldn't mind learning that."

Eagan said, "Me either."

"No problem," said Mila.

Mila knocked back the last of her whiskey then hopped up from her chair. She looked at Gram and said, "Let's get you some air, buddy. You'll recover faster if you walk it off." She tugged on his ear until he stood up—sort of. He was doubled over, which worked fine for Mila, who held onto his ear and used it to tug him all the way out the back door.

Fuzzy followed them out, glaring at Gram the whole way.

Carmine, Eagan, Sadie, and I sat there for a few seconds, blinking, and then Sadie sighed and said, "You have no idea how long I've wanted to shut him up like that."

I nodded and said, "Me too."

Eagan raised his hand and said, "Me three."

Carmine said, "It was quite…satisfying."

Sadie started giggling. "I don't think he's ever been shut down like that." She giggled harder. "And then she dragged him out of here. By his ear!"

Eagan cracked a smile. "Too bad we didn't get a picture."

Sadie said, "Or video." She giggled harder. "Can you imagine?"

Eagan started snickering too. "I bet it'd go viral."

They both burst into full laughter.

It was contagious because Carmine started chuckling and then I succumbed.

Sadie managed to gasp out, "The look on his face."

There was a pause where we all pictured it and then we were all laughing, including Bayley who chortled as loud as the rest of us.

As our laughter died back, Sadie sighed, "I swear I'll never forget that look on his face." And then she sobered, a melancholy, resigned expression replacing her smile. "Not that forgetting is going to be an issue much longer."

The smile evaporated from Eagan's face, replaced by worry.

"Sadie, I—"

She shook her head. "Don't. Just don't, okay?" She forced a small smile. "Or you might wind up like Gram," she said, pointing her finger at his belly.

Eagan hesitated, searched Sadie's eyes for a moment, then nodded.

The sound of rain distracted us, everyone turning to glance out the window at the sudden storm.

Mila came in the back door, trailed by Fuzzy.

With Gram gone, Fuzzy headed off on his own, while Mila walked into the kitchen.

Mila said, "Gram's decided to have a little bit of a reset. I persuaded him to go home, shower, and take a quick nap."

I was more than a little curious how she'd managed to convince him, but I decided to just take the win. The fact that he was gone was going to make things much easier for the moment.

Mila reclaimed her chair, straddling it again. "Now that he's gone, let's have a little chat so we're all on the same page."

By the time Nor joined us an hour later, Mila had talked Sadie and the rest of us through what was likely to happen next with the Murphy clan and their "extradition," and we discussed the best way to handle it.

Nor arrived at the tail end of the discussion and provided a summary of the legal side of things.

By the time we were done talking, the laughter we'd experienced earlier felt like a distant memory.

"Come for a walk with me?" Eagan asked Sadie.

"Sure why not," she said. "It's a beautiful day. Might as well enjoy it."

The "since it'll be my last" hung unsaid in the air.

"Okay with you, Finn?" Eagan asked.

"Yup. There's a couple of paths you can take. I recommend the one that way," I pointed, "that leads towards Zo's."

"Thanks," he said. He and Sadie grabbed their coats and headed outside. I monitored their red and blue dots until they found and followed the path I'd suggested.

Carmine said, "Good thinking heading them away from Sibeta's pond."

I shrugged. "It'd be fine if they did go to the pond—we didn't see Sibeta till she wanted us to. But still, I was hoping to avoid the risk, if I could."

Carmine said, "If you don't need me, I'm going to head outside too—check on Sibeta's plants and a few other things."

I knew we needed to talk, but it didn't seem like the time. So I said, "Sure thing. Have fun."

As Carmine went outside, Fuzzy reappeared and trailed after him, leaving me alone with Mila and Nor.

Mila and Nor had been talking quietly. They exchanged a look, then turned and focused on me.

Nor said, "We need to talk."

I said, "Uh oh. That doesn't sound good. About what?"

Mila said, "About how to kill Sadie."

Chapter Fifty-One

There's a lot of things that coffee can make better. Turns out planning someone's death isn't one of them. No matter how much extra cream and sugar I heaped in there, thinking about playing with the Grim Reaper was…well, grim.

With an "I'm sorry, Finn," Mila left to make some calls.

I sat there feeling a weird combination of exhausted and wired. I looked at Nor. "I'm wrecked, and it's not even noon. How are you feeling?"

Nor said, "I'm fine. The extra sleep really helped. But I'm sorry I wasn't here to help with Gram."

I waved a hand. "Mila had him in hand." I gave a half-hearted snicker. "Literally."

Nor grinned. "Yes, it sounds like she had plenty of her own Mila brand of fun." Her expression turned serious and she said, "But now that we're alone, I have one more thing I want to mention." When I nodded she said, "You may have noticed that I talked with Sibeta last night."

"You looked like you were on a mission."

Nor nodded. "I was." At my questioning look, she said, "At the beginning of the meeting with the Grack, something about the way Sibeta was speaking caught my attention."

The memory of Nor standing with her head tilted, studying Sibeta, flashed in my head.

"Okay," I said.

"When I approached her, I told her that I thought we might have some things in common. I briefly explained to her what it is that I do—both my work with you as the Housekeeper, and my work as a whole."

I nodded again, and she continued.

"I was correct. We do have some things in common." Nor paused and looked at me closely. "Finn, do you know what Sibeta's job is?"

"She's some kind of translator and liaison for her people."

"She's that and more. I think she's closer to some type of diplomat. It was the way she opened the ceremony that first got my attention. There was something about the way she spoke that reminded me of a legal proceeding. And even though I couldn't understand exactly what she was saying to the Grack, there was a particular formality to the way she was going back and forth between the two of you. Then the proceedings themselves, well she wasn't simply translating. She was mediating, acting as a negotiator for you and the Grack."

I thought back to the previous night. Sibeta hadn't simply repeated what she'd heard like a translator would. She'd asked and answered questions for both me and the Grack. She'd also helped us find a middle ground that worked for both of us.

Nor continued, "I asked her about being a diplomat. She didn't know the word, but when I explained that a diplomat represents their country, making agreements for it and negotiating on its behalf, she got excited—she said that might be the word she's been looking for to describe her position. But she said it would be more accurate to say she represents her people, not a country."

I said, "Does that mean she's negotiated for her people with other Housekeepers in the past? Or did she mean she negotiates for her people with things like the Grack?"

"I have no idea. But I might be able to find out. When I explained more about how I negotiate on your behalf, as well as on behalf of clients with global interests, she did that thing where she froze momentarily. Something about my description must have struck a chord with her because when she started moving again, she did one of her bows and, in a very formal manner, requested a meeting with me soon. I said yes, but I wanted to run it by you first. So, this is me running it by you."

"You don't need my permission," I said, waving my hand.

"But I appreciate you looping me in. Hmmm. It seems like she's feeling quite chatty toward you. I wonder what else she wants to talk about."

"I'm quite curious myself," said Nor.

"Well once we get the killing Sadie thing over with—and I can't believe I just said that, by the way—maybe you can hang here an extra day and talk with her?"

Nor said, "I was thinking the same thing."

I drummed the table with my fingers as my leg jiggled under the table.

Nor said, "This Sadie thing is really bothering you."

"Well, yeah." I got up to refill my coffee cup, realized that for once I didn't really want more coffee, and started to pace.

Nor watched me for a minute and then said, "If we don't do this, the Murphys will get her, one way or another."

I threw up my hands, "I know that. I get it. Really. It's just…magical morons keep dragging me and Bayley into one quagmire after another. And this particular swamp pit…it really sucks." I sighed. "You'd think living in a magical world would be all unicorns and rainbows. Instead, I feel like I'm constantly trying to escape a cloud of troll farts."

Nor grinned, "Magic can be fun. But this is still real life, and real life is complicated."

"So much for a magic wand to make everything better," I muttered.

Nor said, "I can get you a wooden stick if it'd make you feel better."

"Can I play 'Whack-a-Murphy' with it?"

"Probably not."

"Never mind then. Troll farts it is. I guess I'll just have to learn to hold my breath."

Chapter Fifty-Two

Nor and I were just finishing up when Zo blipped onto my mental map and came walking out of the tree line in the backyard.

I peeped out the kitchen window and said to Nor, "Zo's here."

Nor said, "Need any help with that?"

"Nope. I got it."

"Okay, then I've got a lot to do. I'll be upstairs if you need me."

While Nor headed upstairs, I snagged my coat and went outside.

Fuzzy followed me out.

Zo approached the back porch and I called out, "Want to come inside for some tea?"

As I expected, she shook her head. "No thank you. I'm not staying long."

I frowned. She never seemed to want to come inside Bayley unless she had to. Well, it was a sunny day. Might as well enjoy the weather while I could.

Bayley popped up a couple of chairs from the porch, but Zo didn't sit down. In fact, she didn't even climb up on the porch, and instead stopped on the lawn in front of me. She nodded hello to Fuzzy, who blinked at her.

I tilted my head and eyed her. "You know, if you're in a hurry, you could've texted."

She shook her head. "Not a good idea."

I waited for her to elaborate but when she didn't, I said, "Okay. Well. How can I help you?"

She looked around the backyard.

Bayley had hidden the circles we'd made under a layer of grass, but her eyes snagged on the spot where the circles were hidden just the same. Then she scanned some more until her gaze landed on the greenhouse.

Some emotion I couldn't identify flashed through her eyes and was replaced by her usual I'm-hiding-all-the-things expression. She said, "I see Sibeta's been at work." She glanced toward the greenhouse and then nodded her head toward it. "New guest?"

My forehead crinkled hard as I said, "I'm not even sure if I'm surprised that you know about the, uh, guest." I played a sudden hunch and said, "Or about the other, the um, Talers."

"Talers?"

It'd taken some brain-wracking for me to come up with a collective noun that fit. I explained, "Well, if the others are anything like Sibeta and the Grack, they're going to remind me of figures from a fairy tale. So, I'm calling them Talers."

Zo gave me a dry, "That makes a very Finn kind of sense."

"Were you going to tell me about them?"

She said, "Not my job. If you were supposed to find out about them, you would."

I mulled that over for a second before I asked, "Any chance you want to tell me how you know about them? And how many of them there are? Or what they are or how they got here?"

"What's the fun in that?"

I sighed and rubbed at the frowny spot between my brows. "At some point, you and I need to have a conversation about your idea of fun."

Zo snorted, and when I looked up she looked amused in a way that felt slightly disturbing, as though she was contemplating her idea of fun and whatever it was, it was going to give me hives.

I decided to focus back on the subject at hand. "So, what's up?"

"I ran into Eagan and Sadie."

I checked my mental map, and they were, indeed, at the pond near Zo's property.

"Okay," I said.

"They told me about Sadie's extradition later."

I shouldn't have been surprised that she'd somehow pried that information out of them, even though the whole situation was supposed to be super hush-hush. She seemed to have a knack for getting people to tell her stuff. I sure did. All the time.

I ignored the knot in my stomach that clenched when I thought about Sadie and said in a mostly level voice, "I don't suppose you have a way out of this that doesn't involve killing her off?"

"Nope. Only way out at this point is for her to be dead."

I nodded and tried to push back the rising anxiety.

Zo said, "Oh don't look so worried. I've been dead before. It's not that big of a deal."

I just stood there blinking at that for a few seconds.

Unsurprisingly, it did not help my anxiety level.

Zo gave me an exasperated look. "Look, if you do this right, it won't be so bad. Just don't screw it up, and everything will be fine."

"Is that why you're here? To tell me not to screw it up?"

"No."

"So…?"

"I'm here to tell you I'm going to help."

I raised my eyebrows. "Uh…really?"

Zo got a wicked gleam in her eyes. "Do you think I'd miss a chance to stick it to the Murphys? I still owe them for what they did to my yard."

When he'd helped me fight off the Fosters, I'd thought Gram had paid off the debt he owed her for wrecking her yard. Apparently, the rest of the people who had helped him, including Kate, hadn't made sufficient amends. Zo could really hold a grudge.

I asked, "What do you have in mind?"

"Depends. I haven't gotten any details about the plan from Sadie and Eagan yet. But when they explain it to me, I'll let you know how I can help."

"Um. Okay. We'll have to run any changes by Nor and Mila," I said.

"They'll agree."

I said, "You seem sure."

"About the others? Yes. But you." She pointed at me. "You're the wild card. The others are more…pragmatic…about these kinds of things."

"I'm pragmatic!"

"Sure you are. But you get all," and she swept her hand up and down, from my head to my toes.

It took me a minute to realize what I looked like to her. I was frowning, my shoulders were stuck next to my ears, my arms were crossed in front of me, and I was slightly hunched over, like someone had just slugged me in the stomach. As usual, I was telegraphing how I felt, in this case distressed.

"Well pardon me for having a feeling."

"Having feelings is fine. Makes you a good Housekeeper. But it also means that you need a little…finessing…sometimes."

I couldn't decide whether I was offended or grateful that she was actually taking some time to explain things to me rather than steamrolling over me like usual. Maybe a little of both.

I said, "If everyone is okay with your plan, I will have no problem with it."

"Good." She started to turn to leave then turned back, her eyes straying to where Fuzzy was watching us at my feet. "How's it going with the door?"

"DeeDee? Um, hi, I've been a little busy, in case you haven't noticed."

Zo looked pointedly at Fuzzy, then up at me and said, "Figure it out, Finn." She turned and strode toward the woods, tossing over her shoulder, "Sooner rather than later."

I stomped inside, gnashing my teeth in frustration. I looked down at Fuzzy and said, "I'm going to figure it out, I swear. Things have just been a little nuts the last couple of days."

Fuzzy brushed his body along my ankles, and I instantly felt a little better.

We went up the back stairs and traversed the length of the

house to the master bedroom.

Mila must've heard us coming because she opened the door as we approached. I could hear Nor typing somewhere in the background.

"Zo was here," I said to Mila. "I need to talk with you both."

Nor appeared at the doorway. "What happened?"

I recounted my conversation with Zo and before I even finished, the both of them were nodding.

I said, "I take it you're fine with her participation, then."

Mila said, "Better than fine."

Nor said, "Are you okay with it?"

I sighed. "Let's be real. I'm not 'okay' with any of this. But if Sadie's good to go, then so am I."

Mila pushed off the doorway she'd been leaning on and said, "Excellent," and disappeared back inside the room.

Nor lingered a moment, studying me and said, "You don't look happy."

"I don't think 'happy' is on the table for me today."

"Well, not to pile on, but I was going to come find you. I need you to do something."

"Given the look on your face, I'm guessing this isn't something fun."

"It could be. If you frame it right."

Definitely wasn't going to be fun. "What do you need?"

"I think I can get the legal concessions you want."

I started to feel a bit of excitement until she held up her hand and squashed it with, "But, to hedge our bets, in addition to using the Sadie situation, I need one other bargaining chip."

"Okay."

"Finn, we need to find out more about what's behind the door. And you need to show that you can open it. And that means calling Wil."

Coming on the heels of Zo's parting words, Nor's mention of DeeDee felt a little like everyone was ganging up on me when I already had a lot on my plate.

"Fine, I will," I groaned.

"Now, Finn. Today. Before all the Sadie stuff goes down. I

need as much ammunition as I can get in order to negotiate the concessions we want from the Fosters."

Fuzzy head-bumped my leg. I looked down at him and he said, "Meow."

"Oh jeez. You too, huh? Okay okay. Three against one, I get it. I'll go call him now."

"Good. We need him here anyway when we deal with the Sadie situation," said Nor. She looked at me then reached out and gave my shoulder a squeeze. "It's a hard day, I know, but try to think of how much better things will be tomorrow once we get through all this."

"Yippee," I said, but I couldn't dredge up any enthusiasm.

I trudged down the stairs to go call Wil, Fuzzy at my feet. He brushed against my legs again, and I picked him up.

"I know we're doing the best we can, and that it's *pragmatic* to treat Sadie this way," I said into his fur. "I just wish it didn't make me feel like I'm not that different from the Council."

Fuzzy leaned in and nuzzled my chin. With a sigh, I dialed Wil.

Chapter Fifty-Three

Wil answered the phone on the first ring. He sounded relieved and anxious when I asked him to come over. In fact, he couldn't get off the phone fast enough so he could head out the door immediately.

That left me with a good twenty minutes before he got there. I checked on Eagan and Sadie, and I wasn't that surprised to find Zo with them.

I texted Eagan to let him know that Wil was coming by. Not that it mattered—we didn't need to hide Sadie anymore—but I thought I should give them a heads-up.

There was a pause, then Eagan texted back that he and Sadie were going to go have lunch at Zo's, and they'd be back in a couple of hours.

I spent a few seconds imagining what that little tea party was going to be like, then snapped myself back to the present.

I realized I should probably get lunch going for everyone still at the house. I texted Nor, but she declined my offer, saying she and Mila were "in the middle of things," so I made sandwiches for me and Carmine.

I ate mine quickly then decided that when I brought Carmine his sandwich, I should check one more thing off my "I really don't want to do this" list.

As I headed out to the greenhouse, Fuzzy trotted along beside me, staying close.

I looked down at him as we crossed the lawn.

"You planning on staying with me the rest of the day? Cuz I gotta tell you, things are just going to get weirder. I wouldn't blame you if you wanted to peace out and sleep through it all in my room."

Fuzzy swerved to brush my leg and then resumed his pace.

I sighed, torn between the desire to put him in lockdown till the crazy passed, and yet craving the comfort I felt having him around. Not that putting him in lockdown was really an option. He'd just convince Bayley to let him out.

My musing came to an abrupt end when we reached the greenhouse. I took a deep breath and let it out slowly, then stepped inside.

Warm air greeted me when I walked through the doorway. Carmine was humming tunelessly as he worked with Sibeta's plants near the door.

At the far end, it looked like we'd set up a decorative landscape of some sort. The dirt had been pushed and bunched into little hills surrounding a big hill in the middle. The big hill had a cave dug out on one side, into which it looked like we'd placed a big, craggy rock. The overall effect was of a bumpy hillside with a cave in the middle that had a big boulder in front of it.

Except of course it wasn't a rock, it was the Grack.

I found it oddly charming.

"Hi Carmine, I brought some lunch," I said, placing the sandwich plate and a bottle of water near him on the table. "I'm just going to say hi to our guest. Be right back."

He nodded at me as I walked past him.

Cautiously, I approached the Grack. Out of the corner of my eye, I could see Fuzzy ghosting along beside me.

I stopped when I was several feet away from the Grack's cave.

Fortunately, Fuzzy stopped too. He wasn't growling, so it seemed like he'd resigned himself to the Grack's presence, but he was giving the Grack his full attention.

I faced the Grack and said, "Um, hi." And I waved at her.

There was a pause and then a small movement. I realized she'd shifted slightly and was looking at me.

I said in my talking-to-scared-animals voice, "I'm not sure how much you can understand me, but I wanted to say 'hi' anyway. And welcome." I looked around the greenhouse as I said, "I hope you like it here. I think this little area you've made is really pretty. And if there's anything you need, I hope you'll let us know."

I did a little Sibeta bow.

After a moment, the Grack inched forward a bit, paused, and then inched back again.

I decided to take that as a win. With a little wave, I said, "Okay, have a good day," and made my way back to where Carmine was working. After a last long look at the Grack, Fuzzy followed along behind me.

I stepped up beside Carmine and began helping him with the potting he was doing. Having my hands busy made me feel a little better.

I eased into the conversation with "How has it been, working in here with the Grack?"

Carmine said, "Fine. I walked up and said hello, like you did, when I first got here. Then I got to work. She doesn't seem to mind. Eagan told her what we use this structure for, so I rather think she was expecting company." He patted the dirt in his pot for a few seconds then added, "But that's not what you're here to talk about."

So much for easing into things gradually.

I sighed and said, "No it's not."

We worked in silence for a minute while I tried to find the right words. Finally, I just blurted out, "Why? Why didn't you tell me about the seeds?"

Carmine gave a deep sigh. "I'm sorry I didn't tell you what I'd figured out about the seeds. It...took me longer than it should have to put two and two together."

He hung his head, shook it, then stared down at his pot as he continued. "I don't like to talk about what happened with Leilani. It's too hard. But out of respect for you," he looked at me and then looked away again, "I'll do it. This once. I feel like I owe you that much."

Part of me felt crappy for making him talk about something so painful, but I needed to know why he'd been withholding such important information, so I nodded.

"As the Master Gardener, I was one of a very few people who knew about the existence of the seeds. It's a huge secret. I know that to you it seems like a whole bunch of people know about it. But that's just because of the type of people you've been meeting. The information really isn't common knowledge."

Which made me curious all over again how Neil had found out about them. Or found out about Bayley for that matter. But I didn't want to sidetrack Carmine, so I kept my questions to myself and nodded for him to continue.

Carmine said, "When I became Master Gardener, the Council told me that there were these extremely rare seeds, and they explained that a single seed could cure anything. Anything."

"How is that possible?"

"No one knows. And believe me, they've tried to figure it out. But it's true."

"That's...that's a lot of power right there," I said. "Power over life and death? That's...a scary level of power."

Carmine nodded. "It is. So they told me the seeds existed, but they refused to tell me where the seeds were from."

I nodded. "Of course, they'd keep that as secret as possible."

My mind flashed back to Carmine explaining about the seeds to Neil—while Sadie, Lou, and Pete were listening. He'd been very careful to emphasize that the seeds did not come from the House, that they were only stored there temporarily, so they wouldn't think there was a secret cache somewhere in Bayley. Gratitude speared through me at his thoughtfulness in protecting me and Bayley.

Carmine brought my attention back to him as he said, "The Council said that there were precious few of the seeds and that none of the other families had them. Over the years, they gave me a single seed here and there to see if I could get it to grow—they were desperate to make more seeds. But even I couldn't coax them awake." He smiled bitterly. "They took the seed back, of course, every time the experiment failed. Told me that I didn't need to worry. As Master Gardener, I was guaranteed a single seed. I could have one to use at any time of my choosing."

"Oh no. Carmine," I said, because I knew what was coming next.

"They lied." His hands fisted and unfisted in the dirt for a few seconds. Eventually he gave another pained sigh and said very quietly, "Have you ever known someone with ALS? Or someone who is terminally ill?"

I shook my head.

"They fight so hard, you both do, and it doesn't matter. Every day there's a little bit less of them. And then they're gone," his voice cracked, and he stopped. Fists clenched, he closed his eyes and took a deep breath, letting it out slowly as he fought for control.

I swallowed around the lump in my throat and said, "I'm so sorry Carmine."

He gave me a sad smile. "I know you are, Finn. And the misery of it all is that if you'd been Housekeeper at the time, Leilani would still be alive and healthy. I know it in my bones."

The heartbroken look in his eyes had my own filling with tears. "I don't know what to say."

He shrugged. For a few minutes, he fiddled with the plant he was potting while he wrestled his emotions under control. When he managed to squeeze out, "They let Leilani die. And I quit," his voice dripped with so much bitterness that the leaves on the plant he was touching curled back away from him.

He noticed and stroked a soothing hand over the plant, and the leaves unfurled.

I wanted to rage at the Fosters who did this to him. I felt sick. And horrified. And if I felt as bad as I did, I could only imagine how Carmine felt.

Carmine cleared his throat. "And then we had that fight with Alexander Foster." He looked at me again. "I should have figured it out sooner, that he was after the same seeds that had been denied to me. But when I did figure it out, I," he shook his head, "I just needed time to process it, I guess. I'd never associated the seeds with Bayley House. It felt like an overwhelming revelation. I could have just come here, had I known, bargained with the Housekeeper maybe," he shook his head again, "which is why they don't say where the seeds come from, of course. They don't want people bothering the Housekeeper or making side deals."

Carmine finally lifted his head to look at me as he said, "When I figured out about the seeds and Alexander, I was so angry, Finn. I'm not proud of it. And logically, I know it's not your fault. You had nothing to do with what happened to Leilani—you weren't even involved with the Fosters back then. But realizing the seeds are linked to the Housekeeper...it brought all those feelings up. And I've been trying to sort it out."

And then it dawned on me. "Oh. That's why you've been staying away so much lately."

He nodded, "I needed some time. I didn't want to take my feelings out on you." He sighed. "I've been trying to find a way to tell you since I got here. But things have been...well, you know how things have been the last couple of days. It just never seemed to be the right time. Anyway, I'm sorry. I should have told you sooner."

I hugged him and said, "*I'm* sorry Carmine. So so sorry. For all you've been through."

He hugged me back. Hard. I felt a tremor roll through him, before he stepped back. When he pulled away, he said, "One more thing. I've been thinking. If it's been this hard for me, at my age, can you imagine how hard it must be for Neil?"

An image of Neil's face, twisted with rage and misery, floated to the front of my mind. I sighed and said, "Yes. Yes I can."

Chapter Fifty-Four

Thoughts of Neil and Carmine plagued me as I trudged back inside. When I slumped against the counter, Bayley murmured around me, and Fuzzy jumped up next to me, nudging me until I picked him up.

I buried my face in Fuzzy's fur and listened to Bayley croon to me as I fought back the wave of despair.

"Stupid Fosters," I said into Fuzzy's fur. "I know none of this is my fault. But I can't help wondering, how many people have they screwed over do you think?"

Bayley grumbled around me.

"Yeah, I'm thinking it's a lot, too." My next thought made me swallow hard. "You know, from now on, this is partly on me. I'm going to be the one giving seeds to the Fosters."

Bayley and I groaned at the same time.

I put Fuzzy on the counter, where he sat watching me as I started to pace.

"But what's the alternative? No seeds, so no one gets cured? Not that that's even an option—the Fosters would lose their minds and find a way to replace me as Housekeeper if I flat out refused, and no way am I leaving you alone, Bayley," I said, my hand trailing along the counter.

Bayley sighed.

"Well, looking on the bright side, at least this way, some people get a second chance." I shook my head. "It's not like I have any say over the seeds anyway. I don't get to pick who they go to."

I stopped in front of Fuzzy. "I wouldn't want the responsibility of playing god with people's lives, I really wouldn't.

But I don't trust the Fosters. Ugh, this sucks." I ran my hands through Fuzzy's fur for comfort.

A green dot blipped onto my mental map.

"And speaking of suck, here comes Wil for my DeeDee lesson." Bayley moaned, and Fuzzy meowed.

"It's okay guys. We all knew I'd have to learn sooner or later. And it's becoming increasingly clear that for everyone's sake, it'd better be sooner." I muttered, "But I don't have to like it."

I met Wil at the front door. His lips were compressed, his eyes narrowed, and both his hands were clutching the strap of his messenger bag really tightly.

"Oh jeez, now what?" I asked as I let him in. At his confused look, I said, "You're wearing the look of doom."

He didn't even bother dissembling. "They'll be here around five to get Sadie."

Bayley and I muttered at the same time. While Bayley's muttering just gave the impression of a disgusted tone, my muttering used actual words. I was pretty sure Wil caught my references to "flocking idiots" as we headed down the hallway.

But instead of going to the kitchen, I stopped short. Right in front of DeeDee.

Wil jolted to a stop next to me, eyebrows raised, whether in reaction to my muttering or in surprise at my abrupt halt, I wasn't sure.

I jerked a finger at DeeDee. "Okay, what's the deal? How do I open it? Without killing myself," I amended.

Wil shot a look toward the kitchen then looked back at me. "This is going to take a few minutes. Do you want to sit down?"

"Fine." I stomped into the kitchen.

Wil followed and set his bag down on the kitchen table. As he took off his coat and sat, he watched me pacing around the kitchen.

Fuzzy hopped up on the table near Wil, then turned to watch me as well.

"Are you sure you want to do this now?" Wil asked.

"Yes."

"You look a little..." he waved his hand to follow my

movements as I stalked back and forth in front of the sink.

"And?"

"And it's never a good idea to practice magic when you're… in a state," he said. "Please, come sit down and let's talk."

With a huff, I flopped into the chair near Wil and Fuzzy.

"Why are you so…" again he waved a hand at me.

"They're coming at five," I ground out. "You know what they're coming to do?"

A look of understanding passed over Wil's face. "Yes. Look, I can see where you'd find this difficult. But it's—"

"If you tell me that it's the way things are done," I glared at him.

He raised his hands in surrender.

"I don't care if it's the way things are done. It's stupid. The ways are stupid." I realized I sounded like an angry, petulant teenager—an image of Neil flashed in my head—and I felt a moment's empathy for him.

I really just wanted the whole day to be over, but for me to have the day end in any kind of a win, I had to get past this huge hurdle first. So I shrugged off some of my tension and said, "Well, there's nothing I can do about the epic amount of stupidity that'll happen later. So let's talk about the door now. Tell me about DeeDee."

"DeeDee?"

"I can't keep calling it the Demon Door."

"I see." Wil slipped into professor mode and asked, "So what is it you want to know?"

"Everything. But let's start with the basics. What is it, where does it go, and how did it get here?"

Wil blew out a breath and said, "We don't know."

"What do you mean you don't know? The whole point of you being here is to fill me in."

With a sigh, Wil clasped his hands in front of him on the table, and said, "I know that I said I'd explain the door to you if you agreed to me tutoring you. But that might have been a little misleading."

I was pretty sure I must've been telegraphing the fact that I wanted to throw something at him because he sat back in his chair, his hand held up in front of him, as though to ward off any blows.

"Just hear me out," he said.

Like I had a choice. I crossed my arms over my chest and nodded.

"I'll tell you what we do know. But I think you'll find there's...well, there's a lot missing."

"Missing."

He sighed. "You know how they lost Bayley's name?"

I nodded, frowning.

"It's not the only thing that's been lost over the years." At the look I gave him, he nodded, "I agree. They...good care has not been taken. The record keeping! Ah, Finn, if you saw the mess the family's historical documents are in...anyway, I digress. My point is, that I wanted to prepare you before I dive in."

"Consider me prepared."

He nodded. "Okay. Well, then, to answer your questions: we don't know what the door is, exactly. I mean, technically, it functions as a door—you can open and close it, and stuff can go through it."

This was about as useful as picking poison ivy and about as irritating. I tried to hold onto my temper. "Uh huh. Where does it go?"

"We don't know."

That did it. I hid my face in my hands and let out a strangled, "You've got to be kidding me."

"What we *do* know—" Wil said over me.

I looked at him from between my fingers.

"—is that wherever it leads, it isn't here." He looked me in the eye and said, "We're fairly positive it's not on this planet."

I dropped my hands and sat up straight. I wasn't completely surprised, but it was still a little shocking to hear him say it so matter-of-factly.

He nodded. "We don't know if it's another planet, another dimension, hell it could be some alternate universe for all we know. But we're reasonably certain it's not here."

"Reasonably certain?"

"Well, I mean, technically, it's possible it's a magically

crafted area somewhere on Earth, but no one really thinks so because it would take way more talent to create something like that than people actually have. Someone also floated an argument that it's a pocket dimension, anchored to this planet, but the main consensus is that, even if that were the case, it's still not part of the Earth, so it counts as not here."

"I see." My mind raced, trying to scramble through the possible implications. I slid a quick glance to Fuzzy, who was watching me closely.

Wherever "not here" was, Boots had asked Fuzzy if he wanted to go home when he sent Fuzzy through the door. So somehow, Fuzzy had gotten from "not here" to Bayley without anyone noticing. And "not here" wasn't Earth, so that meant that Fuzzy was…oh dear.

Wil was watching me think, which didn't seem like a good idea, so I said, "So you don't know where it goes, precisely. How did you find out about the seeds?"

"We don't know—"

"Oh for the love—"

"Just wait. We don't know how, exactly, the first Foster found out about them, we just know that she did. And every Housekeeper since has been tasked with retrieving them."

"Lucky us." I rubbed at the ache forming from my crinkled forehead. "So, to sum up, you don't know much. Do you know who put the door here or why? Or when?"

"The who and why, no. But the when corresponds to the first records of Bayley."

Well, that made sense, since the door was in the house. A thought occurred to me. "Wait. I thought we—the Fosters—made Bayley. Did we make Bayley?"

My eyes widened as I took in his expression, and I said, "Oh no. You don't know do you?" at the same time as Wil said, "We don't know."

I checked in with Bayley. He was being very quiet, but he was riveted on our conversation.

You and I are gonna have to talk about this, I said to Bayley in my head.

He was suspiciously quiet.

"Well, this has been about as enlightening as sitting in a cave at night, praying for a candle," I said. "Is there anything useful you can tell me? Anything at all?"

"I can tell you how to open the door," he said. Then added, "Without killing yourself." He gave me his slightly patronizing professor smile. "My guess is, you've been doing it wrong, that's why you've gotten hurt."

It took a real effort, but I held onto the "no duh" I wanted to hurl at him and managed a nod instead.

That was all the encouragement Wil needed. He leaned forward, eyes alight with eagerness. "Finn, I'm sure that you can do this. No doubt in my mind at all. You just need to learn the process and to get some confidence in using your skills."

Then he put a hand on my arm and said, "One of the reasons I want to work with you, Finn, is that I think you and I have a real opportunity here. By working together, we can expand our understanding of the…DeeDee. With my research skills and your Housekeeper skills, we can thoroughly study the situation from a modern perspective, in a way that hasn't been done in years."

A feeling of concern from Bayley made me ask, "Why hasn't it been done in years?"

Wil didn't meet my eyes as he said, "Well, in the past, opening the door has been somewhat of a drain on the Housekeeper and the house. Not the kind of serious drain you've been experiencing," he added quickly. "But still, a drain. However, I feel confident with me to guide you, we can mitigate any effects that you experience and really make the most of this opportunity."

"That's a nice idea, but I think you're getting a little ahead of yourself."

"You're absolutely right," Wil said. He sat back and rubbed his hands together as he said, "So let's get right to it then. Let's crack open that door."

Chapter Fifty-Five

An hour, ten pages of notes, and a massive hand cramp later, we still hadn't moved from the kitchen table. It turned out that Wil's idea of "cracking open the door" had more to do with cracking open my brain with an endless lecture than with actually touching DeeDee.

That was okay. I wasn't about to experiment with opening the door in front of him anyway, so it saved me from having to kick him out while I tried.

Wil was convinced that my lack of foundational instruction in magic was my main stumbling block. So instead of giving me the hands-on practicum I'd been expecting, he gave me a lecture, crammed with so many details that my head was swimming after the first ten minutes.

But by the time we were finished, I had a step-by-step simple technique to use to help me open the door. Wil then spent another full fifteen minutes admonishing me that I needed to complete every last inch of the mountain of homework he'd given me before he'd even consider letting me try opening DeeDee using the technique he'd given me.

Wil had to hurry off to a meeting, thank the book gods, or we probably would've been at it all day. Before he left, he said, "I'll see you at five for the, well, you know," patted me on the shoulder in what I think was supposed to be sympathy, and headed to his car.

I shut the door behind him and leaned back against it.

As I listened to him drive away, I said to Bayley, "Is any of that going to help?"

Bayley gave me the equivalent of a mental shrug. I had the feeling that it was up to me whether I could make Wil's suggestions work or not.

With a sigh, I tromped back down the hallway and stood in front of DeeDee. She didn't look particularly demonic.

Maybe it was a sign of how agitated I was about Sadie, or Neil, or the Grack, or all of the above, but as I stared at DeeDee, the insanity of the last couple days—and the crazy that was going to take place in a few hours—started spinning around in my head.

I just wanted control over *something*.

And DeeDee was something I could control.

Potentially.

Bayley moaned softly.

"Thanks for the vote of confidence, pal."

I checked my mental map. Nor and Mila were upstairs, Carmine was outside, and Eagan and Sadie must've still been at Zo's because they weren't on the property.

Fuzzy padded over and sat next to me, so close he was nearly sitting on my foot.

I looked down at him.

He looked up at me and said, "Meow."

"What do you think? Should I give it a go?"

He looked at the door, looked at me, and then washed a paw.

"What is it with you two? You're supposed to be supporting me, not throwing shade my way. Jeesh."

I went into the kitchen, grabbed my stack of notes, and returned to standing in front of the door.

I was still standing there reading through them when Mila came down the front steps and joined me.

"What are we doing?" she asked, standing next to me and staring at the door.

I flapped my sheath of papers at her. "We're seeing if this technique Wil just gave me is good for anything more than paper cuts."

Mila nodded and looked thoughtful. "I see. And is this a good time for that?"

"Oh come on. Not you too."

She raised her hands in surrender. "Just asking." She paused and then said, "Need any help?"

"Nope. Just need a few minutes alone."

"Got it." Mila popped into the kitchen for a few minutes. I spent the time reading my notes and trying to visualize Wil's instructions.

Mila exited the kitchen with a stack of food and some sodas. "Working lunch," she said as she squeezed by me, adding "Have fun!"

"Thanks," I said. "Um," I called after her retreating back, "would one of you mind checking on me in, say, half an hour, if you haven't heard from me? Just in case."

"No problem," she called as she trotted up the stairs.

As I put the stack of notes on the floor, Fuzzy moved to stand back a few paces, clearing the space between me and DeeDee.

"Okay, lady. Let's make friends."

I scooched closer until I could reach out and touch the door easily, adjusting my stance so that I was standing the way I remembered Boots standing in front of the door, careful to keep my weight balanced evenly. Closing my eyes, I pictured the door in front of me. I reached out and put my hand flat against the door.

This was the tricky part. I couldn't picture what was beyond the door because I hadn't actually seen it yet. But I remembered what the energy of the door felt like and I pictured that.

Of course remembering the energy of the door meant remembering how it felt to be nearly fried by it—twice. My palms got all sweaty, my heart hammered in my chest, and my mouth went dry with just this small bit of contact.

Fuzzy meowed behind me, and Bayley whined in concern.

I tried to steady my breathing, realizing this was where Wil's technique might help. I practiced the sequence he'd given me, counting my inhales and exhales until I could breathe past the panic clawing at my chest.

I focused my attention on the way the door felt under my fingertips. Then I reached out with my mind, trying to see if I could sense anything else. All I sensed was the door, which was to say, I sensed Bayley, since the door was part of him.

I frowned, chewing on my lip, and then I had an idea. Instead of focusing on the door itself, I tried feeling for what was behind the door.

At first, I didn't feel anything. But then Bayley gave me a little nudge, and I remembered this wasn't all about me. I needed him if I was going to do this. I visualized reaching out a hand to him. He answered back with an image of clasping my hand with a golden, glowing energy.

I let that energy flow through me as I refocused my attention on the door. I felt the wood, scratchy under my fingertips, then I pushed beyond that feeling.

For one breathless second, there was darkness.

Then all of a sudden I could see it.

Hidden beyond the wooden door, a door of pure energy pulsed. Light skittered and danced across its surface.

I gasped, dropping my hand and opening my eyes in surprise. I let out a delighted whoop and danced around in a circle for a few seconds, celebrating my victory.

Bayley and Fuzzy watched me with amusement.

I calmed myself enough to go back to DeeDee and try again. This time, I knew what I was looking for, so I was able to see it much faster.

I slid my hand down to the doorknob, grasping it without turning it. I felt for the connection between the physical handle in my hand and the phantom handle of the energy door that I could only see. When I found it, I slowly turned the doorknob.

Both doorknobs turned. On the first try.

My eyes sprang open as green light flared around the edges of the door.

"Stop! Stop! Stop!"

Startled, I lost my focus, and my connection with the energy door snapped. The ghost image of the door vanished at the same time the green light guttered and went out.

With an aggravated growl, I let go of the doorknob, stepped back from the door, and hauled my necklace out from under my shirt. It was glowing bright blue.

Percy sounded for all the world like he was panting, and the glow from the necklace was pulsing in time to the panicked breathing. Since as far as I knew he didn't have a body, never mind lungs, I wasn't sure if the panting was for effect.

As I was looking down at the necklace, I caught sight of Fuzzy looking up at it. He looked as perplexed as I felt.

I glared at the necklace and said, "Seriously Percy? What?"

"Get me away from the door." Percy's voice shook a little, and something about the sheer amount of desperation in it made me think he wasn't faking. When he added, "Please," my eyebrows hiked up so high they nearly got altitude sickness.

With a sigh, I did as Percy asked and walked away from the door and into the kitchen. I pulled the necklace over my head and set it on the kitchen block. Fuzzy hopped up and sat next to it.

"What's going on?" I asked Percy.

When he didn't respond immediately, Fuzzy nudged the necklace with his paw.

"Alright, alright. No need to get rough." But then Percy didn't say anything further. Fuzzy lifted his paw after a few seconds, but before he could bat at the necklace again, Percy said, "I'm thinking! Give me a minute!"

"Think faster please. I haven't got a lot of time." And a glance at the clock told me that was all too true.

After a long minute, Percy said in a quiet voice, "You can't wear me when you open the door."

"Why not? I was wearing you the other times I tried to open it."

"Yeah, but you weren't doing it correctly. You had no chance of actually opening it properly and keeping it open."

That brought me up straight. An icy chill traveled up my spine and came out in my voice when I said, "You knew I wasn't opening it properly?"

Percy sounded a little worried when he said, "Yes."

"I see." I drummed my fingers on the butcher block. "And did it not occur to you to tell me? Or to try to help me? Because you have to know that opening it wrong nearly killed me. Twice."

Percy said, "It's...it...wasn't—isn't—in my best interests for you to open the door."

"I see." I did not see. And now I trusted Percy even less. I stared at the necklace as I sorted through my thoughts.

Percy said, "What are you thinking?"

"I'm wondering if locking you in a drawer would count as punishment or a vacation for you."

"Very amusing."

"You think I'm joking?"

"I'm already trapped in a necklace. Putting me in a drawer is kind of overkill, don't you think?"

I tilted my head. That was new information. "Trapped? You're not in there voluntarily? Trapped how? And why?"

Percy muttered, "I don't want to talk about it."

"Well you'd better talk about something useful, or you're looking at a long stay in a dark box. Right now, I can't think of a single reason that I should keep wearing you, er, the necklace." Other than the fact that it would hurt something fierce to let go of this last link to my mom, but I wasn't about to mention that.

"I'm too useful to leave in a box," Percy said primly.

Which, unfortunately, was true. Although I could just take the necklace out when I needed Percy's help.

"You're not talking," Percy said after a long moment.

"I'm waiting."

I heard a soft sigh. "You can't open the door while you're wearing me."

"You said that already."

"It would be...bad." Percy added quickly, "For you, too. Not just for me."

"Bad? Bad how?"

"I'm...noticeable."

"Noticeable."

"Now that I'm awake. I'm noticeable, yes."

"I see," although I still didn't, not really. I said, "And that's not a good thing?"

"No." Was that a hint of regret I heard in Percy's voice? "Not good. For either of us."

"Noticeable how? And who or what is going to notice you?"

Percy didn't say anything.

Fuzzy whapped it with his paw.

Percy said, "You can whack me all you want. I've told you what you need to know."

"Have you? Really?"

Fuzzy thwacked the necklace harder, and Percy burst out with, "It's dangerous! Don't you understand? Really dangerous!" In a slightly calmer voice, he added, "Just...take the necklace off when you open the door. That's all I'm asking." In a pleading voice, he added, "Please."

The truth was, my general annoyance with Percy aside, it wasn't a difficult request to fulfill, and it wouldn't cost me anything to take the necklace off when I opened the door.

"Okay," I said.

"Thank you."

"But you have to answer one more question."

It was a sign of how desperate Percy was that he didn't even argue. "Yes."

"Why are you awake now? You didn't seem to be awake before." In all the years I'd been wearing the necklace, Percy hadn't said a peep to me until I'd come to the house.

"I wasn't. I haven't been in a long time. You woke me up, when you fed me your blood."

"I did not!"

"You did. In the cell. You fed me. I woke up, and I helped you escape the cell."

My mind scurried back to when Sarah had me locked up. I'd been covered in blood at the time. My necklace had been caked in it.

"It wasn't on purpose," I said.

Percy didn't reply. I guess it didn't matter whether it was on purpose or not, now Percy was awake and I had to deal with him.

"Are you going to go back to sleep?" I asked.

To my surprise, Percy answered. In a quiet voice, both haunted and regretful, he said, "I'm fairly certain the time of rest has ended."

Before I could follow up on that comment, Zo blipped onto my mental map. Since she was zipping down my driveway along with red and blue dots, I assumed she was driving Eagan and Sadie to Bayley House.

I said to Percy, "We'll talk more about this later."

Of course, he didn't respond.

With a sigh, I put the necklace back on and went to greet the arrivals.

As I walked outside to meet them, I did a quick inventory. Rather than feeling drained the way I usually did when I tried to open DeeDee, I felt fine. A little bit tired, sure, but also a little exhilarated by my success. Bayley seemed fine, too. It made me hopeful that I could actually handle DeeDee after all.

I met Zo's car when it pulled up in front of the house.

Eagan and Sadie piled out, and Eagan said, "She wants to talk to you."

Zo didn't get out of the car, so I dutifully walked around to the driver's side window and said, "You rang?"

"Your Sadie plan sucks."

I didn't disagree, but it still stung to hear it stated so baldly. "I'm aware," I said.

"New plan. They'll explain. I'm pretty sure it'll work. Just go with it. And don't mess it up."

And with that helpful bit of advice, she rolled up the window and drove away.

Chapter Fifty-Six

One family confab, some hasty MacGyvering, and a pot of coffee later, we were ready for Operation Sadie Killer.

While the others scurried off to their assigned tasks, I grabbed my coat and went out on the front porch.

Mila had flown the helicopter off the lawn, leaving the grove in front of the house empty. The sun was already low in the sky, so that the front lawn was painted in the soft golds that preceded twilight.

I'd thought it was a little on the nose to do away with Sadie at sunset, but I'd been overruled.

Fuzzy hopped up on the porch railing next to me, while I wrapped my arms around Bayley's porch post, resting my forehead against the wood.

"You sure you're up for this?" I said into the post.

The entire porch chirruped around me. I raised an eyebrow. "Glad you think this is exciting." I shook my head. "You've been spending too much time with Mila."

Bayley wiggled the porch boards so that they giggled at me.

I looked at Fuzzy. "You know I'm counting on you to keep an eye on the things that I can't."

Fuzzy reached out a paw and patted my arm. It made me feel better.

A pile of blue dots blipped onto my map. Two cars' worth, judging from the spacing. A car full of green dots followed.

Bayley boomed out three loud knocks that echoed through the house and out onto the grounds, signaling everyone that we had incoming.

Nor joined me on the porch. Where I'd dressed for comfort in jeans, a sweater, and peacoat, she'd dressed for clout. She wore a long, camel-colored coat and an exquisitely tailored suit underneath.

I looked at her feet and smiled. "Boots for butt-kicking?"

Nor grinned. "Damn right. Shall we?"

Nor, Fuzzy, and I walked over to stand in the middle of the driveway to the left of the house, by the parking area. As I walked, Bayley heaved a grassy mound across one side of the driveway, which would force the cars to drive over to the parking area.

An SUV pulled into the grove, stopped, then drove toward me. A large passenger van trailed it, followed by another SUV.

I waved the cars toward the parking area, and all three vehicles parked as instructed.

A little voice in my head tried to convince me that it was a good sign that they were following directions. Maybe everyone would behave. My gut told the little voice to go back to dreamland where it belonged.

The Murphys and Fosters swarmed out of their respective vehicles, and I fought down a nervous giggle. They reminded me a little too much of a bunch of clowns piling out of clown cars.

Nor nodded to the Murphys milling around Kate and said quietly, "One lawyer, three low-level magic users that are more like bodyguards, and the other ten are Offensive Wizards—um, OWs—of varying skill sets."

I smiled at Nor as she used my acronym. I'd taken to calling the Offensive Wizards "OWs" and the Improvised Enchantments they cast as "OWIEs."

Looking at the Murphys, I was betting the three guys that were sporting an impressive amount of muscle were the bodyguards. It seemed a little ridiculous that they also could use magic when they were that muscled-up. Talk about overkill.

Not that the Fosters were any better. They'd brought two big muscle dudes of their own.

Nor tipped her head toward the Fosters that Wil was corralling and murmured, "One lawyer, two low-level magic-user bodyguards, three OWs representing the Council.

I grimaced. Of course the Council would insist on having a presence.

Studying the assembled group, I had to stop myself from shaking my head at them all in disgust. Murphy OWs. Foster OWs. We were being overrun by MOW-FOWs, and there was nothing I could do about it.

Wil took the lead of the flock of Fosters.

Kate took the lead of the murder of Murphys.

Both led their groups toward me.

I held up a hand in a stop gesture. Thankfully, they stopped.

"Hi," I said. "I'd say thanks for coming, but I think everyone's pretty clear on how unhappy I am about this situation."

Wil tensed and gave me a warning look. I ignored it and waved my arm toward the front lawn and said, "This way please."

Kate and Wil exchanged a look.

"Finn," Wil said.

"It's freezing," said Kate. "You can't possibly expect us to stand around outside."

"Oh, on top of forcing this extradition and flaunting your extreme prejudice, you thought all you Murphys were going to get treated to a visit inside the house?" I asked. I could see from the looks the Murphys were exchanging that was exactly what they thought. I wondered if that was why so many of them had turned up.

"Sorry. No. I'm being forced to agree to this, but in no universe am I allowing you...people...inside Bayley." I said "people" in a way I hoped made clear that I meant "asshats."

To my surprise, my statement earned me some approving looks from the Fosters. Right up until I added, "You either." At their looks of shock, I said, "You're forcing me to go through with this just as much as they are. No treats for you either."

I could see Nor nodding out of the corner of my eye. She stared down a few Fosters who looked like they were going to object.

Wil looked pained, but I ignored him and pointed to the grassy front lawn again and said, "This way please."

Kate crossed her arms. "This is unacceptable. It's too cold."

"I've taken care of that. Eagan?" I called.

Bayley opened and closed the door for Eagan, who jogged down to meet us.

Kate looked appalled. "Not him again. You brought a Smith?"

Eagan beamed at her. "Personally, I figured you'd feel right at home in the frigid weather. But Finn thought otherwise."

Kate's face turned an interesting shade of red, but before she could find a retort, Nor said, "It's the Housekeeper's right to have impartial witnesses."

Kate opened her mouth to say something, closed it, and looked back over her shoulder. The Murphy that Nor had indicated was the lawyer nodded at Kate, confirming that Nor was right. As he caught Nor's eye, he gave her a single nod of respect, which she returned.

Not to be left out, the guy Nor had identified as the Foster lawyer said, "I concur."

Kate huffed in annoyance and crossed her arms.

"Yippee, now that everyone's on the same page, this way please." I swept my arm toward the lawn again.

As I pivoted to face the lawn, I said loudly enough that everyone could hear, "Bayley, if you please?"

We could have prepared ahead of time, but we'd decided a show of strength would be a good idea, and Bayley had eagerly agreed to help. In fact, he had made it clear to me that he wanted to make this particular creation on his own, leaving me to focus on the assembled group.

I could practically see him rubbing his hands together with glee as a huge, wide, wooden pole popped up out of the exact middle of the lawn.

The pole split into sections that bent down toward the ground like the peel on a banana. Each peel flowed outward across the lawn, and they all stopped equidistant from the center pole, looking like the spokes on a bicycle wheel. Then the individual spokes widened until they butted up against each other. Within moments, Bayley had formed a perfectly circular platform that stretched fifty feet from side to side.

It should have looked roughshod at best, but instead it was arrestingly beautiful. The wood itself was a rich, warm maple-syrup color that glowed softly in the fading sunlight. And each spoke of wood had a vine-and-leaf design running up the middle.

But Bayley wasn't done yet. A railing sprouted up from the edges. It mirrored the vine-and-leaf pattern on the floor, the vines twining and wrapping in a delicate, intricate pattern to form the railing.

I couldn't suppress the small smile that sprang to my lips. The vine-and-leaf pattern was Bayley's private message to me that if these bozos got out of hand, he was ready to bind them in ivy and haul them off the property.

I sent Bayley a mental, *Thank you! That's beautiful. You outdid yourself. Just look at their faces.*

Behind me, the Murphys and Fosters were staring at Bayley's creation in stunned silence.

Bayley sent me the mental equivalent of a mischievous grin.

I glanced at Nor who shot me an approving look back.

I nodded, squared my shoulders, and marched across the lawn toward the platform.

Bayley had left one opening in the railing, and that was what I walked toward.

Nor, Fuzzy, and Eagan came with me, and the Murphys and Fosters trailed behind us. I wasn't sure if it was nerves, but I had to fight back the urge to snicker at how much they reminded me of a bunch of ducklings waddling after their mom.

I stepped onto the platform and walked to the middle. Where the initial pole had sprouted, there was now a round, flat circle, just big enough for me, Nor, and Fuzzy to stand on.

Eagan went to the far side of the platform and turned so that he was facing me and Bayley. At my nod, he raised his hands and started whispering his spell. Immediately, the air on the platform warmed.

As he worked, I turned my back to Eagan, so I could face Bayley and watch the Murphys and Fosters as they filed onto the platform.

As they entered, they split into family groups, with the Murphys on my right and the Fosters on my left.

It was like they had rehearsed this all before. There was no milling about. Everyone seemed to know exactly what they were doing.

The thought that they'd done this before made my stomach drop. How often did they do extraditions with extreme prejudice?

Each group backed themselves close to the railing, leaving a wide, open space between them and my little group in the center.

With both families on either side in front of me, I could see everyone. That left Eagan as the only person behind me—both families gave him such a wide berth that it was like they thought he had cooties. I felt reassured to have him at my back, which was likely what Mila intended when she suggested where he should stand.

Nor stood next to me on my left, so I could easily catch her eye if needed. Fuzzy sat by my right foot, watching everything closely.

Kate walked forward from the Murphys, and Wil came forward from the Fosters. They stopped in front of me, a good ten feet from each other, and about ten feet from me, so that we formed a big triangle.

The Murphy lawyer moved to stand a few feet away from Kate, and the Foster lawyer mirrored him, moving to stand a few feet from Wil.

Kate said, "As representative of the Murphy family, I claim the right of extradition with extreme prejudice."

Wil responded, "Whom do you claim?"

"Sadafea Carsey Murphy."

Wil said, "So noted. The Foster family recognizes your claim and agrees to surrender Sadafea Carsey Murphy into your custody," he paused and his eyes slid to me with an apology in them, before flicking back to Kate to add, "for extradition with extreme prejudice."

Nor said, "Out of respect for the Housekeeper and Bayley House, the Murphys agree to exercise the 'extreme prejudice' portion of the extradition once they have exited the property."

All the Murphys said, "Agreed," at the same time.

Nor looked at the Foster contingent. They said, "Agreed," at the same time.

Kate said, "In exchange for our restraint—"

"Lack of any and all violence," Nor corrected.

Kate looked put upon, but her lawyer nodded. All the lawyers had worked out the wording for this fun-fest ahead of time, and Kate knew it.

"Fine, whatever. In exchange for 'lack of any and all violence' on the property, the Housekeeper and the House agree not to interfere."

She didn't even bother to use Bayley's name. I clenched my fists and counted to ten.

"Agreed," said Wil and the Foster clan, a bit too quickly.

"Agreed," said the Murphys.

Then everyone looked at me.

I swept the group with my best you-should-be-ashamed-of-yourselves look, before I growled, "So be it."

Nor looked at me and nodded.

Mentally, I gave Bayley the go-ahead, and he opened the front door again.

Sadie stepped outside.

Head held high, she descended the porch and strode across the lawn.

I felt a kind of awe as I looked at her strutting toward us. There was no hesitation, no noticeable fear whatsoever. So much confidence was radiating off her that she could have been stomping her way across a runway.

As Sadie mounted the platform, a ripple went through the assembled crowd as both the Fosters and Murphys tensed at the same time.

I shot them another dirty look and walked forward to hug Sadie as she neared Wil and Kate. She stiffened in surprise but then hugged me back.

"I'm so sorry you have to go through this," I said into her hair.

She nodded once, and I stepped back.

"Are you ready?" I asked.

She sent a truly terrifying grin toward the Murphys and said, "Yes."

A few of them flinched backwards. It made me smile.

I walked back to stand next to Nor again, leaving Sadie standing with Wil on one side and Kate on the other.

When I reached Nor, I swallowed hard, then turned to glare at Kate. "Here she is," I said, slicing a hand toward Sadie.

Kate looked Sadie up and down and shook her head. "Had to make it difficult, didn't you? And you swear you're a good Murphy. You're a disgrace to the family name."

A few of the Murphys, and to my dismay, a few of the Fosters nodded in agreement. I shook my head in disgust.

Sadie just grinned wider. "Your turn will come, Kate."

Kate's smile was hard enough to cut a diamond. "Not likely."

"Well this is fun and all," I said, "but I don't need to hear you insult Sadie. So let's just get on with it already."

Kate opened her mouth to say something, but she never got the chance.

I heard an alarm go off in my head and then the sky near the entrance to the grove abruptly clouded over.

A torrent of rain poured from the sky, and Gram stepped into the grove.

Chapter Fifty-Seven

Everyone spun to watch as Gram made his entrance.

The tension radiating from the Murphys and Fosters ratcheted up so much that I felt like I could reach out and twang it like a taut string on a bow.

I thought I'd seen Gram angry before, but nothing I'd seen so far compared to the sheer rage exploding off him as he stalked to the platform.

I let out a low whistle. Shaking my head at Kate, I stage-whispered, "He look mad to you? Cuz he looks kind of mad to me."

Kate's jaw was clenched so hard that she looked in danger of cracking some teeth.

It took me a moment to realize that the big, black rain cloud had stopped raining but was following Gram across the lawn.

I looked at Nor and darted my eyes between the cloud and Gram.

"Is that normal?" I whispered.

She gave a scant shake of her head. Then whispered back, her lips barely moving, "Show of power. That takes enormous control."

As Gram approached the back of the platform, Bayley unbraided some of the branches in the railing, making an entrance for Gram to walk through. Normally, Bayley and I would have gotten a lot of satisfaction out of making Gram walk the long way around. It said a lot about how crappy things were that Bayley was trying to make Gram's life easier.

Eagan shifted out of the way to let Gram pass. Gram stepped onto the platform, gave Eagan a nod, and then stalked forward. He nodded at me and Nor as he passed us, then went to stand next to Sadie.

Once Gram reached Sadie, his cloud stopped above him. It was already twilight and adding the cloud made it suddenly much darker, giving the whole platform a funereal feel.

I shivered at the thought.

Bayley closed the railing again, and Eagan resumed his spot at my back.

Gram stared down the assembled Fosters, then the Murphys. A lot of foot shuffling, arm crossing, and looking away ensued, especially from the Murphys. Eventually, Gram's glare landed on Kate. He gave her a look of utter disgust then turned his back on her, effectively dismissing her, and focused on Sadie.

A flicker of some emotion flashed in Kate's eyes, but she quashed it fast.

To Sadie, Gram said, "Are you okay?"

"For the moment," she said.

Gram kept his eyes on Sadie as he said in a loud voice that boomed across the platform, "It's my right to attend. Why wasn't I informed?"

Kate glanced at the Murphy lawyer, who said, "It wasn't deemed advisable. You may, of course, issue a legal objection to the procedures that are followed today. *After* we've concluded."

And by "after" he meant "once Sadie's dead and there's nothing you can do about it." I wanted to ask what the point was, but Nor gave me a small shake of her head.

I took a small bit of comfort when Gram said, "Oh I will, you can count on it" and all the Murphys collectively winced. Whatever legal action he was going to take, apparently it wouldn't be pleasant.

I looked at Gram and I said, "I'm sorry. This sucks."

He nodded.

There was an awkward moment where nobody said anything, then Kate stepped forward and said, "It's time."

The Murphy and Foster lawyers backed away from Kate and Wil.

The three muscular Murphy bodyguards moved up to bracket Kate, with one behind her and one on each side. The MOWs split into two groups of five and raised their hands to indicate they were ready to zap Sadie with some OWIEs if needed. They moved in unison, reminding me of a bunch of people doing tai chi.

Gram said, "Sadie," and reached for her.

Sadie took a step toward Gram.

And the Murphys let loose.

Or at least they tried to.

As the MOWs began gesticulating, Sadie stepped forward and raised her own hands, murmuring at the same time.

It took me a moment to realize that Sadie was utilizing her Murphy-neutralizing desiccant skills. Nobody could summon any water. Not Kate, not Gram, and certainly not the MOWs. Oh, the MOWs were gesturing frantically, but the moment they managed to gather even a droplet, Sadie made it disappear again.

It would've been funny if the situation weren't so dire.

And I knew it couldn't last. Sadie was only delaying the inevitable. Still drained and wounded from her last battle, she couldn't hold the MOWs and their OWIEs at bay for long. The best she could do was run down their batteries so they wouldn't be as strong.

The MOWs doubled-down on their efforts, and I could see the physical strain on Sadie. But she was making the MOWs pay as well. Faces beaded with sweat, the MOWs were in various states of distress, some grimacing with pain, some looking like they were going to barf, and at least one dripping blood from his nose.

Two of the MOWs stepped toward Sadie, their faces creased with effort.

Sadie flung one of her arms toward them, and both crumpled to the ground unconscious.

But it cost her. "Gram—" Sadie squeezed out.

He nodded, and she released her no-water-for-anyone spell with a gasp.

The remaining MOWs struggled for a few moments, but they rallied. With an effort, they managed to conjure a collection of wicked-looking water darts and heaved them as hard as they could. One second the air was clear. The next, a barrage of deadly darts hurtled at Sadie and Gram.

With a howl, Bayley zoomed me, Nor, Fuzzy, Wil, Eagan, and the Fosters out of the way. We shot away from the action, the platform underneath us growing so fast that we zipped several feet across the lawn, out of range, in an instant. I felt it coming, so I grabbed Nor and braced, but Wil and the Fosters all fell over with a bunch of satisfying thuds.

Fuzzy, of course, remained perfectly balanced.

I looked back behind me to see that Eagan was clinging to the railing, still on his feet.

I didn't waste time seeing if any of the Fosters were hurt. I spun around and focused on the action, now a good twenty feet away.

Even at my distance from the MOWs, I could see the looks of frustration and exhaustion on some of their faces.

Sadie might not be able to totally disable the MOWs, but she wasn't completely out of juice either. She was using her desiccant powers to dismantle the onslaught of water darts. Any dart that had any chance of reaching her or Gram evaporated before it could get anywhere near them. The rest of the darts went wide and crashed into the platform with loud "thunk-thunk, thunk-thunks" that reminded me of gunfire.

While Sadie took care of the MOWs, Gram faced off with Kate, running interference so she couldn't get at Sadie. Now that Sadie wasn't blocking her access, Kate was summoning entire walls of water. With a swipe of her hand, she sent each wall slamming toward Sadie, but Gram stood in the way, swiping with his hand and sending the water crashing harmlessly to the side.

Every time Kate swiped a new water wall toward Gram, he swiped it away.

It was the weirdest version of "wax on, wax off" that I'd ever seen.

After several rounds of water darts failed to get by Sadie, some of the MOWs decided to switch tactics. While a few kept Sadie busy by heaving more darts at her, the others tried something new. I stood there, gaping, as whips made of water appeared in the air. Kate stopped casting water walls, dashing out of range as the water whips slashed toward Gram and Sadie.

Unbidden, Devo's "Whip It" started playing in my head, providing the world's most inappropriate soundtrack to the fight.

Sadie continued to make any water darts that neared them disintegrate, while Gram swiped the whips out of the way, so they lashed the platform instead of him or Sadie.

Bayley? Are you okay? I frantically thought at him as I watched the water smashing into the platform. I was tempted to throw the plan to the wind and toss all the Murphys out, ending the madness.

He gave me a cheery *Ding* and focused my attention on Sadie, reminding me who we were there for in the first place, so I gritted my teeth and stood my ground. As planned, I didn't interfere.

Watching Gram and Sadie, I couldn't help but be amazed seeing them work in tandem, disarming their brethren with stunning efficiency. It took me a second to realize that beside Sadie's first desiccant spell, neither of them had launched offensive spells back. I wasn't sure if that was because they were too busy reacting to the onslaught, or if they were pulling their punches in an attempt to protect their family.

Two of the MOWs near the back caught my eye. I was startled to realize they were entirely focused on aiming spells at the cloud above Gram, and it suddenly occurred to me that they were trying to keep him from grabbing Sadie and leaving.

My gaze shifted to the muscle guys around Kate when they moved to face outward from her, acting as shields and blocking anything that came her way.

That brought my attention to Kate. She stood still, but I could see her lips moving, her hands twitching at her sides, as she stared at Sadie.

"Stop," I hollered, but no one listened to me. I wasn't even sure they could hear me over all the water crashing about.

Then Kate raised an arm in the air. It must've been some kind of signal because three MOWs broke off assaulting Gram and Sadie to focus on her.

I hauled on my and Bayley's magic and yelled, "Sadie!" To my shock, my voice rang out as though it had been amplified by a bullhorn. Sadie looked at me, and I waved frantically toward Kate.

Kate circled her hand in the air. While the two MOWs who were on cloud duty kept up their barrage, and the three helping Kate stood watching her, the three remaining MOWs grouped together and hit Gram with a hurricane of whipping water bullets, forcing him to defend himself and turn from Kate.

Sadie stepped toward Kate, putting herself between Kate and Gram.

Smiling at Sadie, Kate sent up a small fountain of water.

It acted like a liquid signal flare.

Kate's three waiting MOWs jumped into action. One whipped a band of water around Sadie's mouth, while simultaneously another wrapped a band around her arms, pinning them to her sides, and the third wrapped a band around her legs, snapping them together.

I could see holes appearing in each of the restraints as Sadie evaporated sections of them, but the MOWs filled them in as fast as she could make them.

As the three MOWs fought to keep Sadie bound, Kate raised both hands, mouthing something as she sliced both hands down.

A huge cage of water slammed down on Sadie.

My brain tried to make sense of what I was seeing. It reminded me of a Houdini-style water escape box, without the box. She was walled in, underwater, but the water was just standing there on its own.

Sadie pummeled the box with her magic, disappearing chunks of water until it looked like it was being eaten by acid. But Kate kept filling in the holes as Sadie struggled to make them.

Sadie looked like she was struggling to raise her arms, and I could see her mouth moving, but she was underwater so she couldn't really speak.

The next part happened lightning fast, like someone pressed time's fast-forward button.

The water started to compress, shrinking and squeezing Sadie.

I saw her throw back her head and open her mouth to scream.

"Stop!" I shrieked and started running forward.

Gram yelled, desperately holding off the five MOWs targeting him by tossing up a water shield with one hand while he threw out a hand toward Sadie.

Kate flung both her hands toward Sadie.

For a frozen instant, I could see Gram and Kate, hands extended, flinging their magic toward Sadie, caged in the shrinking water cube between them.

There was a huge surge of magic.

Then the water cube exploded.

Chapter Fifty-Eight

The force of the explosion slammed into me, knocking me backward, and drenching me as water sprayed outward.

Bayley softened the platform where I landed, cushioning my fall.

Still, as he re-solidified the platform under me, I was too stunned to try to stand. I sat dazed on the platform, blinking and dripping, my ears ringing.

A red mist drifted in the air. The platform in front of me was coated in a red spray. When I looked down, I was covered in red droplets.

There were a lot of them.

I spent a few seconds trying to count how many before Bayley sent me a gentle, reassuring nudge, telling me everything was okay.

Fuzzy, who had managed to keep totally dry, padded over and chirped at me. It helped me to look up and focus.

Despite Bayley's reassurance, everything was not okay.

Nor and Mila had prepped me extensively on what to expect, on what might happen, but as I wiped at my dripping face, and my hand came away red, my stomach lurched. This was so much more gruesome than anything I had imagined.

It took me a minute to realize that Nor and Eagan were standing over me, talking to me.

I felt a wave of concern from Bayley and a warm pulse of his magic, then my ears stopped ringing.

"—are you alright?" Eagan said as he squatted in front of me to look me in the eyes.

"Finn?" A concerned Nor leaned over me.

"How come you're not covered in...red?" I asked them.

"We were out of the blast range," Eagan said.

Nor looked behind her toward the Fosters, then looked back at me. Reaching a hand down for me, "Can you stand?"

From the way her eyes were shifting toward the Fosters, I gathered it would be a good idea if I didn't show any weakness. I was suddenly so furious that standing seemed like an excellent idea.

As I clambered to my feet, Nor and Eagan watched me with worry. When I stood up and got a good look at the entire platform, I kind of wished I'd stayed sitting.

A look behind me confirmed that the Fosters had formed themselves into a nice huddle where they were arguing and pointing toward me and the Murphys. It looked like Wil was frantically trying to calm everyone down.

All the Murphys were down, but the lawyer and some of the OWs were squirming and struggling to get up again.

In contrast, Kate, her bodyguards, the three OWs who'd been helping her, and Gram were all prone and unmoving. I had a terrified moment where I thought they might all be dead, but Bayley nudged them with his magic and reported back to me that they were all alive. How damaged, I had no idea, but alive.

That left one last thing to look at.

In between Kate and Gram, the only thing that remained of Sadie and the water cube was a big, red, wet spot.

A lot of loud emotions welled up, and I grabbed onto the loudest: anger.

"Ivy!" I snapped. I guess I said it louder than I intended because everyone who was moving froze.

Everyone but Bayley. In my mind, I directed him to bind all the moving Murphys.

The wooden vines and leaves in the platform's banister came alive. The banister unraveled into individual wooden vines that whipped around the platform, wrapping the dazed Murphys like mummies. Bayley made sure to cover their mouths and bind their hands, just in case anyone got spell-happy.

Given the amount of magic they'd all expended, I doubted

anyone could summon a raindrop at this point, but I wasn't taking any chances.

I turned to Eagan. "Can you please check on the ones that aren't getting up?"

Eagan, looking pale and a little ill, nevertheless nodded and trudged off toward Gram.

I spun to face the Fosters, not bothering to hide how angry I was. One look at my face, and they all went still.

I looked at Wil. "They going to behave, or do I have to bind them, too?"

A few of the Fosters gaped and looked offended, but Wil said, "We're good. We'll just stand here till we're needed." He shot a meaningful look at the group who all eventually nodded in agreement.

I turned back to the Murphys, trying not to wince at the fine red droplets coating everything. I looked at Nor and said, "Now what?"

"We need their lawyer."

I zeroed in on the ivy-cocooned lawyer and asked Bayley to bring him to me. Bayley shifted the lawyer onto a plank and raced him across the platform, stopping in front of me.

The lawyer looked back and forth between me and Nor, wide-eyed.

I asked Bayley to uncover his mouth then said, "If I let you out, will you behave?"

"Yes, of course."

"No magic."

He nodded.

Bayley unwrapped him by spinning him around a few times, so the lawyer stumbled to regain his balance before facing me.

I heard footsteps and huffing behind me, and the Foster lawyer came stomping up.

He started, "I should be—"

I turned my glare on him. "Did I or did I not just ask you if you could behave?"

He looked taken aback. He sputtered for a moment, then tried again with, "As a lawyer for the Council—"

"Oh buddy. Are you new? Wrong thing to say." I thumbed toward Nor. "She's my lawyer. Not you." I leaned forward, and he flinched back as I growled, "And as for what you and the Council can do—"

Nor put a hand on my shoulder. "Finn. It would be a good idea to allow the Council lawyer to act as a witness." She pinned him with a look that made him swallow hard. "He will, of course, follow protocol and act as a *silent* witness."

The lawyer looked back and forth between us, swallowed again. His sense of self-preservation must've kicked in because he nodded, stepping back slightly and folding his hands in front of him in fig-leaf position.

I turned to the Murphy lawyer who was trying hard not to smile.

I pointed over his shoulder to the bodies lying prone on the ground. Eagan was doing some sort of magic over Gram, but he didn't look overly alarmed at anything.

"Did you bring a medic?" I asked.

The Murphy lawyer shook his head. "No Housekeeper. We did not."

"Of course you didn't. This was supposed to be a *peaceful* exchange. In fact, this was supposed to *only* be an exchange. Did you or did you not agree to exercise the 'extreme prejudice' portion of your extradition *after* you left?"

"Yes Housekeeper, we did."

"I don't know about you, but this," I gestured to the red-covered platform and downed Murphys, then to my red-covered self, "looks pretty extreme to me."

He didn't respond.

I continued on, "And wasn't this supposed to be an extradition that had a," I looked at Nor, "what was it?"

"Lack of any and all violence."

"Lack of any and all violence, yes. And you Murphys *swore* to those stipulations. They signed a legal document, right?" I looked at the Foster lawyer who nodded and looked a little smug, and then at Nor who nodded as well.

She added, "Signed and magically notarized."

The Murphy lawyer winced a little but didn't waffle. "That is correct."

I pointed at the big red splat where Sadie had been, "Does that look like a lack of any and all violence to you?"

I spun on the Foster lawyer, who'd started grinning. "I don't know what you're smiling about, pal. You and the Council messed up. Again."

He sputtered, "I don't see how—"

I said, "Of course you don't—"

At the same time, Nor said, "The Foster Council agreed to, and indeed insisted upon, this extradition. Had you not caved to the Murphys' demands, we wouldn't be in this situation."

The lawyer looked like he was going to argue again when Nor said loudly, "By your actions, you and the Foster Council have put the Housekeeper and Bayley House in mortal jeopardy."

The Foster lawyer went pale, and the entire Foster contingent, who'd been listening in, reacted as if they'd just been slapped. There were looks of fear and shock on all of them.

Wil and the Murphy lawyer wore identical expressions. Both of them had hiked up their eyebrows and looked so grave you'd think we'd just sentenced them to life imprisonment.

Nor said, in the same loud, carrying voice, "This is a family matter. We'll discuss it later. But be sure, we *will* discuss it."

Then she shifted her gaze away from the Foster lawyer, who sagged a bit and took a half-step back. She turned her attention to the Murphy lawyer, who was watching her the same way you watch a coiled rattlesnake.

"As for the Murphys," she said.

The Murphy lawyer said, "You wish to discuss restitution?"

I rubbed my forehead and shook my head. "Are you nuts? Seriously, what's wrong with you? You have people unconscious and probably injured over there. You want to hammer out legalese now?" Before he could answer, I said, "What I *wish* was that none of this ever had to happen. But since that's off the table, how about you admit that you guys royally screwed up, apologize, get your people out of here, and agree to sort out the details later."

The Murphy lawyer said slowly, looking back and forth

between me and Nor, "You want an admission that we made a mistake?"

Nor said, "Not sufficient. For now, we want an admission that you are in full breach of contract."

Such a cold way to describe what just happened, but apparently it was sufficiently dire in the magical lawyer world because the Murphy lawyer's face shut down and went into poker-face mode.

"A moment, please," he said. Nor nodded, and the lawyer stared off into the distance. It looked like he was thinking through the ramifications. It would've been nice if he'd made the idiots in his family do that before anything had started. But oh well, if wishes were candy, I'd have been bouncing around the lawn on a sugar high right then.

While the Murphy lawyer thought, I looked at Eagan. He'd made his way to Kate and her bodyguards and was going from person to person doing...something. Neither they, the three downed OWs, or Gram were moving, so whatever he was doing wasn't fixing whatever was wrong.

The Murphy lawyer shifted, bringing my attention back to him. He looked between Nor and me and said, "Agreed. As the representative for the Murphy family, I agree that we are in breach of contract. How would you like to proceed?"

Nor looked at the disaster behind the lawyer and said, "Legal proceedings will have to wait until we're ready."

The Murphy lawyer nodded.

Eagan rejoined us to say, "They're all alive. I was able to keep them warm and comfortable, which should help keep them from going into full shock, but beyond that, there's not much I can do."

I looked at Nor and the Murphy lawyer. "Call some medics. I revoke the Murphys' invitation. I want all of you out of here as soon as possible." I turned to look at the Foster lawyer and then at Wil and the Fosters, "You guys, too. Everyone out. Now."

Chapter Fifty-Nine

Getting ambulances to the property took more time than I would have liked, but the Murphys stayed quietly in their cocoons, and the Murphy lawyer spent the whole time on his phone.

I hoped the Murphys were taking the time to think about what they'd done and to gain a new appreciation for the Smiths. They should have been counting their lucky stars that Eagan was there because it was full dark now and getting colder by the minute. The ambulances would've found a bunch of Murphysicles if Eagan hadn't kept his spell going.

Nor helped keep the dark at bay. She disappeared inside and came back out bearing industrial-strength lanterns that Mila armed her with, so at least we weren't sitting in the dark the whole time.

I guessed the Fosters decided the entertaining part was over because they let Wil pack them up and hustle them out without a fuss.

All the growling Bayley did probably helped.

On his way out, Wil came over to me. He looked me over and shook his head. "Finn, I'm so sorry. I…I don't even know where to start. I need some time to process all this." He shook his head again as he stared at the mess on the Murphy side. "I'll call you later to check on you, okay?"

"Sure, thanks," I said. If I sounded unenthusiastic, Wil couldn't really blame me.

While we waited for the medics to arrive, Nor, Eagan, and I stood near Gram's unconscious body and had a discussion. By the time the ambulances rolled in, we'd come to a decision.

The ambulances lined up around the circular driveway, forming a ring around the lawn. Bayley helpfully removed the barrier he'd put up earlier so they could exit easily. I unwrapped the OWs, and various paramedics loaded them into the lead ambulances.

Soon, the only Murphys left on the platform were Kate, the bodyguards, Gram, the lawyer, and five medics.

When a Murphy medic started working on Gram, we walked over to her.

"How bad is it?" I asked.

The medic shook her head. "He has a small lump from hitting his head when he went down, and a few of his ribs are bruised—no major breaks, but there may be some hairline fracturing. I'll need an x-ray to be sure. He's still unconscious due to massive magic drain. Hopefully, not enough to cause permanent damage."

I nodded. "And the others?" I swept my hand, taking in the ambulances as well as Kate and her bodyguards.

"Likely the same. Some bruising, maybe some minor breaks or sprains. Most everyone has various degrees of magic drain. Too soon to really know yet about any long-term damage."

She waved and a medic wheeled a gurney over to Gram.

"So he's stable?" Nor asked, looking down at Gram.

"More or less."

I said, "Then he stays."

The medic looked stunned. "What?"

"He stays."

The Murphy lawyer wandered over.

I looked at him and pointed to Gram. "He stays."

The lawyer looked nonplussed. "He's a Murphy—"

"No kidding. And given what you did to his sister, I don't feel real great about you guys taking him. I don't trust you guys not to try to make this all his fault and take it out on him." The look on the lawyer's face made me think that was definitely on the table.

Score another one for Nor—she'd called it.

I said, "I think you've done enough damage to his family for one day, don't you? He stays."

The medic's eyes zipped back and forth between us as if she were watching an interesting show.

Nor stared the lawyer down. "You're not going to win this

one. Just take your people and go."

The lawyer studied me and whatever he saw there made him nod at the medic.

I might've been mistaken but I could've sworn I saw a look of approval flit across the medic's face when she glanced at me and the lawyer wasn't looking at her. In any event, she waved off the guy with the gurney and left to help the other medics.

The Murphy lawyer looked between Gram and Nor then said, "We'll be in touch."

Nor gave him her shark smile and said, "Looking forward to it."

The Murphy lawyer wisely turned and walked away.

"Bayley, can you please put Gram in the living room on the couch?" I said.

Fuzzy came to sit next to Gram, and Bayley lifted the section of wood with them on it away from the rest of the platform and then extended that section across the platform and all the way to the house. He opened the door, and they disappeared inside. A few seconds later, Bayley withdrew the wooden arm all the way back into the platform, shutting the front door behind him as he went.

The medics on the platform all stopped to stare while this happened. A few shot nervous glances at me and the house.

I ignored them while I texted. By the time I was done, all the remaining Murphys had been loaded onto gurneys and were being put in the ambulances.

The ambulances pulled away, followed by the lawyer driving the SUV he'd come in, with a paramedic driving the other van following up the rear.

We watched them leave the grove and I stared after them until they blipped off my mental map as they left the property.

My shoulders sagged. "They're gone."

Eagan exhaled and let go of the last of his spell, which had continued to keep us warm. The cold came rushing in to slap at my face and stiffen my damp clothes.

Nor went to put her arm around me, then thought better of it as she took in my soggy mess. "Let's get you cleaned up," she said.

I nodded.

We all trudged toward the house. Bayley opened the door, and Fuzzy came racing out.

I held out a hand. "Not yet, pal. I don't want to get gunk all over you. Then we'll both need a shower."

Fuzzy slowed his roll and instead of leaping into my arms, trotted along beside me at a safe distance.

We mounted the porch stairs, and Mila greeted Nor and Eagan at the door, while I turned and looked back over the lawn, Fuzzy at my feet.

A groan emanated from the porch.

"You said it. That's exactly how I feel in a nutshell. Okay. Can you get rid of the platform now? Excellent job, by the way. As always," and I patted the porch railing.

Bayley sighed and sent me a nudge of affection through our bond, along with some concern about the state I was in.

"I promise to go take care of myself after we finish up here," I said.

With that, Bayley made the entire platform disappear into the lawn.

I blinked.

One minute it was there, the next I was staring at the completely undisturbed lawn.

"Wow Bayley. You never cease to amaze me."

The porch gave a cheerful chirrup.

I turned to walk inside and found Mila waiting for me in the doorway. She looked me up and down and winced.

"Ooh, that went a lot rougher than planned. I might have gotten a little carried away with the red corn syrup."

"You think?" I said, as Fuzzy and I walked into the foyer, and Bayley closed the door behind me.

"You alright?"

"I guess. I'm not sure yet. Depends. How'd things go on your end?"

Mila perked up and grinned. "You've got to see this."

Chapter Sixty

A quick peek into the sitting room assured me that everyone was in fine shape, and, in fact, experiencing post-battle jollies. Before I could join them though, Mila rerouted me, convincing me that before I did anything else, I needed a quick shower.

I trudged upstairs, Fuzzy following me.

A quick check-in with Bayley told me his battery was really low from expending all that magic. But he felt really pleased at being able to help and didn't seem to mind the drain at all. Still, I could feel his fatigue dragging on me, adding to my own. I hadn't used enough magic to be knocked on my butt the way I usually was, but I had used some, and I could feel the combined fatigue from me and Bayley fighting with the stress and adrenaline still bounding through my body.

Stepping into the shower, I let the hot water wash away some of the tension along with all of the gunk.

Fuzzy stood guard on the sink.

"I'm fine, Fuzzy. Honest," I said, wincing only a little as the aches from the explosion twinged when I moved the wrong way.

Fuzzy gave me a look and maintained his post.

Thoughts came swarming into my head.

The violence of the Murphy attack.

Fear that Bayley would be harmed in the onslaught.

How close Nor and Eagan had been to being collateral damage.

Images swam before me. Of Gram and Sadie, fighting for their lives. Of the bodies on the platform, unmoving. Of all those red droplets.

"You know, guys, I'm about done with random morons barging in here and throwing their weight around like a bunch of drunk baboons."

Fuzzy said, "Meow," and Bayley grunted in a "you said it" kind of a way.

With an effort, I swatted all the thoughts back and carefully blanked my mind, then tipped my head back to let the hot water work its magic.

I made it back downstairs to the sitting room in about fifteen minutes, and by then, there was a mixture of voices filling the air.

I stood in the doorway and surveyed the room.

Carmine, Eagan, Lou, Pete, Nor, and Mila were clustered together behind the left-hand couch, where Gram sprawled unconscious. His head was propped on a pillow near the fire, and he was covered with a blanket. He was still unconscious.

Someone had taken care of refreshments while I was in the shower because there were snacks laid out on the coffee table, and everyone seemed to have beverages.

Neil stood right in front of the blazing fireplace, one hand crammed in his pocket, the other gesturing with the cup he was holding, as he talked animatedly.

His conversation partner turned to give me a small wave when she saw me and Fuzzy standing in the doorway.

"Hi Sadie," I said.

Mila bounced over and gave me a one-armed hug. "You're looking much better," she said.

I was still looking Sadie over. She didn't seem to have incurred any new damage, to my relief.

I shifted my gaze to Mila and said, "I'm fine."

Both Fuzzy and Bayley made a small "harrumph" sound at the same time, which had Mila pursing her lips.

"Well the boys seem to disagree, so why don't you have a seat?"

I made my way to the right-hand couch, sitting down at the nearest end, across from Gram's blanket-covered feet. Fuzzy immediately hopped onto my lap.

It was like everyone took me sitting down as a signal.

Sadie sat at the other end of the couch I was on, across from Gram, where she had a clear view of his face. Neil seemed torn, his gaze darting between Sadie and me, but before he could make up his mind, Eagan took the spot between me and Sadie.

Nor shoved the armchair over and sat to my left, at the corner of the coffee table. Mila dragged a chair into the space Nor had created, seating herself between Nor and the end of the couch with Gram's feet on it.

Lou, Pete, and Carmine formed an old guys' group, warming themselves in front of the fire. Carmine sank into the rocking chair near Gram's head, and Bayley slid two chairs over for Lou and Pete. They all sat, backs to the fire, facing Nor and Mila.

That left Neil. He dragged a chair over next to Sadie's end of the couch, so he wound up sitting next to her, but near Lou and Pete.

I looked around the circle we'd formed. With all of the immediate crises averted, for the first time in days, a little space opened up in my brain. And all of the strain of the last few days came crashing down on me like a pile of boulders.

Bayley murmured, then tilted the coffee table so that one of the glasses slid toward me.

I smiled when I realized it was filled with the Shake-It-Off concoction. Taking his advice, I had a drink. I immediately felt some of the exhaustion lift.

A quick glance to my right confirmed that Neil and Eagan were drinking some of the Shake-It-Off too.

Neil saw me looking and said grudgingly, "It's not bad."

"Glad you like it," I said.

Carmine cleared his throat and said, "I figured it'd be useful. Hope you don't mind me whipping some up."

"Thanks Carmine. You're a lifesaver. I appreciate it."

Eagan waggled his cup at me. "This stuff is better than a beer and a pizza. I feel like a new man."

As I slugged back the Shake-It-Off, my eyes focused on Gram. I gestured to him and said, "How is he?"

Sadie said, "Sleeping it off, from what I can see."

I turned so I could look at her better. "And you? How are you? That was…I really don't have words for what that was." I ran my hands through Fuzzy's fur, trying to keep from clenching them.

Mila said cheerfully, "That was an epic miscalculation is what that was. Well, no one's dead, so live and learn."

I just blinked at her.

Nor looked pained.

Mila said around a mouthful of pretzels, "What? None of the damage is permanent so I take that as a win."

Nor said, "I think you underestimate how…appalling…it was to be in the middle of it."

Neil muttered, "Well it wasn't my fault," as he crossed his arms and huddled into his chair. "I did my part."

Lou and Pete looked like they were both about to say something, but Mila beat them to it. With a shake of her head she said, "Nope you did just fine. Excellent in fact."

Neil ducked his head, but not before I caught the glint of pleasure in his eyes.

"From what I can tell," Mila said, "everyone did their part." She held up her hand and began ticking things off on her fingers. "Bayley dug the tunnel from the house to the platform, and he also created the underground room where Lou, Pete, Neil, and I hung out under the platform. Really good job, Bayley. We had plenty of space."

Bayley made some happy creaks that made me smile.

Mila smirked at me. "No one had any idea we were down there."

Eagan nodded. "I was listening really closely, and I never heard a peep from you guys. I'd never have guessed you were right under us."

Neil snorted. "Don't know why you guys were so uptight about being quiet. A herd of elephants could've come by, and you wouldn't have heard us. What?" He said when Lou and Pete started shaking their heads. "The stupid Murphys—er, sorry Sadie—but they went berserk with those water missile things. Those little bastards were *loud*."

I stared at Neil, bewildered. This was a totally different kid from the rageball I'd met the other night. I'd never heard him speak so many words in a row. And he wasn't done yet.

As I stared in amazement, Neil leaned forward, growing more animated as he relived his adventure. "Sadie you should have seen it. So like, one minute we're in this neat room that Bayley dug out, right? And then, the whole dirt roof over us just sort of goes sliding off. And now I'm looking up, and I can see the underneath of the platform, right? And at first, I'm like 'why is the platform moving' and then I realize that the whole room we're in is sliding around under the platform."

"Bayley was moving us around to follow where you were on the platform, Sadie," Lou supplied.

"Right! That's what I was saying," Neil said. "So I'm looking up at the platform, and I can hear everything you guys are saying, then all of a sudden, that bitchy Murphy lady—"

"He means Kate, and language please," interrupted Pete.

Neil rolled his eyes, but said, "Whatever. That, er, Kate, says 'It's time,' and then some dude says 'Sadie'—"

"Gram," Eagan and I said at the same time.

Neil rolled right over us. "Right, Gram says 'Sadie' and blam, everything goes batsh—, er, crazy."

Neil was bouncing on the edge of his chair, vibrating with so much energy I was afraid he'd fall off. I glanced at Lou and Pete, and they looked unperturbed, so I guessed they'd already seen him like this, but to me it was like I was meeting a totally different person.

"So like, it happens really fast. Bayley pops a hand out of the bottom of the platform, right? Like, a wooden hand. And he waves it at us! And Mila goes, 'You're on' and a window opens in the platform, like right above me, but see, I make it look like there's no window, like the platform is still there. And no one even notices!"

Neil leaned toward Sadie. "But see, the cool part is, I had to do a see-through glamour so, like, you guys on top saw one thing, but from underneath we could see what was really going on."

"Like a one-way mirror," said Eagan.

Neil gave him a dismissive look. "Kind of. It's more complicated than that." He concentrated on Sadie again and said, "Okay, so at the same time Bayley opens the window, and I'm doing my thing, Lou and Pete, they're doing their thing so you don't fall through the empty space under your feet yet."

"Air cushion," Lou supplied.

Sadie said, "It was really good. I couldn't tell the difference between standing on your camouflaged air cushion and standing on the actual platform."

Lou and Pete grinned at her.

Neil continued, "So like, we can see all the crazy that's going on through the window under your feet. There's darts and whips—I didn't know you guys could make whips out of water, that's so cool—and it's so *loud* with all this like whamming and sloshing as the water is going everywhere. So cool."

Neil's experience of events was so far from the gut-clenching, terror-filled experience I'd had that all I could do was sit there and blink as I tried to reconcile the two versions of what happened.

Neil continued, "This is where it gets really good. Suddenly there's this water jail thingy that you're in right above us, Sadie. And then you do your thing, and all the water under your feet disappears. And I see it start to go, so I super quick make it look like it's still there."

Sadie nodded at him and said, "You were fast. No one noticed."

Neil shrugged to hide it, but I could see him puff up a bit with pride. "No biggie," he said. "The fun part was next. So I'm standing there, waiting, and Mila's all, 'Get ready,' and then Sadie, you toss your head back, and wham!" Neil pantomimed wildly with his hands, acting out the next part as he said it. "Lou and Pete drop the air cushion, and Sadie, you drop in our room. I'm standing off to the side so I'm casting a second glamour to make it look like you're still in there. And then Mila tosses in her magic bomb, which I hide—so now I've got two illusions running at once, the window and your doppelgänger—what a rush! And then boom!" Neil mimed the explosion with his hands. "It all blows up. Fake blood everywhere. I drop the glamour, Bayley closes the platform, and just like that, we're outta there." Neil cackled. "It was epic. We were right under their noses, and they had no clue!"

Mila looked at me apologetically. "The explosion should have been much smaller. I underestimated the amount of magic Kate was able to throw at Sadie and Gram. Sorry."

"Did there have to be so much 'blood' in it?" I asked. Even knowing it was fake, being covered with that much red gunk—seeing the "blood" coating everything in a fine mist—had been shocking. Not to mention disgusting.

Mila shrugged. "It added verisimilitude. Besides," she said. "it really freaked you out, and since you have no poker face, you being all wigged out and upset really helped sell the whole thing. So I'm counting that as an unexpected bonus."

I didn't know what to say to that, so I hunkered into the couch, and clutched Fuzzy.

Neil might think the whole day was a lark, but my day had been very different from his.

The whole time on the platform, I'd been worried that Sadie would actually die. So many things could have gone wrong, not the least of which was Neil's part in the whole thing. So much had hinged on his illusion talent, and I'd been terrified he'd screw us over.

But two things had made me agree to the plan.

Sadie had wanted to do it.

And Zo had vouched for Neil.

Chapter Sixty-One

After Zo had dropped off Sadie and Eagan, they filled me in on their visit with her.

Sadie said, "I know Mila has been working on a plan to fake my death, but Zo said it won't work."

I couldn't decide what was more alarming. That Zo knew what we were up to, or that she somehow knew it wouldn't work.

Eagan said, "Let me start from the beginning. We were walking in the woods near Zo's property, and all of a sudden she just sort of showed up."

I said, "She does that."

"So she invited us to her house for a cup of tea. And I sort of had the impression that 'no' wasn't an option." He looked at Sadie, who nodded in agreement.

Eagan said, "'I promise you'll be perfectly safe,' Zo said, and started walking away, making it clear that we were supposed to follow after her."

Sadie said, "I got a look at her front yard when we climbed up the steps to her porch. No wonder she's pissed at Gram. That yard is huge. If he did even half the damage she claims, that must've been a nightmare to fix."

I said, "Oh it was bad, believe me. He and his merry little band pelted it with so much hail that it looked like the army had been using it for artillery practice."

Eagan said, "So Zo sat us in her kitchen and fed us tea."

"Did she read your tea leaves?" I asked.

Sadie looked at me in surprise. "She did. She read mine."

"Me too. What did she tell you?"

Sadie hesitated, then said, "It's private."

Before I could dig for more info, Eagan jumped in with, "But the important part is that Zo informed Sadie that she was going to help."

Sadie said, "She...has plans for me."

"Oh...and you're okay with that?"

Sadie nodded vigorously and her eyes lit with a gleam. "I'm looking forward to it."

Eagan added, "So Zo has...plans for Sadie. And then Zo says 'Of course, if you're dead, none of that is going to happen.' And she tells us that she's sure Mila's plan isn't going to work. But then she says she has an alternate plan." Eagan squirmed in his seat. "*If* we can get you on board with it."

Looking at how uneasy Eagan was, I suddenly had a bad feeling. "I already told her I'd be fine with whatever."

Eagan and Sadie traded a look.

"What?" I asked.

Eagan said "Finn...I don't know how to tell you this...she wants to use Neil to help Sadie."

"Neil?"

"Yes," said Eagan and Sadie at the same time.

"Stalker Neil."

Eagan nodded.

Bayley groaned.

"Just-tried-to-burn-down-Bayley Neil? Stop nodding like this is completely normal and fine. This is not normal. It is not fine. I feel bad for the kid, but I think his cheese has totally slid off his cracker. His eggs got scrambled somewhere along the way, and no way am I going to trust him, particularly with something as important as Sadie's life. No. Uh uh."

"Actually, he's not that bad," said Sadie.

I goggled at her.

"Just listen," she said.

So I'd listened.

Now, as I sat watching Sadie smile at Neil, I was glad I'd let Sadie talk me, Bayley, and Fuzzy into working with Neil. Partly, it came down to the fact it was Sadie's life and if she wanted to take the chance on him, that was her call.

But mostly, I trusted Zo.

As usual, she'd been right. Neil had performed better than I would've dared to hope.

I said, "You did a good job today, Neil."

Neil gave a one-shouldered shrug and muttered, "It's not like it was hard or anything."

Lou shot him a look and then said to me, "We paid a visit to Zo after yesterday's fiasco."

Neil hunkered deeper into his chair, staring fixedly at his feet.

Pete added, "We're working on a plan for him. And Zo has some ideas on how he can both hone his skills and make amends. Today was a start in that direction."

Neil looked like someone had just asked him to lick a snail, but he didn't comment.

I nodded and I said, "Well, thank you for the help, Neil. And you too, Lou, Pete. We couldn't have pulled this off without you."

Neil gave the barest of nods to me, but when his eyes shifted to Sadie and she smiled at him, he grinned back.

The gray dot that I'd been monitoring on my mental map approached the front door.

I put Fuzzy on the floor and said, "Be right back," reaching the front door just as a knock rang out.

I opened the door and was greeted by a stack of pizza boxes. Dr. Paige peeked her head around the side and said, "Someone order pizza?"

Mila appeared behind me and said, "Yes! Real food!" and relieved Dr. Paige of her pizzas.

I smiled and stepped forward to hug Dr. Paige, who had a huge bag slung over one arm. "Not only do you make house calls, but you deliver food in our time of need. Thank you so much," I said.

"Food is a kind of medicine," Dr. Paige said, hugging me back. "And pizza is extra good medicine," she added with a wink as she stepped into the house.

"Pizza in the kitchen!" hollered Mila as she walked down

the hallway.

Neil beelined after her, followed at a more sedate pace by the others.

On her way by, Nor nodded approvingly at me, then waved at Dr. Paige and said, "Good to see you."

Eagan walked over and hugged Dr. Paige. "I take it you're here about Gram?" he asked.

She nodded.

Eagan stepped back and looked at me. "Smart thinking. I'll keep everybody in the kitchen till you're done. Holler if you need anything," then he sauntered after Nor.

"Hi Doc," said Pete.

"Paige, good to see you," said Lou. Lou looked at me and said quietly, "We need a minute, if you have it." He looked in the direction that Neil had gone, then back to me as he said, "We've got some more information."

I nodded, motioning for them to stay put.

Carmine tried to slide by me, but I snagged him by the arm and motioned for him to stay too.

I made introductions as Sadie drifted over. "Sadie, this is Dr. Paige Alexander. She's a really good doctor. I figured we should have somebody take another look at Gram, just in case. Dr. Paige, Sadie is Gram's sister. You didn't see her. As far as everyone outside this house knows—well everyone but Zo—Sadie is dead."

Dr. Paige took that in stride with a cheery, "Okay." I supposed she'd spent so many years hanging out with Zo, Lou, Pete, and Eagan that all of this seemed normal.

And then I added, "And this is Carmine—he's a Foster like me. He's got a great salve he's been using to help Sadie. Carmine, do you think it might help with Gram?"

"I might have something that'll help. It depends on what you think, Dr. Paige," Carmine said a bit shyly.

She smiled at him reassuringly. "Generally, I'll take all the help I can get with you magical people. Let's see what we're dealing with." She turned to Sadie, looked at the bruise on her head and scanned down to the ginger way Sadie was holding herself, and said, "You too. Let me get a look at you while we're at it."

Sadie opened her mouth to object, but Dr. Paige shook her head and said in a no-nonsense voice, "Don't even bother arguing. You'll lose, and it'll just make you feel worse. In there, please," and she pointed to the sitting room.

Sadie closed her mouth and did as Dr. Paige instructed.

Dr. Paige looked at me and Carmine and then she said, "You're looking a little peaky, Finn. Why don't you both go eat some pizza. I'll come get you when I'm done."

With that Dr. Paige shut the sitting room door, leaving me, Fuzzy, Lou, Pete, and Carmine in the hallway.

"Carmine, why don't you go ahead and grab a bite. We'll be there in a sec."

Carmine looked between Lou, Pete, and me, noted the serious expressions on their faces, nodded, and trundled off down the hallway.

Fuzzy stayed put, sitting close enough to lean against my leg while I talked to the guys.

"From the looks on your faces, I'm guessing this is not gonna make me happy."

Pete said, "Did you happen to notice a change in Neil?"

I said, "Hard to miss. It was like he was a totally different person."

Lou said, "There's a reason for that."

Pete sighed. "It's not good news Finn."

"Just tell me, guys."

Lou, sounding extra grim said, "You know how we took him to see Zo after we left your house last night? Well between Pete, me, and Zo we were able to find out some things. First of which was that coming after you wasn't exactly his idea."

I nodded. "When Sadie was convincing me to let Neil help, she said that the whole stalker thing wasn't entirely his fault. She didn't have a lot of details though, just that Zo told her the kid had been pushed into it."

Pete said, "It's true. He's been...influenced."

"Influenced? Is that code for 'spelled'?"

Pete said, "That was part of it."

"Part of it?"

Lou said, "Basically he was groomed. Someone approached him online while his father was sick. They've been working on him for months. They fed Neil the info about the Housekeeper, Bayley, the seeds—all of it. Gave the kid hope that his dad could be saved, then watched it crush him when of course it didn't happen."

Bayley moaned.

I couldn't even manage that. My mouth was hanging open. Finally I managed to squeak out, "That's...that's...sick. Who does that to a grieving kid?"

Lou said, "It gets worse. From there, they basically brainwashed him. Really effectively. Stoked his existing grief and anger over his dad, not to mention his sense of alienation from the Guthries. Then they used the resulting emotional turmoil to fuel a spell that focused all that misery on you and drove him to act on it. To top it off, they plied him with suggestions to make sure he followed through on those actions."

I could only stare at them. I had no words.

It was terrifying. Who'd want to wind someone up like that just to get at me?

Pete said, "Given the type of spell they used, the combo of mind manipulation and camouflage, we think whoever is involved has some Best and Guthrie talents in the mix. Why they're targeting you—or whether they're targeting you, specifically, or just the current Housekeeper—we don't know."

Lou said, "Yet. We've only started looking into this. The fact that they targeted a Guthrie, and a minor at that, well now we're involved in this, and we're not going to stop until we have some answers."

I shook my head. "I don't know what to say. I mean, thank you for your help." Laughter turned us toward the kitchen for a moment. I looked at Lou and Pete. "Is Neil different now because you broke the spell?"

Lou nodded. "Yes. We were able to neutralize it, and then one of Zo's teas really helped him to rebound."

Pete added, "He's suffering from a bit of backlash at the moment—that's why he seems a bit—"

"Hyperactive," Lou supplied.

Pete said, "Yes. Think of it as an overcorrection for being so angry and miserable for so long. Sort of like a mood swing from one extreme to the other. It'll wear off in another day or so, and his mood will even out to wherever he would be naturally. He'll still have his grief to deal with, of course, but his emotions will be far less severe."

Well, that explained why Neil seemed so different today. It also explained why Zo was so sure he would do okay helping us—she'd been able to see the real kid under all the bad influences Neil had been under.

Lou added, "It will take a while to undo all the damage, not to mention all the programming—he's still got residual anger toward you that'll take time to root out."

Pete said, "But as you can see, there's a normal kid under there. A grieving one, but we don't think he's the, uh—"

"Crazed lunatic," supplied Lou.

"—yes, he isn't at all what he seemed he was yesterday."

"Glad to hear it." I sighed and rubbed my forehead. "This is a lot to process, guys. I'm going to need some time to think."

Lou said, "Of course. And we'll keep digging."

Pete added, "We just wanted to let you know."

"Glad you did. Really. Thank you. Why don't you guys get some pizza? You sure deserve it. I'll be down in a minute."

They nodded and headed off to the kitchen.

I looked down the hallway as a peal of laughter poured out of the kitchen. No way was I ready to be Party Finn, so I went and plunked myself on the stairs with Fuzzy on my lap.

To Bayley and Fuzzy, I said, "Brainwashing? What the hell guys?"

Chapter Sixty-Two

I was still sitting on the steps stewing over everything that had happened in the last couple of hours when Carmine came down the hall a few minutes later.

He looked between me and the kitchen and said, "Not ready to join the fun?"

"Not quite."

"Mind if I join you?"

I nodded, and Carmine shuffled over to the stairs, lowering himself to sit on the step next to me.

We listened to the buzz of conversation drifting down the hallway from the kitchen.

Eventually he looked at me and said quietly, "You do know this is a win?"

I nodded and kept patting Fuzzy.

Carmine made an "Mmm" sound. There was a pause then he added, "But it doesn't feel like it."

I shook my head. I tried to sort through my feelings. A part of me knew I should be taking a victory lap with the people in the kitchen. Against the odds, we'd pulled it off. It was just that…

I sighed and hugged Fuzzy closer. "On that platform," I shot a glance down the hallway then looked back at Carmine, "I know it wasn't Mila's fault. But that explosion…for the love of vampires, there was So. Much. 'Blood.' It felt so real that for a few seconds, I thought we'd actually killed Sadie."

I was swamped with the sense memory of sitting, my whole body stunned and tingling, my ears ringing, all the while feeling the wet drip, drip, drip sliding down my face and neck.

I shook my head and buried my face in Fuzzy's fur. "Bayley told me she was okay. Logically, I knew she was safe. But…I…it could so easily have been for real, you know? While I was sitting there, I realized how close we came to total disaster. And it's not like we got out of this with no damage." I slid my glance to the sitting room and back, realized I was rubbing my aching temple, and with an effort went back to patting Fuzzy.

"It took all our combined magical mojo and a whole bunch of smarty-pantses to get out of this mess and still—with all that power, all those smarts at our disposal—still we couldn't stop the Murphys or the Fosters from forcing this whole showdown in the first place, couldn't stop them from breaking the rules once they got here, and couldn't stop them from escalating things to the point where people got hurt." I gestured toward the sitting room, where Dr. Paige was working on Gram, and said a silent prayer that Kate and her goons were also getting help. They all sucked, but I didn't want anyone to die.

"So yeah. It's a win in that Sadie lives and gets to fight another day. And don't get me wrong. I really am thrilled about that. But," I shook my head.

Carmine waited a full minute before he prompted, "But?"

I looked around the walls that had become so dear to me, felt the warmth of my sweet Fuzzy in my lap, heard the laughter of my friends down the hallway. The fact that they all mattered to me clashed with everything that had happened and—

"I don't feel safe."

It slipped out of me before I'd even fully acknowledged the thought. I was surprised to find myself blinking back tears.

I'd been leaning back against the riser of the step behind me. I felt it soften and shift as it grew and wrapped around my shoulders, like a pliant, wooden Linus blanket. As Bayley hugged me, he let out a quiet croon.

At the same time, Fuzzy stood and put his head against my neck so that his purr could rumble through me.

I held onto Fuzzy with one hand and patted Bayley with the other. "How am I going to protect you guys—not to mention everyone else on the property—when the families can just do whatever they want?"

Carmine sighed, rubbing his eyes with a weary hand. "It's... not an easy question. I won't insult you by giving you platitudes."

Then, to my surprise, Carmine took hold of my hand and held it.

He said, "But if it's any help at all, you're not alone. We'll help you figure it out. If you like."

And I realized it was a help. A huge help. As I sat there holding Carmine's hand, the knot in my stomach eased, and some of the pressure on my heart lifted.

I squeezed his hand and let out the breath I hadn't realized I was holding onto. "Thanks, Carmine. I can use all the help I can get."

Nor overheard me as she came striding up the hallway. She stopped next to the stairway with, "Is it something I can help with?"

"Actually...yes," I said.

Carmine smiled. "I'll leave you ladies to it."

He gave my hand a final squeeze, then he stood up and headed back into the kitchen.

Bayley dropped the wooden blanket around me as Nor sat next to me, so I could turn and face her as she said, "You're not eating any pizza."

"Not yet, no." And I filled her in on what Lou and Pete had told me. I felt kind of bad that I did as I watched all the happiness drain out of her face.

She said, "We'll need Mila's help with this. She can coordinate with Lou and Pete."

I nodded and lapsed into silence.

Nor studied me and said, "That's not all, is it."

"No." I thought for a minute. "I was trying to explain to Carmine. Nor, I can't get past the thought that none of today's insanity should have happened."

Nor folded her hands on her knee and said, "Explain."

"This is Bayley House. It's a special place. I mean, seriously, look at the magical mumbo jumbo that Bayley comes with: the place is protected like Fort Knox, there's the whole special bonding thing with the Housekeeper," I pointed down the hallway, "and, let's not forget DeeDee over there."

Nor nodded. "All true. And your point?"

I petted Fuzzy, trying to get my thoughts in order. "It doesn't seem to matter to the Fosters—or the Murphys, for that matter—that Bayley has thoughts, feelings, or opinions—or that I do. They don't care. They treat this place like they can do anything they want with it, treat Bayley as a…thing. And me? I'm just an inconvenient tenant they can push around. Which I guess is true, I am a tenant. But…"

"But you're not a typical tenant. You're the Housekeeper."

"Right! And you guys keep telling me that the Housekeeper is supposed to have special status. Oh they think I'm 'special,' all right—and not in the nice way. The truth is, I don't have any real authority, special or otherwise. If this position was ever more than a fancy title, it isn't now. In reality, I have a very limited say over what happens here. And this whole Sadie thing hammered home how little I can actually do. And, you know what? I'm not okay with that. Things need to change."

The house creaked around us as I felt Bayley physically tense. When I tuned into him more closely, it was like he was holding his breath.

Nor got the intense, focused look she got when her genius brain was firing on all cylinders. "Power."

"What?"

"Power. You want to be in a position of power."

"Um, maybe? I hadn't thought of it like that."

Nor pinned me with her gaze and said, "So what kind of power do you want?"

Suddenly all the stuff that had been swirling in my brain the last couple of months clicked.

I said, "Reese asked me what it was that I wanted to do with my life as Housekeeper. And I've been thinking about it a lot. I was thinking that I wanted to continue working to make this a place where everyone—no matter what family they're from—is welcome."

I leaned toward her, gesturing with my hands, as I tried to

explain. "Now I'm not sure it's enough to just be welcoming. It's not just the Sadie thing—though she's the very extreme cherry on top. I mean, think about how badly Reese needed this place."

Nor nodded.

I said, "And now I have Sibeta and her people, and the Grack and her babies to worry about. Not to mention whoever else is hanging out."

Nor said, "It sounds to me like you want protections in place that you can enforce."

"Yes! Bayley is very well protected, in terms of security. But I need to be able to intervene on his behalf better—and I want to be able to care for whoever stays here."

Nor said, "To clarify, you want a say in what happens here. You're talking about setting up legal authority and legal protections."

"Yes."

Bayley hummed as a vibration of excitement flowed up the steps.

I patted the step, letting him know I was glad he was on board.

Blowing out a long breath, I said, "I'm tired of feeling like I'm being dragged from one crisis to another. Like things are happening to me, and I have no control over them."

Nor said, "Agency. You want agency."

"Yes. I do." My mind flashed to the conversation I'd had with Zo the other day when she berated me for not taking charge of my tutoring. And I realized that the reason it had stung so much was because she was echoing what I'd been feeling on a subconscious level—not just about the tutoring, but about my whole position as Housekeeper.

"I've always prided myself on being a responsible person, Nor. And it's time for me to take responsibility for this job. My adjustment period/settling period—whatever you want to call it, it's over. I'm done with being a pawn. From now on, I get to choose. And the first choice I'm making is to get some damn rules in place to make sure a forced extradition like today never happens again. I choose to make Bayley a safe place—for him, for me, and for anyone else who is here. To make sure that if people come here, there's no way that any of the families can interfere."

Bayley and Fuzzy both purred loudly at the same time.

A gleam lit Nor's eyes. "I thought you might be heading in this direction. And I have some ideas."

"I sense a 'but.'"

She hesitated slightly then said, "But you may not like this...I think there's a way we can use the Sadie situation to our advantage."

"You know what? If there's a way to get some extra good out of the nightmare that happened today, then hell yes. Let's do it."

When Nor smiled, I heard R.G. in my head muttering "Leopard." It was the kind of smile that promised a world of trouble for the Fosters as she said, "Oh this is going to be fun."

Chapter Sixty-Three

After my conversation with Nor, I finally felt ready to join the group in the kitchen. Between talking with Nor and the general joviality of the group, my spirit finally felt much lighter.

By the time Dr. Paige and Sadie joined us in the kitchen, the group was mellowing due to a combination of magic drain and pizza coma.

"Well, what's the verdict?" I asked. Everyone quieted to hear what Dr. Paige had to say.

"Gram woke up long enough for me to do a quick cognitive exam and get some of your shake into him. He was lucid, just tired. I agree with the Murphy medic—I think he'll be fine. Despite that lump on his head, he didn't show any signs of a concussion, and there are no obviously broken bones; some bruising, and maybe a hairline fracture. He'll be sore, but he'll recover."

I released a pent-up breath and relaxed a little. As much as Gram wasn't my favorite person, I didn't want him to die on my couch.

General conversation in the kitchen resumed as Dr. Paige turned to Carmine. "Now let's talk about that salve of yours. It's doing a wonderful job on Sadie," she said.

"You okay?" I asked Sadie quietly.

"Feeling pretty good for a dead woman," she said and gave me a little wink. She drifted toward the pizza and was immediately bracketed by Neil and Eagan.

Dr. Paige's okay seemed to give the others permission to wrap things up. Lou and Pete corralled Neil and made their farewells.

"Thank you guys again," I said.

Pete said, "Glad to be of service."

Lou said, "Never a bad thing to be able to help the Housekeeper."

Neil still refused to meet my eyes, standing off to the side, staring at his feet as he fidgeted.

"Bye Neil," I said.

"Bye."

Sadie came over and hugged him. He stiffened for a second and then hugged her back. She whispered something to him, and he just shrugged. But I caught a glimpse of his flushed cheeks and the gleam in his eye.

After Lou, Pete, and Neil left, Nor, Mila, and Carmine took their leaves as well and disappeared upstairs.

That left me and Fuzzy in the kitchen with Sadie and Eagan. Without me even asking, they helped me clear up.

As we were working, I asked Sadie, "If you don't mind my asking, what did you say to Neil?"

She said, "I told him it gets better."

I said, "That was kind of you. It looked like it meant a lot to him." I looked at the shadows lurking under her smile and added, "Do you believe that? It gets better?"

On a long sigh, she said, "I hope so."

When we finished up, Eagan came over to stand at Sadie's side. "I don't know about you, but I'm wiped. I'll meet you bright and early?"

Sadie smiled and said, "You don't have to drive me to Zo's. I can walk there by myself."

"A gentleman always sees a lady to her door," Eagan said.

Sadie rolled her eyes, but a grin tugged her lips.

"Wait, so soon?" I asked. I knew that Sadie going to Zo's was part of the plan, but I hadn't realized that she'd have to leave right away.

Sadie nodded. "I would've gone tonight, but I want to talk to Gram before I leave."

I nodded as I watched the way that Eagan and Sadie were standing so close to each other. Trying not to grin, I said as casually as I could, "You know Eagan, it doesn't make a ton of sense for you to drive all the way home just to turn around and come right back. You're welcome to crash here tonight."

Eagan looked startled. He slid a glance to Sadie, who was busy trying to look nonchalant. Then he said, "I, uh, have a change of clothes in my car. For the gym. So yeah. Thanks Finn. That would be great."

As Eagan hustled out to his car, I caught Sadie watching his retreating backside.

As innocently as possible I said, "Good thing these walls are so thick that they're basically soundproof." When Sadie spun to me, eyebrow arched, I added smoothly, "Otherwise having all these people sleeping so close together could get noisy."

Sadie snorted. "Good to know. With my luck, he'll pick the room next to mine and spend the whole night snoring like a water buffalo." Sadie cast an eye toward the sitting room. "I was thinking about sleeping on the couch to keep an eye on Gram—"

I waved a hand at the same time Bayley grumbled. "Not necessary. Bayley's keeping an eye on him," because neither of us trusted him to behave, wounded or not. "Go get some rest. You sure earned it after the day you had."

Eagan reappeared just as she said, "You too."

I nodded and sent them both upstairs with instructions for Eagan to help himself to the linen closet and whatever free room he wanted. My guess was he'd pick the room next to Sadie's.

That just left me and Fuzzy alone in the kitchen with Bayley.

I was leaning against the butcher block and let myself slide down it until I was sitting on the floor, leaning against it. Fuzzy immediately climbed into my lap.

Without anyone around to look after, the exhaustion I'd been holding back kicked down its holding pen and roared through me, chasing away my last bit of energy.

"It's probably not a good thing that I want to just lie down here, is it?" I asked Fuzzy and Bayley.

Bayley cooed to me, and Fuzzy patted my face with his paw.

Bayley sent me a mental image of him scooting me upstairs to my room so I didn't have to walk.

"No that's okay, Bayley. There's nothing physically wrong with me. I mean, I'm tired, sure. Okay fine, I'm exhausted. But so are you. I just don't want to go upstairs to bed yet. I…need to stay here for a bit, keep an eye out for Gram."

The truth was that I felt most comfortable in the kitchen. And here on the floor, with the butcher block at my back and the kitchen sink in front of me, with Bayley and Fuzzy, I felt the most secure and relaxed that I had in days. If I looked up, I could even see Sprout on the windowsill, like a little green beacon of hope.

Bayley sighed and murmured.

I put my head in Fuzzy's fur, and we all soaked up the solacing quiet.

Chapter Sixty-Four

The next thing I knew, Bayley was nudging me awake in my mind while Fuzzy was taking the more direct approach by sticking his cold, wet nose in my face.

After a blurry few seconds, I realized Bayley was warning me that Gram was awake.

I sat up and realized I was sleeping on the kitchen floor.

It took me another second to realize Bayley had molded the floor to my body shape and heated it so that I was comfortable. He'd also snuck my pillow under my head and covered me with a blanket for good measure. I'd been sleeping so hard I didn't notice any of it.

"Thanks, Bayley, thanks Fuzzy" I said, patting the floor as it flowed back into its usual shape.

Bayley chirped at me in response, and Fuzzy nuzzled me.

Gram rounded the corner into the kitchen.

He stopped short when he saw me and blinked a few times before he said, "You're on the floor."

"Thank you, Captain Obvious," I said, but without any real heat.

He didn't respond, and instead walked over and reached a hand down to help me up.

I grasped it, but he winced when I started to tug, so I let go and used the butcher block to lever myself up.

Fuzzy looked back and forth between me and Gram. He must've decided that Gram wasn't a problem at the moment because he yawned, padded over next to his kibble dish, curled up, and went back to sleep.

A quick glance at the wall clock told me it was just after five a.m.

"Sadie?" he asked, face pinched.

"She's okay. Upstairs. Sleeping."

A wave of such stark relief passed over him that I actually felt bad for him for a second. His eyes got suspiciously shiny as he muttered, "I was afraid I'd dreamed it. Seeing her. After." He scrubbed a hand over his face as he reined in his emotions, growling, "What a cluster."

"Speaking of which, how are you feeling?" I asked.

"Thirsty," he said. "I was looking for some water."

Good luck with that, I said in my brain, imagining him trying to get water out of the faucet and Bayley blocking him. But aloud I said, "Sit down. I'll get you some," and motioned to the table.

I brought him a bottled water from the fridge and, while he was chugging that, I poured him some Shake-It-Off.

Handing it to him, I said, "Drink that. It'll help."

He must've really been hurting because he slammed the whole thing back without hesitation.

"How are your ribs?" I asked.

"Feeling like they went a round with Leatherface." At my blank look, he said, "The guy with the chainsaw in *Texas Chainsaw Massacre*? You know, because a couple of those whips got through and whacked me?"

"Ah," I said. "Also, ouch. Well, good news is if your ribs are broken, it's only a hairline." He nodded and I said, "And the rest of you? How are you doing?"

He thought about it. "Well I'm not dead. Which is good, because now I've got to go kill some people in my family."

He said it so matter-of-factly that I couldn't tell if he was joking or not.

"Er, not that I blame you, but maybe don't plan a murder in my kitchen, if you don't mind. I don't want to be an accessory."

He nodded and was silent for a moment. Then he said, "What happened? Last thing I remembered was Kate putting Sadie in a Water Torture Cell."

So that was what it was called. I filed that away and said, "The way Mila explained it to me, Kate tried to cast something at the same time you did—I have no idea what. But there was an explosion."

"Is Kate dead?"

I shook my head.

A truly scary smile twisted his lips and he said, "Good."

I held up my hand in a "wait" motion. "It's not like she was doing the victory dance. Last I saw, she was unconscious. The Murphy medics took her and the rest of the Murphys away."

"But not me."

"Well, they were going to take you, but we decided that might not be a good idea. Their lawyer as much as admitted they're going to try and pin this whole thing on you."

That scary smile was back. "Something to look forward to."

I didn't know how to respond to that, so I didn't say anything.

We sat in silence for a few minutes before I decided to make myself some coffee. As I was puttering around, Gram broke the silence with a quiet, "Thank you."

I was so surprised that I bobbled the coffeepot, clanking it against the counter. I rallied fairly quickly with "For the coffee? No problem. I can whip up some food too—"

"Not the coffee. Well, yes the coffee. But Sadie." He hung his head. "I didn't…I couldn't…" he sighed, staring at the table as he collected himself, then said, "I tried. But I couldn't ever… fix her…situation." Still refusing to meet my gaze, he said softly, "Thank you."

It was probably just as well that he wasn't looking at me. I was pretty sure that my discombobulation was written all over my face. Gram freaking Murphy was sitting in my kitchen having a butt-crack-of-dawn heart-to-heart with me. What was the world coming to?

I turned to face the coffeepot before he caught the look of disbelief on my face.

After a pause, I said, "I know I'm supposed to say 'happy to help' and all that, but we both know I'd be lying." I said it matter-of-factly, and a glance at Gram showed me he wasn't offended so I plowed on. "None of this should have happened," I said, snapping the coffee filter into place a little harder than necessary. "Sadie doesn't deserve the way she's been treated, Gram."

"Agreed."

"These rules the families have, the way they treat people based on their powers, it's wrong. And icky."

"Icky?" A grin tugged at the corner of his mouth.

I rolled my eyes. "Fine. How about disgusting. Or insulting. Or degrading. Or just plain wrong. Is that better?"

"Not disagreeing."

"Mmm," I said, watching the coffeepot brew. "Well you're at the top of your family's pack. Do something about it."

He lounged back in his chair, tilting it so it rested on two legs, started to cross his arms, winced, and settled for clasping his hands in his lap. He still somehow managed to look like his usual arrogant self.

That didn't take long.

"Not that simple," he said.

"Did I say it would be?" I shot back.

He pursed his lips. "What about you?"

"What about me?"

"Why don't you do something? You're the damn Housekeeper."

And there it was. The thing that had been getting me all twisted up. He was right. I was the damn Housekeeper. It was a title that hinted at all this power. But I needed it to do more than hint. I needed it to be more than just a title, more than the position had been for years.

Determination poured through me all over again.

I was the Housekeeper all right. And that was about to take on a whole new meaning.

Good thing I had Nor to help me make it happen. I sent a silent thanks to the lawyer gods that I had Nor in my life.

Of course, Gram couldn't know what we were up to, so I just sighed and threw his own words back at him with, "It's not that simple."

He smirked and said, "Told you."

I managed to stifle another eye roll and poured us some coffee.

A little nudge from Bayley had me checking my mental map. Sadie and Eagan were headed downstairs. I hid my grin when I realized they had exited the same room. The last thing I needed was for Gram to go all big brother on Eagan.

Sadie and Eagan came into the kitchen and stopped short on seeing me and Gram.

Eagan looked at Sadie. "Told you she might be up already," and went to help himself to some coffee.

Sadie nodded and walked toward Gram, whose eyes were zipping back and forth between her and Eagan.

Gram stood up as Sadie approached. They looked at each other for a long moment, then he wrapped his arms around her. She hugged him back, her head on his shoulder, reminding me of how I'd first seen them.

They held each other for a long moment.

I looked away, feeling like I was intruding, and busied myself by feeding Fuzzy. He blinked open an eye, glanced at his food dish, then went back to sleep.

As I stalled, petting the sleeping Fuzzy, I could hear Gram and Sadie whispering something to each other, but I didn't try to make it out. Whatever they were saying, it was obviously private. When they stopped whispering, I returned to the table.

Eagan brought coffee over for himself and Sadie, then topped off my and Gram's cups before joining us.

Bayley chirped at Eagan, and I smiled at him. Eagan smiled back at us.

Sadie and Gram let go of each other and sank into chairs next to each other.

"Let's have it," Sadie said. "How bad?"

Gram shrugged, tried to hide the wince it caused, and said, "I've had worse."

"Where is it on the list?" she asked.

Gram said, "I don't know. I'm still walking, so definitely

not the top five. You?"

She waved a hand. "Eh. Not even in the top ten."

I couldn't decide if I was impressed or disturbed that they each had a running "how bad is my boo-boo" list.

We all sipped our coffees for a few seconds before I said, "Okay, so what now?"

Eagan and Sadie exchanged a look. Eagan looked at the clock and said, "We need to get her to Zo's soon."

Gram's mouth tightened, Bayley groaned, and I said, "Already?"

Sadie nodded. "I probably should have left last night," she turned to Gram, "but I wanted to make sure you were okay."

Gratitude flashed in Gram's eyes and he reached out, gave Sadie's hand a quick squeeze, then let her go.

With a reluctant sigh he said, "It's probably wise not to delay too long. Who knows who will show up here—plus I wouldn't put it past Kate to post some people to watch the property."

Sadie said, "If I were in her shoes, I would."

Gram said, "Me too."

Eagan said, "They'll be expecting me to leave eventually. And Zo gave Sadie a charm that'll cloak her, so I can sneak her out."

Gram said, "They might try to check out Zo's."

Eagan's smile had an edge as he said, "If they want to try and force themselves onto Zo's property, they're welcome to try."

Gram and Sadie both shivered at the same time.

We all sat sipping quietly for a few seconds. Eagan and Sadie had some sort of silent conversation across the table, then Eagan swallowed the last of his coffee and stood, "Sadie, I'll grab your stuff and meet you by the door when you're ready."

"Thanks Eagan," Sadie said.

Sadie and Gram were looking at each other in a way that made me want to give them a moment alone.

"I'll help," I said, finishing my coffee, too, and following after Eagan. On my way out, I glanced at Fuzzy. He lifted his head, looked at Gram and Sadie, then looked at me. I had the sense that he'd keep an eye on them. I leaned down to give him a pat of thanks.

Eagan and I were silent as we climbed the back stairs and made our way to Sadie's room. Her things were already packed up in the duffle bags they'd arrived in. She'd also stripped the bed and stacked the linens and towels in a neat tower to make it easier for me to do the laundry.

It struck me that the room already had the feeling of being deserted.

Eagan hefted all the bags but the smallest one, which I grabbed, then I followed him along the hall and down the front stairs to the door.

We could hear the murmur of Gram and Sadie's voices from the kitchen, but not what they were saying.

I looked at Eagan. His hands were stuffed in his pockets, and he wore a thousand-yard stare. His usual cheery grin had been replaced by compressed lips, and the crinkles around his eyes were from some darker emotion than laughter.

I said quietly, "Anything I can do?"

He snapped out of his reverie to look at me. He shook his head. "Nothing to be done. She's got to go."

I reached up a hand and patted his shoulder. "I'm so sorry, Eagan." I paused and then said, "Any chance you can go with her?"

He gave me a wistful smile. "I can't. Not now at least." His eyes shifted in the direction of the greenhouse and back. "Too many responsibilities."

"I can take care of the Grack—"

"I know. It's not just that." And he sighed, shaking his head. "Besides, it's too soon. We barely know each other."

I nodded, not sure what else to say.

He got back a bit of his usual mischievous glint in his eyes when he added, "But not now doesn't mean not ever."

I smiled at him.

Sadie walked out of the kitchen.

Gram didn't follow.

She strode down the hallway, saying, "Ready," as she reached us. She turned to me and said, "Thanks, Finn. Totally inadequate, given all you've been through because of me, but thanks, nonetheless." Then she endeared herself to me even more when she looked around the hallway and said, "And thank you, Bayley. I wouldn't be standing here without you."

Bayley chirruped, making us all smile.

"You're welcome," I said. "And you're welcome back at Bayley House anytime you like. Hopefully, next time will be a lot less eventful."

"Oh I don't know," Sadie said, "this was rather fun." And with a saucy wink, she snagged a couple of bags and headed out the door.

Eagan grabbed the remaining bags and said, "Really, thank you Finn. See you soon?"

"Sure thing. Be safe."

And with that, Eagan and Sadie got in the car and left.

I went into the kitchen and found Gram leaning on the sink, staring out the kitchen window.

"They're gone," I said.

He nodded.

"Are you going to be able to keep in touch with her?"

He shook his head. "Maybe. But maybe not. For the short term, definitely not. Then we'll have to see."

I figured the Murphys would have Gram under a microscope for a while and that avoiding Sadie would be prudent. But it looked like it was paining him.

He muttered, "She's alive, though. Whether I get to see her again or not, at least she's alive."

He pushed off the sink and turned to face me fully.

"Time for me to go," he said. I moved out of the way so he could walk past me toward the kitchen doorway.

"Is that safe? Do you have a place to go?"

A ghost of the arrogant Gram that I knew and loathed resurfaced to drawl, "Why Housekeeper, I didn't realize you cared."

I shook my head at him. "Seriously, do you have a safe place to go?"

"That's for me to know."

"Don't be a weenie, Gram."

"A weenie?"

"Hey, if you're going to go all little boy," I mimicked him, "'that's for me to know'," then resumed my normal voice as I pointed at him, "I'm going to use little boy names and call you a weenie."

A genuine smile twitched his lips. "Finn, you really are one of a kind."

And he walked out the back door. Rain poured down from the sky, Gram stepped into it, and then he was gone.

I closed the door as the rain disappeared as quickly as it had come.

Chapter Sixty-Five

Carmine, Nor, and Mila wandered downstairs around seven a.m. We had a mellow breakfast, then while Nor and Mila made some calls, Carmine decided to head home.

I had a moment of doubt about Percy, but when I asked him to open the door to Carmine's, he did it without objection or comment.

Carmine and I stood in the open doorway. But instead of walking through, Carmine turned to me and said, "Are we okay?"

I hugged him and said, "Sure are. I really appreciate you being honest with me."

He hugged me then stepped back. He hesitated a moment and then said, "I meant what I said yesterday, when we were talking on the steps. You're not alone."

"Thanks, Carmine."

He gave me a searching look, then nodded, and walked through the doorway. He turned back and said, "See you next weekend? I have a new spell I think you're ready for."

I smiled and said, "Yes please! Just give me a holler when you're ready."

He smiled and waved, I waved back, then I closed the door.

I held my locket up to eye level. "We're going to talk about your freak out the other day."

I thought Percy wasn't going to answer, but he said. "I'm aware. But not today."

I didn't have the energy to argue with him, so I put the necklace back on and tucked it in my shirt.

Nor came into the kitchen toting her laptop bag and her

briefcase. "We're just about ready to go—Mila's finishing up some Mila stuff—but before we do, you and I need to talk."

"I thought you were going to hang out for a bit and talk with Sibeta?"

Nor shook her head. "I was, but I can't. There's too much going on. But I'm going to see Sibeta before I go and set up a specific meeting time."

I nodded. I knew Nor had other clients to deal with. That workload, plus the whole "Make me a real Housekeeper" challenge I'd dumped in her lap with no warning, probably meant that her plate was overflowing.

"Sorry if I'm screwing things up again," I said.

Nor waved a hand in dismissal. "Please. You know I like nothing better than to hand the family councils their asses." An evil grin spread across her face. "This is going to be a lot of fun."

I shook my head at her. A lot of the people in my life seemed to have very different definitions of "fun" than I had.

Nor said, "Speaking of good times, when I come back to talk with Sibeta, I'll be ready to finalize some details about our earlier discussion." She looked around the room as she said, "We're going to make sure Bayley," she looked back at me, "and you have more say in things."

"Good," I said. There was enough weight behind the word that Nor's expression had a determined edge when she nodded at me.

While Nor was off talking with Sibeta, Mila bounded into the kitchen, snagging a soda as she said her goodbyes. "Bayley, as always, working with you has been a thrill. And Finn, you always show me the best time. You have a real talent for trouble, and I can't wait to see what you get into next!"

That wasn't a talent I really wanted, and I was just fine waiting a good long time before any more trouble found me, but I didn't say that to her. Instead, I just shook my head at her and hugged her.

Nor returned, then the two of them took off together.

And whammo, the house was back to normal. Just me, Bayley, and Fuzzy, hanging in the kitchen.

With all the visitors gone, I checked in with Sibeta and went outside to check on the Grack. Neither of them were feeling particularly chatty. Sibeta took the news of Sadie's departure with a nod of the head, then disappeared back into the pool before I had time to talk with her further. The Grack didn't even nod. I walked up to her, she shuffled forward a little, I said hello, she shuffled back into place. And that was it.

I spent the rest of the day doing household stuff, loads of laundry, and generally tidying up after the guests. By evening, I was still tired, but puttering around the house had gone a long way toward soothing my nerves.

I should have known I wouldn't get off that easy.

I'd just finished a nice candlelit dinner with Bayley and Fuzzy when a green dot appeared on my map.

I facepalmed, elbow on the table, as I groaned.

"This had better not be a freaking Foster lawyer."

When I got to the front door, I realized it was probably worse. Wil was striding up the front steps.

Bayley grumbled behind me, but not so loud that Wil could hear.

"Hi Wil," I said.

Wil said, "Can I come in? I just need a minute."

If he just needed a minute, why didn't he text?

But I said, "Sure," and I let him inside.

Instead of heading to the kitchen like I expected, he started up the front stairs.

"Uh, Wil, where are you going?"

"Follow me."

Bayley let out a low growl when Wil's foot hit the next step. Wil stopped, shot me an exasperated look, and said, "Please."

I folded my arms and said, "Wil, I'm really tired. Yesterday was...well you were there. I'm really not in the mood for games."

"Neither am I. Look, this will only take a minute. Then if you want me to go, I will."

I shook my head but figured I might as well find out what was going on, so I gestured him forward and followed him up the stairs. Fuzzy appeared beside me, trotting along next to me as I trailed Wil, who beelined down the hallway, straight to the attic stairs, and up into the attic.

I felt Bayley tense.

"Wil," I said, entering the attic behind him. "What are you doing?"

Bayley still had all the attic's bits and bobs arranged the way they were when Kate had barged in, so they were still stacked into an impenetrable wall on each side of a narrow central aisle.

Wil walked part way down the aisle, turned and stopped. He stared at the mountain of stuff for a few seconds, and then his whole face lit up. I could see him twitching with eagerness. Pointing, he said, "Can you have Bayley make me a path through here?"

Bayley was ringing alarm bells in my head.

Picking up his warning, I shook my head at Wil. "Usually, yes. But he's still really tired, and I don't think that's a good idea. What's this all about Wil?"

"Do you know what's over there?"

I squinted at him in the dim light. "More junk? I haven't had time to catalog the attic yet."

Wil studied me. "I can't tell if you're lying or if you really don't know. But either way, I do. I know what's in that corner. And you need to give it to me."

And all at once I remembered when we were in the attic with Kate, how Wil's attention had been focused on something in that direction. And with a sinking feeling, I was pretty sure I knew what it was.

Bayley flashed an image of the star thing that Mila had stolen, confirming my suspicion.

I rubbed my forehead and tried for patience as I said, "Okay, one, how dare you accuse me of lying. Two, how can you possibly know what's under all this junk? And three, I'm not giving you anything. You're acting really weird."

"I have no problem digging for it myself," Wil said, and he started shifting boxes out of the way.

I had a few seconds of staring at him, gape-mouthed, before I growled, "Bayley!"

Bayley made the section of floor under Wil like an elevator. One second Wil was in the attic, the next he was plunging toward the ground floor.

"Take him to the front door, please," I said, dashing back down to the front door, with Fuzzy at my heels.

Wil was standing in front of the door, pulling at the wooden hands clamping his legs in place.

"What the hell, Wil?" I said, as I ran down the stairs.

He looked at me and said, "I thought Bayley was too tired. He seems fine to me."

"He is tired, you butt, and now he's more tired because he has to deal with whatever damage you have going on. Again, what the hell, Wil?"

Wil ran a hand through his hair, making it stand up at odd angles. "You think I don't know that you and Nor are going to use yesterday as an excuse to change the rules for the house?"

Nor and I were hoping to do exactly that, but I was surprised that he had guessed it.

Wil said, "Oh don't look so surprised, Finn. You keep forgetting that I'm not an idiot. Hell, given how things went yesterday, coupled with the whole Alexander mess, I can even see where you have grounds for legitimate concerns."

Not exactly a resounding endorsement. I didn't have a chance to respond because he continued, "But before you start making waves that are going to tie my hands, you need to let me deal with," he pointed toward the attic, "that."

"What, exactly, is 'that'?"

Wil scrutinized me for a moment before he said, "It's an... artifact of sorts. One of a kind."

"And what makes you think it's in my attic?"

Wil got a calculating look. I could practically see the wheels spinning in his head before he finally said, "It's my gift. I'm good at...finding things. Old things. Magic things."

I waited for him to explain more, but when he didn't, I said, "So your 'gift' says there's a thing in the attic. Got it. And why do you want it?"

"That's not important."

"Oh I think it is. You just barged in here and tried to seize it. I think some explanations are in order."

"No."

"No?"

"No. I'm sorry Finn, but there are just some things you're not ready to be read in on."

"You're sure about that?"

Wil said, "I am. You're just going to have to trust me on this. I'm the best person, maybe the only person, to deal with it. I know its lore. I know how to…keep it safe."

The pause before "keep it safe" was slight, but it made me think that he was going to say something else. Maybe something more like "I know how to use it."

I said, "No."

"What do you mean 'no'?"

I shrugged. "You say to trust you, but you don't trust me enough to tell me what's really going on. So no. Whatever is in the attic is perfectly safe here in Bayley House. In fact, I can't think of a safer place for it to be. So no."

Wil growled in frustration. "Finn, you don't know what you're saying. I know it's not your fault—you're just so far behind in your training—you have no idea of the ramifications some things can have. But I do. You really need to listen to me. Please. Just give it to me." He stared me in the eyes as he repeated, "Please Finn."

I took in his clenched hands and said, "I get that this is important to you. I do. But until you feel like you can tell me more, the answer is still no."

His face turned cold. "I didn't want to have to do this, but you're leaving me no choice. Either you hand it over, or," he straightened, crossing his arms, "I'll stop tutoring you."

"That seems kind of low, Wil," I said slowly.

"I'm not playing around Finn. If I'm not tutoring you, no one will be. No one wants to. And if you're not making progress in your training, the Council will not be happy with you."

"Because they're so happy with me now?"

Wil snorted. "You think you've had it hard? You've only seen the tip of the iceberg. You have no idea how much work I've been doing on your behalf."

"Work you volunteered for," I said quietly.

"I did," Wil acknowledged. "But I expected it to be more of

a two-way street. Now's the time for you to uphold your end of our arrangement."

"By giving you the artifact."

"Yes."

"And then we live happily ever after?"

Wil smiled. "Then I give you the best training you can possibly get in the Foster family. And I continue to advocate for you with the Council." Wil reached a hand toward me. "Finn, this is a win-win. I get what I want, and more importantly, you get what you need. C'mon, Finn. Don't you want to make the most of your magic?"

I stared at Wil. I reached out and grasped his hand.

I saw a look of triumph flash through Wil's eyes before he replaced it with a look of affection.

"Wil, I respect you," I said, giving his hand a squeeze, before withdrawing mine. "And I'm so sorry you feel this way. The answer is still no. Unless and until you can tell me what the artifact is and why you want it, it stays here."

The affection in Wil's eyes evaporated, and I found myself staring at a cold, calculating stranger. He shook his head. "Mistake Finn. You've already made several. But I don't know if you can come back from this one."

"Well, I'm not dead yet, so there's still a chance," I said in a joking tone that I didn't feel. "Now, I think it's time you go. And please call or text first before you return. Do you need help to your car, or can Bayley let you go?"

Wil's lip started to curl in a sneer, but he tempered it into a sardonic grin. "Oh, I can behave."

"Bayley?"

Bayley muttered as he released Wil.

"Good night Wil. Drive safe," I said.

"Finn," he said, with a nod. I'd never heard so much meaning layered into my name. It felt like a farewell, a challenge, and a warning all rolled into one.

Wil left without a backward glance.

Epilogue

Zo showed up a week after Sadie left. As usual, she declined to come in, but at least this time, she sat on the back porch. I brought us some hot cocoa and blankets, and between those and the heat Bayley added to the porch, we were able to cozy-up comfortably.

Zo and I sat quietly, sipping cocoa, and watching the snow begin to fall in soft, lazy flakes.

"How's Sadie?" I asked.

"Fine."

"What's she doing now?"

Zo shook her head.

"Oh come on. At least tell me something."

Zo pursed her lips. "She's off having adventures."

That seemed like it might be a good thing. So far as I could tell, Sadie was the adventuring type.

Zo asked, "What's going on with you and the Foster Council?"

I didn't bother asking her how she'd heard. I gave her a quick summary of my visit with Wil. When I mentioned the artifact, her face became carefully neutral.

She said, "It's a good thing you didn't give it to him."

"You know what it is?"

"I can guess."

"And are you going to tell me?"

"It isn't time."

"Time for what?"

Zo stared at the falling snow.

"Can you at least tell me if it's dangerous?"

"Not now," she said carefully.

"What does that mean?"

Zo just sipped her cocoa.

I sighed in frustration. "So anyway, the day after Wil left, Nor called to let me know that Wil filed something called an 'Isolation Brief' with the Council. Apparently, he's trying to use my harboring Sadie as further proof that I need some alone time to ruminate on what it means to be a Foster. At least they're not threatening to cut off all my food and supplies this time—the Council has just decided to try to limit my contact with outside people."

Zo snorted. "Good luck to them. You've got the necklace." She sipped her cocoa, then added, "And people are welcome to access the property from my house, if you need it."

Startled, I said, "What? Really? Thanks Zo!"

She waved me away. "Well, you and Bayley need to make a clear path through the forest to make it easier for people. Maybe get some carts or something so people don't have to walk the whole way."

Bayley squeaked the porch floorboards.

I smiled. "Bayley's excited to have a new project."

Zo said, "Good. Eagan's got to be able to get back and forth to keep an eye on the Grack—"

"And he's tutoring me."

Her eyes gleamed. "Is he?"

"Yup. I've officially asked him *and* Carmine to be my tutors. I've got a regular schedule set up and everything. In fact, I've decided to find tutors from all the magical families." *And Wil can suck it,* I said in my head.

"Really."

I was prepared for the suspicion in Zo's eyes. I wasn't ready to tell her about my being a balance yet, so I'd thought up an explanation ahead of time in case she asked questions about my tutoring plan. I said, "I know the other families' magic is different from the Foster magic, but I figure it can't hurt to learn how each family does their thing. I mean, there's got to be some overlap, especially at the basic level where I am. Plus, since I'm planning on being around all the families, not just the Fosters, it seems like a good idea to know more about how each family works."

Zo grunted but didn't ask any questions. Instead, she said,

"So your training has commenced—finally."

"And I'm taking legal steps to make some changes."

Zo gave me the side eye. "I see. I take it Nor's handling the legal side?"

"Yeah. She's amazing. She's already counter-filed against the Isolation Brief with an avalanche of stuff that probably has the Council lawyers popping antacids. They think this is bad, wait'll they get a load of what we have planned next. I'm sure they're going to fight us hard, though."

"My money's on you and Nor."

"Mine too."

We sipped in silence for another minute before Zo said, "You know the Fosters will have to get in touch eventually. They need you to open the door." She slid her gaze to me. "Can you?"

"What is it with you and DeeDee?"

Zo just looked at me.

I couldn't help my grin. "Yes, I finally figured out how to open the door."

Zo went still. "Really."

"Yup. I had to stop though because my necklace freaked out. You should have heard it—what?"

Zo looked a little ill. "I hadn't thought of that." She looked at me. "You'll keep it away from the door now that you know what you're doing?"

I nodded.

"Good."

I was about to ask her to explain when she waylaid me with, "Well I suppose it's time for me to pay up."

"Pay up?"

Her lips quirked. "Unless you don't want to know about Fuzzy."

As though she'd summoned him, Fuzzy came out the back door, padded over to me and hopped in my lap.

Zo looked from him to me and said, "The deal was, you learn to open the door, I answer your question about Fuzzy."

I clutched my mug in one hand and placed the other on Fuzzy's back. "The *what is he* question?"

She nodded.

When she didn't continue I prompted, "Well? What is he?"

Zo answered immediately. Unfortunately, I couldn't understand the word she said.

"Uh, could you say that again?"

"Sure. He's an," and then she said slowly, breaking it into syllables, "Oh-ret-por-tam-fee." She laughed at the look on my face. "We call them Orrets for short, if that helps."

"What language is that? Whatever it is I don't speak it. Could you translate it into something I do understand?"

"Knowing the name of the language won't help you." Zo stared at the falling snow while she thought. "Sibeta's people call him Travis. Do you know why?"

I shook my head.

"The last one of his kind was here more than two centuries ago. At the time, the Housekeeper called her Travis." Zo speared me with her gaze. "I'm guessing you don't know the origin of the word 'travis'?"

I shook my head.

"It comes from a word meaning 'to cross over.' It was given to people who were gatekeepers."

My mouth felt dry. "He's a gatekeeper? You mean for DeeDee?"

She nodded.

"A gatekeeper. Who...crossed over...from the other side of the door, erm, gate."

"Yes. And you already knew that. Ask me something you don't know."

I had so many questions. I was terrified I'd sound like an idiot if I said it out loud, but I said, "Is it true he can really talk?" I blurted the rest. "I mean not just talk, but *talk*—you know, really understand what I'm saying—and not just me, but Bayley, and the Grack, and Sibeta?"

"Yes. But again, you already knew that."

There was knowing in your head, and then there was saying it out loud and having someone confirm it. I gaped at her. "So he's a...talking gatekeeper. And now he's here to...what?"

"Help you."

As Zo drank her cocoa, I asked, "You said it's been centuries since one of his kind was here. Why show up now? Why help me? And help me with what?"

Zo held up her mug. "I'm out of cocoa." She handed her mug to me as she stood.

I put Fuzzy down as I scrambled to my feet. "I'll get you more cocoa! Don't go. You've barely answered my questions."

"Ask Fuzzy. When he can tell you and you understand him, then you'll deserve the answers."

"But Zo—"

"I've already told you more than I should." She sighed. "I might be getting soft in my old age." She shifted her gaze to me and away as she fussed with her coat. "Or it might just be you. Hard to say."

I wasn't sure, but I thought she might have just complimented me. I stood there searching for something I could say to make her stay.

Wrapping her scarf around her neck she stared through the snow into the distance. "Things are going to start happening more quickly now." She turned and patted my shoulder. "Try to keep up."

She leaned down and patted Fuzzy, then patted the banister as she said, "Gentlemen." She walked off the porch, calling, "See you soon, Finn." Then she strode off toward the woods, disappearing as soon as she stepped into the forest.

I stared after her until Fuzzy bumped against my leg, and Bayley sighed around me.

I picked Fuzzy up. "So you're an Orret. And a gatekeeper."

"Meow."

"At some point, you're going to have to explain all this to me."

Fuzzy reached up with one paw and patted my cheek.

I sat back down in the rocking chair Bayley had made for me, tucking the blanket around me and Fuzzy. Bayley hummed with contentment, and Fuzzy purred, as we all watched my first snowfall.

"Okay boys, let's see what kind of wonders this winter will bring."

Acknowledgments

I'm publishing this book in September 2020 and my goodness, what a year it's been so far. Even Finn would admit that there's not enough coffee in the known universe to balance the crazy that this year has wrought.

Given that nobody has a lot of extra bandwidth these days, I'm all the more grateful for the help and encouragement I've received in creating this book.

My deepest thanks to Michael Tangent, editor and cover artist extraordinaire, for all the hard work and creativity he continues to lend to this series. Your sense of humor kept me from pulling all the hair out of my head more times than I care to count.

Many sincere thanks as well to all my friends and family who offered me encouragement along the way.

In particular, thanks to my alpha reader and general cheerleader Moira DeNatale. Having you tugging at my sleeve to find out what happened next helped keep me going through some of the bumpy bits.

A huge thank you to my advance readers for your eagle eyes and your excellent feedback. I am really fortunate to have such enthusiastic and kind helpers who are so generous with their time.

A belated but heartfelt thanks to Mary Jesch for all the Latin help. You dove right in when I called to consult on how to use existing Latin naming structures to create the names for the Best magical powers. Every time I write "mustela" or "sanguinursus," I smile.

An extra thanks to Michael Duhan for reminding me about the Monty Python "Penis Song" from *The Meaning of Life*. It makes me chuckle every time I hear it, and it made the scene where I named the necklace an absolute gigglefest to write.

Sanford Meisner said that "An ounce of behavior is worth a pound of words." Alesha Howe, my fellow creative and *Buffy*-watching buddy, is the kind of go-getter, ride-or-die boss babe that Meisner had in mind. (I could totally see her, Sadie, and Mila going for a pint!) And fortunately for me, I get to be the beneficiary of some of her awesome. Whether I need her keen insight into character, some moral support to get me over my latest creative hurdle, or some real talk about life's latest snafu, she's got my back. Thanks for helping to make my life and my writing better, Alesha.

And last but never least, thanks to you, Reader, for continuing on this journey with me. I hope this latest chapter of Finn's story gave you a magical respite from the real world and made you smile. I'll be back before you know it with Finn and Fuzzy's next magical adventure.

Printed in Great Britain
by Amazon